CHAIN REACTION

CHAIN REACTION

A Lucinda Pierce Mystery

Diane Fanning

This first world edition published 2013
in Great Britain and 2014 in the USA by
SEVERN HOUSE PUBLISHERS LTD of
19 Cedar Road, Sutton, Surrey, England, SM2 5DA.

British Library Cataloguing in Publication Data

Fanning, Diane author.
  Chain reaction : a Lucinda Pierce homicide investigation.
  – (A Lucinda Pierce mystery ; 7)
  1. Pierce, Lucinda (Fictitious character)–Fiction.
  2. Women detectives–Fiction. 3. Bombings–Fiction.
  4. Detective and mystery stories.
  I. Title II. Series
  813.6-dc23

ISBN-13: 978-0-7278-8341-4 (cased)

All Severn House titles are printed on acid-free paper.

Severn House Publishers support the Forest Stewardship Council™ [FSC™],
the leading international forest certification organisation. All our titles that
are printed on FSC certified paper carry the FSC logo.

Typeset by Palimpsest Book Production Ltd.,
Falkirk, Stirlingshire, Scotland.
Printed and bound in Great Britain by
TJ International, Padstow, Cornwall.

Dedicated to the new love of my life, Simon Jacob Fanning

ONE

Routine. Ordinary. Typical. Just what Bob and Elsie Cornwall did every Sunday morning. They pulled out their walking shoes, snapped the leash on the harness of their sable Sheltie, Herman, and went on their regular walk. Two blocks east, two blocks south, a circumnavigation of the high school, then back the way they came.

All was quiet and peaceful in the neighborhood as they strolled through on the way to the campus. Walking past the east side of the building, approaching the front of the school, they startled at an unexpected sound. With a rumble, a jacked-up, red pick-up truck tore away from the front, spraying dirt and clumps of grass.

Bob and Elsie stopped where they stood. If they had been ten feet further along, Elsie wondered, would the vehicle have run them down in its rush to flee? Herman barked loud and high, frightened and disturbed by the interruption of the morning's quiet peace.

Still parked by the entrance, a large flatbed with wooden plank sides held containers partially filled with bins of grass clippings and leaves. On the steps leading inside, a man in a red flannel shirt, blue jeans and a ball cap stood abruptly. In one hand, he held a big, browned biscuit. A slice of ham slid out of his partially eaten breakfast and fell on the ground.

Blaring horns and squealing brakes drew their attention back to the red truck that had just run a stoplight as it pulled into the highway. It all happened so fast that Bob and Elsie didn't have enough time to process their surroundings before the fury roared outward from inside of the school.

Bricks fell off the facade. The pillars at the entrance crumpled, burying the man on his lunch break. The shock knocked the two walkers to the ground. Bob dropped the leash as he fell and Herman ran off as fast as he could, his tail tucked between his legs.

For a moment, neither Bob nor Elsie could hear as the explosion reverberated in their ears. They looked at each other and blinked, then gingerly pushed up from the ground. Elsie screamed for Herman but the Sheltie was focused on his escape and could not hear the sound of her voice. He seemed to be heading in the direction of their home. She could only hope she'd find him there later. She rushed over to the rubble where the man had once stood.

Blood spattered over the busted bricks. The man's legs, pinned under the fallen pillars, twisted at unnatural angles. His face was battered and his eyes wide open as they stared, visionless, into space. Elsie felt her head spin and a surge of bile rising in her throat. She threw her hand over her mouth and staggered away at a fast clip. She disgorged the contents of her stomach on the asphalt parking lot.

Bob rushed to her side and wrapped an arm around her as she continued to heave even after there was nothing left. 'He's dead?' Bob whispered.

Elsie nodded her head. As a retired emergency room nurse, she'd seen a lot of gruesome injuries in the past but somehow, outside of the hospital environment, it felt more shocking and had a much greater emotional impact. She could smell the primitive scent of blood mingled with the construction-site scent of concrete, mortar and brick dust. Her eyes stung from the particles in the air. The sounds around her echoed in her ears, creating an internal roar that seemed louder than the blast itself.

In the apartment building across the exit road, windows flew open, people ran outside. Blocked from coming any closer by the tall chainlink fence that separated the building from the school, they wrapped their fingers through the holes as they stared in disbelief. Approaching sirens wailed, drowning out the sound of shouted questions from the spectators. By the time Elsie was erect again, marked and unmarked vehicles were screeching to a halt around her. An ambulance pulled up to the front of the school. And EMTs quick-stepped out of it, carrying bags of equipment and supplies.

Police officers asked Bob and Elsie for their names and then placed them in the back of separate cars. Elsie objected loudly to being parted from her husband. A young, freckled officer apologized, telling her it was necessary to keep them from talking together until they had been interviewed separately. Elsie knew it was senseless to argue but she resented her isolation just the same.

The wait felt interminable to Elsie. Her mind wandered to worries about Herman, making her oblivious to the approaching detective. She shouted out involuntarily when the front door of the vehicle jerked open and a woman with a face that bore subtle traces of old scars slid into the seat and leaned back towards her. Holding out her identification, she said, 'I'm Lieutenant Pierce, Mrs Cornwall. I need to ask you a few questions.'

Elsie nodded mutely. Lucinda blew out a frustrated puff of air when Elsie said that she had not noticed the license plate number of the fleeing pick-up.

'Was there anyone else in the area?' Lucinda asked.

'Herman,' Elsie said.

'Herman who? And where did he go?'

'I wish I knew. He's our dog. He ran off. He was frightened by the loud noises.'

Lucinda blew out another puff of air.

Elsie felt like an ass – an unhelpful ass. And now that Herman's name was mentioned, she felt irresponsible for not grabbing his leash immediately, before he could run off down the street. What if he got lost? What if he were run over by a car? He had never run off before. Would he know how to find home? Would he know to wait for us?

'Ma'am. Ma'am. Please focus over here. Please answer my questions. The sooner you do, the sooner you can go home.'

'Excuse me?'

'Please answer the question, ma'am.'

'I'm sorry. What question?'

'Did you see anyone else in the vicinity before or after the explosion?'

'No. Not until the police cars pulled up. Well, except for the people on the other side of the fence by the apartments.'

'Did you see the deceased before the building blew?'

'Yes. When the truck pulled away, he jolted to his feet. He was holding a biscuit. There was a bite out of it. He looked confused.'

'Did he say anything?'

'No. I don't think so.'

'Did you speak to him after the explosion?'

'No. I didn't really understand what was happening. It all happened so quickly. The truck squealed out and then the loud noise. I didn't even realize it was an explosion at first. It was odd seeing the bricks blow off the side of the building and the pillars start to tilt. Then I was on the ground. I don't remember falling. I remember feeling off balance and then I was down. And my dog was running away. He wouldn't stop. You have to let me go. I don't know where he is. He's frightened. He needs me. I need to see if he got home. I really need to go,' she said, twisting at the door handle. It wouldn't budge. She pounded on the glass and shouted, 'Let me out of here!'

'Ma'am, don't panic. I just need to ask you a few more questions—'

'No. I'm not answering anything – nothing more. I'm done until I know Herman is OK. I'm not saying another word until then.'

'Ma'am, please be patient. We'll get you home soon.'

'No. Now.' Elsie's eyes flashed with anger and she jerked her head away, refusing to look at the lieutenant.

Lucinda sighed and stepped out of the car, closing the door behind her. Elsie checked the door handle again then watched as the detective went over to the vehicle where Bob sat being questioned. As Lucinda approached, another plain-clothes officer stepped out of that sedan.

She watched the two women talk together and then heard Lucinda calling over to a uniformed officer, 'Please give Mr and Mrs Cornwall a ride home, Collins.'

Lucinda returned to the vehicle where Elsie sat waiting and opened the rear door. 'You sure you're not injured, ma'am? That's a nasty scrape on your left arm.'

Elsie raised the limb in question and looked at it, stunned. She hadn't noticed it before. 'Oh, that must have happened when I fell.'

'There's still an ambulance here. Do you want the paramedic to patch it up?'

'No, no,' Elsie said, shaking her head. 'I just want to get home.'

'Are you sure?'

'Don't worry; I'm a nurse. I know how to care for this. It's nothing, really.'

'OK, if you're certain. Come on over to the car where your husband is. Officer Collins will give you a ride home. I'm sure I'll need to talk to you later. And here's my card if you think of anything that you don't recall right now.'

As Elsie stepped out, she heard an alarmed yell from a distant entrance to the school. 'Lieutenant! Lieutenant! We need you in here now!' the voice shouted.

Elsie watched as the detective took long, rapid steps, almost running, across the grass. She marveled at Lucinda's sense of balance and ability to move so quickly over rough terrain in a straight skirt and higher heels than Elsie ever felt comfortable wearing, even when she was standing still.

TWO

'This way,' a male forensic evidence tech said to Lucinda. 'Ms Spellman needs you.' He spun around and went back through the door.

Inside of the building, the dust was so thick that Lucinda coughed and choked on it as she followed the retreating back. As they neared the internal side of the entrance where the pillars had fallen and crushed the man eating his breakfast, the hallway obstructions multiplied. Lockers that used to be fastened to the inside wall were down, their contents sprawled across the floor. The concrete blocks of the exterior wall were pitted, stripped of paint, and here and there a combination lock had embedded into the hard surface from the force of the explosion.

The tech picked his way through rubble and into the remains of an office. Venetian blinds hung crooked and bent over busted windows facing an enclosed courtyard. An avalanche of papers had fallen like snow over every surface. Acting like shrapnel, pieces of metal from file cabinets stuck out of walls, furniture and demolished countertops. Most of the broken glass had been forced outward and now decorated the grass lawn like shiny slivers of ice.

Marguerite Spellman stood over a mutilated body in the middle of the space. The male corpse was missing the lower half of one leg as well as one arm. His neck twisted to the left, the right side of his head was cratered and the pieces of bloodied bone were unrecognizable as human. Virtually nothing remained of the facial features on his right profile.

Marguerite and Lucinda exchanged a glance. Lucinda asked, 'Innocent victim or participant in the crime?'

Marguerite shrugged. 'It's hard to tell, Lieutenant. Maybe I'll find a clue in this mess. Maybe there will be an indication in the post-mortem. At this point, it appears as if that might be a question you'll have to answer on your own.'

Lucinda grunted in acceptance and said, 'If we ever find an answer.'

Marguerite sniffed the air. 'Do you smell that?'

The lieutenant drew a deep breath in through her nose, picking up the scent of dust and blood but nothing more. 'What?'

'Ammonia, I think.'

Lucinda inhaled again. 'No, I don't.'

'Maybe it's just my imagination; I thought I picked up a faint trace of that acrid odor but I can't smell it now.'

'If your first impression was right, what would that mean?' Lucinda asked.

'Perhaps an ammonium nitrate bomb – a fertilizer bomb – like the one that took down the federal building in Oklahoma.'

'People can still get that stuff?'

'It's pretty common,' Marguerite said. 'But there are inert markers in most of the product sold since Oklahoma. If that's what was used, we may be able to trace the source through that. Hopefully, gas chromatography will identify the fuel used to initiate the combustion as well.'

Doctor Sam grumbled as he stepped into the room, 'Geez, Lieutenant, do you try to make things difficult for me? I'm past retirement age and way too old to be climbing over mountains of rubble like some young billy goat. Why can't you be more considerate about where you leave your victims?'

'Hey, Doc Sam, sorry. It is what it is,' Lucinda said with a shrug.

'You can do better than that, Pierce.' He crouched down by the body. 'You could have left me a little more to work with here. Identifying this body is going to be nigh near impossible unless you come up with a name that we can match with DNA.'

'Give me something to work with, Doc.'

'I'm not a miracle worker, Pierce.'

'Yes you are, you old codger. Give me an age, a height, something to narrow the identification process.'

'Has anyone ever told you that you are one demanding woman?'

'Almost every day, Doc – what's your point?'

'You are exasperating,' Doc said. He huffed and puffed his displeasure as he examined the body.

Lucinda exchanged a glance with Marguerite over Doc Sam's head, folded her arms across her chest and waited for a pronouncement from below. Marguerite stifled a laugh and walked off to check on the progress the techs were making with evidence collection.

With a loud grunt, Doc Sam pushed himself up off of the floor. 'It's a male. Might be high school age. Could be a bit past that but

I'd guess we have a student here. Average height. The one eye that remains is blue; hair brown.'

'Victim or bomber?'

Doc Sam spread his hands wide. 'Why do you even ask a question like that? You think the answer is tattooed on his chest?'

'No, sir, Doc. I was just hoping you'd seen something I'd missed.'

'Of course I have. I always do. But, in answer to your question, no. I'll look for it at autopsy but doubt I'll find it. You're gonna have to identify him first and figure it out from there.' He turned away from Lucinda and shouted to the two white-coated men standing in the doorway. 'Bag the body, load it up and get it to the morgue, post-haste.' Turning back to Lucinda, he said, 'Yes, Lieutenant, it's a priority for me. I'd like to get the post-mortem done before the damn Feds barge in.'

'The Feds?' Lucinda asked.

'C'mon, Pierce. An explosion? An act of terrorism? You think the Feebs are going to let you handle this?'

'There's no proof, at this time, that this is a terrorist act.'

'Go ahead. Anchor your boat in the sea of denial. Isn't going to change the situation one little bit,' he said.

Lucinda knew he was right. The thought had already crossed her mind. But she didn't want to accept it. If she called Special Agent in Charge Jake Lovett, maybe she could work out a compromise that would still keep her on the case. She knew he could call some of the shots with the FBI involved in the case, but would Jake be able to keep ATF and Homeland Security at bay? She punched in his cell number.

'Lovett. Oh, is this you, Lucin— uh, Lieutenant Pierce?'

Obviously, he was not alone. 'Yes, Special Agent Lovett. I have a situation here—'

'Wish I could lend a hand, Lieutenant, but I'm on the way to a possible terrorist incident with an explosives expert from the ATF. And the State Secretary of Veteran Affairs and Homeland Security is sending someone over there to meet us at the scene.'

'Are you going to Woodrow Wilson High School, Special Agent Lovett?'

'Oh, you've heard about it?' Jake asked.

'You might say that,' Lucinda answered.

'Oh. Don't tell me. You're already there?'

'Yes, Special Agent Lovett, this is my case. Is that understood?'

'Uh, listen, Lucy . . . uh, Lieutenant Pierce. We'll be there in ten minutes or less and we'll talk then.'

Then a click, silence and a dial tone. He'd hung up on her. He's going to pay for that one way or another, she vowed. And I will continue to work this case no matter what Mr Special Agent Lovett or the AFT goon or the Homeland Security bureaucrat thinks about that. She stomped outside to check the progress at the exterior of the blasted-out entrance.

THREE

L ucinda was outside observing the techs as they worked around the collapsed entryway when Jake Lovett pulled up with a toot of his horn. Lucinda used her hand to shield her eyes from the sun and watched Jake stretch his long legs out of the car. She wanted to deny the flutter in her chest that his presence induced but it was a useless effort.

Another person emerged from the right side of the vehicle wearing an ATF ball cap and windbreaker. His face bore the indicators of a lifetime out in the sun: dark, leathery skin, deep creases from his cheekbones to his mouth, harsh, permanent furrows on his brow, and his eyes squeezed in a perpetual squint. He was a bit shorter than Jake but his stride was longer and more purposeful. She imagined that he always appeared as if he was in a rush to get somewhere.

Approaching her, Jake said, 'Lieutenant Pierce, ATF Resident Agent in Charge Connelly.'

Lucinda stuck out a hand and shook Connelly's firmly. 'Agent Connelly,' she acknowledged with a nod. Then she turned to Jake. 'I thought you were bringing an explosives expert.'

Connelly wheezed out a laugh. 'Don't let my bureaucratic title throw you off, Lieutenant. I spent more than seventeen years in the field investigating bomb sites for the ATF before I got this desk job. And earlier on, I was army, detailed on an explosive ordinance disposal team.'

'He knows his stuff, Pierce,' Jake said.

Lucinda stared at Jake. 'Pierce.' He called me 'Pierce'. Is he trying to out-macho the ATF man? We're gonna have a lot to talk about when I get him alone. 'Good, Lovett. Shall I show you gentlemen where it appears the explosive device detonated?'

'Lead the way, ma'am,' Connelly said.

Lucinda walked to the far entrance and guided the two men over the rubble. She wasn't sure what to think of the ATF guy. *Was his use of 'ma'am' a sign of respect or a way to put me in my place because of my gender? Am I going to have to prove myself, yet again, to another backward male in authority?* She didn't know what to think, but she knew one thing for sure: she didn't like the effect his presence had on Jake.

Lucinda pointed out the blood-smeared spot on the floor where a young man had lost his life in the explosion. 'We don't know his identity yet but we do believe it is a male of high school age, possibly a student here.'

'Or an embittered dropout seeking revenge. Someone angry enough to be used as a tool by terrorists?' Connelly said.

'Perhaps,' Lucinda said, 'but until we know that he was involved, we are treating him as a victim.'

Connelly grunted. 'Might not be the most effective way to get information from family and friends.'

'Maybe not, Agent, but it is clearly the most compassionate way,' Lucinda snapped.

Jake raised his open palms up in the air. 'We'll just play it by ear. See where the evidence stands once he's been identified. No need to make a decision now.'

Connelly shrugged. 'Who's in charge of the forensics here?'

'That would be Marguerite Spellman. She's in the Tyvek suit over by the bank of windows,' Lucinda said, pointing in Marguerite's direction.

'Mind if I speak to her about protocol and what I need to analyze the device?'

Maybe Connelly's not so bad. That certainly sounded like an acknowledgement of my authority. 'I think you'll find Ms Spellman is extremely competent and thorough,' Lucinda said, still not convinced of his good intentions. 'But sure, go ahead, knock yourself out.'

Jake jerked his head towards the doorway and walked out into the hall. As Lucinda joined him, he said, 'What is your problem?'

'My problem?' Lucinda objected.

'Yes, your problem. Your hostility to Connelly is pretty obvious.'

'No, it's not. You are seeing my hostility to you reflecting on the hapless ATF guy.'

'Hostility? To me? I thought we had a great time yesterday. I had a lot of fun. I thought you did, too.'

'Oh, really, you had a good time? Then why were you already gone when I woke up this morning?'

'I told you I had to go into the office and take care of some paperwork. I thought I'd be back by now.'

'And going into the office couldn't wait until after we had breakfast?'

'Ah, c'mon, Lucinda. I thought I could get back before you woke up. I didn't expect this,' he said, waving his arms around. 'C'mon. There's something else. What did I do?'

'We need to get back to work,' Lucinda said, turning around and returning to what was left of the office.

'Lieutenant,' Connelly said, 'Ms Spellman here thinks this is the only administrative office in the high school. Is that correct?'

'I think so, Agent, but the school principal is on her way here. She can provide us any details we need on the building. From our brief conversation on the phone, I think that office over there – the one with the door hanging half off its hinges – is hers.'

Connelly walked over to the gaping entrance and leaned inside. 'It's a mess, Lieutenant, but far less of one than this main office area. Couldn't have gone off in there. Might be useful to bring her inside to walk us through what normal might have looked like.'

'She should be here any minute. Sergeant Colter will call me when she arrives.'

'Good,' Connelly said. 'And, ma'am, whatever I did to get off on the wrong foot with you, I'm truly sorry. I'm a strong believer in inter-agency cooperation. I believe it leads to quicker resolution when we aren't squabbling with one another.'

'I am sorry, Agent. My beef is with Agent Lovett. I'm afraid I allowed that to splash over on you.'

'Hey, don't give Lovett too hard of a time. For a Feeb,' he said with a wink, 'he ain't half bad.'

Lucinda was saved from a response by a buzz on her cell. She looked down at the readout. 'It's Sergeant Colter. The principal is here. I'll go bring her in.' She walked out into the hall, brushing past Jake on the way. He called out to her but she didn't glance in his direction.

FOUR

Lucinda stepped outside and easily identified the principal who stood on the other side of the yellow tape, her mouth hanging open. The woman was nearly as tall as Lucinda, with a short, tight haircut, a sharp nose and café-au-lait skin. She wore a royal-blue suit with a skirt that ended just at her knee. Approaching her, Lucinda stuck out her hand and said, 'Ma'am, I'm Lieutenant Pierce. We're hoping you'll be willing to come inside and help us understand our surroundings.'

The woman jerked her head toward Lucinda but didn't seem to see her outstretched hand. 'Is it as bad in there as it appears to be from out here?'

'In places, yes, ma'am.'

'And two people died – one outside and one inside?'

'Yes, ma'am.'

'Who were they?'

'The man on the landing was Fred Garcia. The one in the office, we don't know yet.'

'Oh, Mr Garcia. He'd been maintaining the grounds for long before I got here. He has three children – I've forgotten their ages but they're not in high school yet. Does his wife know?'

'Not yet, ma'am. Someone will be visiting her shortly.'

'Could I – may I – accompany whoever goes to see Mr Garcia's widow? I want to be there for her.'

'I am sure that can be arranged,' Lucinda said with a nod. 'We will appreciate the assistance and I am certain that Mrs Garcia will be grateful to see a familiar face.'

'Just let me know when. Can I see the other victim? Maybe I'll recognize—'

'Sorry, ma'am, the body has already left for the morgue. But the damage to the face was so severe that I doubt anyone would recognize him. We do suspect, however, that it may have been a student.'

'A student? What was a student doing in the building on a Sunday?'

'We're hoping you'll be able to help us answer that question, ma'am,' Lucinda said, lifting up the tape.

The woman ducked under and when she stood back up again, she stretched out her right arm. 'Forgive my manners, Lieutenant. I'm Rose Johnson. I've been the principal at this school for three years.'

Lucinda shook her hand and said, 'No need to apologize. Your reaction is understandable.'

As they turned into the hall with the dismantled lockers, Rose gasped and mumbled 'Ohmigod, Ohmigod' again and again as they picked their way through the obstacles.

Entering the office, Lucinda said, 'Ms Johnson, this is Resident Agent in Charge Connelly from the Bureau of Alcohol, Tobacco, Firearms and Explosives. And that is Special Agent in Charge Lovett from the Federal Bureau of Investigation. Gentlemen, this is Rose Johnson, the principal of this school.'

Rose's face blanched as she looked over the ruin of her workplace, her eyes roaming from one side to another. 'May I?' she asked, pointing toward her corner office.

'Certainly, ma'am,' Connelly said.

Jake reached out a hand to steady her as she stepped around a fallen, twisted file cabinet. In the doorway of her space, her hand flew to her mouth as she took in the scene in front of her. She knelt down and picked up a framed photograph. After shaking off the broken glass, she ran her fingers over the face of a man in uniform and clutched it to her chest. 'My son,' she said. 'I lost him in Iraq. An IED. I imagine the scene there looked a lot like the devastation here.'

Everyone within hearing mumbled condolences and Rose said, 'Thank you.' After a short silent pause, she asked, 'Where did you find the body of the person you thought was a student?'

At that inopportune moment, a tech shouted, 'I found a leg!'

Rose threw a hand over her mouth and lurched. Jake grabbed a metal trash can, dumped its contents and held it under her chin. When she had finished disgorging her breakfast, Connelly handed her a handkerchief and Marguerite rushed up with a bottle of water.

'I am so sorry,' Rose said. 'That was very unprofessional of me.'

'Nonsense,' Connelly said, 'it was very human. And no harm done. Don't give it another thought. However, there is quite a bit of blood where the body was; are you sure you are up to it?'

Rose swallowed hard and nodded. 'I need to be, sir.'

Lucinda led her over to the spot and pointed. 'Just to warn you, in case of the discovery of another body part, the victim also lost a hand in the explosion.'

'Ohmigod. And you think it was a student.'

'He was the right age but we really don't know if he attended school here currently or ever.'

'If he is a current student, tomorrow morning's attendance records should narrow down the field of possibilities.'

'Ma'am, I don't think it will be possible to open school tomorrow.'

'Oh. Of course not,' Rose said. 'The PTA has a phone tree, I can have them call around about the school closing and also ask about any students whose whereabouts are unknown. That should help. And, of course, we'll put an announcement up on the school's Facebook page. And send out word to the radio and television stations and the newspaper.'

Agent Connelly said, 'I'm not so sure that's a good plan. It might be better if you say nothing about the situation here.'

'Are you crazy, Agent? I can't just shut down the school and not give the parents a reason for it. And I certainly will not lie to them.'

'I do have the authority—' Connelly began.

Lucinda held up a hand. 'Hold it. Hold it right there. Let's not get emotional about this – we are going to have enough of that from the community as it is. I'd like to suggest an alternative. Ms Johnson, if you will write a script for the callers and for your Facebook message and give it to Agent Connelly for approval, I think that will solve the problem.'

'But—' Connelly objected.

'The principal is right, Connelly. She does need to give an honest reason for the closure. And we will have a serious advantage in this investigation the sooner we identify the unknown victim.'

Connelly turned to Jake. 'It sounds like time for the FBI to step in and take charge here, Lovett.'

Jake folded his arms and looked Connelly in the eye. 'Lieutenant Pierce is in charge of this case. It is in her jurisdiction. This is her community. The FBI is here to assist with resources and manpower in any way we can.'

Lucinda struggled to keep a placid face. She didn't want to antagonize Connelly further by appearing to gloat – besides, it may be premature. She certainly didn't comprehend the inter-agency politics on the federal level – even the machinations on the local level were far too byzantine for her to understand or accept.

Connelly stepped forward and poked a finger in Jake's chest. 'This is a Homeland Security matter. This may be an act of terrorism by Muslim extremists.'

Jake wrapped one hand around Connelly's finger and flung it away. 'Possibly. But considering that one of the possible perpetrators flew out of here just before the explosion driving a classic Bubba truck, I think we are looking at a local problem.'

'But we need to explore all possibilities.'

'Of course we do,' Jake said, 'and we will. But until we know for certain that this is the act of international terrorists, Pierce is calling the shots.'

'I'm going to take this up with my superiors.'

'Fine, Connelly, you do that. But, for now, get your priorities straight. You are here to help identify the components and determine the type of device we are dealing with.'

'Have you gone native on us, Lovett?' Connelly taunted.

Jake turned his back without answering.

Lucinda had an urge to rush up to him, hug him and thank him, despite the fact that he called her 'Pierce' again. Although she was suspicious of his reason for that earlier, now the logic of that professional distance was clear. Jake had probably seen this one coming.

FIVE

'Lieutenant Pierce,' echoed down the hallway.

Lucinda stuck her head out of the office and spotted Sergeant Robin Colter. As Lucinda walked towards her, Robin said, 'There's a suit outside claiming he's from Homeland Security. He asked to speak with the person in charge of the investigation.'

'I imagine, from the look on your face, he's already proved to be a pain in the ass.'

'Oh yeah. He was not pleased to learn a local cop was in charge.'

'Oh joy,' Lucinda said with a sigh. 'Lead the way.'

In the outside doorway, Robin pointed to a stout man with a flushed face standing on the sidewalk. His arms were folded tight across the front of his boring navy-blue suit. Lucinda approached him, holding out her hand. 'Lieutenant Pierce,' she said.

The man did not move or introduce himself. 'Is no one here from the FBI or the ATF?'

Lucinda withdrew her rebuffed palm and said, 'Of course, we have one of each.'

'Then why are you in charge of this investigation?'

Lucinda stepped close to him, her heels giving her a distinct height advantage as she looked down on his slicked, thinning hair. 'Because it is our jurisdiction, it is our high school and the victims are likely residents of our city. And because this is my case.'

'We'll see about that,' he said. 'Take me to the federal agents now.'

'Before I take you on to the scene, I need to see your ID.' Lucinda mirrored his folded arms with hers.

For a moment, he glared at her without moving. Then he slowly unfolded his arms and reached into an interior pocket of his suit jacket. Lucinda resisted her instinctive protective reaction to unfasten the snap on the holster holding her weapon.

Pulling out his badge, he flipped it open long enough for Lucinda to read his name – 'Franklin Wesley' – but nothing more before he snapped it shut. 'Satisfied?' he asked.

Not exactly the word Lucinda would have used to describe her feelings at that moment but she said, 'Yes, sir,' anyway. 'Follow me.'

Lucinda took long strides going inside, pleased to hear Wesley grunting as he struggled to keep up with her. At the check-in point, Lucinda signed in and pulled on a pair of Tyvek booties and latex gloves.

Wesley just stood there as if he had no need to follow proper procedure.

'Sign up and put on shoe coverings and gloves or you are not walking any further,' Lucinda ordered.

Wesley scowled at her but complied. He was still pulling on his gloves when Lucinda walked away from him.

In the office, Lucinda pointed to the federal investigators, one at a time. 'Special Agent Lovett. Resident Agent Connelly.' Pointing over her shoulder, she said, 'This guy's named Wesley and he claims to be from Homeland Security.'

'Sir, good to see you here,' Connelly said, as Lucinda walked away from the men and over to Marguerite Spellman.

Lucinda listened as Marguerite explained her theory that the explosion originated in a file cabinet, keeping an eye on the men across the room. Wesley's face scowled in impatience or exasperation – Lucinda wasn't sure which one motivated that sour expression. Connelly fidgeted in agitation, waving his arms wildly while he spoke. Jake's face bore a bland expression. He had both hands in his pockets as he rocked back and forth from heel to toe. He appeared as if he didn't give a damn and that ticked off Lucinda.

A couple of minutes later, Wesley spun around and walked away, his lips pursed and his brow furrowed. Lucinda raised an eyebrow at Jake who merely shrugged in response, raising Lucinda's irritation level up another notch.

Connelly walked away from Jake, approaching Lucinda and Marguerite with stiff steps. 'Lieutenant,' he said, 'please inform me if the ATF can put any resources at your disposal to help with your investigation.'

'Thank you, Agent Connelly. You could be most effectively utilized if you would coordinate the testing of the explosive device evidence with Ms Spellman.'

'Certainly,' Connelly said with a condescending grin. 'After all, I am the explosives expert here.'

'As you said earlier,' Lucinda responded. 'But I think you'll find that Ms Spellman has had intensive training in that area; however, our lab might not have the same state-of-the-art testing equipment that I am sure you can access.' Lucinda turned away and went looking for Principal Rose Johnson. Lucinda escorted the principal outside to Robin Colter.

'Ms Johnson,' Lucinda said, 'Sergeant Colter will need to ask Mrs Garcia a few questions after she absorbs the shock of her husband's death. It's never easy to do that but we need all the information we can get as soon as possible. Any help you can give her would be appreciated.'

Rose nodded. 'I'm hoping the sergeant will give me a sign if I get off track,' she said, smiling at Robin.

Lucinda watched the two women climb into Rose's car and got back to work.

A little after six that evening, Lucinda started feeling useless. All she could do was observe until the forensic techs had cleared one area or another. So she was greatly relieved when Jake approached

her and said, 'Let's get away from here for a few minutes – a dinner
break would do us good.'

Lucinda smiled, 'Terrific. It will give us time to talk away from
everyone else.'

Jake grimaced. 'I'm going to have to ask Connelly to join us.'

'Really, Jake? He is the main thing I need to get away from.'

'It will look suspicious if I don't.'

'Oh, screw it. I don't care who knows about our relationship.'

'I wasn't talking about that as much as I was concerned that he
might get the idea that we are shutting him out of the investigation.
He could use that to get you thrown off the case.'

Lucinda sighed. 'If you have to, you have to . . .'

Jake shrugged and walked away. When he returned, he had a
bounce in his step. 'Well, Connelly didn't think it was a good idea
if we were all absent from the scene at one time. The two of us
can go with his blessing. I think he's planning on asking Spellman
to go with him after we get back.'

'Really? Marguerite and – what is his first name anyway?'

'Clarence. But he hates it. Don't use it unless you're desperate.'

Lucinda laughed. 'Certainly is a nice piece of ammunition to
save for a rainy day.'

After a short debate, they decided to eat at the nearby
Commonwealth Diner, where the food was traditional American
fare and the ambiance conducive to quiet conversation. After
ordering, Lucinda fiddled with her silverware and the condiments
tray until Jake asked, 'What's troubling you, Lucy?'

'Well, gee, Jake. We have a young victim, a destroyed high
school, the ATF breathing down my neck and the man who lives
with me is referring to me by my last name. Why would anything
be troubling me?'

'You know I only do that as a sign of respect – to show others
that I have high regard for your abilities.'

'Oh, sure, Jake. We work together frequently and you think
refusing to acknowledge that you know my first name is the equiva-
lent of the Good Housekeeping Seal of Approval. Give me a break.'

'Lucy, come on. I didn't want Connelly to think we had anything
more than a professional relationship when we worked in the field.
You grabbed on to that because you were looking for a reason to
be angry. What gives?'

'Right. Never your fault, is it, Jake?'

'Lucy, that's not fair and you know it.'

'What I know, Jake, is that you and your good buddy—' Lucinda cut herself off when the waitress approached with their platters.

They mumbled their thanks to her and then stared down at their plates. Both of them picked up forks and dropped them. Simultaneously, they said one another's name.

'Go ahead, Lucy. What were you going to say?'

'I'm sorry, Jake.'

'Sorry about what, Lucy? What's the problem?'

Lucinda sighed and lowered her head. 'I wasn't really paying attention to how I was acting today. I was denying the problem. I was refusing to accept the power that this day still has over me.'

'What power? What are you talking about?'

'What day is it, Jake?'

'Sunday,' he said, furrowing his brow as he answered.

'Oh, please, Jake. The date.'

'May fifth.'

'Yes, and why is that significant?'

'Uh,' Jake stalled, casting his eyes around the room as if he'd find the clues on the wall. 'Oh, yes. Cinco de Mayo. Is that it?'

'Aw, geez, Jake. Why would Cinco de Mayo be significant to me? I'm not Hispanic and I'm not from Texas. I thought you would have remembered.'

'Oh, Lucy, please. Give me a break.'

Lucinda sighed even more deeply. 'Today is the anniversary of my mother's murder.'

'Oh. You're right. I should have remembered. I'm sorry.'

'No, no,' Lucinda shook her head and stared down at her plate. 'That's crazy talk. This is all on me, Jake. I always think: this year, it's not going to bother me. This year, I won't let it affect me. Then I shut down my self-awareness, go off the rails and get ticked that everyone around me doesn't get it. I do this every year and every year I tell myself not to repeat it the next year. But here I go again. The calendar changes and I started reacting like some crazed Pavlov dog. I'm sorry I put you through this. I'd say it won't happen again but I seem powerless to stop it.'

Jake reached across the table and laid a hand on Lucinda's. 'Don't worry about it. If we're together for fifty more years – a hundred more years – and every year you act out on this one day, I can handle it. It was a traumatic experience to be present when your father shot your mother and it doesn't surprise me that this day still casts a dark shadow over your life. I will promise you, though, that I will never let this day arrive again without being there for you – I will never let the date leave my mind again.'

Lucinda kept her head down. She loved him for what he was saying. She appreciated the sentiments he expressed. Still, she felt guilty for the weakness in her character that put him in this position. She was ashamed of her inability to get past that one moment in her life.

'Lucy. Look at me, Lucy. Please.'

She raised her head, revealing the track of tears down one side of her face. 'I'm sorry, Jake.'

'You do not need to apologize to me for being human, Lucy. C'mon, force a little smile on to the face I love.'

She made a funny face at him and they both broke into quiet laughter. 'Our food is getting cold, Jake.'

They both picked at their plates and exchanged a smile before throwing themselves wholeheartedly into devouring the comforting meat loaf and mashed potatoes before they grew cold.

SIX

It was daybreak on Monday morning before the techs finished gathering evidence. Lucinda, Jake, Marguerite and Connelly were the last four remaining in the building. Outside, they checked to make sure guards were in place at each entrance and around the perimeter. They were grateful to see that the police department's public information officer had arrived on the scene to handle any situations arising from students who came to the school that morning, ignorant of the previous day's news.

At home, Lucinda talked to her cat Chester as she headed into the shower. He followed behind her, making plaintive responses. When she turned on the water, he raced out of the room looking for satisfaction elsewhere. When she finished and left the bathroom, Lucinda slid her palm across Jake's as he passed her on his way to clean up. She tossed her towel on the end of the bed and slid under the sheets. Just as she dropped her head to the pillow, hoping to get a few hours of sleep, her cell phone rang. She groaned and hit the answer button. 'Pierce,' she said.

'Lieutenant Pierce, this is Jumbo Butler in Missing Persons.'

Lucinda thought, *Why now? Why me?* But she said, 'Hey, Jumbo. I've been up all night and I really need to get some sleep. Will this keep for three or four hours?'

'I don't need you to do anything right now. I just want to update you on a development that might have a bearing on the explosion at the high school.'

Lucinda swung her legs out of the bed and pressed the phone closer to her ear. 'You've got a lead?'

'Maybe. We've had two reports of missing high school students—'

'Either one a male with brown hair, blue eyes?'

'Both of them but—'

'We have a body at the high school.'

'Yes, Lieutenant, I know. If you'll let me finish—'

'Yeah, sorry, Jumbo,' Lucinda said, wondering if he'd ever get to the point.

'I got the dental records for both of them and a forensic odontologist is on his way here right now to examine the body in the morgue and compare it with the X-rays. Doc Sam wasn't sure if there was enough of the jaw intact to make a comparison so I also obtained DNA samples from both sets of parents and sent them down to forensics.'

'Wow. You've been busy.'

'Go ahead and catch some sleep while you can; it'll be a couple of hours before we have the dental comparison results and longer for the DNA. I'll keep an eye on the progress. Just call me when you wake up.'

'You get an ID, Jumbo, you call me. I'll keep the phone on and right beside me. I won't care if you wake me up.'

'You got it, Lieutenant.'

'Who was that?' Jake asked as he emerged from the shower.

'Jumbo from Missing Persons. You remember him from the dementia case a couple of years ago, right?'

'Short, round guy?'

'Yes,' she said and summarized the reason for his call.

'Best thing we can do while we wait is get some sleep,' Jake said.

'Don't know if I can sleep now, Jake.'

'You've gotta try, Lucy.'

Lucinda sighed, laid her head on the pillow and was gone. She awoke with a start and looked at the clock. Ten twenty-seven. 'Jake, wake up, it's been more than three hours and Jumbo hasn't called.'

'Maybe we just didn't hear the phone ring.'

Before he finished the sentence, Lucinda had punched in Jumbo's number and put the cell to her ear. As soon as she heard the answering click, Lucinda said, 'You didn't call.'

'Lieutenant Pierce?'

'Yes. You didn't call.'

'I didn't have anything definite.'

'Special Agent in Charge Lovett is here. I'm going to put you on speaker.'

'Oh. Well . . .'

'The agent's cool, Jumbo. You remember him, right? He's not gonna step on us. What do you have?'

'The forensic odontologist said that if we knew with certainty that the body in the high school was one of the two missing students, then he could make a determination of which one it was since he was able to eliminate one of them. But the jaw and teeth were so damaged from the explosion that he could not identify the victim definitively.'

Lucinda sighed. 'What about the DNA?'

'Beth Ann Coynes is working on that – she made it a priority first thing this morning and she's doing a rush analysis to get preliminary results.'

'Audrey is not interfering?'

'No. Dr Ringo is pushing her harder than anyone to get results as soon as possible.'

'That doesn't sound like Audrey. She always seems to follow a "first in, first out" priority system.'

Jumbo chuckled. 'This time's a bit different. Her authority has been brought under question.'

'What does that mean?'

'Some guy named Connelly from the ATF has been demanding the DNA samples and ordering her to stop the testing immediately.'

'You're kidding me?'

'No, he wants to take everything up to an FBI lab – even showed up in person demanding it. Dr Ringo ran him out.'

'I know Audrey has a forceful personality, but I sure can't imagine Connelly being intimidated by her.'

Jumbo laughed. 'That's where it gets really rich, Lieutenant. According to Beth Ann, Dr Ringo chased him out with a beaker that she claimed was filled with hydrochloric acid. Said if he didn't get out, she'd splash it in his face.'

'Ohmigod! She threatened him with acid?'

'No.' Jumbo paused to laugh again. 'The beaker was filled with tap water. But Connelly has filed a complaint. Dr Ringo put the lab on lockdown. The powers that be are deciding whether a SWAT team is needed to breach the entrance.'

By this time, Jake was out of bed and pulling on his clothes. 'Hey, Jumbo, this is Agent Lovett. I'm heading out the door. I'll corner Connelly and see if I can de-escalate the situation.'

'I'll see if I can talk some sense into Audrey,' Lucinda said.

'Great. You'll keep me posted?'

'Sure will,' they said in unison.

They barreled past the neglected Chester and headed off to slay their respective dragons.

SEVEN

On the way to his office, Jake flipped open his phone, turned it on and saw eight voicemail messages – all but one of them from Connelly. Without listening to the backlog, he called the ATF agent. 'I'll be in my office in ten minutes or less. Meet me there.'

'I've got a situation here, Lovett.'

'I know all about your situation, Connelly. My office. Nine minutes.'

'I can't walk away from this, Lovett. I've got to get this resolved now.'

'Do you want me as an ally or an obstacle?'

'You won't stand in my way, Lovett.'

'When you single-handedly went into that lab to confiscate samples for the FBI forensic lab, you went over my head. My office. Eight minutes.' Jake disconnected before Connelly could respond.

His phone buzzed at him. He checked the readout, saw Connelly's name and ignored it.

He wasn't sure Connelly would show up, but when he pulled into the FBI parking lot, there he was, standing by the elevator, fists on hips and an intense scowl on his face. As Jake approached, Connelly barked, 'Now, you see here, Lovett. You have no right—'

Jake pressed the elevator button and said, 'My office, Connelly.'

'Right here,' Connelly said, thrusting an index finger toward the ground. 'Right now.'

The elevator doors opened and Jake stepped inside. 'You coming?'

Connelly glared at him. As the doors began to shut, he threw an arm through the opening, pushed back the doors and stepped inside. Pointing a finger at Jake, he said, 'You have no authority over me, Lovett. None.'

'I know that, Connelly. But you're out of line.'

'That woman threatened—'

'My office, Connelly. Not here. Not now. End of discussion until we are there.'

Connelly glared at Jake again. Jake turned his head away and stared at the wall, refusing to be baited.

Jake walked out of the elevator and through the small lobby, smiling and greeting the receptionist on his way. When he reached the office, he turned and saw Connelly following him, fists clenched at his sides.

'Shut the door, please,' Jake said as he stepped behind his desk and took a seat.

Connelly loomed over Jake's desk. 'You are out of line.'

'Let's stop the macho posturing right now. There is no one here to observe. No one can overhear our conversation. Let's just get down to it. OK?'

'That woman—'

'Dr Ringo?' Jake asked.

'Whatever.'

'I just want to make sure I know which woman we are talking about.'

'The red-headed bitch.'

'That does narrow it down considerably. Still—'

'Dr Ringo. Yes. Dr Ringo. The bitch threatened to throw acid in my face.'

'Yes, but it was an idle threat. There was nothing but tap water in that beaker, as I am sure you know by now,' Jake said.

'I didn't know that at the time. I was in fear for my life,' Connelly shouted.

'So, why didn't you shoot her?'

A dumbfounded Connelly stared at Jake with a stupid and astonished look on his face. 'You can't be serious?'

'If a law enforcement officer is in genuine fear for his life, he is within his rights—'

'Cut the crap, Lovett. It was a figure of speech. I knew hydrochloric acid wouldn't kill me.'

'Good to know you do have some scientific background,' Jake said and allowed a patronizing smile to slither across his face.

'Lovett, you know she committed a criminal offense when she threatened me. I want her arrested and charged.'

'And how do you propose to execute that action?'

'SWAT team. They can force their way into the lab.'

'Really? You think force is an appropriate response to use on someone who threatened to throw a beaker of water in your face?'

'I figured a show of force would be all that was needed to pressure her into surrender.'

Jake laughed. 'You don't know Dr Ringo very well, do you?'

'No. I just had the unpleasant misfortune of meeting her today.'

'There is nothing she likes more than a good fight. She spends every spare moment looking to pick one with somebody – anybody. If you do even the smallest damage to her lab, she'll sue your ass from here to China and make the ATF look like a bunch of bumbling, power-happy buffoons. And she has friends in high places. Her uncle is a federal judge. How does that scenario play into your future career plans?'

Connelly blanched. 'I didn't know about her uncle. But, Lovett, we cannot trust those hicks to run the tests we need. They could ruin our case in the courtroom.'

'That's where you're wrong, Connelly. Dr Ringo never lets anyone go into the courtroom without getting the results verified in an independent lab. She has a network of university-based labs across the country ready to test her accuracy at no charge, in the name of research.'

'But she couldn't possibly have all the state-of-the-art equipment she needs.'

'Ah,' Jake said, 'that's where Dr Ringo has been the most effective. She formed a private foundation to raise funds for just that purpose. If it doesn't fit into the budget allowed by the city, she throws a fundraiser event or makes a few major donor calls.'

'A private foundation? Is that legal?'

'The city council is rather pleased with her ability to supplement her own budget without a constant plea for additional funding every budget cycle. They wish all the agencies operated like hers. Thanks to the foundation, although she doesn't have everything the FBI has, she has more than enough to handle most jobs. She's a bit short in the explosives analysis department but I'm sure she'll prioritize correcting that deficiency right away. And I do believe that is the area where Lieutenant Pierce requested your assistance.'

'Pierce has no authority over me.'

Jake dropped his head and swayed it slowly side to side. 'Don't repeat that outside of this room. It makes you sound like a spoiled child. Pierce is the lead on this investigation. In that context, she certainly does have authority over you.'

Connelly shook his head. 'Can you see her putting that lab bitch in her place? I can't and Ringo's behavior just cannot be tolerated. Can you imagine what would happen if all the locals treated us that way?'

'But they don't. There is only one Dr Ringo. Be grateful for that and let this go.'

'No can do, Lovett. This is a matter of principle.'

'What principle? The maintenance of your macho integrity? Check your ego at the door, Connelly. Let's just focus on solving this case and worry about all these peripheral issues later.'

'I don't think this is peripheral, Lovett.'

Jake sighed. 'I'll tell you what, Connelly. Lieutenant Pierce has gone over to the lab to talk to Dr Ringo. Let's give her a little time to work this out.'

'I don't like this. I've already filed a complaint against that Ringo woman. I'll file one against you, too, if I have to.'

'Fine. You do that. But let's make solving the case our priority. When that's done, you can drag me off in handcuffs for all I care. I am promising not to resist arrest. Or to threaten you with water.'

Connelly pointed a finger in Jake's face. 'That is uncalled for.'

Jake shrugged. 'Just go see Jan at the front. She'll find a desk where you can work. See if you can develop some leads. I've gotta make a couple of phone calls and then I'll brief you on the latest in the investigation.'

'When?'

Jake tilted his head and stared at him. 'As soon as I make my calls. And the sooner you get out of my office, the sooner I can get that done.'

Connelly turned and walked away. He paused at the doorway and said, 'You haven't heard the last of this, Lovett.'

'Yeah, yeah, yeah,' Jake said under his breath as Connelly stomped down the hall.

EIGHT

Lucinda found two uniformed police officers outside of the doors to the forensic lab. 'What are your orders?' she asked. 'We were told to stay here, make sure no one goes in or out and to remain at our post until we are relieved or receive new orders,' said an officer wearing a badge that identified him as 'Porter'.

'Are you expecting a SWAT team?'

Both of the men shrugged. 'Not at the moment,' Porter said.

'But that could change at any time,' added the one labeled 'Dunn'. 'We've heard they are talking about the possibility.'

'I'm going to try to communicate with Dr Ringo. If I can, I want to negotiate my way inside. If you're going to have a problem with that, get approval to let me enter now.'

Porter and Dunn looked at each other and shrugged again. 'Our orders came from our sergeant,' Porter said.

'And you're a lieutenant,' Dunn added.

'We're cool,' they said together.

'You certain? I don't want to get stopped at a critical moment.'

Both men nodded. 'No problem, Lieutenant,' Porter said.

Lucinda pulled out her cell and called Audrey, who answered the phone, 'Dr Ringo.' Lucinda was grateful of that reminder. She'd have a far better chance of success if she addressed the head of the forensic lab with her formal name rather than her first name.

'Dr Ringo. This is Lieutenant Pierce.'

'I am certainly not going to surrender to you.'

'I don't want you to surrender, Dr Ringo. I want you to let me in. I'm on your side here.'

'If I open the door, they'll force their way in.'

'Right now, Dr Ringo, is the best time to open the doors for me. The two officers here have acknowledged my authority and have agreed to follow my orders. You wait much longer and there might be a SWAT team here and God knows what kind of damage they will do.'

Audrey Ringo did not respond on the phone. Instead, she waved a blue lab towel out of an open doorway.

'It's all clear, Dr Ringo, but please hurry.'

A red head stuck out into the hall and Audrey scanned the entrance to her lab. 'Is anyone hiding around the corner?'

'No, Dr Ringo. It's just the three of us.'

'Tell those officers to put their hands in the air.'

'I can't do that, Dr Ringo. You're going to have to trust me.'

'Ha! That's a good one.'

'Aw, c'mon, Dr Ringo. This has nothing to do with our past conflicts. This has to do with forensic chain of evidence and local jurisdiction. You know my stand on that. Let me come in and help you fend off the Feds.'

'OK. I'm coming out. If I get shot, I will never forgive you.'

Lucinda threw up her hands. 'I swear, Audrey, if anyone pulls a gun, I'll step into the line of fire.'

'Audrey! At this life-and-death moment, you minimize my authority?'

Lucinda cringed. She knew that had been a mistake the moment the name buzzed across her lips. 'No, Dr Ringo. I am sorry. Please open the doors. I hear the elevator on the move. Who knows who might be coming?'

With darting eyes and furtive moves, Audrey made her way to the door, unlocked it, grabbed Lucinda by the elbow, jerked her in, slammed the door, flipped the dead bolt and raced back to her office.

Lucinda mouthed, 'Thank you,' to the officers outside and followed Audrey down the hall.

As Lucinda stepped into the other woman's office, Audrey said, 'Speak your piece.'

What a drama queen. Audrey's normal every-hair-in-its-place appearance had suffered serious damage. Stray red hairs sprang out of a collapsing up-do. The bright blue jacket of her suit was wrinkled and had a coffee stain on one lapel. Audrey appeared genuinely fearful but still defiant. 'Dr Ringo, as things are escalating now, this situation is not destined to turn out well.'

'You think I don't know that? You had me risk my life to tell me the obvious?'

'Dr Ringo, your life is not in danger. Your liberty may be. You could be arrested but no one is going to kill you.'

'Oh, I'm sure you believe that but I'm talking the ATF here. They even have firearms in their name so what makes you think they won't use them?'

Lucinda sighed. 'OK, I won't argue that point with you. I'll just say this: we need to find a way to extricate you and the lab from this current conflict before things get out of hand.'

'I will not turn any evidence in this lab over to that odious man.'

'Why can't you give him some of the remainder of the samples? Enough to keep him happy but still leave you with enough material for confirmatory testing?'

'Because he will not be satisfied with that. He wants to bring me down. He wants to discredit this lab. I will not allow that.'

'He wouldn't be so adamant now if you hadn't threatened him, Dr Ringo.'

'Oh, poor baby, threatened by a beaker of water! Does he think he is made of sugar crystals?'

'Don't be disingenuous, Doctor. You told him it was acid.'

Audrey's mouth spread into a malevolent grin. 'You should have seen him back-pedal. I didn't think that nasty fat man could move so fast.'

'Right now, this is not funny, Dr Ringo. Maybe we'll be able to laugh about this later but right now—'

'Do you realize what that man is threatening? Do you realize how hard I've worked to get all the necessary equipment, personnel and an outside network of specialists in specific fields of forensics?'

'Yes, Dr Ringo, but—'

'The final results out of this lab are impeccable. They've never been effectively challenged in a court of law under my tenure. That is certainly not something the FBI lab can say.'

'I know this, Dr Ringo.'

'And that ATF hooligan called it a backwater facility. He accused me of compromising the investigation and prosecution of this case with sloppy testing. Me! He accused *me*.'

'Listen. I don't particularly care for Connelly, either, but I have to work with him.'

'You should refuse.'

'If I do, I'll be off the case.'

'Refuse to release your files. Refuse to release my reports. I certainly won't turn them over to that man.'

'You can't withhold evidence, Audrey.'

Audrey's lips formed a thin line and she stared at Lucinda as if the lieutenant had just defaced a priceless piece of art.

Oh jeez, there I go again. 'Sorry, Dr Ringo. That was an unintentional slip.'

'Really, Lieutenant, you need to exercise better control of your tongue.'

The child in Lucinda wanted to scream, 'Audrey, Audrey, Audrey!' as she ran circles around the woman but her more mature side prevailed. 'Dr Ringo, I don't want to argue with you. I agree that Connelly had no right to come in here and demand you turn over the evidence. He was out of line. You, however, have made the situation worse with your threat.'

'What was I supposed to do? He was bigger than me and he wore a gun and wasn't shy about flashing his shoulder holster at me. What was I supposed to say? "Yes sir, Mr ATF man, ransack my lab to your heart's desire. We're so ignorant and backward here we want you to take this awesome responsibility off of our hands."'

'No, Dr Ringo, I wouldn't expect that. I have no problem with anything you've done to protect the sanctity of your lab – well, maybe that acid threat thing but I have to admit it stirred up a pretty funny image in my mind. Nonetheless, right now, we need to sit down, set aside our outrage at the actions of the ATF bully and find a way to extricate you from this mess without damaging the lab or your professional reputation.'

'That man has the manpower and firepower to cause damage to the lab but my reputation is sterling – he'll get nowhere on that front. But, for the sake of the lab, I am willing to try. Let's go to the break room. I desperately need a cup of mint tea.'

NINE

J ake was fuming as he walked through the Justice Center on the
way to the forensic lab with Agent Connelly. The explosion at
the high school created a volatile situation – hysterical parents,
a ravenous media and a lot of pressure from above. And instead of
focusing like a laser on developing leads and searching for answers,
he was caught up in a political power play – an inter-agency war
game that damaged the progress of the investigation. He wasn't sure
what irritated him more – the belligerence of the ATF agent or the
stubbornness of the city forensic lab head.

When the two men reached the outer doors to Dr Ringo's kingdom,
Connelly exploded. 'Two uniformed officers. That's it?'

'No one wanted to escalate this situation any further, Connelly.'

'This is ridiculous. I'm calling for more manpower.'

'Connelly,' Jake said, injecting as much calm into his voice as
he could muster. 'Your call for a SWAT team has been rejected by
the police chief, the ATF and the FBI. Get over it.'

Connelly ignored him. He shouted into his cell phone. 'I want
every available agent in the state to proceed here stat.' He disconnected the call and glared at Jake.

Jake stared back at Connelly, pulled out his cell and called his
office. 'Send all available agents in the office down to the city
forensics lab right away. I do not expect that there will need to be
a show of force unless the ATF gets out of hand.'

'Sir, do you want to leave the last part of your request off the
record?'

'No. I wanted it stated very clearly that the purpose of this
deployment is to serve as a check on the ATF and to minimize any
problems they might create.'

'You are out of line, Lovett,' Connelly snapped.

Jake turned away from him without responding. He went to the
far wall and remained facing it as he called Lucinda. 'I'm out here
with Connelly. He's called for reinforcements. I've got agents on
the way to stop him from doing anything stupid. But the sooner
you can offer a solution to this stalemate, the better.'

'We'll be out in no more than half an hour, Jake.'

'See if you can cut that time a bit.'

'I'll do my best.'

In his peripheral vision, Jake noticed that Connelly had inched closer to him while he talked. It was obvious that the ATF agent was trying to eavesdrop on his conversation. 'Listen, I've got to go. Just get out here as soon as you can.' He disconnected and spun to face the other man. 'Can I help you, Agent?'

'Yes, you could – by getting the hell out of here and letting me handle this situation as I see fit.'

'The FBI and local law enforcement have – or should I say *had* – an excellent relationship of mutual inter-agency cooperation before you tried to steamroller them. I hope we will be able to repair the damage done and solve this case without further interference from you.'

'Interference? This is my turf, Lovett, and these puffed-up locals are in *my* way. Homeland Security will hear about your obstruction when this is all over.'

Jake leaned with his back against the wall, crossed one turquoise Chuck over the other in feigned nonchalance. Inside, he was boiling but he looked away from Connelly, riveting his gaze on the lab doors, hoping for any sign of Lucinda and Audrey.

Connelly made a rude noise, pointed at Jake's shoes and shook his head. Then he positioned himself against the opposite wall. They remained in their respective positions without talking until they heard the elevator doors open. Jake and Connelly straightened up and turned toward the sound.

Jake hoped that some of his agents were about to walk out. He was disappointed when two men emerged in black ATF windbreakers, then relieved when they were followed by four FBI agents in suits and ties.

Jake tried not to smile as Connelly ranted. 'Two? That's it? Two agents?' He heard soft murmurs from the men with Connelly but could not discern the words. Then he saw Connelly throw up his hands. 'OK, OK,' Connelly said. 'When? When? When will they be here?' Another response, too quiet for Jake to hear, followed by Connelly's irritated exclamation: 'You've got to be kidding me!'

TEN

After Lucinda and Audrey reached a tentative agreement on how to proceed, Audrey insisted on changing into a fresh laboratory coat and repairing the damage to her deteriorating upswept hair. Lucinda waited impatiently until Audrey finished and was ready to accompany her. Then they walked side by side to the double doors. Through the glass, she saw a fuming Connelly, a relieved Jake and a large mix of uniformed and plain-clothes officers and agents.

Audrey started to insert her key into the lock but stopped. She stretched up on tiptoes to whisper to Lucinda who bent down to hear what she had to say. Lucinda nodded and shouted through the door. 'Everyone get away from the front entrance – at least twenty feet back.'

The policemen instantly obeyed her order. Jake started to comply, then stepped forward to lay a hand on Connelly's upper arm. The ATF agent shrugged him off. Jake pointed at the four FBI agents standing behind him and signaled for them to step back. Then he touched Connelly on the forearm. Connelly shoved him.

'Are you really ready for an ATF–FBI war?' Jake hissed at Connelly. 'You're outmanned and outgunned. How do you think this is going to end?'

Connelly turned and looked at the two men remaining at his back.

'Really, guys,' Jake said. 'You want to have this confrontation here and now? You really think inter-agency politics is more important than solving this case?'

The ATF agents looked down at the floor. First one, then the other took a step backward. They kept walking back until they were beside their FBI counterparts at the proscribed distance.

'C'mon, Connelly. You're the chief reason that Dr Ringo doesn't want to unlock that door.'

Connelly stomped away from the doors, joining the other two ATF agents. Jake, too, stepped back. Audrey unlocked the door and after she and Lucinda entered the hallway, she turned and locked it again.

'Here's the deal,' Lucinda said and turned to look at the three whispering ATF men. 'Connelly, are you ready to listen?'

The ATF agents took three steps toward the door before the FBI men stepped in their path and blocked their progress.

Audrey turned away toward the doors. Lucinda reached out a hand to restrain her. 'Wait, Dr Ringo.' Facing the agents, Lucinda said, 'If you all would just back up to where you were, we can talk this out like adults.'

The FBI agents moved towards the ATF men. Connelly snarled Jake's name. 'Not now, Connelly,' Jake said. 'Let's resolve this disagreement here so we can get back to the investigation.'

Outnumbered, Connelly and his agents backed up.

'Dr Ringo has a reasonable offer. She will maintain control of the evidence—'

'This is getting us nowhere,' Connelly objected.

'Hear me out first, sir,' Lucinda demanded. 'This is workable. There are no questions about the professional conduct of this lab during Dr Ringo's tenure here. There have been no successful judicial disputes over her results. She will be allowed to do the work without interference and the ATF and FBI will accept that. In return, Dr Ringo agrees that all reports will be distributed simultaneously to our homicide department, the regional ATF office and the field office of the FBI.'

'So we have to trust her?' Connelly said.

'Not exactly. In addition, Dr Ringo agrees that, upon completion of the testing, she will provide samples, wherever possible, for additional testing. She will present these samples to representatives of both the ATF and the FBI, when there is sufficient quantity remaining to do so. And the material will be released following strict chain-of-custody protocols.'

'I don't like it,' Connelly said.

'All I want to do,' Jake said, 'is get back to the investigation and stop playing these games. If you want to fight me on that point, Connelly, I will file an immediate complaint and the FBI will seek a court order to stop you in your tracks. Now, do you want to get back to what we are all supposed to be doing here or do you want to continue being a jerk?'

A sharp knock on the glass drew everyone's attention back to the lab. Beth Ann said, 'I have identified the victim.'

'Open the doors, Dr Ringo,' Lucinda ordered.

Audrey pointed at Connelly and said, 'I don't trust him.'

'Audrey, cut the crap,' Lucinda snapped. 'You need to open those doors and get three copies of that report and distribute them to all three agencies. You got most of what you want so it's time to start cooperating. We have a case to solve and maybe parents to inform. Let's do it.'

The look Audrey gave Lucinda could have withered a freshly emerged blade of grass but she stuck her key in the door anyway. As she eased it open, Lucinda reached for the paper in Beth Ann's hands and said, 'I'll make copies right away.'

As Lucinda walked to the copy machine, she looked at the name: David Baynes. The victim was one of the missing students. Was he an accomplice or just a person in the wrong place at the wrong time?

ELEVEN

Lucinda was delighted when Jake volunteered to go with her to inform David's parents of his death. She was dismayed when Connelly insisted on coming along as well. Before getting into the car, she called Jumbo Butler to inform him that one of his missing persons was found deceased.

Jumbo exhaled loudly and said, 'Hopefully, the other student will be found safe and sound.'

'I hope so, too, Jumbo. Good luck,' Lucinda said.

At the Bayneses' home, the three investigators gathered at the end of the sidewalk. 'Since I am in charge of this investigation, I trust that you will all honor that and follow my lead.'

Jake nodded in agreement but Connelly just stared.

Lucinda rolled her eyes and led them to the front door. It flew open before Lucinda had a chance to pull her finger off of the doorbell. In front of her, a woman with wild eyes and even wilder hair was dressed in an old cardigan, worn jeans and a T-shirt, its design washed out from years of running through the laundry cycle. 'Mrs Baynes?' Lucinda asked.

The woman's eyes bounced to each of their faces. 'No. No. I don't want to hear it,' she said and started to slam the door.

A sorrowful-looking man, badly in need of a shave, stepped into view and stopped the closing and opened the door wide. He said, 'C'mon, Sarah, we need to deal with whatever they have to say.'

'No, no, we don't. Look at them,' she said, swinging her arms in wide arcs. 'They didn't come here with good news. Look at their faces. If they found David alive and well, they would be smiling. David would be with them. I don't want to know what they have to say.' She turned her back and ran off.

'I'm sorry,' he said. He reached out a hand to shake all three of theirs. 'Chuck Baynes, David's father. Please come in.'

They followed him into the living room and took seats on the sofa. 'I'll go get Sarah – if I can.' In a few minutes, he returned without his wife. 'I'm not sure if she's coming. I'm sorry but . . .'

'That's OK, Mr Baynes,' Lucinda said. 'Have a seat, please.'

'I guess I should,' he said, slumping into the nearest easy chair. 'I suppose you've found David – where was he?'

'You heard about the explosion at the high school?'

'The high school? Yes. You found David at the high school? What was he doing there on Sunday?'

'We were hoping you'd be able to answer that question. Do any possibilities come to mind?'

'Not one. I have no idea. It makes no sense to me. Are you sure it was David?'

'Yes, sir. The DNA tests confirmed that it was. Unfortunately, he did not survive the blast.'

They all looked toward the foot of the stairs at the sound of Sarah's voice. 'I want to see him. I want to see my son.'

'No, you don't,' Lucinda said. 'You really do not want to see him.'

'He's my son. I have my rights. You can't deny me this.'

'Mrs Baynes, please trust me: you do not want to see him now. You will not recognize him and you will never get that image out of your mind.'

'I demand that you take me to my son.'

Lucinda turned to the woman's husband. 'Please, sir, no parent should have to see this.'

'Was he near the explosion?'

'Yes, sir. He was very badly injured.'

'I don't care,' Sarah shrieked.

Chuck rose and went to her side, but when he tried to put an arm around her, she squirmed out of his reach. 'He is my son,' she shouted. 'I want to kiss his forehead, touch his cheeks, tell him goodbye.'

Connelly bounced to his feet. 'Good grief, woman, there's not enough of his forehead left to accommodate a chicken's lips.'

Sarah moaned and collapsed to the floor.

Lucinda and Jake glared at Connelly and jumped to their feet, hurrying over to the fallen woman. By the time they reached her, Chuck was kneeling by her side, holding one hand and gently patting her cheek.

'Sarah, Sarah,' Chuck said.

Sarah's eyes blinked open. 'No, Chuck, no. Please tell me it's not true.' She struggled to sit up.

'Easy, easy,' Chuck said as he slid an arm behind her back to support her.

Her eyes darted back and forth between the faces of Lucinda and Jake. 'I need to get up, Chuck. This is embarrassing.'

Jake stretched out a hand to help her and said, 'Ma'am, you've had quite a shock. Your reaction was normal.'

Sarah grabbed Jake's hand as Chuck wrapped an arm around her waist. Once she was up on her feet, Chuck walked her over to a chair and eased her down.

'Now that we've gotten past your hysterics, tell me what you know about your son building a bomb,' Connelly said.

'What?' Chuck and Sarah said together.

'You heard me. Don't play dumb. You had to know what he was up to—'

'Enough, Connelly,' Lucinda interrupted.

'I want answers, Lieutenant, and I want them now. And you,' Connelly said, pointing a finger at Sarah, then Chuck, 'you people need to give us some answers.'

'Agent Connelly, can we please step outside for a moment?'

'Not unless you're putting those two conspirators in cuffs first.' Connelly pulled his pair out of his waistband.

Jake stood and stepped between Connelly and the shocked parents. 'Cut it out, Connelly.'

'What's wrong with you people?' Connelly said, glaring at Lucinda and Jake. 'There's no way that boy could have built that bomb without his parents' knowledge and possibly their blessing. Don't tell me a few crocodile tears and a phony fainting spell have blinded you to reality here?'

Lucinda put her hand on the butt of her gun. 'Agent Connelly, you are out of line. Step outside and wait for us until our conversation here is over.'

'Are you threatening me, woman?' Connelly snapped.

'Come on,' Jake said, pushing against his back with a shoulder. 'Let's go. Let's go now.'

Connelly tried to brush him off, but Jake pressed harder. 'She's not going to draw a gun on a federal agent.'

'Don't press your luck, Connelly,' Jake said as he manhandled the other agent outside.

Once the door shut, the loud exchange was muffled and indistinct but still audible. 'I'm sorry for the agent's behavior,' Lucinda said.

'But is that what you all think? That we helped him build a bomb?' Chuck asked.

'No, sir, I do not.'

'But you think he was responsible for what happened?' Sarah said.

'I don't know, ma'am,' Lucinda admitted. 'I am trying to figure out exactly what happened. And the first questions are: what was he doing at the high school Sunday morning? And how did he gain access to the building? Why was he there? Once I have those answers, I can determine if he was in the wrong place at the wrong time or if he was responsible for what happened. And, of course, there is the possibility that he did play a role in the explosion but had no awareness of what he was doing.'

'You mean someone used him without his knowledge?' Chuck asked.

'Possibly. But at this point, I can't assume anything. We will need to search his room and see if we can find any leads there.'

'You'll probably want his computer, too,' Sarah offered.

'Yes, ma'am.'

'Don't waste your time getting a search warrant. We'll sign anything you need to authorize your access. Won't we, Chuck?' Sarah said, turning to her husband who nodded his agreement.

Lucinda had the form documents ready. She pulled them out, filled in the blanks and handed them over to the couple to sign. 'Take your time. Feel free to read them over and discuss as much as you need.'

'No need to read it. I don't care what it says. I want you to find out what happened to our son. Honestly, I can't believe that he had anything to do with the explosion but I want to know why he was in that building at that time.' His pen, however, still hovered over the signature line. 'I do have one condition, though.'

Lucinda tensed. Oh dear. There were a lot of things a father in this situation could ask and a lot she couldn't promise. 'What is that, Mr Baynes?'

'That man does not enter my son's bedroom,' he said, pointing toward the front of his home.

'Just for clarity, Mr Baynes, exactly which one of the two agents do you want to be kept out of David's room?'

'I'm surprised you have to ask,' Chuck said. 'But for clarity's sake, I will answer: Agent Connelly with the ATF.'

'Hand me the document,' Lucinda said. On the bottom, she wrote, 'This agreement is automatically null and void if ATF Agent in Charge Clarence Connelly sets foot inside of the Byneses' home.' She handed the piece of paper back to Chuck. 'Does that satisfy you, Mr Baynes?'

Chuck grunted. 'Yes indeed, Ma'am.' He signed and passed it over to his wife.

Sarah added her signature, handed the form back to Lucinda and said, 'The son I knew would not build or place a bomb anywhere. But we have to accept the possibility that he is not the person we believed him to be. I want the truth, no matter how painful it is.' Tears rolled down both of her cheeks as she spoke.

Lucinda swallowed hard to keep her own empathetic emotions from slipping out of control. 'If one of you could show me to his room, I'll get started.'

Chuck led her upstairs and into David's room. 'Well, I'll go downstairs with Sarah. Feel free to do what you need to do. I just ask that you try not to mess things up too much. Sarah would feel the need to put everything back in its proper place and I don't think she's up to that yet.'

Once Lucinda heard Chuck's descending footsteps and knew she was alone on the second floor, she called Jake. 'They've given me permission to search their son's room and to confiscate the computer. I'm going to call the Regional Computer Forensic Center and see if Ted Branson can get down here to take direct possession of David's laptop. Please get Connelly out of here before he causes any further complications. I'll get a ride from Ted or whoever he sends down from Charlottesville.'

'Are you sure? I could help you in there.'

'I know you could but my greater need is to get Connelly out of here before he causes any additional turmoil.'

'You think he could cause them to revoke the permission.'

'They said as much, Jake. In order to get them to sign the release, I had to add that as an automatic response if he walks through their door again. So get that insensitive jerk off of their property before that happens.'

'Oh jeez . . .'

'What?'

'The blinds on one of the windows: someone has pulled up a slat and is looking our way.'

'Get that man out of here now, Jake. They were very emphatic about that.'

'That's not going to be an easy job.'

'Cuff him or do whatever is necessary. Just get him out of here now.'

'I will not draw a gun on him.'

'I did not draw my weapon,' Lucinda objected. 'I simply rested my hand on the butt of my gun.'

'Technicality, Lucy. I think you really stepped in it.'

'Won't be the first time, Jake.'

TWELVE

Lucinda was pleased with the results of her call to Ted. He promised to be there in two hours to take the computer to his lab for forensic analysis. Even more pleasing was Ted's eagerness to take time when he got there to update her on how his kids and wife were doing. It sounded as if his marital situation was now on a firmer footing. She hoped that was true because it would mean he wouldn't be attempting to make her feel guilty for pushing him away from the possibility of renewing their high school romance.

She opened up the lid of David's laptop and was surprised to see that it was not password-protected. Wouldn't a kid with something to hide make sure that no one else could get access? She pulled up his internet search history and saw no mention of anything that was even remotely connected to bombs or explosive devices. She also found nothing that suggested an interest in violence, except for a few action movies. There was no indication he ever visited any website with racist sentiments or of militia organizations or conspiracy theorists of any stripe. Not at all what she expected. But, then, if he was involved with any of that, wouldn't he know to erase his tracks?

She went next to his Facebook page but that asked for a password. She opened his email inbox and found it was populated with a slew of YouTube links that led to music or humorous videos, communications from the school or teachers at the school and lots of spam. She checked his deleted messages folder but it was empty. Was that a sign of good email maintenance? She doubted it. If that were the case, he wouldn't have had all that junk mail in his inbox. Whatever had been deleted would have to be ferreted out up at the computer forensics lab.

Lucinda looked around for a cell phone but didn't find one. Perhaps it was destroyed in the explosion that took David's life. Maybe he didn't have one. She'd have to talk to his parents. If he did, she would need to get a search warrant to get a copy of his billing records. Or maybe Mr or Mrs Baynes would do that for her and save her the hassle.

Exploring the top of David's desk, Lucinda found only one thing that raised any questions: a folded-up note. With gloved hands, she pressed it open on the surface. It began with a salutation. 'Hi Davey!' There was a heart over the 'i'. Had to have been from a girl. 'You need to speak to Kev,' it continued. 'It has to stop! Please!' It was signed with a smiley face followed by a loopy 'E'. She'd have to ask David's parents if they knew who wrote the note. In fact, she needed to get a whole list of the boy's friends. Someone had to know something.

Lucinda got down on her hands and knees to peer under the bed. Dust bunnies, empty freezer pop packages, energy drink cans and dirty socks. She stood up and pulled down the bed linens: nothing stuck in the sheets but one discarded pair of tighty-whities. Nothing under the pillows, either. She flipped up the mattress. Two often-handled issues of *Playboy* but nothing more. She wondered if she should just leave them there and then thought of Sarah finding them and slid the magazines into a paper bag.

She remade the bed, taking care to make it look as it did before she entered the room, down to sprawling the same T-shirt across the lower part of the quilt. Next, she tackled the dresser, looking under everything, inside of rolls of socks and into every pocket. A few notes, a bottle of breath spray – but no drugs, no cigarettes, no booze.

Lucinda turned to the closet, carefully inspecting all the clothes on hangers. Then she kneeled down and went through the pile of fallen clothing and one by one through all seven pairs of shoes, turning each shoe upside down and shaking it. Her whole haul from the inspection there yielded one quarter, two pennies and a pile of candy wrappers.

Finally, she hoisted his heavy backpack on to the bed. She pulled out textbooks and notebooks and shook each one upside down. School assignment papers, a permission slip, a couple of bookmarks and another folded note fell on the surface. She set the latter aside as she explored the remaining contents of the bag. Pencils, pens, a ruler, another pile of wadded-up candy wrappers, an iPod and an unopened energy drink. When she was certain it was empty, she set it aside and spread open the note. It read: 'Saturday night at 10 by the dumpsters behind the Walking Dog.' It was unsigned – not even an initial.

Unless something was hidden inside the recesses of the laptop or there was sinister intent behind the two written messages she'd found, the room contained absolutely nothing that pointed to David as the bomber – not even one clue to why he was at the high school on a Sunday morning. She had hoped for a solid clue leading to the people she needed to question. All she had were two notes of unknown provenance. She could only hope that talking to David's friends would lead to some usable information but there was no guarantee of that.

A dead teenager, two grieving parents and soon a school full of shocked friends and acquaintances. What could she tell them? How could she comfort them when she had no answers and no idea of where to find them?

'David,' she said to the empty room. 'Please, David, point me in the right direction. I need some help here. Who is "E"? And why did she turn to you for help? What was her problem? Who was Kev? What was your involvement? Why are you dead, David? What went wrong?'

Caught up in the moment, Lucinda had not heard the doorbell

ring and was unaware of Ted's presence until he spoke. 'Glad I got here as quickly as I did. You must be desperate if you're talking to yourself.'

Lucinda laughed and said, 'Good to see you, Ted.' They hugged briefly – and platonically, Lucinda hoped. She then explained all that had ensued up to that point.

Ted collected the laptop, its cord, a few flash drives and a stack of CDs and DVDs. Then they headed downstairs.

'Yes, he did have a cell phone,' Sarah said, an exasperated look on her face.

'You didn't want him to have one?' Lucinda asked.

'I knew it was best that he did,' Sarah said with a sigh. 'But it was a constant source of conflict. Every night at dinner, we had to tell him to put it on the table and turn it off.'

'And if we wanted to talk to him,' Chuck added, 'we had to take possession of the phone first or he'd never stop texting.'

'He texted a lot?' Lucinda asked.

'He texted more than he talked,' Chuck said. 'Are you saying that his cell wasn't with him?'

Lucinda winced. 'If it was, it didn't survive the explosion. It would help a lot to have a copy of his bill to see whom he called and texted. I can apply for a search warrant to get his records from the phone company but that will take time. Would you, by any chance, have a copy of his bills?'

'His bills? His bills?' Sarah asked.

Chuck interjected, 'We have a family plan. His records are on our bill.'

'Did you just toss them after you paid them or would you keep it on file?' Lucinda asked.

'We hold on to everything for at least a year, right, Sarah?' Chuck said.

'Oh, yes, of course,' Sarah said. 'I can get those for you.'

'That would be a big help, Mrs Baynes. Thank you. When did your last billing cycle end?'

'Oh, my, I don't know. I . . .'

'Well, when do you usually pay the bill each month?'

Sarah shook her head and tears formed in her eyes. 'I can't remember. I know I should. I'm sorry.'

'No apologies are necessary. I can figure that out from the bills and file a search warrant for the most recent records.'

'Wait a minute. Sarah, didn't you tell me you could get those records online now?' Chuck said.

'Oh yes, yes. What was I thinking? I can print that out.' Sarah wiped away tears with the back of her hand. 'I'll go do that right away.'

After Sarah left the room, Chuck stood and walked over to an antique oak washstand, pulled open a deep drawer and removed a photo album. He sat back down with the closed album resting on his knees and stared into space.

Lucinda gave him some time and then asked, 'Is there something you wanted to show me in that album, Mr Baynes?'

Chuck sighed and, without looking at Lucinda, said, 'I thought I did. I wanted to show you his pictures growing up. But now – but now – I just don't know if I can bear to look at them.' Chuck's head jerked upward. 'Sarah! Sarah, what's wrong?'

Lucinda spun around and saw Sarah standing with a hand over her mouth and a look of horror in her eyes. Then Chuck was standing beside her, an arm around her shoulders.

'What is it, Sarah?'

Tears coursed down the woman's cheeks. Through her sobs, she choked out, 'I went into the office for a reason. But I couldn't remember why I was there.'

Chuck pulled his wife tight against his chest and held her close, whispering comfort into her ear. After a couple of minutes, he eased back from her, planted a kiss on her forehead and said, 'I do that all the time, Sarah. We all do. It was David's phone records. You were going to get them for the lieutenant. Come on, let's do it together.'

Lucinda watched them walk out of the room, arms around each other. Sarah leaned hard on Chuck's side, causing them to swerve while her husband re-established their equilibrium. Lucinda wanted to say something soothing but she was incapable of speech. A lump in her throat threatened to erupt in sobs. She swallowed several times to regain her composure.

By the time the Bayneses returned with a manila folder in hand, Lucinda felt in control of her emotions but she knew it wouldn't take much for them to flare up again. She struggled to remain calm and steady as she pulled out the plastic sleeve with the note from 'E'.

Neither parent knew the identity of the mysterious author with

any certainty. Sarah suspected Emily Jarvis; Chuck thought Elizabeth
Harding. When Lucinda asked about Kev, Sarah said, 'Kevin
Blackwood, probably. They were close in middle school but I didn't
think they were in touch much lately – so maybe it's not him.'

Lucinda asked if they knew who wanted to meet with David the
night before he died. 'He did spend a lot of time at the Walking
Dog,' Chuck volunteered. 'A lot of the kids do. Inexpensive food
and a company tolerance for kids just hanging out. It doesn't really
point to anyone specific.'

Lucinda asked the couple about David's friends and watched the
painful process as they brainstormed the names of anyone they could
ever remember visiting David at the house, along with all those
he'd mentioned on a regular basis. They couldn't recall the last
names of all the kids. Lucinda could only hope that Ted would be
able to dig that information out of the computer.

Sarah and Chuck looked haggard by the time they finished.
Lucinda looked at her notes and hoped that one of those kids would
know something – anything that would lead to the person responsible
for David's death, even if it turned out that it was David himself.

Lucinda felt as if all the oxygen in the home had been consumed
by their bottomless grief. She left the Bayneses holding on to one
another on the sofa and let herself out of the house. On the porch,
she inhaled a deep breath.

THIRTEEN

Lucinda felt devoid of energy when she slid into the passenger
seat of Ted's car. 'It is never, never any easier. No matter how
many times I do it.'

'I know,' Ted said. 'It's one thing I certainly don't miss about
my job on the force. Computer forensics doesn't have as many
adrenaline-churning moments but it also takes me out of the death
notification business. Anything I need to prioritize for you in my
analysis?'

'Yes,' Lucinda said, pulling out the legal pad with David's list
of friends and extracting a blank sheet. 'The Bayneses did not know
some of the last names for David's friends. I am going to write

down some first names. If you can pull out any indications of their identity in his email or Facebook, that would be very helpful. Also, I am trying to identify a girl with the initial of "E" who needed David's help with some problem or other regarding someone she referred to as "Kev", who might or might not be Kevin Blackwood, and I am interested in any references to the Walking Dog.'

'Walking dog?' Ted asked.

Lucinda chuckled. 'That's right. The Walking Dog is a fairly recent addition to town. It wasn't here when you moved up to Charlottesville. It's just a fast-food teenage hang-out specializing in hot dogs. Mind if we talk about something else? I am drained right now.'

'Course not. You want a family update?'

'I'd love one. How's your dad . . . Ellen, the kids?'

'The kids are great. Good grades, lots of friends; they really like it up there. Dad? Well, I feel like we lose another piece of him every day but the good news is that he remains pleasant and still remembers all our names most days. When he temporarily forgets one of the kids' names, he calls them "Buddy" and they don't have a clue.'

'And Ellen? Your marriage?'

'That's best of all.'

'Really?'

'We've both been doing a lot of healing. We've been able to talk about the loss of the baby without getting angry or pointing fingers. We still walk on eggshells a bit with each other but that's getting better. And we're sharing a bed once again.'

'That's terrific, Ted.'

Ted blushed a bit and said, 'Yeah. I finally got to the point where I accepted the fact that the high school romance you and I had was just that – a thing of the past. That helped a lot and it made me realize that I was as much a part of the problem in our marriage as Ellen was. I had been placing all the blame on her.'

Lucinda didn't express the total relief she was feeling, afraid that it would sound too much like rejection. She just patted his arm and said, 'Good, Ted. That is what you needed to do.'

'And you? Look at you. You look fabulous. Only traces of the scarring remain. I bet those will fade even more with time.'

'Thanks, Ted. I no longer cringe when I look in the mirror but they still stand out like flashing lights to me.' For the rest of the ride, they shared the latest news about mutual acquaintances. Before getting out of the car at the Justice Center, Lucinda leaned across the seat and placed a kiss on Ted's cheek. 'Thanks for everything, Ted.'

'The least I could do,' he said.

Lucinda walked into her office with a list of fifty-seven names. including one girl named Emily, two named Elizabeth and one Electra – what were her parents thinking? She looked up addresses and phone numbers. She called those five girls first – although she found all but one of them at home, the parents were at work. She'd gotten times when she could interview them with a parent present. She went back to the list gathering information about the remaining students identified by last names.

She was halfway through it when Captain Holland barked, 'My office, Pierce.'

She reluctantly rose from her desk and followed him down the hall. What are the odds, she wondered, that this summons was related to Connelly? He's probably been whining about me since he left the Bayneses' house. Then again, maybe the captain just wants an update on the progress at the high school.

'Sit,' Holland barked as Lucinda walked through the door.

The look on his face told Lucinda that she was not going to like what he had to say.

'You're off the case,' he said and stared at her with an expressionless face.

She was certain what he meant but didn't want to believe it. 'What case, sir?'

Holland lowered his head and glared at her. 'You know what case. The case at the high school. The explosion. You are no longer involved.'

Lucinda sighed. 'Jeez, Captain, are you really going to cave in to a little whining from an obnoxious federal agent?'

The captain bolted to his feet and slammed both hands down on the surface of his desk. 'A little whining? A little whining? Oh, give me patience. You threatened a federal officer with a firearm and you describe his reaction as a little whining? You are lucky that you still have a job, Lieutenant – even luckier that you still are, at least for now, a lieutenant. What were you thinking?'

'Sir, I did not threaten him with a firearm.'

'Really? What do you call it?'

'Sir, I rested my hand on my gun. It was in the holster. The holster was still snapped shut.'

By now, Holland's face was blood-red and veins throbbed in his throat and at his temples. 'If you don't call it a threat, what do you call it, Pierce?'

'I just wanted him to know I was serious.'

'Oh, he got that. He said he was in fear of his life.'

Lucinda rolled her eyes. 'BS,' she said.

'Do you want me to charge you with insubordination, Pierce?'

'No sir, I—'

'Then clean up your attitude.'

'I'm sorry, sir. I know my reaction was extreme but Connelly was badgering two parents who had just learned about the death of their son. He was leaping to unwarranted conclusions and he was undermining my investigation.'

'Well, it's not your investigation any longer. Connelly's the lead now. Lovett is assisting him. And you are out of the picture. Go to your office right now, forward any digital evidence you have to me and pack up anything and everything else in your office connected to the case and bring it in here.'

'Is this really necessary, sir?'

'The decision has been made, Pierce. They didn't even tell me until it was a done deal. The police chief called me after he hashed it out with Lovett's FBI supervisor and ATF Deputy Federal Security Director Wesley. And just for the record, Pierce, I am really pissed off at you this time and haven't decided what I am going to do about it. And, no, it's not the political embarrassment of being ultimately responsible for you that has my dander up; it's the fact that an explosion at one of our high schools – the one closest to this office – has been taken out of our hands; one of our kids is dead and we cannot be involved in solving the case – that is all because of you. It's all on you, Pierce, and that pisses me off. Now, get out of here and go get those files together.'

As she was walking through the doorway, the captain said, 'One more thing, Pierce.'

She turned around and said, 'Yes, sir.'

'Lovett has been ordered not to discuss the case with you. Don't pressure him or he might end up out of a job. And while we're at it, you all ought to stop seeing each other socially until this case is wrapped up.'

Socially? He doesn't know we're living together? We haven't gone out of our way to publicize that fact but we also haven't tried to hide it. I had assumed everyone knew. Maybe I should call Jake and make sure he doesn't volunteer the information unless he's directly asked.

When she reached her office, she continued to think about the wisdom of making that call or waiting to talk to him that evening. She first emailed every case-related file on her computer to Holland. Then she got an empty business envelope box and stacked documents in it. She picked up one of the two notes she found in David Baynes's room but her hand hovered over the pile. She set the piece of paper off to the side. She did the same with the other message as well as her handwritten list of David's friends. When everything else was in the box, she sat down to think.

It was important evidence but they needed the cooperation of David's friends. If Connelly goes in there with his hostile, suspicious attitude, the kids will balk at cooperating and the parents might hire attorneys. That would cut off all communication and stop any possible answers in their tracks. No defense attorney on the planet would want a teenager talking to law enforcement when Homeland Security was raising the threat of terrorism charges.

Lucinda picked up the notes and her lists with notations about addresses, phone numbers and times of parental arrivals, slid them into a manila folder and walked down the hall to the copier, grateful that she could get there without going past Holland's office. She made copies of all the documents and returned to her office where she slipped both the copies and the originals into her satchel.

Putting the lid on the box with the other evidentiary documents, she lifted it and carried it down to Holland's office. 'Where do you want me to set this down, sir?'

'Over there by the wall. Is that everything, Pierce?'

'That is what you ordered, sir.'

Holland looked at her with indecision etched in his brow. If he demanded a direct answer to his question, she knew she couldn't lie to him but she hoped it didn't come to that. 'Is there anything else, sir?'

His wariness still showed in the expression on his face but he waved his hand and said, 'No. That will be all. Why don't you call it a day? If the chief comes down here while he's still in a fever pitch, it won't be good for either of us if you're still here.'

'Yes, sir.'

'You're deskbound for now, Pierce, until I say otherwise. Understood?'

'Yes, sir,' she said and spun on her heels, making a fast exit. She needed to get out of there before she said something she'd regret.

In her car, she pulled out her cell and hit the button for her favorites list, then pressed Jake's cell number.

'Lieutenant Pierce,' Jake answered, 'I cannot discuss the case with you. Please don't call this number again.'

FOURTEEN

L ucinda's heart felt as if it stuttered and stalled before it began beating again. Her hands shook as she guided her car into a parking space on the side of the road. *Don't call his cell ever again. Did he really mean that? No. Of course not. Someone must have been with him. He was warning me and acting tough for his audience. Who was with him? Connelly? Or his supervisor, the Wicked Witch of Washington, DC? Or ATF Deputy Regional Director Wesley? Whoever – it doesn't really matter who it was, does it? He'll explain it all when I see him. I just need to go home and wait until he gets there.*

After feeding Chester and snacking on Havarti, stoned-wheat crackers and a glass of Pinot Grigio, she got restless and anxious. What if he doesn't come home? What if it's all over? What if he did really mean it?

She went out on the balcony and paced. Which one of them would stay in their new apartment? That was easy. *I can't afford it on my own. I certainly will miss this view of the river. I wonder if I can get back into my old building? Until I actually speak to Jake, all I'm doing is creating senseless agitation.*

It was a good time to call Charley, the twelve-year-old girl who'd become a big part of her life since Kathleen Spencer, Charley's mother, had been murdered.

'Hey, Charley,' she said when the girl answered the phone.

'Lucy! It's been a horrible day.'

'What's wrong, Charley?'

'Well, I just missed getting an A on my algebra quiz. One stupid question. And I don't know how I got it wrong.'

'You'll make up for it. Those things happen.'

'Not to me. Not in algebra. It's sooo easy. I can't believe I was so dumb.'

'You're not dumb, Charley.'

'Duh. I know that. But I put down a really dumb answer. And that's not all.'

'What else happened?'

'You remember Madison?'

'One of the girls involved in the vandalism last year?'

'Yes. She's back. They made her repeat eighth grade.'

'Is she bothering you?'

'Yes.'

'Did you tell the principal?' Lucinda asked.

'Lot of good that did. She told me it wasn't charitable to diss someone who's trying to suck up to you.'

Lucinda conjured up an image of that language coming out of the principal's mouth and chuckled. 'She used those words?'

'Not all of them. She did say I was being uncharitable for not accepting her apology.'

'Oh, so she was apologizing to you?'

'Yes. Do you realize how annoying that is?' Charley asked.

'Maybe she's changed. Maybe she's sincere.'

'Puh-leez! Not you, too.'

Lucinda realized that wasn't an argument she could win and changed the subject. 'The reason I was calling is that I was just thinking that it was about time we did something together.'

'Yes, yes, yes. Sunday is Mother's Day. Me and Ruby made cards for you.'

Lucinda felt an ache deep in her chest. 'I think that would be a great idea, Charley. Since the three of us all lost our mothers, we ought to stick together.'

'Well, I kinda wanted some time just with you but we can do that another day. Ruby would be real sad if we left her with Dad on Mother's Day. What do ya wanna do?'

'I thought we might go for tea at the Olde English Shoppe. There will be a lot of mothers and daughters there but I don't mind that if it wouldn't bother you and Ruby.' Lucinda mentally crossed her fingers. It would be a good sign of healing if Charley didn't object.

'That would be fun. And Ruby's still just a little girl so she'll probably want to pretend that you're her mommy. Would that be OK?'

'Yes, Charley, it would be perfectly OK,' Lucinda said as a tear dropped from her one real eye.

'Oh, but do we have to wear white gloves to go to tea?'

Lucinda chuckled. 'I don't think that's necessary.'

'Oh, good. Ruby had to wear white gloves when she was a flower girl last year – and boy did she make a mess of them!'

'All right, then, make sure it's OK with your dad and I'll drop by for you and Ruby at three o'clock on Sunday afternoon.'

'Cool. But, Lucy, mean girls are mean girls forever. Just like some of the bad men you lock up. They don't stop being mean; they just learn better ways to trick people.'

Sounded like a good working definition of a sociopath, Lucinda thought but she said, 'You don't think people can change, Charley?'

'Oh, sure,' the girl answered. 'But they have to have some good inside their hearts – and Madison? Her heart is as black and rotten as a banana left in a locker all semester.'

FIFTEEN

For another hour, Lucinda stewed and fretted. She thought of calling Jake despite what he said but then thought better of it. She couldn't bear it if she called and got the same response as the last time.

Finally, the front door opened and Jake entered the apartment. She rushed towards him and exchanged a kiss. He pulled back and put his index finger up to his lips.

'Jake, what's—'

He raised his finger again and shook his head. 'How about we go for a walk down by the river?'

'A walk?'

'We'll put on some suitable shoes and take a nice walk,' he said, stepping past her to the bedroom. He sat on the side of the bed, pulled off a pair of green Converse high-tops and slipped on a pair of Rockport walking shoes. 'Get a move on, Lucy. Time's a-wastin'.'

'Times a-wastin'? Are you feeling all right?'

'Never felt better,' Jake said with a cheeriness that struck Lucinda as false.

'Jake, what is—'

Jake emphatically pressed his index finger to his lips. 'I'll wait for you downstairs.'

Lucinda watched him leave. She was totally perplexed but she knew the only way to get any answers was to pull on her shoes and meet him outside. And he was still wearing his suit. He was going to take a walk dressed like that? Something was wrong. Instead of waiting for the elevator, she took the stairs down. She wasn't sure if it was any quicker but at least she wouldn't be standing around doing nothing.

'Jake?' Lucinda said as she approached him.

He put an arm around her shoulder and said, 'Listen, I know you probably think I'm nuts. And I am probably being excessively paranoid. But when the Wicked Witch forms an alliance with her counterpart in the ATF, anything is possible.'

'You think they bugged our apartment?'

'It's possible.'

'Really?'

'The Wicked Witch has my home address, and from what I saw of the two of them today, I'm sure she'd have no reluctance about sharing that information with Deputy Director Wesley.'

'Oh jeez,' Lucinda moaned. 'My captain told me not to socialize with you until the case is resolved.'

'You don't need to worry about that.'

'Why not?'

'Both the FBI and the ATF are pretty ticked off at your police chief.'

'But he took me off the case.'

'Yeah. But that's where he drew the line. He refused to fire you. He told them that they had no control over his department and hiring and firing decisions were internal matters not subject to their review or approval.'

'He did? That's a surprise. The captain made it sound like everyone was one big happy family.'

'They want everyone to think that. They don't want to risk seeing the conflict blaring in headlines or on television. But there's a lot of animosity brewing on both sides, which is probably for the best as far as our job security goes.'

'But what if they find out we're living together?'

Jake shrugged. 'We'll deal with that when it happens. But, quite frankly, if they haven't already bugged the apartment, that will give them a reason. As long as they never hear us discuss the case, they'll be too busy trying to figure out how to turn the situation to their advantage.'

'By having you spy on the police department through me?'

'Maybe. But just because they ask and just because I might agree, that still doesn't mean I'd do it.'

'And you think your cell might be tapped, too?'

'Mine and yours. Maybe. I just don't want to take any chances.'

'Well, I took a big one today, Jake.'

'What did you do?'

'I held on to some of the case information I had and didn't turn it over to the captain. I wanted to give it to you.'

'Risky. Risky, Lucy. What is it?'

'I found two notes in David's room when I searched. One was from a girl only identified by the letter "E", asking for his help with a problem. The other was a note from an unidentified person asking for a meeting behind the Walking Dog the night before he died.'

'Oh, c'mon, Lucy. That's actual evidence. You're withholding actual evidence. And what about the chain of custody?'

'I handled the notes only with gloves on and I placed them in separate plastic sleeves. I labeled and sealed them.'

'Where are they now?'

'In the safe in our walk-in closet.'

'You've got to turn that in. Tell the captain they were in the trunk of your car and you just remembered them.'

'No, Jake. I will not. Not with Connelly involved in the case. Listen. I have one more thing that probably will help identify who wrote the notes. The Bayneses gave me a list of David's friends – fifty-seven of them. I started getting addresses and phone numbers and even called a few of them. But I don't want Connelly bullying those people. Either he'll terrify the kids into shutting up or the parents will hire attorneys and slam the door.'

'You're probably right about that. It's not going to be easy to hide what I'm doing from Connelly. I'll have to run two simultaneous investigations – one for his eyes and another that's not. Hopefully, if I get results in the latter, I'll be able to think of some way to slip it unnoticed into the former. Man, this could get really complicated. Hey, you want to keep walking up to El Sol and La Luna and grab some dinner and a margarita before heading back home to get to work on your list?'

At the restaurant, they both ordered crab and shrimp quesadillas and loaded the tops with sour cream, avocado and salsa. The margaritas took the edge off of their anxiety and the good meal left them in a state of contentment that they each contemplated quietly as they walked home holding hands.

Inside, they fell into a work pattern of keeping legal pads by their sides and using them to communicate everything about the case. They threw in bits of idle, phony conversation about the books they were reading and leaned over to exchange noisy kisses. If anyone was listening, they wanted their activities to seem harmless.

Just after eleven that night, Jake stood, stretched and jotted, 'Well, we've got it all together for everyone on the list with a last name. I'm calling it quits; my brain is fried from the tedium.' He pulled Lucinda tight against him, pressing a hand into her lower back.

'I think I know what's on your mind,' Lucinda said.

'I think you're probably right,' he said before kissing her again.

'So, what if they are listening?' she whispered in his ear.

'What if they are?'

'I can try to be quiet but if, well, you know, if that happens, I doubt if I can,' she continued in a *sub rosa* voice.

'Let 'er rip,' Jake whispered back. 'Let them think we're having wild, monkey sex – better than anything they've ever imagined.'

Lucinda laughed out loud and then put her mouth back to his ear, 'Wild monkey sex? Where did you come up with that?'

'I read it in a book somewhere. Not completely sure I know what they meant but I'm up for defining it in any way you see fit.'

'As long as I'm not going to have to scratch under my arms and make those weird monkey grunting noises.'

'Everything is optional, Lucy. It's time to pick and choose and enjoy.' He pressed her against the wall and kissed her breath away. When he let her up for air, she raced down the hall, discarding pieces of clothing as she ran.

SIXTEEN

Lucinda sat at her desk in the Justice Center, sorting, filing and filling out forms. She startled when she heard her name. She looked up and saw Captain Holland in her doorway.

'Need you on a suspicious death,' he said.

'Look like homicide?' Lucinda asked.

'Nope. Looks like a suicide but we've got to investigate it until we're sure.'

'You want me to investigate?' Lucinda said, pointing a finger to her chest. 'I thought I was deskbound.'

'Give me a break, Pierce. Considering how stretched we are manpower-wise, you must have known that couldn't last long.'

On her feet, Lucinda slipped her arms into a khaki blazer. 'Didn't know but I did hope,' she said with a grin. 'Who is it?'

'Looks like the other high school student that went missing last weekend.'

'Could it be—'

'Don't get your hopes up, Pierce. It doesn't look like it. It sounds like a suicide from the responders at the scene. But just in case, if you see any hint of a possible connection to the explosion, come straight to me. Stop what you are doing and come straight to me. Is that clear?'

'Yes, sir,' she said.

Holland pointed a finger at Pierce. 'I'm serious now. I'm not playing games. You find a link, we'll talk it over, see how far you can run with it. You overstep without my seal of approval and you'll be out on the street.'

Lucinda nodded. 'Yes, sir, I understand.'

'Just be sure you do it,' he said. He turned around and walked away.

Grateful of her release from the desk and eager to poke around for a connection to the explosion at the school, Lucinda rushed out of the parking lot to the site where patrolmen now watched over the body of a teenage boy. Partway to the location, more sobering thoughts supplanted her excitement. A young man was dead and, whether it was a suicide or a homicide, his parents would be devastated – even if he was a constant source of problems, the emotions of his mother and father would crumble like a termite-hollowed log.

Lucinda pulled into a quiet neighborhood and on to Guinevere Lane. The road ended in a cul de sac where two police cars were parked. She pulled her car to the side behind them. A uniformed patrolman stood a short distance away 'in the grass between two houses. Neither of the backyards had fences, making it easy to walk between them down to a grove of trees. Looking at the ground, Lucinda saw a faint but obvious flattening that indicated it was a well-traveled path.

On the way back, Lucinda asked, 'Gruesome scene?'

'Actually, not,' the officer said. 'He looks very peaceful, maybe even content.'

'Doesn't sound like any kind of attack.'

'Doesn't look like one at all.'

Entering the wooded area, Lucinda felt a sense of irony. Here she was investigating death while, all around her, life seemed to be erupting with vigor. The deciduous trees had all leaved out but still bore the bright, vibrant green of new growth. Old brown undergrowth was now overrun by a fresh crop of green shoots. A blackberry bramble off of the beaten path was covered with white buds not yet opened in full blossoms.

In a small clearing to the right, Lucinda saw the body. At first glance, the boy appeared to be sleeping, his mouth hanging open with the corners of his lips turned up in a shy smile. His arms rested flat on the ground. The curled-up fingers of one hand held a prescription container, the other a bottle of water. Next to him, she spotted a makeshift fire pit, a ring of soot-covered rocks surrounding a circle of blackened earth.

Lucinda made a broad circle around the perimeter and approached in a straight line to minimize the disturbance of the site. Crouching down, she peered at the pharmacy label: OxyContin, prescribed for Barbara Matthews. It clearly was not the woman's body but it definitely indicated to Lucinda that she was looking at the remains of Todd Matthews, the other student missing from Woodrow Wilson High School.

She looked over the body and saw no signs of injury. She couldn't flip him over and check his back, though, until Doc Sam or one of the other forensic pathologists arrived. Although some perpetrators try to mask a homicide with the appearance of suicide, at this point Lucinda was not seeing any evidence indicating that this was anything more than a tragic, self-inflicted loss of life.

As she rose, she visually followed the path that brought her here and saw it continued on through the woods, slipping out of sight. 'Any idea of where it leads?' she asked the officers.

Both of the men shrugged their shoulders and said, 'No, Lieutenant.'

The patrolman who led her back added, 'You want me to go check?'

'No, one of you needs to stay with the body. The other one needs to be out near the street, directing new arrivals. Whoever that is can start running yellow tape from the street, up the path and around this location,' she said and took off to follow the beaten earth of the trail.

As soon as Lucinda went around the small bend that blocked the rest of it from her view earlier, the path crossed a narrow trickle of a creek and headed up a small rise. She dodged the muddy spots by the running water and trudged uphill. When she reached the crest, she was surprised to realize that she was behind the high school. She felt a flutter of excitement in her chest. Did that indicate a connection to the explosion? Or was it serendipity?

Walking back to the body, she spotted two new patrol officers rolling out the yellow tape, wrapping it around trees. She approached them and said, 'Run the tape all the way down this trail and block it off at the far edge of the woods. The high school is back that way and I imagine this path was made by students so I want both entrances blocked off and an officer posted at each end.'

Back at the body, Lucinda pulled out her iPhone and snapped a close-up photo of the dead boy's face for confirmation of his identity. As she put it away, she spotted a man approaching, wearing a medical examiner's windbreaker, followed by two men in white uniforms. The first man held out his hand, I'm Dr Perry, but you can call me Mike.'

Lucinda shook his hand and said, 'Lieutenant Lucinda Pierce, but you can call me whatever you like.'

Perry chuckled. 'I have a message for you from Doc Sam. He said, "Tell Pierce I truly regret not being able to join her for a picnic in the woods but at the moment, I am elbow deep in viscera." And he wanted to know if he could get a rain check for another forest rendezvous.'

Lucinda rolled her eyes. 'Leave it to Doc Sam to add the romantic touch to any occasion.'

Perry kneeled down beside the body, examining it *in situ*. When he leaned back, Lucinda asked, 'Do you need a hand turning him over?'

'Yeah, sure. Thanks.' Together, they gently placed the body face down. 'No sign of trauma back here, either,' Perry said.

'Look like a drug overdose?' Lucinda asked.

'That's a good possibility at first glance, but I won't know for sure until I get toxicology. It wouldn't take much with OxyContin if that's what he used.'

Rising back up, Lucinda said, 'Well, I'd better go see Mr and Mrs Matthews, get confirmation that this is their son.'

'Good luck, Lieutenant. I wouldn't wish that experience on anyone.'

SEVENTEEN

After contacting dispatch, Lucinda had an address for the Matthews, just one street over on Lancelot Lane. She pulled up in front of a split-level ranch and walked up the sidewalk. When she touched the doorbell, the door flew open as if programed to do so. Standing on the other side was a T-shirt-and-sweatpants-clad woman who appeared to have gone to hell but hadn't completely found her way back. Lucinda held up her badge.

'Did you find him?' she asked.

'We should talk inside, Mrs Matthews.'

The woman doubled over as if Lucinda had punched her in the stomach. A high-pitched keening rose from her throat. A man ran down the half-flight of stairs. 'Barb, Barb,' he said, then turned to Lucinda. 'What did you do to her?'

Barb sucked in a breath and tried to speak. 'They, they – oh, Jeff.' She spun toward her husband and wrapped her arms around his waist.

'Sir, Mr Matthews, sir?' Lucinda said.

'What do you want?' he snapped.

'Could I please come in? I need to talk to you and Mrs Matthews.'

'What did you tell Barb? What did you say to upset her? And where is my son?'

'Sir, that's what I want to talk to you about,' Lucinda said.

'May I see your badge?' he asked.

Lucinda pulled it out and held it up.

'Homicide? Someone murdered my son?'

'Sir, may I please—'

'I'm sorry. I'm sorry. Neither one of us has had much sleep. Please come in. We'll go up to the living room.'

Lucinda followed up the steps. The couple huddled together in the middle of the sofa. Lucinda took a chair a short distance away. On the mantelpiece was an assortment of photos of their son at all ages of his life. There was no doubt in her mind that the discovery in the woods was Todd Matthews. 'I am sorry to say that we believe we found your son's body this morning.'

'He was murdered, Barb,' Jeff said.

'Sir, we don't know that. We are treating it as a suspicious death,' Lucinda said.

'Maybe it's not him. Maybe it's someone else. Just 'cause we reported him missing doesn't mean it's him,' Barb said, her voice getting more shrill with each word.

'Ma'am, I do have a photo I can show you to confirm his identity.'

'Ohmigod! I couldn't bear that. I couldn't look at a dead child. Any dead child. And if it's – if it's . . .' Barb said before breaking down in sobs.

'Is it gruesome? A lot of blood? Or . . .' Jeff said before stalling out.

'No, Mr Matthews,' Lucinda said. 'In fact, I thought he looked very peaceful.'

'OK,' he said, inhaling deep and holding the breath in his chest for a moment before releasing it in a quivering sigh. 'I'll look at it,' he said.

As Lucinda pulled out her cell, Jeff pressed his wife's head to his chest in a protective gesture. Lucinda held up the photo.

Jeff gasped. 'Yes. Yes. That's Todd,' he said and turned his head away. 'But he just looks like he's sleeping.'

'Yes, sir. That's one of the reasons that we do not think it is a homicide. We saw no injuries on him.'

'What's the other reason?' Jeff asked.

'In one hand, he had a water bottle. In the other, he held a plastic prescription container labeled OxyContin. The name on it was Barbara Matthews.'

Barb jerked her head up. 'OxyContin? That's from a while back – after my accident.'

'I thought you threw them away, Barb,' Jeff said. He turned to Lucinda. 'She only took one of them and it really knocked her for a loop. She got another painkiller from the doctor and didn't take any more.' He spun his head back to his wife. 'I thought you were going to throw them out.'

'Well, I was going to,' Barb said, 'but then I thought, what if the pain gets too bad? What if I need them? And then I forgot about them.'

'And now our son is dead,' Jeff said as he rose to his feet and began pacing the room. 'I can't believe you didn't throw them out.'

'Mr Matthews, excuse me,' Lucinda interrupted. 'This is not helpful. Please sit down. I really need to ask you a few questions.'

For a moment, Jeff looked as if he was going to ignore her. Then he slid on to the sofa as far from his wife as possible.

'When did you last see Todd?' Lucinda asked.

'We already told that missing persons detective,' Jeff snapped.

'Please, bear with me, Mr Matthews—'

'Saturday night,' Barb said. 'A little bit after midnight when he got back from the Walking Dog.'

'The Walking Dog, Barb? I thought we decided that he shouldn't be going to seedy hang-outs like that.'

'It's not seedy, Jeff. And that's why he didn't ask you. You are too rigid.'

'Yeah, your permissiveness was the right thing, wasn't it? You let him do what he wanted and now my son is dead.'

'He's my son, too,' Barb shrieked.

Lucinda stood, holding out her hands, 'Please, please, I need your help. Todd needs your help.'

They both looked down at the floor.

'Now, did you hear from him after that at any time?'

Barb and Jeff's heads popped up. They looked at each other as a bright flush rose in their faces. Jeff hung his head back down. Barb jutted out her chin and said, 'Yes. He called our landline when we went down to the police station at two a.m. Sunday night or Monday morning, whatever. Anyway, we went to report him missing and missed his call.'

'Did he leave a message?' Lucinda asked.

'Yes,' Barb said with a nod.

'Did you give the tape to the missing persons detective?'

'No,' Barb said. She turned a withering glance on Jeff. 'My husband did not think that would be a good idea. I foolishly listened to him.'

'Mr Matthews, why did you think that?' Lucinda asked.

Jeff did not look up and did not respond.

With a deep sigh, Barb rose to her feet. 'Come on,' she said. 'You should listen to it. It's on our computer.'

Barb led Lucinda into a small, neat office with a computer work-station on one wall and a long work table on the opposite one. Barb woke up the computer and punched a telephone icon. She scrolled to a message received at two seventeen a.m. and opened the file.

She pressed the audio start button and Todd's voice came out of the speakers, sounding slow and a little slurred. 'Mom, Dad, just wanted to let you know I love you. You don't need to worry about me anymore. And you don't have to stay together for the sake of the kid.' He chuckled without humor. 'Go ahead and split up. You should have done it years ago. With me gone, there's no need to try to fake it.' The call clicked off.

Barb appeared to shrink as she listened. If a human being could melt at will, Lucinda was certain that Barb would have done so right before her eyes.

'I shouldn't have listened to him,' she said and shuddered. 'I wanted to cut a copy to a disk and take it back to the station right away. But Jeff said it wouldn't look good – it would reflect badly on us. He said it would just prove that he ran away and the cops would stop looking for him. Oh God, I wish I hadn't listened to him.' Barb sank to her knees and buried her face in her hands.

Lucinda laid a hand on her shoulder and let her sob. When Barb raised her tear-ravaged face, she said, 'Maybe if I'd gone back to the police, maybe he'd still be alive. Maybe he could have been found and his life saved. I said that we needed to do something – something was wrong, I said. He doesn't sound right. Jeff said, "He's just been drinking – all teenagers do that at one time or another. When he sleeps it off, he'll be crawling back here, promising never to do that again." And I had my doubts, but I didn't push. I should have. I will never be able to forgive myself for that.'

Lucinda kneeled beside her. 'I have a couple more questions, Mrs Matthews.'

'Yes, please, whatever you need,' Barb said. A slight tremor in her speech made each word seem as fragile as spider web.

'Did Todd have his own car?'

'Oh, no. He's only fifteen,' she said, her voice cracking. She sucked in a sob and looked Lucinda in the eye.

'How did he get to the Walking Dog on Saturday night?' Lucinda asked.

'A friend picked him up.'

'Do you know who?'

'I'm sorry, no. All I know is that he was driving a red pick-up truck,' Barb said.

Lucinda's heart raced. 'Are you sure of the color?'

'Oh, yes. He stopped right under the streetlight.'

'Did he come home in the same vehicle?'

'I don't know. I didn't see him until he came up the steps.'

'And the last time you saw him? You didn't see him in the morning?'

'No. He was still asleep when I went for a walk in the park and he was gone by the time I returned. But Jeff saw him that morning.'

'I'd better go talk to him, then,' Lucinda said as she rose. She extended a hand to Barb who grabbed it and pulled herself upright.

Returning to the living room, Lucinda saw Jeff sitting where she'd left him. He looked up and she saw tears in his eyes. 'Did you see Todd Sunday morning?'

'Yes. He came into the kitchen, guzzled a glass of orange juice, slammed a banana in his mouth and mumbled, "See you later, Daddio," through the food. I almost told him not to talk with his mouth full but I didn't want to start another quarrel.'

'Where did he go?' Lucinda asked.

'Don't know,' Jeff shrugged.

'How did he get there?'

'Somebody picked him up.'

'Do you know who that was?'

'No. I asked if he was going somewhere with David and he said, "Nah, but I'll catch up with him later."'

David? There was a Todd on the list of friends she'd gotten from the parents of David Baynes. Lucinda's heart pounded hard. 'David who?'

'Umm, umm, can't remember.'

'Baynes,' Barb said. Lucinda turned and saw her leaning against a wall, her arms crossed tightly across her chest.

Lucinda struggled to keep her voice calm and smooth. 'David Baynes who lived over on Guinevere?'

'Yes,' Barb said. 'Wait a minute. You said "lived"? Has something happened to David, too?'

Lucinda nodded, 'Yes, but I am not at liberty to discuss that at this time.' She turned back to Jeff. 'Did you see the vehicle that picked up David?'

'Sure. A Ford pick-up. Looked new.'

'The color?'

'Red. Bright red. What we woulda called candy apple red when I was a kid.'

Lucinda felt as if she had a coiled rattlesnake inside of her chest. 'Did you get the license plate number?'

'No,' Jeff said, hanging his head. 'I'm sorry, no.'

After expressing her condolences and saying goodbye, Lucinda walked away from the home. Her ears were ringing from her speeding thoughts. She felt as if she were about to explode. There was a connection to the high school explosion. The captain would have to let her follow it through and find out exactly where it led.

EIGHTEEN

Charley didn't know what to think anymore. Her whole world had been turned upside down and shaken hard. She didn't know men did things like that to girls. She had a vague idea of what men and women did together from her health and personal hygiene class last semester – but that was something grown-ups did with each other. She never thought a man could do anything like that to a little girl. But she knew Amber wasn't lying. And it made all those warnings about strangers make more sense.

Before homeroom, she'd found Amber sobbing in the girls' room, locked inside a booth. It took a while for Charley to convince her schoolmate to unlatch the lock. Amber said, 'It hurts so bad and I'm still bleeding.'

Charley asked what happened and almost wished she'd never heard the answer. The sickening details about what the boyfriend of Amber's mother did to her poured out in strangled sentences broken up by sobs. It made Charley feel light-headed and nauseous. What was forced on Amber shouldn't be done to anyone. Why would any man want to do that?

The teacher had scolded Charley when she slipped into her first-period English class fifteen minutes after the bell. Now that the period was almost over, she felt relief. She'd paid no attention to anything that had been said. She only hoped she'd make it a few more minutes without Mrs Hanna calling on her for anything.

All Charley could think about was how to help Amber. She did not want her friend to go back home. But Amber had sworn Charley to secrecy so Charley couldn't tell anyone. Amber said, 'He told me if I said anything to anybody, he would kill my little brother.' When Charley tried to get her to go see the school nurse, Amber would not even consider it.

Amber was in Charley's third-period algebra class. She had to think of a plan before then. She had to get Amber away from that man.

At that moment, the teacher looked in her direction. 'What do you think about their decision, Charley? Should they have given up or kept trying?'

Charley tried not to look as stupid as she felt. 'Gee, Mrs Hanna, I just think the whole thing has me confused.'

'That's understandable, Charley. Anyone in class have any thoughts they want to share?'

Not one hand went in the air and no one made a sound.

'OK, then,' Mrs Hanna said, 'I want you all to read the story again tonight and be prepared to share your ideas with the class tomorrow. I will expect everyone to have something to offer to the group.'

Charley couldn't believe faking it had been that easy.

NINETEEN

A s soon as Jake pressed the button on the receiver, he heard, 'We got a hot lead. I'm heading out to follow up with observation of the suspects.'

'Connelly?' Jake asked.

'Yeah, yeah, yeah. Thought you'd want to come along to eyeball them.'

'What've you got?'

'Suspected Muslim extremists who weren't where they were supposed to be on the Sunday morning the high school blew,' Connelly said.

'Muslim extremists? Why would they target a school when it was supposed to be empty?'

'You got mush for brains, Lovett? Terrorists blow things up. Who else would we be looking for?'

'What about David Baynes?'

'He was a suicide bomber, of course, recruited by the terrorists. Listen, you coming along? I'll be there in five. Meet me outside. If you're not there, I'm not coming to look for you,' Connelly said and clicked off from the call.

It didn't quite fit together for Jake. Don't suicide bombers go into crowded places? Don't terrorists want to cause as many deaths as possible? And why would they pick a white middle-class kid to carry out their mission?

Shaking his head, Jake left his desk and walked outside to wait for Connelly. A black SUV screeched tires as it pulled into the parking lot and came to halt beside him two minutes later. Jake couldn't see through the heavily tinted windows but when the passenger door popped open, he knew it must be his ride.

He clambered in and asked, 'Who are we checking out?'

'Ibrahim and Fatima Irfan.'

'Names sound Pakistani,' Jake said.

'Yes. Unfortunately, they are here legally so we can't call in INS to assist. In fact, they've been US citizens for the last eleven years.'

'Citizens? Doesn't sound like Muslim extremists to me,' Jake said.

'They could be part of a deep-cover sleeper cell.'

Is Connelly stretching the facts to fit some bizarre scenario in his head? Or is he just jerking me around? 'You really think that?'

'I think that's possible,' Connelly said with a nod.

'What do you have tying them to the explosion?'

'A tip, Lovett.'

'How do you know it's solid?' Jake asked.

'Because the Irfans did not open their convenience store until just after noon last Sunday.'

'Maybe they do that every Sunday.'

'Aha! Nope! Sunday mornings, they're usually there by seven before the churches open their doors. Apparently, a lot of people buy gas on the way to services.'

'That sounds a little thin. There's an infinite number of reasons: illness, a family problem, oversleeping . . .' Jake said.

'Thin, Lovett? Thin? They own a red pick-up truck. They are Pakistani. That means they must be Muslim. And they place regular phone calls to Pakistan every month.'

'Maybe they have family there.'

'My point exactly. Divided loyalties. The man who called in the tip said he's heard them making comments denouncing America and that they threw a party after 9/11.'

'You got a name for that tipster?'

'Nah. It was anonymous. You know how people are reluctant to get too involved.'

'There is another possibility, Connelly. Maybe the person responsible for the explosion is trying to divert our attention. Or maybe someone with a beef against the Irfans is using you to get even with them.'

'You've been watching too much TV. Why don't you just reserve your judgment until we check them out?'

Might as well, Jake thought as they pulled up to a small ramshackle building, whose windows were blocked by new and older, curled advertising posters. Connelly parked between the front door and the gas pumps. An old red pick-up, nearly faded to pink, sat on the side of the building.

'Does that look like the red pick-up truck we're looking for?' Jake asked.

'Sure looks like it.'

'Ah, c'mon, Connelly. The witnesses referred to the truck as new and jacked-up.'

'You know how unreliable eyewitness testimony can be, Lovett. Just relax. We're not going in there to be confrontational. This is just to size them up. We'll grab drinks from the cooler as if we're just two regular customers.' Connelly led the way inside and Lovett followed.

It looked like hundreds of little mom and pop stores Jake had seen before: tight aisles crammed full of product that left little room to maneuver. It was the kind of place where you could find almost anything if you were willing to look long enough. Behind the counter, a couple stood side by side. Both were in their late fifties or early sixties, of the same short height, with dark skin and black hair. He wore a white short-sleeve shirt and khaki pants on a thin, fragile-looking frame. She was pleasantly stout in a matronly blue, flowered shirtdress and old-fashioned tennis shoes.

'Welcome, gentlemen,' Ibrahim Irfan said as they walked past the counter.

Connelly ignored the greeting. Jake said, 'Good morning.' They both grabbed a soft drink from the glass-front cabinets that lined the wall.

While they paid for their beverages, Jake noticed a necklace around Fatima Irfan's neck. A gold chain bore a series of small, round medallions with blue stones set in the center. A solid gold crucifix hung in the middle.

'Lovely piece, ma'am,' Jake said pointing to his own neckline. 'Is it Pakistani?'

A smile crossed Fatima's face as her fingers touched the chain. 'This, oh, yes – Kundan, to be precise. Thank you. It was my mother's.'

'Unusual for Pakistan, isn't it?'

'Not among the Catholics – there are quite a few of us there. Most people in this country, though, are surprised to know there are Christians in our native land.'

'It is one of the reasons we came to this country,' Ibrahim added. 'It is difficult to practice our faith there without fear.'

Jake nodded and said, 'Have a good day,' before following Connelly out to the car. 'Satisfied?' he asked the other agent.

'With what?' Connelly asked.

'They're not Muslim – they're Catholic.'

'Nice cover story for a pair of terrorists, don't you think?'

'Next you'll be saying Fred Garcia was a suicide bomber.'

'Don't be ridiculous, Lovett. With a name like Garcia, the dead groundskeeper had to have been a Catholic – they have serious prohibitions against suicide. His faith would not allow him to set off a bomb that would take his own life. Besides, he's Mexican, isn't he?'

'Actually, I think he is an American citizen just like the Irfans. American and Catholic, Connelly.'

'Don't be a PC monkey, Lovett. It's blinding you to the facts before your eyes. We still don't know why the Irfans didn't open their store Sunday morning. Until we find that out, they are suspects. We'll put the possibility that Fred Garcia's death was a Mexican mafia hit on the theoretical list. Right now, we need to focus on the Mohammed factor and the whereabouts of the Irfans at the time of the incident.'

'Oh, Jeez,' Jake said as he got out of the car and headed back into the store. Approaching the counter, he said, 'Excuse me. I meant to ask you about your hours of operation.'

'You did not see them listed on the door?' Ibrahim asked.

'Oh yeah,' Jake said. 'But, you see, it says you open at seven on Sunday mornings and when I stopped by here last Sunday morning, you were closed.'

'I am sorry for your inconvenience, sir,' Ibrahim said. 'We were both ill. We think it was the food we picked up for our dinner on our way home from the store Saturday night. We had a neighbor put up a sign on her way to church that morning. You must have arrived before she did.'

'It was around eight thirty, I think.'

'You must have just missed her. Again, I apologize for your inconvenience.'

'No problem,' Jake said, flashing a smile. 'I wanted to know just in case I was out this way again on a Sunday morning. Thanks.'

Sliding back into the car, Jake said, 'They had a bit of food poisoning last Sunday morning. And before you dismiss it as convenient, they do have a witness – a neighbor who put a sign up on the door.'

'I still think we need to get a tap on their phone line.'

'I won't support you in that warrant request, Connelly. In fact,

I'm telling you up front, if you ask for one, I'll argue against it. These are grandparents who came here seeking religious freedom. Sounds like a pretty all-American story to me. And considering the details of the incident at the high school, the idea of it being the work of Muslim extremists strikes me as pretty loony.'

'Loony? Don't get on your high horse, Lovett. Although I am aware that we have plenty of lunatic fringe domestic terrorist groups out there, I know all Muslims harbor the ability to commit violent acts of terrorism.'

'Why are you insisting that it's an act of terrorism?' Jake asked.

'It's obvious, Lovett, that's why. And I am going to uncover the terrorist plot that led to this tragedy. If you don't want to assist, that's fine. I won't have to share the glory. But I am determined to get to the bottom of a terrorist plot before I retire, and that's coming real soon – I won't let you get in my way.'

'Relax, Connelly, I'm here, aren't I?' Jake said. The ATF agent's strange logic made sense to Jake now. Connelly was consumed by his career bucket list and knew his time was limited. Until he scratched that item off of his list, he'd be seeing terrorist plots everywhere. Jake hoped that Lucinda was making progress on a more productive line of inquiry and could carry through to the end before someone shut her down.

TWENTY

Lucinda returned to the Justice Center and went straight to Captain Holland's office. Holland was on the phone but when he saw her standing in the doorway, he waved her inside and gestured to a chair.

Lucinda could tell from his end of the conversation that Holland was squabbling with someone over budgetary over-runs. She hoped that financial concerns would not limit her ability to investigate.

After hanging up, Holland muttered about bean counters and asked, 'You find something?'

'Yes, sir. I—'

'Shut the door,' Holland ordered.

Lucinda rose, closed it and returned to the chair. She explained the connection between David Baynes and Todd Matthews as well as the presence of a red pick-up truck. Holland nodded through her explanations of those two overlaps but then winced when she told him about the notes she'd found in David's room.

'Dangerous, Pierce.'

'Necessary, Captain.'

Holland put his hands on the desk, interlaced his fingers and stared down at the surface. When he raised his head, he said, 'Is that it?'

Lucinda said, 'You asked me to find any link between Todd's apparent suicide and the explosion at the high school and report back to you.'

'Yes, but they all seem to be rather nebulous connections, don't you think?'

Lucinda looked over his face, trying to read his thoughts. Holland's countenance was placid with no signs of anger or disappointment. What was going on here? 'Sir, maybe I wasn't that clear.'

'Oh yes, you were very clear, Pierce. I appreciate you reporting back to me as I requested but, as you can see, the vagueness that is still present in your findings strongly indicates the need for you to continue to follow up on your leads.'

A smile slowly slipped across Lucinda's face. It sounded as if the captain was justifying her continued investigation. 'Well,' she said, 'we cannot conclusively determine whether or not it was a suicide until we have the toxicology results.'

Holland nodded, smiling back at her. 'Of course you can't. We've seen our share of homicides staged to look like suicides and because of that you need to keep working on this case. We sure wouldn't want to get so enthused about these coincidences that we leap to premature conclusions, would we?'

'No, sir,' Lucinda said. She wanted to jump up and click her heels together but she remained seated with a rigid control on her decorum. The captain had her back after all.

'Where do you need to go from here?' Holland asked.

'The big question, as you've pointed out, sir, is whether or not this was an actual suicide. That will largely mean simply waiting for results from the lab. But, in the meantime, I want to find out more about the relationship between Todd and David and whether or not they saw each other on Saturday night or Sunday morning – computer data and information from cell phones would help. We also need to know who picked up David the night before the explosion and who, then, is presumably the owner of the red pick-up truck. Maybe "E" who wrote the note to David is also a friend of Todd's – or perhaps the "Kev" she mentioned is a vital part of the equation. Could Kev be the driver of the truck?'

'Take tonight to plan out your course of action. We don't want to rattle any cages with unwarranted speculation and we don't want anyone outside of this department to think we are overly enthused about any particular theory, if you know what I mean.'

'Absolutely, sir. I will keep the whole situation as low-key as possible until you decide we need outside assistance.'

'Keep me in the loop, Pierce. I can't help you if I don't know what's going on. If the crap hits the fan, I need to know where to find the off switch.'

'You got it, Captain.' Lucinda was relieved but exhausted. The day had felt much longer than it had been. Tonight, she needed to brainstorm with Jake. She hoped he got home in time to do that and to relax with her over a bottle of wine afterwards. All she wanted was a little peace and quiet.

TWENTY-ONE

The first thing Lucinda saw when she opened the door to her apartment was Chester flying over the back of the sofa and heading her way. Next, she saw two heads pop up from the same spot. She instantly recognized one of them. 'Charley?'

'Hi, Lucy,' Charley said, jumping to her feet. 'I want you to meet my friend Amber.'

The other girl rose cautiously and slowly faced Lucinda. Amber had a solemn face framed by a short haircut. She wore a striped polo that Lucinda thought looked like a hand-me-down from an older brother. Amber's jeans were loose and rolled up at the ankles – more passed-along duds?

Lucinda stepped forward and held out her hand, 'Hello, Amber.'

Amber wedged her hands in the front pockets of her jeans and didn't look up.

Charley looked back and forth between the two of them, unsure of what to do. 'Amber, this is the police I told you about who can help you, who can keep everybody from getting hurt. This is Lieutenant Lucinda Pierce.'

''Lo,' Amber mumbled without raising her eyes.

'Charley,' Lucinda said, 'come help me get some drinks for all of us. Then we can all sit out on the balcony and relax. Amber, you can wait right here or go out and wait for us there. We have a lovely view of the river.'

In the kitchen, Lucinda asked, 'What is going on here, Charley?'

'Amber has a problem. She needs your help.'

'What's the problem?'

'I can't tell you. I promised.'

'Is Amber in danger?'

'Yes. It's serious, Lucy.'

'Charley, listen to me. It is not always good to keep a promise of silence if, by doing so, you'll leave the other person exposed to harm.'

'I know,' Charley said with a sob. 'That's why I begged and pleaded with her to talk to you. And she said she would. And I got her away from her house – at least for the weekend. Daddy said she could spend it with us.'

'Is Amber being abused at home?'

'I can't answer that without breaking my promise. Please don't make me break my promise,' Charley pleaded.

'I might have to, Charley. I'll try not to but I may not have a choice. C'mon, here's three glasses, fill them with ice and take them out to the table on the balcony. I'll grab the iced tea and the ginger ale.'

When Lucinda and Charley returned to the living room, they saw that Amber had already wandered outside where she was leaning against the banister and looking down at the water below.

'Amber,' Lucinda said, 'would you rather have iced tea or ginger ale?'

Amber shrugged her shoulders without turning around.

'C'mon, sweetie, pick one. It doesn't matter to me.'

Amber looked back over her shoulder. 'I never had ginger ale.'

'You want to try it? If you don't like it, you can change your mind.'

Amber turned all the way around and nodded. She accepted the glass and took a sip. 'Oh!'

'Do you like it?' Lucinda asked.

Amber nodded. 'It sparkles on my tongue.'

'Good,' Lucinda said. 'Now, let's all sit down round the table and talk about your problem, Amber.'

Amber spun toward Charley and glared.

'Amber, I didn't—'

'Amber,' Lucinda interrupted, 'Charley told me you had a problem but that's all. If you want me to know more – if you want me to help – you'll have to tell me exactly what it is.' Looking at the young girl, Lucinda had a pretty good idea. Withdrawn and dressed boyishly – was she always like that? Or was that the outward manifestation of a sexually abused girl trying to assume protective coloring in a hostile environment?

For a moment, Amber didn't move. Then she lifted one leaden foot after another and joined Charley and Lucinda at the table but didn't look at them. She kept her eyes focused down in her glass.

'Charley,' Lucinda began, 'why don't we start by you telling me how you found out Amber had a problem?'

'I found her crying in the bathroom at school. She was crying so hard it made my heart ache. It took me forever to get her to open up the stall. She didn't want to talk to me at first but finally she did. And I believed her but it still was so unbelievable – I never knew things like that happened.'

'Things like what, Charley?' Lucinda asked.

'I can't tell you, Lucinda. I promised Amber. I promised.'

Lucinda saw tears welling in Charley's eyes and gave her an encouraging smile. 'Amber, see what a good friend you have? She believes in you. She wants to help you. And she made a promise to you that she is determined to keep.'

Amber lifted her head and looked at Charley. Her lower lip quivered but she did not say a word.

'Amber,' Lucinda continued, 'you've put Charley – your good, loyal friend Charley – in a very difficult spot. She wants to keep her promise to you but she wants to help you. Charley thinks that the best thing for you to do is talk to me – to tell me what is going on in your home. Are you going to trust her on that? Or are you going to let her sit there in turmoil, knowing that whatever she does, she'll be doing something wrong.' Lucinda leaned back in her chair and waited.

Two minutes passed, with Charley becoming more and more

fidgety with every passing second. Every time Charley parted her lips as if ready to speak, Lucinda motioned to her to remain quiet.

Finally, Amber broke the silence. 'He said if I told anybody, he'd kill my little brother.'

'Amber, I understand and respect your fear,' Lucinda said. 'But I promise you that won't happen. Every single action I take to protect you will be done carefully and deliberately with the safety of both you and your little brother in mind. I understand the danger and I won't put either of you at risk.'

Amber shuddered and sighed.

'Amber, please,' Charley begged. 'You trusted me but I can't do anything. You need to trust someone who can.'

'What if she doesn't believe me?' Amber said, choking on her own words. 'My own mother didn't believe me.'

'You told your mother?' Lucinda said.

'Yes,' Amber said, tears sliding down her face. 'She slapped me and called me a liar. She said I was a selfish little girl who didn't care about anyone's happiness but my own.'

'I will believe you,' Lucinda said. 'I know we don't know each other, Amber. But I know Charley and I know Charley believes you. That's good enough for me.'

Amber's small chest heaved as she exhaled and began recounting the theft of her innocence. Lucinda was repulsed at the details of her abuse – progressing from fondling to forced fellatio to anal rape over the last two years. Lucinda worked hard to keep that feeling of revulsion off of her face because she knew how vulnerable Amber was – she knew the child would interpret any expression of distaste as being directed at her.

Amber's sobs made her nearly incoherent as she finished her horrific tale. Lucinda opened her arms and Amber fell into them. Lucinda pulled her into her lap, wrapped one arm around the girl's frail shoulders and placed the opposite palm on the side of Amber's head. Looking over at Charley, Lucinda's saw that her young friend was swallowing hard as she tried to keep her tears at bay.

Once Amber stopped sobbing, she gently pulled back and said, 'I'm scared.'

'Of course you are, Amber, but I am going to take steps to make you safe. Still, it will take a while for you to stop being afraid but it will come in time. Now, when did your mother say that you had to come back home?'

'She said it would be good not having me around causing problems for everybody, but I had to get back by Monday after school because she starts a new job and I need to be there to look after my little brother Andy after school.' Amber rubbed the back of her hand across her nose.

'OK. That's good. That gives us a few days to take care of everything. What is the name of your mother's boyfriend?'

'Eddie. Eddie Springer.'

'Do you know where he lives?'

'He lives with us.'

'Does he have a job?'

Amber nodded. 'He works at some pool hall but I don't know where.'

'OK. One more question, Amber. Are you hurting physically right now?'

'Yes, ma'am,' she said, her lip quivering.

'Where does it hurt you, sweetheart?'

'My bottom hurts and it's bleeding a little.'

Lucinda fought to stay calm. She wanted to storm out of there, hunt down Eddie Springer and put a bullet between his eyes. 'Now, you two just relax for a bit. I have to make some phone calls. You can stay out here, or if you want to go inside, that's fine. Charley knows where to find some snacks if you're hungry.'

As Lucinda eased up from the chair, Charley put her arm around Amber and patted her friend's back. They were whispering together as Lucinda went inside.

In the bedroom, Lucinda shut the door before pulling out her cell and calling Charley's father, Dr Spencer. 'Evan, Charley's little friend has a serious problem. She needs to be seen by a physician immediately. I could take her to the emergency room, but I'm worried that might be too traumatic for her. I was hoping you might know a female physician who'd be willing to see her in a more private setting after hours.'

'What's her problem?'

Lucinda detailed the trauma of Amber's abuse and explained the pain problem. 'Do you know of anyone who might be able to help at this time of the evening?'

'I do. Actually, I know just the doctor for this situation. Let me see if I can reach her. I know she'll want to know if a police report has been filed. Are you taking care of that?'

'Yes, Evan. I'm going to see to that and to getting both Amber and her little brother into a safe situation.'

'OK. I'll call you right back.'

Lucinda left the bedroom and found the girls in the kitchen, sitting at the counter, eating bowls of ice cream. It would probably ruin their dinner but that felt very insignificant under the circumstances.

'Is Daddy on his way, Lucy?' Charley asked.

'He's got to make a phone call first.' Lucinda poured a glass of Merlot and stepped back on to the balcony to wait for Evan's call. She startled when the phone rang.

'I got hold of her. I'll be there in just a few minutes and we're going to meet the doctor at her office in half an hour,' Evan said.

'Good, I'll explain to them what's going on so you won't have to deal with any panicked reactions.'

'Good luck with that. Sometimes, I am flat out ashamed to be a man.'

TWENTY-TWO

On the way home, Jake stopped by the Happy Dragon to pick up dinner. He almost called Lucinda when he couldn't decide whether or not to get the kung pao shrimp or the triple delight for her. But, since he really wanted to surprise her, he just bought both along with his favorite, the sweet and sour shrimp plate.

He had second thoughts on his way home. What if she's in the middle of fixing dinner? Maybe I should have called first. Then again, heated up, the Chinese would all work well for the following night. Nonetheless, when he entered the apartment, he looked first at the kitchen, relieved to see no preparation in progress.

He set the food down on the counter and found Lucinda out on the balcony. Slouched in one of two lounge chairs, she sprawled like a liquid spill across the cushions. 'Man, you look more tired than I feel,' he said.

'Hey, Jake,' she grinned. 'Got a kiss for a weary warrior?'

He placed a peck on her lips and said, 'Looks like you had as bad day as I did.'

'Actually, I thought it was a good day until I got home. After I got in the door, I had to change my assessment really fast,' she said, swinging her legs to the side and standing up for a hug.

Jake embraced her and asked, 'Was something wrong here? Where's Chester? Is he hurt?'

'Chester is fine. He's sitting in the bedroom window soaking up the sun. When I came home, Charley was here with a friend. I'm famished, Jake, come into the kitchen with me while I throw something simple together for our dinner and I'll tell you all about it.'

'You don't have to fix a thing.'

'What? You're cooking?'

'I can, you know.'

'Oh yes, Mr Special Agent Man, you are an expert at pulling food from the freezer and popping it into the microwave.'

'I did better than that tonight. I brought dinner home. Let's fix plates and come back out here to eat. So what's wrong with Charley? Is she in trouble again?'

'No, Charley's fine. It's her friend who has a problem but I don't think I can talk about it while we're eating,' she said as she walked into the kitchen and opened the take-out boxes. Seeing the selection, she poked fun at Jake for his indecisiveness over the order. When they sat down, she said, 'Update me on your day with Connelly.'

Jake ran through the events and said, 'Connelly is not going to pursue anything that does not point to a Muslim terrorist conspiracy and that's not what it looks like to me.'

'I agree – the scenario is all wrong from the timing and the people involved. David Baynes as a suicide bomber sounds ludicrous to me. Was he serious about the Mexican mafia as an alternative theory?'

'I believe he is,' Jake said with a sigh.

'Sounds like Connelly is in need of intervention.'

'Agreed. Unfortunately, it is out of my hands. If I were to attempt having him removed, it could result in them taking me off the case. So are you following a more productive line of inquiry or did the captain shut you down?'

'Definitely the former – Captain Holland is backing me up all the way.'

Jake waited for her to continue but when she didn't, he said, 'That's it? That's all you're going to tell me?'

Lucinda looked at the plate and set down her chopsticks. 'I told the captain about the notes. And about the information I learned today.'

'What information?'

'I need your promise – like the notes, this stays between you and me. I can't have Connelly mucking this up.'

'Of course, Lucy. I'm not going to jerk you around.'

'Even if it means you're stuck running down rabbit trails with Connelly?'

'Yes. Can't say I like my role. But it is what it is and anything you tell me I will keep between the two of us.'

Lucinda talked about the connection between David Baynes, who died at the high school, and Todd Matthews, who seemed to have committed suicide. Then she moved to the red truck connection with Todd. 'It appears as if they are all tied together. I think what I need to do next is find that red truck. I was thinking about going to the high school in the morning and getting a list of all faculty and student parking permits for red pick-ups, but I don't want to run into Connelly.'

'You won't, particularly not if you go there in the morning. We, too, are looking for a red pick-up. We're taking a list of red pick-up owners and matching them to people on the terrorist watch list and making a circuit of those people. Connelly said if that doesn't work, we might have to resort to a street-by-street grid search, starting with the area around the mosque. He has no plans to go up to the high school tomorrow because he wants to wait until students are back in school so he can go through the parking lot. Your plan certainly makes more sense but he doesn't want anyone at the school to know what he is looking for. He's driving me crazy.'

'I think he's already gotten there,' Lucinda said. 'I'll go to the school first thing in the morning. Now that the undamaged part of the building has reopened and temporary trailers have been installed to house the wrecked office and classrooms, the staff will be there in full force for an in-service day devoted to the plan to care for the kids' needs when they return.'

'Usually, when you have a productive day like that, no matter how long or tiring it is, you're charged up with energy when you get home. But tonight you seemed drained. The problem Charley's friend has must be pretty serious. Is that what's making you keep looking at your phone?'

'Yes, I'm expecting a call from Evan.'

'Evan Spencer? But I thought you said Charley was fine?'

'Yes, she is.'

Jake folded his arms across his chest. 'Then why the interest in Spencer?'

'Jake, are you jealous?'

'Maybe. All I can get from you is a month-to-month commitment.'

'Oh, please, Evan is the last person you need to worry about,' Lucinda said. 'I needed Evan's help with the difficult situation facing Charley's friend. Quite frankly, it's absolutely awful. The little girl needed a discreet examination by a female doctor and Evan found one.'

'That doesn't sound good.'

'It's not,' Lucinda said and then, after a heavy sigh, explained about Amber.

'No wonder you're wiped out.'

'Now, I'm anxious to hear from Evan about how the doctor's visit went. I can't make any decisions on where to go next to protect this child until I know what I have to offer social services and the sexual crimes unit.'

'Are there people you can trust in both departments?'

'I think so. The timing of this is so delicate. We need to make sure that the children are both safe when that bastard is arrested. And we need to be sure that they'll keep him away from them afterwards.'

'No way you can get a guarantee of no bail.'

'No, but there are alternatives. Personally, if he gets out, I think he should be monitored with restrictions on where he can go and the kids need to be stashed someplace where they will be safe from harm.'

'So, all you are asking for is common sense and logic. Sounds easy but in practice it's often impossible.'

'I know but I will be relentless.'

'Would you go so far as to run off and take the children with you?'

'If it comes to that, Jake.'

TWENTY-THREE

After Amber's examination by Dr Carson Winters, Evan's first priority was getting Amber to his home and settled into bed. He made arrangements to call the other doctor at home after he'd accomplished that.

Charley showed Amber up to her room while Evan relieved Kara, the babysitter, and checked in with his younger daughter, Ruby. 'Now, Rubikins,' he said as he tucked her into bed, 'you stay out of Charley's room tonight.'

'But I want to meet her friend,' Ruby objected.

'There will be plenty of time for that. Amber will be here all through the weekend.'

'But, Daddy—'

'And don't go in waking them up tomorrow morning. Amber has had a very hard day and she needs her sleep and she's just not up to meeting another new person tonight.'

'OK, Daddy . . .'

'Promise?' he asked, lifting up two fingers in a modified scout pledge.

'Promise,' she said, mimicking his actions.

'That's my girl,' he said, giving her a peck on the forehead. 'Sleep tight.'

He went down the hall to Charley's room and knocked on the door. He heard a gasp inside and knew it must be Amber.

'Come in,' Charley said.

'No, no, no!' Amber objected.

'It's OK, Amber. It's Daddy.'

Evan opened the door a crack and said, 'Don't worry, I'm not coming in. Charley, you two can stay up as late as you want tonight and just sleep as long as you need to in the morning.'

'But, Daddy, it's a school night,' Charley said, the surprise at his leniency apparent in her voice.

'So call this an exception to the rule. If you need to go in late in the morning or even stay home all day, I'll write your excuses. Come on out here and give me a kiss goodnight, Charley. I'm heading off to bed.'

Charley bounced off her bed and out into the hall. Evan eased the door shut behind her.

'Charley, I know I've always had a house rule about not locking your door at night in case there is an emergency, but if it makes Amber feel safer, go ahead and do it.'

'Are you sure, Daddy?'

'I don't like the extra responsibility it puts on your shoulders, Charley, but right now Amber's feeling of security is really the most important thing to consider.'

'OK, I'll let Amber decide. But I'm not a little kid anymore, in case you haven't noticed.'

'Oh, I certainly have,' Evan said as bittersweet emotions flooded over him. 'Good night, Charley.'

'Wait, Daddy. Why did he do that to Amber? What made him do that?'

'I don't have an answer. I don't think any decent man understands why some men do things like that. You're not worried about me doing anything bad to you, are you?'

'No, I don't worry you'll do something bad – it's just sometimes you are so embarrassing. I wish you could try not to be so dorky when we're at the mall.'

'OK, I'll try,' he said, walking off and shaking his head, wondering how his self-esteem would survive Charley's teenage years. In his bedroom, he called Dr Winters. 'Hi, Carson,' he said when she answered.

'Well, Evan, it's obvious that the girl was telling the truth. I found clear evidence of rape and collected a sperm sample. The good news is that although there is some physical damage, it should heal with time. Just give her some Tylenol when she experiences any pain. The bad news is that she may never completely recover from the emotional damage. She's going to need the care of an adult with a lot of love to give and mountains of patience if she has any hope of a normal life after this ordeal.'

'I think the best I can do for her right now is keep my distance and let Charley take the lead as her friend. I'd like to wrap my arms around her and rock her to sleep, but I know if I tried, she'd be terrified.'

'Yeah, it's going to be a while before she trusts any man. Tell your lieutenant that I'm ready, willing and eager to testify at any hearing or trial. Amber should never return to that home and her little brother needs to get out of there as soon as possible, too.'

After hanging up, Evan called Lucinda and relayed the information from Dr Winters. 'And listen, Lucinda, I can't take on Amber and Andy permanently – I'm already worried that I'm not up to the challenge of raising my two girls on my own – but if there is a need for a temporary placement until the right home can be found for Amber and her brother, I am willing to take that on.'

'Evan, I can't tell how much I appreciate that. My schedule is so erratic that I knew I couldn't do it but it just might be the solution to getting them into a safe environment without delay. Is Charley doing OK?'

'Right now, Lucinda. But I'm worried about how this will affect her ability to have a good relationship with a man in the future.'

'I wouldn't worry about that Evan. Charley has a great father watching over her – she'll know a good man when she sees one.'

'You couldn't say that when we first met.'

'No, Evan, I couldn't. At times, you were a bit of a jerk – but you'd just lost your wife to an act of violence and were under suspicion for her murder. All things considered, you did pretty damn good. Now, if you can only survive the teenage years with two girls – glad it's you and not me.'

TWENTY-FOUR

In the morning, Lucinda set up an eleven a.m. meeting in the conference room with a social work supervisor from Child Protective Services, a CASA volunteer attorney and a detective from the sex crimes division before driving over to Woodrow Wilson High School.

The student parking lot in the back was empty but the space on the side for faculty and administrative personnel was packed. Lucinda walked through there, noting the presence of three red pick-up trucks before going inside.

Lucinda didn't blink at the sight of high chainlink fence around the exterior of the damaged portion of the building but, inside, the same barrier looked out of place. The demolished hallway was blocked and a long table with two chairs rested in front of it. Sitting on the floor, in neat stacks beside the table, were sealed boxes filled with the contents of the intact lockers marked with a unit number and a student's name. On the surface were containers holding the items rescued from those that had blown to bits. Each box was piled high with a pathetic and jumbled assortment of mangled textbooks, battered binders, all sorts of school supplies and a collection of shoes and clothing whose continued use was doubtful.

She followed the handwritten signs to the makeshift office that was nothing more than a repurposed closet with a desk, telephone, computer and one staff person. The handwritten sign on the front of the desk read: 'Administration Office Outpost – full services available in trailers 201 and 202 on the west side of the building.' Fortunately, the woman in the small cubicle was able to direct Lucinda to the cafeteria where all staff had gathered for a meeting. She eased open the doors and slipped inside. A psychologist was talking to the group about the impact on students and preparing them to anticipate wide reactions from boisterous acting out to total withdrawal.

Principal Rose Johnson spotted the detective before Lucinda located her. Rose left her seat and walked to the back of the room and the two women stepped out into the hallway. 'What can I do for you, Lieutenant?' the principal asked.

'I was hoping you could provide me with a list of parking permits for red pick-up trucks. Would that be possible?'

'Thank heavens that the school district tech guru insisted on a rigid schedule of computer back-ups. The desktop where that data was inputted was totally destroyed but we were able to restore it all on to a laptop. We'll need to go outside to the temporary office – oh my, what a mess.'

'The staff seems to be taking it well.'

'Ha! You should have arrived ten minutes earlier. They were acting like a bunch of twelfth graders ready to escape the system. Shouting questions at me and demanding answers I simply do not have. A few thought that we shouldn't start classes up again until there was a memorial service for Fred Garcia. I told them that Mrs Garcia planned an early-evening celebration of her husband's life that they all could attend but they objected, saying that we should have a remembrance here on campus. The moment I had that under control, a few others voiced their outrage that we were still in this building, but, honestly, there is no place else for us to go. The school-age population has been exploding in the district and there's no room anywhere. I did get one good and reasonable suggestion out of the shouting match, though. We have maintenance workers on their way with plywood to block the sight of the ripped-apart hallway from the students' view. That should be completed right after lunch. Well, here we are,' she said, pulling open the door of the trailer marked 201.

Inside, three frazzled-looking women all talked on phones while non-stop ringing continued in the background. 'Oh dear,' Rose said. 'I'm going to have to recruit a couple of teachers to help out in here.'

Before picking up another call, a gray-haired woman said, 'Rose, it's been non-stop all morning.'

'Sorry, Meredith, I'll go get some back-up for you but, unfortunately, right now I need to pull someone off the phones to get some data for Lieutenant Pierce.'

'Tiffany was the first one in this morning and probably needs a break from the calls more than anyone.'

'Thanks, Meredith,' Rose said and turned to Lucinda. 'Meredith is our office manager and you're in luck, Tiffany is our go-to computer nerd so you shouldn't have any trouble getting what you need.' After making introductions, Rose excused herself to find more staff to answer the incoming calls.

Lucinda explained what she needed to the short-haired blonde with intense brown eyes peering from behind a boxy pair of black glasses. In less than five minutes, the detective had a print-out of the staff names for the drivers of red pick-up trucks and another one with the students who drove the same type of vehicle.

Before going back into the main building to talk to any of the teachers on the list, Lucinda went to the parking lot to see what she could learn from looking over the vehicles. The first one she located belonged to Tilly Campbell, a math instructor and 4-H Club sponsor. She drove a full-sized pick-up with a crew cab. The bed had a black liner that was scratched and pitted as if it had seen a lot of hard use. It sat up a bit higher than the average truck, making it a good fit for the witness description. Although not brand new, it was only a couple of years old and its paint was still bright and shiny. Inside, the cab was a rolling disaster with piles of paper and dozens of pens and pencils scattered on the floorboards.

The next red truck, owned by chemistry teacher Chet Bowen, was a small, faded red, older-model Ranger. It had quite a few years on it and the bed was nearly scraped clean of paint. The cab, though, was spotless. The dash appeared polished, the steering wheel wrapped in leather and not a single piece of trash or paperwork could be seen anywhere. The only visible article inside was a neatly folded T-shirt that read 'If you're not part of the solution, you're part of the precipitate'.

The third vehicle in question was the most likely suspect of all. A GMC Sierra Denali in metallic red with large, chrome-laden wheels. The rear sat up higher than the front, giving it the appearance of a sprinter ready for take-off. The bed was as spotless as if it never carried anything heavier than a grocery bag. The interior was clean with black perforated leather seats and a shiny, reflective peace sign dangling from its visor. The owner was Brittany Schaffer, an English teacher.

Lucinda went into the building and located Rose Johnson who set her up in a classroom and sent someone to find Annie Potts, a cafeteria worker who could assist Lucinda by rounding up the teachers she wanted to question. Before Rose left, Lucinda showed her the list of teachers and said, 'Do any of them seem likely to have been involved?'

Rose thought for a minute and shook her head. 'Chet Bowen sure isn't – he's the most boring man I've ever met. Oh, don't get me wrong. Put him in front of a classroom to talk chemistry to students and he transforms into the most animated instructor you've ever seen. Let him talk about his favorite subject and his eyes twinkle, his hands fly and he bounces around the room as if every instant leads to a new and dramatic discovery for mankind. Anything else and he's a major yawner.'

'Maybe the chemistry of explosive reactions would interest him?' Lucinda suggested.

'Nah, not Chet. There's not an extreme bone in his body. An unenthused Presbyterian, moderate Republican with a placid wife and two very well-behaved and equally boring children.'

'So what about Tilly Campbell?'

'She's a real pistol from Texas: down-to-earth, with an uninhibited laugh and a devotion to livestock. She sees herself as an urban missionary for the wholesome farm life – but try as she might, she never seems to round-up more than a handful of students for the 4H Club. I doubt that she'd never get caught up in anything dicey.'

'Brittany Schaffer?'

Rose rolled her eyes. 'I swear I do not know how that woman managed to get a degree. I don't think she's capable of plotting anything but a party. She's flighty and too flirty with male teachers and students alike – I've had to talk to her about that on more than one occasion since I came here as principal three years ago. And the way she dresses! I have had to speak to her about that more times than I can remember. In fact, I spoke to her about it this morning. Told her that dress she was wearing was perfectly acceptable for an all-staff day but I didn't want to see it on a class day. She got all pouty with me, whining that it was a brand-new dress she bought especially to wear to school. I finally got her to promise not to wear it on campus when students were here but I doubt if she'll remember that commitment for more than a week. As the common wisdom suggests, look up "sieve-head" in the dictionary and you'll see her picture.'

'Do any of them have any grudge or problem with Fred Garcia?'

'Fred? You think he was the reason for what happened here?'

'Just covering all the bases – no matter how unlikely.'

'I can understand that,' Rose said with a sigh, 'but I think that avenue of inquiry is a waste of time. Fred was everybody's friend. Even though it wasn't his job, he's the one they all turned to when they had a flat tire, a car that wouldn't start or something heavy to carry into the school. And Fred helped them all, every time they asked. Well, look, here's Annie. I'll leave you two to get your job done.'

Annie appeared young enough to be one of the students. Her dark blond hair was pulled back in a perky ponytail and a meteor shower of freckles spread across her cheeks and nose. She wore jeans, a T-shirt and a big white apron folded over and tied tight behind her back.

'Annie, you can take off that apron and leave it here if you like,' Lucinda said.

'Shoot, ma'am, nobody would recognize me without it,' she said with a big grin. 'Fact is, they'd probably hustle me outside and tell me that classes won't start till tomorrow. I learned at the beginning of the school year that the apron is all that stops me from being sent to the office when I'm caught in the hallway in the middle of class periods.'

'You do have a point,' Lucinda said with a laugh. 'I'd like to talk to Chet Bowen first.'

'I'll be right back,' she said and bounced off with her ponytail swinging.

TWENTY-FIVE

Jake grew more and more exasperated with Connelly with every passing mile they drove. Jake tried logic, teasing, reverse psychology but nothing seemed to ease Connelly's obsession with a Muslim plot. They visited a mosque where Connelly threatened and insulted an imam. They stopped in at every Pakistani-owned convenience store in town – even going out of the city limits to badger the handful of shopkeepers in the suburbs.

Connelly topped it all when he went into Dr Abhinav Singh's office and barged into an examination room where a patient sat on the end of the examination table in his street clothes. 'You,' he said, holding up his badge and pointing to the turbaned physician, 'have some questions to answer.'

'Sir, I am in the middle of examining a patient. Please return to the waiting room and I will be with you momentarily,' the doctor said in a measured, calm voice.

A nurse stepped into the doorway. 'Doctor, I am sorry, I tried—'

'Do not worry, Miss Frazier,' Dr Singh said.

'Come on, Connelly. This is highly inappropriate,' Lovett objected, half convinced that if the cuffs belonged on anyone, it was Connelly.

'Cuff him, Lovett,' Connelly ordered.

'No,' Lovett said, shoving the ATF agent back. 'Out of here now.'

'Look at their headdresses, Lovett,' Connelly said, pushing back. 'They are probably conspiring in here right now. Terrorists are always making political statements with their headgear.'

'They are Sikhs, not Palestinians, Connelly. It's religious, not political. Get out of here now or this is not going to end well.' Jake winced when he glanced over at the two other men, now standing side by side, appearing alarmed and uncertain of what to do.

'I'm taking them both in, Lovett. And that's that.'

'Then you are doing it on your own and you won't be bringing them into the FBI office.'

'Fine, Lovett. I'll have you off this case by lunchtime. You might want to start clearing out your desk, too. I'd lay odds that you'll be terminated before day's end.'

Jake thought about trying to overpower Connelly and force him outside. That action, though, seemed destined to escalate the situation into a violent response – someone could get injured or even killed. He spun around, walked out of the doorway, passing the shocked faces of the staff nurses, and went outside. He needed to get help for the ATF agent – Jake was now certain that Connelly was unstable and obsessed. Jake wished they'd taken his car. If they had, he could have left Connelly here without any transportation and easier to intercept.

He headed up the sidewalk in the direction of the coffee shop he'd seen just up the street. Stepping inside, he ordered a coffee with a shot of espresso and sat down to think over the situation. Connelly clearly had an unhealthy obsession with anyone whose skin color and features made them appear Middle Eastern. He seemed willing to believe that they all were Muslim and that every Muslim was a terrorist. And it appeared to Jake as if Connelly had come completely unhinged. Was he having a serious mental breakdown or a psychotic break? Or was it all a symptom of the early onset of dementia?

Jake had worked with ATF agents before and found every one of them to be competent professionals who didn't jump to conclusions or take rash actions. They were analytical, logical and knowledgeable. Connelly didn't appear to be any of the above.

But what exactly can I do about it? Jake wondered. *Should I call the Wicked Witch or should I go directly to the ATF and let them handle what is their internal problem? Would that look like a power play? Or would the Deputy Federal Security Director appreciate my discretion?* It was hard to tell. Wesley clearly had a bias against local law enforcement. Did that extend to every agency but his own?

Jake got up and ordered another cup. He knew he could not sit on the sidelines. Connelly had authority over the general public and he was misusing that power in a way that indicated psychiatric problems of some type.

He stepped outside, coffee cup in one hand, cell phone in the other. He stared at the keypad for a moment and then placed a call.

TWENTY-SIX

Chemistry teacher Chet Bowen did not look capable of speaking to a group of three or four, let alone a whole classroom of teenagers. A red bow tie bobbed on a prominent Adam's apple. His striped shirt struck a discordant note with a plaid sports jacket that appeared to be a refugee from the 1970s.

Lucinda started to stand when he entered the room. Then she noticed his tiny stature and the expression of meek surrender behind his dark-framed glasses and decided that he required gentler handling to get his full cooperation.

Chet stood in the doorway as if waiting for her permission to enter. When Lucinda greeted him, he walked into the room with tiny, hesitant steps as if he was afraid the floor might collapse beneath him at any moment.

'Please have a seat, Mr Bowen,' Lucinda said, gesturing to a chair on the opposite side of the table from hers.

He eased down and folded his hands on the surface. 'I don't really think I know anything about the explosion at the school but I will be glad to answer any questions you have for me.'

'You drive a red pick-up truck?'

'Yes, ma'am.'

'Did you drive it up to the school on Sunday morning?'

Chet furrowed his brow. 'No, I did not. You think my truck was here that morning? That's not possible.'

'Did you loan your truck to anyone else or give anyone permission to drive it?'

'Not since last summer.'

'Who did you loan it to then?'

'My neighbor – but he had it for less than an hour. He needed to pick up a dresser he bought at a yard sale.'

'Could he have made a copy of your key?'

Chet's eyes widened. 'A copy of my key? Why would he do that?'

'Maybe he wanted to use your vehicle without your knowledge in the future.'

'We've been neighbors for nineteen years, I can't imagine—'

'I'll need his name and address, please.'

He provided the information and then added, 'Please make it clear to him that I have not accused him of anything.'

'Certainly, Mr Bowen,' Lucinda said. 'Do you know a student named David Baynes?'

'The boy who died? No, he was never in one of my classes. I can't recall ever hearing his name before learning about his death.'

'How about Todd Matthews?'

'The name sounds vaguely familiar but I can't place it. I don't think he was one of my students. I could check the school records if you like.'

'You did know Fred Garcia, didn't you?'

'Of course. Fred's as much a part of this school as the roof above our heads.'

'How would you describe your relationship with him?' Lucinda asked.

'Well, we weren't friends, we didn't socialize outside of the school, but we had a cordial acquaintance. Exchanged greetings when we passed, like that. He once helped me tie up my muffler tailpipe when it was dragging. Good Lord, Lieutenant, you don't think Fred was involved in this conflagration, do you?'

Lucinda ignored his question and asked, 'Where were you on Sunday morning, Mr Bowen, and what did you do?'

'I was home until sometime after noon. I rose at approximately six twenty-five a.m. Answered the call of nature, brushed my teeth and then brewed a pot of coffee. After putting on my robe and slippers, I walked out front to collect my newspaper. Then I read it while drinking coffee. About nine a.m., I set that down and turned on the CBS *Sunday Morning* show, then switched over and watched the last half of *Meet the Press*. After that, I read a couple of journal articles until the phone rang and I heard about what happened at the school.'

'Would you call that a typical Sunday morning for you?'

'Until the phone call, yes. I am very much a creature of habit,' he said. A weak grin flashed across his face and then faded as quickly as it had arrived.

'After the phone call, you left the house?'

'Yes, I went up to the school but I left right away when I saw all the media there. We're not supposed to talk to reporters ever, unless it's been cleared by the principal.'

'Do you have any students who have demonstrated an abnormal interest in chemical reactions that cause explosions?'

Chet chuckled. 'Adolescents – particularly the boys – are very destructive by nature. Every year, someone asks me how to make a Molotov cocktail or how to blow up an anthill or something like that. But abnormal interest? I wouldn't say that.'

'Anyone specific stand out in your mind?'

'No, Lieutenant. I really don't pay them any mind. Some of them – possibly all of them – ask their questions hoping to shock me. I can't say I have ever had a student who seemed to be serious about actually doing it – except maybe the anthill guy, but that was a while back and I don't remember who that was.'

Lucinda looked at her watch. She was running out of time. She needed to get back to the Justice Center for her eleven o'clock appointment and then return here to interview the other two teachers. She slid a business card across the table. 'If you think of anything, Mr Bowen, please give me a call. What might seem frivolous or pure conjecture, on your part, could open doors in this investigation.'

'I certainly will but I doubt if anything will come to mind,' he said, standing with a look of relief on his face.

'But, sir, just make sure you do not go out of town until we can eliminate your truck as the one that was at the school that morning.'

'I–I–I am a suspect?'

'Everyone connected to this school is a suspect, Mr Bowen. Please do not share our conversation with anyone.'

He nodded and hurried out of the room in his short, mincing stride.

Not a likely suspect, Lucinda thought, but, then again, a lot of bombers are introverts. It can be their way of making a statement without having to speak.

TWENTY-SEVEN

J ake hesitated before he finished inputting Deputy Federal Security Director Franklin Wesley's number. He decided that having a delicate conversation with him about Connelly standing on a sidewalk wasn't a good idea. He'd rather be in the confines of his office. He decided to call a taxi instead but stopped when he saw Sergeant Robin Colter pull up to the curb.

'Need a ride, Agent Lovett?'

'Sure do,' Jake said. 'And I could use your help with a few other things, too.'

When Jake entered the office, one of his agents intercepted him with an urgent message from Marguerite Spellman. He sat behind his desk and called her first.

'Hello, Special Agent Lovett,' she said. 'I'm up in the FBI Terrorist Explosive Device Center in Quantico and I wanted to give you a heads-up on the report that will be headed your way shortly. The experts here agree with me that the explosion most likely originated in the file cabinet. It appears to have been ANFO – an ammonium nitrate bomb. Somewhere between ten and fifteen pounds of the stuff would have produced a sufficient amount of expanding gasses to create a shockwave commensurate with the damage on the site.'

'Ammonium nitrate? That's pretty common stuff. Can we narrow down where the bomber acquired it?'

'Common is right. It's actually a chemical fertilizer – not a problem in and of itself – but combine it with a little gasoline and/ or propane and you've got a disaster in the making. The good news is that since Timothy McVeigh used an ANFO, there's a law requiring that inert markers are incorporated into the ammonium nitrate to make it traceable. They are tracking down that data right now to determine the origin of the explosive. They found a bit of fuel oil residue as well but unless it contained additives that will show up in the gas chromatograph, that won't be much help.'

'Any indications of the trigger that detonated the bomb?'

'The analysis of the debris has uncovered a small piece of the accelerometer which could have been rigged up to a file drawer so that when the victim pulled it open, it would have activated. You'll get a full report when they finish collecting data. Just wanted to let you know where things stood at this moment in time.'

'Thanks, Marguerite. I really appreciate this.'

'Any time, sir. Is it true that Lieutenant Pierce has been pulled off the case?'

'Yeah, unfortunately, it is. But that's probably not the end of the story.'

Marguerite laughed. 'Knowing the lieutenant, I am certain that it is not.'

Jake disconnected the call and started to dial the Deputy Federal Security Director but stopped when his door flung open and an agent shouted, 'Local police chief on line three. He said he didn't care what the hell you were doing but if you weren't talking to him in thirty seconds, he was sending officers over to arrest you.'

Jake grabbed the line. Special Agent in Charge Jake Lovett, sir. How can I—'

'What the hell are you doing in your office?'

Jake held back a smartass answer and waited for the police chief to continue.

'I took my experienced investigator off of this case in deference to you federal jerks and now look what's happened.'

'What has happened, sir?'

'If you'd been with that lame-brained ATF goon, maybe this wouldn't have happened. Or, hell, I don't know, maybe you would have made sure there was a second victim.'

Jake shook his head, trying to make sense of the conversation. 'What do you mean by "victim"?'

'The nurse, you idiot.'

'What nurse, sir?'

'Don't play stupid with me, agent. I know you were there. I know you just walked out on those defenseless, unarmed people.'

'Something happened at Dr Singh's office?' Jake knew Connelly was not thinking clearly but . . .

'That ATF bastard shot a nurse in the foot when she tried to remove him from the doctor's examination room. What the hell where you all doing in there?'

'We had no right to be there. I tried to get Connelly to leave with me but he refused. I wanted no part of his harassment of the doctor.'

'So instead you left that guy to shoot up the place?'

'The nurse – is her injury serious? How is she doing?'

'Of course it's serious. All gunshot wounds are serious. Or don't they teach you that at the academy? She's in surgery right now.'

'What about the doctor? What about his patient?'

'We don't know where the hell they are. Are you satisfied? That so-called law enforcement agent got them out of there at gunpoint, threatening patients in the waiting room.'

'You put out an APB?' Jake asked.

'Of course I did. Do you think I'm stupid? I am so sick of you Feebs assuming our incompetence that I could spit. Who the hell do you think—'

'Sir, sir,' Jake interrupted. 'Just as you called, I was in the middle of dialing the ATF Deputy Federal Security Director to express my concerns about Connelly. I'd like to get off this call and do that right now. Then I'll coordinate with your dispatch to help you locate the agent and his passengers.'

'*Hostages*, Lovett. As far as we are concerned, they are hostages and your cohort is a fugitive. Get busy,' the police chief said before slamming the phone down in Jake's ear.

When Jake tried to contact Wesley, he hit a wall with a gatekeeper who insisted that the Deputy Director was not available. 'I suggest he becomes available real fast. One of his agents has been involved in a shooting.'

Jake heard a click and then Wesley's voice. 'Was the shot fatal?'

'No, sir.'

'How bad is Connelly injured?'

'He's not injured at all, sir.'

'Then what's the purpose of this call, agent? What kind of game are you playing?'

'Connelly did the shooting, sir.'

'What?'

'He barged in on a doctor who was examining a patient. He tried to take them both in for questioning because the doctor owned a red pick-up truck and both men were wearing turbans.'

'What does that have to do with anything?'

'Connelly is obsessed with Muslim terrorists, sir, and he sees them everywhere.'

'Which one of them did he shoot?'

'Neither one, sir. He shot the nurse who was attempting to remove him from the examination room.'

'The nurse? A female nurse?'

'Yes, sir. All five foot and four inches of her.' Silence followed. After a moment, Jake said, 'Sir?'

'You should have been there with him.'

'I left the situation because I didn't like Connelly's tactics and I was not about to assist him. I was preparing to call you when I heard what happened.'

'You shouldn't have left him alone.'

Jake couldn't believe that the blame was being deflected on to him again. 'Sir, if Agent Connelly cannot be trusted in the field alone, why is he still working for your agency?'

'That is an insolent, impudent and impertinent question for you to voice to a superior official at a collaborating agency. I've half a mind to report your gross insubordination to your supervisor.'

Jake sighed. 'I don't think she'd be surprised, sir.'

'Humph. I knew that you were a troublemaker when I first laid eyes on you.'

'Sir, I really need to get going. The locals want me to assist in finding Connelly and his hostages.'

'Finding Connelly? You don't know where he is? Hostages? What hostages?'

'He left the scene where he shot the nurse and took the doctor and the patient with him.'

'Well, you better learn real quick to use your troublemaking skills as trouble-*fixing* skills because I'm telling you right now, the ATF is not going down on this alone.'

Another phone slammed in Jake's ear. He left his office and called police dispatch on his way to his car, hoping they could find Connelly before any more damage was done.

TWENTY-EIGHT

Lucinda rushed into her office, grabbed her notes on Amber's situation and went down the hall to the conference room. She was five minutes late for the meeting and was relieved to see that Lieutenant Barry Washington, Sandy Purvis from CPS and Leticia Fletcher, the CASA volunteer attorney, were just arriving and not already seated and waiting on her.

After a flurry of greetings and the filling of coffee cups, they sat down around the table and Lucinda delivered her presentation about Amber's home situation, the medical report and the desired arrests of the mother and her boyfriend. 'At the moment, Amber is safe – she's staying in the home of a girlfriend. Andy, to this point, has not seemed to be in imminent danger but, with an abuser, we know that could change at any moment.'

'Most of them usually do stick to children of one gender in a particular age group,' Barry said, 'but there's no guarantee of that.'

'I don't like any children to be in that kind of environment. Regardless of whether they are being directly victimized or not, it is still a toxic situation. What kind of timetable are we looking at, Lieutenant Pierce?' Sandy asked.

'I don't want to take the children out of the home until the arrest is made because of the risk of flight. I'd like to do it all simultaneously and before Monday – that's when Amber's mother said she had to return home,' Lucinda said.

'So there will only be one child in the house at the time of arrest?' Sandy asked.

'Exactly. And I have a short-term solution for their housing if you all can make it happen. Dr Evan Spencer, the father of Amber's friend, is willing to take care of both the children until a more permanent placement can be found. Leticia, I thought that you might be able to facilitate that.'

'Emergency orders are my specialty,' Leticia said with a grin.

'Wait a minute,' Sandy interrupted. 'What about Dr Spencer's wife?'

'Deceased,' Lucinda said. 'She was a murder victim actually; it was my case and that's how I got to know the family. I've spent a lot of time with them in their home and with the two girls outside of it.'

Sandy leaned forward and rapid-fired questions. 'Any other adults in the home? Any other children? And what do you know about this man?'

'No other adults live in the home but one person frequently there is Kara, the girls' sitter. She's in her late twenties and very reliable. When needed, she spends the night even for as much as a week at a time when the doctor has to be out of town. The oldest girl, Charley, is Amber's age. The youngest, Ruby, is six years old. Dr Spencer is a well-respected orthopedic surgeon. He used to go out of the country on a regular basis to work with Doctors without Borders. Since he's been a single parent, he's cut back on that – no more than two or three trips a year now. They live in a condominium overlooking the river – the place has more square footage than two or three typical ranch homes. Each of Dr Spencer's girls has her own bedroom and there are two additional bedrooms. When Kara needs to be there overnight, a couple of the girls will have to double up but otherwise each child will have separate space.'

Sandy narrowed her eyes. 'And you trust him?'

'Yes, absolutely,' Lucinda said.

'Ever doubted him?'

'Well, yeah, but—'

'I don't like the sound of that, Lucinda.'

'He was my first suspect in his wife's homicide.'

'Oh dear God!'

'Listen, Sandy, we got the guy who did it. In fact, he's dead.'

'Did Dr Spencer kill him?'

'No, I did.'

'Sorry, I just—'

'Don't apologize for taking your responsibility for these children seriously. Listen, the girls found their mother's body – and it was a gruesome crime. Dr Spencer bumbled about a bit in the beginning, but he soon lived up to the demands of parenting two traumatized little girls. I don't think anyone could have done better. I do not think Amber and Andy could be placed in better hands for the transition.'

'I will have to interview him and Amber and Andy, too, before Leticia moves forward with the temporary custody.'

'I can set you up with Dr Spencer, and I'm sure you could talk to Amber in his home. As for Andy, you're going to have to make a decision without talking to him – we can't risk the mother and boyfriend finding out what is happening. Maybe you could go with fourteen days as a probationary period for custody. I promise you that Dr Spencer will give them a safe, caring environment.'

'Maybe seven days,' Sandy said. 'But I am not making a promise, Lucinda. As much as I trust you and your judgment, I can only commit to taking the necessary steps to make a determination. The best interests of the children trump everything else.'

Lucinda beamed a broad smile. 'I know that, Sandy. That's why I called you. Now, Leticia, once you get the go-ahead from Sandy, how fast can you move to make it happen?'

'Twenty-four hours or less.'

'Sandy, how long do you think it will take you to decide?' Lucinda asked.

'Can you arrange an interview with Dr Spencer and Amber today?'

'By the end of business hours?'

'Not necessarily. This evening will be fine. If you can do that, I can give you an answer in two days.'

Lucinda turned to Leticia, 'So you can get to a judge over the weekend, if needs be?'

'Oh, yeah. I live next door to one. She knows I won't give her a moment of peace if she doesn't listen to me when I say "emergency situation". I've trained her well over the years.'

'Terrific. Let's get busy. Barry and I will be ready to make the arrests as soon as you guys have everything in place.'

After Leticia and Sandy left the room, Lucinda said, 'Barry, can you take care of the paperwork for the arrest warrants and bring the DA up to speed? I've got to get back to the high school.'

'Woodrow Wilson High School?'

As soon as he asked, Lucinda realized her mistake. 'Um, well, actually—'

'I thought you were off that case.'

'What case?' Lucinda asked while she tried to plaster a look of innocence on her face.

'Don't play dumb with me. The explosion, Lucinda. Are you trying to lose your job?'

'How about if you just say, "Gee, I have no idea where Lieutenant Pierce is"?'

'I swear, Lucinda, one day you are going to play too fast and loose and not be able to wiggle out of the way when the axe comes down. And I don't want to be standing there holding your hand when it happens.'

'I won't let that happen, Barry. You know me: if I go down, I go down alone – today, tomorrow, forever. I implicate no one.'

Barry sighed. 'Anybody ever tell you that you're an adrenaline junkie?'

'Hey, you know my personal philosophy of life, don't you, Barry?'

'Lie hard, die young?'

'Sounds a little too preordained for me, don't ya think? Nah, it's this: if you're not living on the edge, you're taking up too much space. See ya later. Keep me posted. I've got some cliff-walking to do.'

TWENTY-NINE

Jake checked in with the desk sergeant in charge of coordinating the search for Connelly. He was asked to visit Connelly's office to speak with the office manager, Maggie Lazarus. He found her at her desk, trying to cope with never-ending phone calls. She went through a dozen calls in record time, answering with a curt 'ATF' and ending the call with a slam of the receiver before saying another word.

Finally, she looked up at Jake. 'Sorry. Media calls just won't quit. If someone was trying to call in an imminent threat, I doubt they'd get through. May I help you?'

Jake held out his badge and said, 'I need to talk to you about Connelly.'

'Doesn't everybody?' she said with a sigh. 'I can't hear myself think with this constant ringing and blinking red lights. Could we go down to the coffee shop on the corner and talk?'

'Sure, let's go,' he agreed.

'Let me grab my purse so I can lock up. There's no one else here and I really need a break.'

They descended in the elevator without a word. Outside of the building, Maggie pointed to her right and said, 'It's just up at that corner. If you want some ideas of where he might be, I may be able to help. If you want answers about why he hasn't been forced to retire before he went totally off the rails, those decisions are way above my pay grade.'

'You have an idea, though, don't you?'

'I'm not supposed to talk about internal ATF matters to outsiders, but under the circumstances . . .' She trailed off without completing her thought.

The Funky Bean appeared as disheveled as an old hippie gone to seed. Tired, over-stuffed furniture with worn-thin upholstery formed groupings around tables crowded with magazines, newspapers and paperbacks. A row of scarred, unpainted tables, with convenient electrical outlets and stools, lined up by a portion of one wall, ready for more Spartan laptop users.

Jake ordered a redeye – a coffee with a shot of espresso – and Maggie chose a vanilla latte topped with whipped cream. They sat down in the furniture grouping furthest from the counter.

Jake opened the conversation. 'I know it is difficult for you to talk about what was going on with Connelly to someone outside the ATF, but I need you to help me. I fear the outcome of this situation could get very ugly. At this point, no one can predict what will happen but I do know the locals are considering all eventualities and every option open to them.'

Maggie stared down into her cup, took a long swallow and said, 'I've been warning them for more than a year. But you've got to understand. Agent Connelly spent time at all three 9/11 sites. He was at the World Trade Center the day after it went down. It scarred him – it scarred everybody who was there.'

'Are you saying he's had a problem that long?'

'Oh no! When I started working in this office six years ago, Connelly was a little bit suspicious of Muslim men in the their twenties and thirties, but not more than anybody else. But then, after his wife died, his concern moved to paranoia and obsession.'

'What happened to his wife?'

'Massive stroke – she lingered, patched into machines for a couple of weeks, and then the doctors convinced him to pull the plug.'

'When was that?'

'About eighteen months ago. It was after her funeral that he started acting odd. He became suspicious of every Muslim person he saw. He once told me that Muslims had pulled a fast one on the doctors. He said he had proof that they administered a fast-acting drug that caused her to have a stroke.'

'Proof?'

'So he said, but he never showed me a thing. And every day, it seemed to get a little worse. Not only was he certain every Muslim he met was guilty of something but he saw Muslims everywhere – even in his own church.'

'What religion is he?'

'Catholic. Every Monday, he started telling me about seeing a Muslim or two sitting in the pews pretending to worship but he knew they were plotting to blow up the church. Then, one week, he came in and told me that the priest of his church was a secret Muslim who was trying to destroy the faith of the whole congregation.'

'Really?'

'Yeah, and sometimes he'd make the oddest statements. Like when he told me he couldn't go back to the church because of the heretic priest, he said, "Got to guard against that at all times, Maggie – garbage in, garbage out."'

'So what did you do?' Jake asked.

'I went over his head. I felt bad about that. I mean, he's been a great boss – even now, he treats me great. Understands when I have personal business, when my daughter gets sick, tells me to stay home on the Monday after Daylight Saving Time hits so I can adjust to the loss of an hour without pressure. Always takes me out to lunch on my birthday, never steals credit for ideas or work – yeah, he's been great. But he was falling apart. I wanted them to force him into retirement before he did anything wacky. I wanted him to go out with his reputation intact – his service to his country appreciated. But now . . .'

'What reaction did you get from the home office?'

Maggie sighed deep and swallowed down the rest of her cup. 'They thanked me. They asked for my patience. They said that Connelly had already agreed to retire.'

'Then why was he still working?'

'Because he agreed to retire on his twenty-fifth anniversary date but that is still a year away now. I didn't know what else to do but try to keep him from acting on any of his nutty ideas. But since the explosion at the high school, he just doesn't listen to me any longer. Oh damn, I shouldn't have told you all of this,' Maggie said, hanging her head.

Jake rested a palm on her lower arm. 'Yes, you should have, Maggie, because I am going to use this information to get Connelly to step down, to walk away from the possibility of a violent confrontation. What you have told me could save his life. Now, you said that you might know where he could be.'

Maggie's shoulders shuddered as she inhaled deeply and looked into Jake's face. 'If I tell you, do you promise me that you will do everything in your power to protect him?'

'Absolutely,' Jake said.

'I imagine someone's already checked his home.'

'Yes, I know they have. They are searching it right now.'

'You probably should stake out his wife's gravesite, if you haven't already.'

'I don't know but I'll check into that.'

'There is one more place where he might be.'

'Where, Maggie?'

'I want you there – don't leave this up to the locals. I don't want you to tell anyone until you are there in person to protect him.'

'Again, you have my promise.'

'His brother has a vacation cabin at Smith Mountain Lake.'

'Do you have an address?' Jake asked.

'Yeah, I even have a map. It's up in the office. And it's probably about time I returned to those damn phones.'

Jake walked her back, retrieved the information about the cabin at the lake and got into his car. He called Lucinda but her cell phone immediately went to voicemail. 'I don't think I'll be home tonight, Lucy. I've got to follow a lead out of town. I'll call back later. Love you.'

Jake lowered the convertible top on his baby-blue 1966 Impala Super Sport and pulled out of the parking lot, knowing he'd enjoy cruising across the state in his vintage car even if the drive out to the lake proved totally unproductive – or even if it turned horribly tragic. He shook that thought out of his head and headed west.

THIRTY

L ucinda returned to the classroom at the high school to continue the interviews. Tilly Campbell walked in wearing a grin and an outfit that spoke of her Texas roots: flared, mid-calf denim skirt with an embroidered vest over a plain white knit shirt with three-quarters sleeves and a pair of red, intricately stitched boots. Her long hair was pulled back in a clip at the nape of her neck revealing large Lone Star earrings dangling from her lobes. 'Howdy, Lieutenant,' Tilly said.

The woman's stereotypical image left Lucinda speechless for a beat, then she said, 'Please have a seat, Ms Campbell.'

'Don't mind if I do.'

Lucinda half expected the woman to spin the chair around and straddle it backwards but she sat in it like a normal person and crossed her legs. 'What can I do for you, Lieutenant?'

'Miss Texas much?' Lucinda asked.

Tilly leaned her head back and laughed. 'Sure do, ma'am, but somehow the beauty of Virginia has kept me tethered here – a whole lot prettier than that West Texas ranch where I grew up.'

'What brought you here in the first place?'

'My mama was from Virginia and she went to Sweet Briar College. She assumed that I would go there, too, and I never considered anyplace else. Can't say I have any regrets. Still get back to the ranch a couple of times a year – my brother and his family live there now but it still feels like home. So, I suspect this little chatty talk is designed to disarm me before the hard-hitting questions start flying?'

Lucinda laughed. 'Not exactly, Ms Campbell, just ordinary human curiosity about someone from a distant place. I guess it wouldn't have been very effective with you if that had been my plan. Anyway, I wanted to talk to you about this past Sunday morning. Where were you?'

'Home. Alone. Well, I did have two dogs and a cat with me but I doubt they can confirm my whereabouts.'

'Where was your red pick-up truck?'

'Oh, so that's why you wanted to talk to me. Well, it was sitting in my driveway – all day long. I thought about coming up to the school when I heard what happened but I decided I'd just be in the way. Didn't go anywhere till lunchtime on Monday.'

'You didn't loan your truck to anyone?'

'I hope you're not suspicious of one of my 4-H Club kids.'

'Why would you think that?' Lucinda asked.

'Because they spend time at farms and would have access to fertilizer.'

The alarm in Lucinda's head pinged its danger signal. 'And what does that have to do with what happened here?'

'Well, shoot, Lieutenant, it looked pretty obvious to me that it was the same kind of explosion as the one by McVeigh in Oklahoma – a fertilizer bomb. Or am I wrong about that?'

At the scene, Marguerite Spellman had theorized fertilizer – ammonium nitrate, to be precise – as the explosive material used. Lucinda hadn't considered Tilly Campbell as a likely suspect before. But now? 'Interesting theory, Ms Campbell. How did you reach that conclusion?'

'Because of the damage, the force of the explosion that caused it, the availability of the material and the fact that it wouldn't have weighed enough to cause a transportation problem – anyone but a small child could carry enough of it in here. That's what it was, wasn't it?'

'I would like to get a list with contact information and parents' names for all the members of your 4-H Club.'

'Lieutenant, I'm telling you that these are good kids. Not a hoodlum in the bunch. I'd bet my life on the fact that none of them were involved.'

'When can you get me that list?'

Tilly exhaled a loud sigh. 'I sure wish you'd leave those kids alone, Lieutenant.'

Silence filled the space between them as they stared at each other. Tilly was the first to look away. 'Fine. I'll go get that information together for you right away. Shouldn't take me long at all. Anything else?'

Lucinda could tell from the look on the other woman's face that any additional cooperation would not be readily forthcoming but she pushed ahead. 'Do any of those kids drive red pick-up trucks?'

Tilly shrugged. 'How would I know?'

'Can you think of anyone capable of setting off that explosion?'

'I told you: my 4-H kids are upright, solid citizens – not criminal misfits.'

'I wasn't just asking about them, Miss Campbell. Anyone, anyone you think might be able to pull this off?'

'At first, I thought about the really bright kids in my calculus class who were strong in physics. But I couldn't think of one of them who was that devious or that bitter. Then I realized that, with all the internet sites out there with step-by-step instructions on how to build everything from a Molotov cocktail to a dirty suitcase bomb, it wouldn't require anything more than average intelligence. That gives you a whole school full of possible suspects.'

'Anyone of your students express interest in any of those devices?'

Tilly shook her head. 'C'mon, Lieutenant, get serious. These are teenagers. Every year, there are bunches of them who are interested – but it's all talk or lame experiments in the woods. I never felt a single one of them was dangerous.'

Lucinda slid a card across the desk. 'Thanks, Ms Campbell; call me if you think of anything. Bring by that list as soon as it's ready. I'm sure we'll need to talk again soon, so—'

'Don't worry, ma'am, I've got no plans to run off to Texas and hole up on the ranch. I do remember Waco.'

Tilly walked out with long strides, her boot heels clicking on the floor tiles. An interesting woman – and great at raising red flags. But did that indicate guilt or guileless innocence?

While Lucinda waited for her next interview, she turned on her cell and listened to the voicemail from Jake. She almost called him back but then remembered that he wouldn't tell her anything about the case over the phone and wouldn't want to hear anything from her, either. It would have to wait. She turned her phone back off when she heard the staccato clip of high heels moving down the hall in her direction.

THIRTY-ONE

As Jake approached Lynchburg, his heart soared at the first sight of the Blue Ridge Mountains. On a clear, bright day like this one, he was always amazed at the aptness of the name of the range – an unexpected and magnificent blue rising up on the horizon, rounded by eons of weather into soft, forgiving peaks that bear little resemblance to the stark, sharp juts of the Rocky Mountains.

He left the interstate highway for smaller state roads, shifting his direction to the southwest as he traveled at a slower pace through rural areas in the direction of Smith Mountain Lake. Just over one hundred miles from his starting point, he turned left, heading south in a near straight line. Two and a half miles later, he reached Smith Mountain Lake Turnpike and traveled southwest to a sprawling body of water. GPS directed him to a property abutting Smith Mountain Lake State Park where a small log cabin sat at the end of a rutted dirt drive.

Jake parked just past the drive by a rusted mailbox and entered the woods. Fortunately, in early May, the undergrowth was not as lusty as it would be later in the summer and finding a spot where he could remain concealed while observing the home was not difficult.

The cabin was an old structure – the logs appeared to be hand-hewn. Someone had kept the place up, though. It was obvious that the mortar had been freshly pointed, the porch was stained a dark brown and the steps leading up to it looked sturdy. The Adirondack chairs arranged in groupings on either side of the door appeared to be of recent vintage.

For a long while, Jake heard nothing to indicate that the cabin was occupied. He started easing his way through the woods, circling around to view the back side of the structure, when a shout rang out, followed by a loud noise that sounded as if something inside had crashed into an exterior wall.

Jake moved quickly as he looked for the shortest approach from the woods to the cabin – the route that would offer the least risk of discovery as he crossed open ground. When he found it, he darted to the building and pressed himself against the wall and listened. All he could hear was the lone rumble of spoken voice – it sounded like only one voice. It seemed that if anyone else was inside, they were not responding.

He crept around to the closest window and slowly eased an eye over to it. He was looking into an unoccupied living room dominated by a tall stone fireplace with a blackened hearth. A wooden chair with a broken leg lay on its side on the floor in front of it. The bright, pointy splinters at the break indicated that it might be that chair he heard crash into the wall.

He eased around the corner and saw Connelly's black Jeep Grand Cherokee, its top draped in a camouflage tarp. Now Jake knew with some certainty that the ATF agent was here and, in all likelihood, had his two Sikh hostages with him.

He approached the next window and peered into a small room containing two bunk beds with stripped mattresses and bare pillows. No one was in that room, either. The next window was high and opaque – probably the bathroom. He couldn't see through the obscured glass but heard no noises of anyone in that room.

The window beside that one opened on another bedroom. One

of the two single beds there had been made, its blanket and linens pulled into place but looking as if someone had slept there.

As Jake approached the next window, he could hear a voice that sounded like Connelly's. 'I don't want to hear any more of your heathen babbling.'

Then Jake heard heavy feet stomping away. He froze in place as he listened, leaning toward the sound of a whispered voice.

'. . . hamri kro hath dai rchcha . . . pooran hoeh chit ki eichcha . . . tav charnan mun rehai hmara . . . apna jan kro pritipara.'

To Jake's relatively uneducated ear, it sounded like Hindi, but he knew that if he were listening to one of the Sikhs, it could just as easily have been Punjabi. He doubted he would know the difference. But something about the speech pattern told him that he was hearing words spoken in prayer.

He heard sounds of movement from another room and took the risk that Connelly was not in view of the window and eased up. He saw a slumped man in a turban handcuffed to an electric range. He saw another standing, still in his white lab coat, cuffed to the refrigerator: Dr Singh.

Dr Singh continued his whisper. '. . . mo rchcha nij kar dai kriye . . .' He stopped abruptly, his eyes widening as he spotted Jake on the other side of the glass. Jake raised a finger to his mouth and the man jerked his head toward his erstwhile patient who was attached to the stove.

The doctor turned back to Jake with a question on his face. Jake dared not make a sound and could not hold up a note since he had no paper or pen, so he did the only thing he knew that could possibly indicate that help was on the way: he gave a thumbs-up.

Jake bent back down and scurried around to the porch, pulling himself up on the side as quietly as he could. He crawled toward the front door, pausing every few feet to listen for any indication of movement inside. Jake reached up to the knob and eased the door open just a crack.

'No! Don't!' rang out from the kitchen.

Jake fell back, rolled and landed on the ground as a shotgun blast tore through the door. Jake stayed down low, raising his head just high enough to watch the entrance.

Connelly came running through it, waving his weapon around.

'Come out, you chicken shit, and face me like a man.' Then he spotted Jake and turned the shotgun in his direction.

Jake shifted to the side of the cabin and ran to the back where he took cover behind the SUV. He heard Connelly's footsteps cross the porch and land on the ground where he once crouched. He raised up one arm with his badge in his hand and shouted, 'Connelly, put down your weapon.'

'Lovett?' Connelly asked.

'Yeah, Connelly. Put down your weapon and we can talk.'

'No. This could be a trick. Come out with your hands up.'

'Can't do that, Connelly. I can make a call for back-up. We might have to wait a bit for them to arrive but things could get really ugly when they do.'

Connelly laughed. 'You gotta be kidding me, Lovett. Have you looked at your cell recently? You won't see a single bar. You're in a dead spot. Throw down your weapon and put your hands on your head. Then ease your way out here. No sudden moves.'

'Hey, Connelly, how are you going to explain to your brother about his front door?'

After a moment of silence, Connelly said, 'Well, if I'm the only one who makes it out of here alive, I can tell it anyway I want it, can't I?'

'Connelly, I'd say this is not exactly in keeping with your oath of office.'

'You know what I have to say to that, Lovett?'

'No, sir, can't say that I do.'

Connelly fired a shot into the windshield of his own vehicle, sending every dove for yards skyward in a loud flurry of agitated wings.

THIRTY-TWO

Brittany Schaffer sashayed into the classroom like the second coming of Marilyn Monroe. One look at the dress she was wearing and Lucinda understood the principal's concern. Dark red fabric swirled with black molded around her body like shrink wrap. The dipping neckline showed more cleavage than most women had.

The teacher's blond hair was fine, wavy and lightly tousled. Her big cornflower-blue eyes and soft smile softened her sensuality with a glaze of innocence. Her childlike speaking voice added to that impression. 'I understand you wanted to see me.'

'Please have a seat,' Lucinda said.

Brittany seemed to melt into the chair. She folded her hands primly on top of the table while crossing her legs to reveal a long stretch of thigh.

'I understand you own a red pick-up, Ms Schaffer.'

'Have you seen it? It's wicked cool.'

'Yes, I have. It seemed like a lot of truck for an English teacher.'

Brittany tittered. 'Daddy was in construction. I worked for him in the summer all through high school and college. Wouldn't have been much use to him if I couldn't manage a beast of a pick-up. Kind of got to like it – and so . . .'

'Where were you on Sunday morning?'

'At home. I slept wicked late. I'd been out late Saturday night and didn't think I'd ever recover.'

'Are you saying you were hung over, Ms Schaffer?' Lucinda asked.

'Oh, c'mon now, that's not a polite question to ask a lady,' Brittany said with a giggle.

'Did you drive your truck Saturday night?'

'Oh no, officer! I would never, ever drink and drive. In fact, I was out with a new dude and he got so smashed that we had to call a cab to get home. You can verify that,' she said, nodding her head up and down. 'The cab company would have a record of it, wouldn't they?'

'So where was your truck Saturday night?'

'In the driveway, of course.'

'And where was it Sunday morning?'

'Still there, officer. You're not going to trip me up. I was drinking and I did not drive that night or the next morning. I did not break the law.'

'I'm going to need the name and contact information for the man you were with Saturday night.'

Brittany's jaw dropped open. 'You're kidding me. This is so embarrassing. It was our first date. If the police start asking questions, he'll never ask me out again.'

'And why not, Ms Schaffer? Is he an ex-convict? A drug dealer? What?'

'Oh, for pity's sake, officer. He is a fine, law-abiding man. But heavens, if you dated someone just once and the police came knocking on your door, what would you think?'

'I guess it would depend on why,' Lucinda said.

'Oh, please! The reason doesn't matter. You know that would be a problem. Where there's smoke, there's fire. You know what I mean?'

'I guess that makes me the smoke.'

'Well, yes, you could look at it that way. You do understand, don't you?' Brittany said with a grin.

'So, tell me, ma'am. What's the fire?'

Brittany's brow furrowed. 'What?'

'What are you trying to hide, Ms Schaffer?'

'Really, officer, really? There is no fire. There is no smoke, either, except for you and that has nothing to do with me.'

'So where was your truck again?'

'In my driveway.'

'You didn't loan it to anyone?'

'No.'

'Why not? You weren't using it.'

'That's not a good reason to let someone else use my truck.'

'No,' Lucinda said, 'but it would be a time that wouldn't inconvenience you. After all, it was Saturday night. Maybe one of your students needed some wheels for a hot date. I know the administration might not look on that too kindly, but there's no need to tell them – just between the two of us.'

'If someone told you I loaned them my truck, they are lying,' she said, rising to her feet.

'Before you leave, the contact information for your date Saturday night, please.'

Brittany tossed her curls, blew out an exhalation of exasperation and pulled out her cell phone. She scrolled through her contacts, hit a name and turned the screen toward Lucinda. 'There.'

Lucinda wrote down the name 'Tom' and his phone number and email address. 'Tom's last name, please.'

Brittany gritted her teeth and growled, 'McCallister. Am I excused now?'

'Yes, Ms Schaffer. But one thing: don't leave town without clearing it with me first.'

'I'm going to the coast this weekend,' she said, her hands on her hips.

'Check with me on Friday and we'll see how things go.' Lucinda held out her business card. 'And, if you'll notice, I'm Lieutenant Pierce, not officer. You might have a difficult time reaching me if you forget.'

Brittany snatched the card from Lucinda's fingers. 'Thank you, officer,' she said in an edgy voice. She spun around and flounced out of the room and into the hall.

Lucinda sensed that Brittany was lying about something or hiding a secret. Was it relevant to the case? Probably not but she had to follow that suspicion until she ran it to ground.

THIRTY-THREE

Charley and Amber holed up in Charley's room listening to music and talking about all the boys – and some of the girls – in their classes. The ring of Amber's cell phone interrupted their banter.

Amber answered the phone and stepped over to the side of the room with her back to Charley. Charley tried not to listen to Amber's end of the conversation, inadvertently picking up only a word here and there, but it was obvious that the longer it lasted, the more agitation was present in Amber's voice.

Amber disconnected, spun around, grabbed her backpack and said, 'I've got to go.'

'Wait, Amber. Why?' Charley asked. 'Was that your mother?'

'No. It was my brother, Andy, and he needs me.'

'What happened?'

Amber said nothing for a moment and then began, 'I hate talking about this but you know even worse about my family, so here goes. My mom is passed out drunk – again. And the boyfriend is there and he's pretty drunk, too. He got mad at Andy for some-thing – I couldn't understand why 'cause Andy was crying too much. The boyfriend was drinking out of a glass and he threw it at Andy. Andy ducked and the glass shattered on the brick fireplace.'

'You have to go home because of a broken glass?'

Amber sighed. 'Yeah, sort of. But no, not really.'

'Did the boyfriend hurt Andy?'

'Not yet. That's the problem. The boyfriend left and told Andy to clean up the glass and said if he found the tiniest speck anywhere he'd make Andy sorry he was ever born. And, Charley, I know he can do that. I gotta go help him clean it up before Eddie gets home.'

'I'm going with you,' Charley said, pulling on a hoodie and dropping her iPhone in her pocket.

'You'll just make him mad,' Amber objected.

'He won't do anything with a stranger there.'

'You don't know him very well.'

'He doesn't scare me.'

'He should,' Amber insisted.

'I've seen worse,' Charley said. 'C'mon, Andy needs us. And my iPhone has a cool app that's the brightest flashlight you've ever seen. We'll be able to find even the teensiest pieces of glass.'

'I don't want him to hurt you, too, Charley,' Amber said.

'Let him try,' Charley said, bristling with a bravado designed to hide the fear that he might put her to the test. She knew herself well enough to know she'd never give in to anyone without a fight, but she also knew that, despite that, men were bigger and stronger – and no matter how dumb they were, she couldn't always outsmart them.

THIRTY-FOUR

As Lucinda turned out of the parking lot, she got a call from Sergeant Robin Colter. 'Lieutenant, in every spare moment, I've been following up on the phone numbers on David's bill—'

'You know we're off the case, right?' Lucinda said. She couldn't help but be pleased that Robin was pushing forward with the investigation but, although she didn't mind putting her own career at risk, she didn't want to encourage anyone else to do the same.

'That isn't stopping you, is it, Lieutenant?' When Lucinda didn't respond, Robin added, 'Agent Lovett passed a copy of the document to me. He suggested that I might want to follow up on my personal curiosity since he was too preoccupied with Connelly to accomplish anything worthwhile.'

'Oh, did he?' Lucinda said, wondering why Jake had not mentioned that to her.

'He told me to call you if I found anything significant.'

'And did you?'

'I think so. I think I've identified the girl who wrote the note to David Baynes,' Robin said.

'He told you about the note?' *What else is Jake doing behind my back?*

'I just happened to run into him when I stopped for coffee. He seemed very distracted. I thought he would have said something to you.'

'Me, too,' Lucinda said through gritted teeth.

'Yes. He said you'd be OK with that.'

No sense in dragging Robin into a conflict between her and Jake, Lucinda thought. 'Fine, fine, Colter, so who is she?'

'I think "E" is Ellie Fitzpatrick.'

'Funny, David's parents mentioned the names of a few of their son's friends as possibilities but never mentioned her.'

'Probably because he was the friend of Ellie's big brother, Paul, who went off to college last fall. According to Mrs Fitzpatrick, David promised Paul he'd look after Ellie and make sure no one messed with her at the high school.'

'Sounds promising,' Lucinda said, 'When can you talk to her?'

'Her mother said that she should be home any minute. I was hoping you could interview her.'

'Really? Do you foresee a problem with the girl that you can't handle?' Lucinda asked.

'Not with the girl, but the mother. See, she went on this rant about the principal, complaining about her inability to protect the children in her care. I can understand that frustration, and maybe I'm being overly sensitive, but it seemed as if there was an undertone of racial sentiment in her criticism of Principal Johnson. Maybe I'm imagining it and maybe when she takes a look at me, it won't matter, but I'm worried it may impact her willingness to cooperate and—'

'Say no more, Colter. Give me the address and I'll meet you

there.' Lucinda muttered as she spun her car around and pointed it in the direction of the Fitzpatrick home. The childhood promise that, one day, people would not be judged by the color of their skin seemed to get further out of reach every year. It eroded her faith in her fellow man even more than any criminal act did. There will always be bad guys but why did otherwise decent people have to have such bad attitudes?

When Mrs Fitzpatrick answered the knock on the door, she immediately turned to Lucinda, extended her hand and said, 'I'm Tara Fitzpatrick. You must be Sergeant Colter.'

'No,' Lucinda said, shaking her hand, 'I'm Lieutenant Pierce. And this is Sergeant Colter.'

'Oh,' Mrs Fitzpatrick said, without offering a palm to Robin, 'do come in.'

Lucinda looked over at Robin and nodded – the sergeant sure nailed that one.

Mrs Fitzpatrick called up the staircase, 'Ellie, they're here.'

As a young, frail, pale girl walked down the stairway, it was obvious why her brother felt she needed protection. Long straight hair hung in her face like a shield from the outside world. Every step she took seemed tentative, as if any loud noise would make her run for cover. She looked more like a fifth grader than a freshman in high school. Her eyes stayed focused on the floor as she muttered, 'Hello.'

'Sit down, Ellie, and speak up,' her mother said. 'They won't bite; they just want to ask you a few questions. Lieutenant?'

'Hello, Ellie. I'm Lieutenant Pierce. Sergeant Colter wants to ask you a few questions about your friend, David Baynes. Sergeant?'

'He's dead,' Ellie said with a sigh.

'Yes,' Robin said, 'we're sorry that you lost your friend. We want to know, did you write David a note before he died?'

'Yes,' she said without looking up from the floor. 'About a week before.'

'What did you write?'

'I asked him to make Kev stop.'

'Stop what, Ellie?'

'Sticking stuff in my locker.'

'What kind of stuff?'

'Dead bugs – mostly cockroaches,' she said through curling lips.

'Just bugs? How did you know he was the one who did that?'

'He stuck them in envelopes with notes. He said he'd set a bomb in there to stink me out.'

Robin and Lucinda exchanged a look of alarm. 'A bomb, Ellie?' Lucinda asked. 'Are you sure about that? Did you keep any of his notes?'

'Yeah, I'm sure but I didn't keep the notes,' she said.

'Where is your locker, Ellie?'

'By the office – well, it was – it was blown to pieces in the explosion.'

'What's Kev's last name?' Lucinda asked.

'And where can we find him?' Robin added.

Ellie lifted her head for the first time and looked at the two women, one at a time. 'If you're thinking Kev blew up the school, you're wrong. He wasn't talking about that kind of bomb; he was talking about a stink bomb. He's just a pest, an annoying geek. He wouldn't do that. He couldn't do that.'

'His full name and address, Ellie,' Lucinda ordered.

'Kevin, Kevin Blackwood, but his address won't do you any good; he's still in the hospital.'

'Still? How long has he been there?' Lucinda asked.

'Two weeks.'

'That's a long time. What's wrong with him?'

'He's stupid,' Ellie said.

'Ellie!' Mrs Fitzpatrick scolded. 'That is not an acceptable word.'

'Well, he is, Mom. He jumped off Creekview Bridge on a dare and broke every bone in his feet and his legs, too. That's stupid.'

'We'll need to verify that,' Robin said.

'His house is just two doors down,' Mrs Fitzpatrick said, pointing east.

'I'll be right back,' Robin said.

'Ellie,' Lucinda said, drawing the girl's attention back. 'Did you know any of David's friends?'

'My brother,' Ellie said. 'But David wasn't really my friend; we didn't hang out or anything. He'd just help me if I had a problem.'

'Do you know anyone who had a grudge against David?'

Ellie shrugged. 'No.'

'What about Fred Garcia?'

'Who?'

'The groundskeeper who died.'

'Oh, Mr Fred, yeah. He was really nice.'

'Do you know any kids who were angry at him?'

'Mad at Mr Fred? No. Everybody liked Mr Fred.'

'Do you know any kids who were angry about school?'

Ellie laughed with a bitter edge. 'Lots of them. But I don't know anybody who knows how to build a bomb – I didn't think David did. Nobody tells me nothing.'

'No one tells you *anything*, Ellie,' Mrs Fitzpatrick said, correcting her daughter. 'But I sincerely doubt that statement is true.'

Ellie rolled her eyes. 'I got homework. Is that all?'

'Yes, thank you, Ellie,' Lucinda said, handing her a card. 'Call me if you think of anything else.'

Ellie shrugged and walked upstairs.

'Thank you for coming, Lieutenant,' Mrs Fitzpatrick said. 'I doubt that sergeant could have handled the interview so well.'

'I did not come here because I had any concerns about how Sergeant Colter would handle the interview with your daughter, Mrs Fitzpatrick. I am here because we could not trust you.'

'Excuse me!'

'Sergeant Colter's very professional, very competent and very bright. I know it is difficult for you to look at the color of her skin and believe that, but it's true.'

'I never—'

'Spare me,' Lucinda said and walked out the door. Returning to the car, she was joined by Robin a few minutes later.

Leaning against the car, Robin spoke through Lucinda's open window. 'Yes, indeed,' she said. 'Kevin Blackwood has been in the hospital since a week before the explosion. His grandmother was there and she said he still has more surgeries before he has physical therapy to walk again.'

'Well, that sure was a dead end. Let me know if you find anything else.'

THIRTY-FIVE

Returning to the Justice Center, Lucinda worked on a hand-written report about her morning's hunting expedition. Across the top of it she wrote: 'For Captain Holland's Eyes Only.' In the middle of writing about her interview with Tilly Campbell, she picked up the phone and called Marguerite Spellman. 'Hey, Spellman, am I remembering correctly that you said the explosion at the high school might have been caused by a fertilizer bomb?'

'I thought you'd been taken off of this case, Lieutenant.'

'I'm just curious. Someone said something to me today and I was wondering if I should report it to the lead investigator, that's all.'

'Knowing you for all these years, I can't help but think that you are spinning the truth a bit but I've never been very good at stone-walling you, have I, Lieutenant?'

'No reason to start now, is there? It might look suspicious.'

Marguerite laughed. 'Yes, that is what I said at the scene and in fact, since then, I've gotten confirmation – the explosive substance was ammonium nitrate, a commonly used fertilizer.'

'Thanks, Spellman. Good to know.'

'Someday I'll get the whole story, right?'

'Scout's honor, Spellman,' Lucinda said and hung up the phone.

That meant that Lucinda still had to include Tilly on her suspect list, even though her instinct told her that it was a very long shot. Brittany Schaffer would go on the top of the list for the moment. On the other hand, Chet Bowen was so unlikely it was laughable.

Captain Holland raced past her office door, shouted, 'Whoa,' then stuck his head through the opening. 'My office, now, Pierce,' and he was off again.

What now? Lucinda wondered as she grabbed her incomplete report and followed him down the hall.

As soon as she set foot in his office, Holland said, 'Where is Special Agent in Charge Jake Lovett?'

'I don't know, sir.'

'Do you have any idea where he was planning to go today?'

'No, sir. I got a message from him saying that he might not get back tonight but he didn't say where he was going.'

'Are you holding out on me, Pierce?'

'No, sir. If it was part of the investigation, he wouldn't have said anything to me on the phone. He wouldn't want anyone to know he was violating orders to leave me out of the loop.'

'Are you saying he thinks his phone's tapped? Is this pure para-noia or does he have something to back that suspicion?'

'He does think his phone might be tapped. When I questioned him on that point, he told me that when the FBI and ATF are working together, anything is possible.'

'Yeah, he's got that right,' Holland said with a nod. 'But you have no idea of where he might have gone.'

'No, sir. What's going on?'

'No one has been able to reach him for hours.'

'Hours?' Lucinda said. She whipped out her iPhone and punched Jake's name on her favorites list. Her heart sank when it went straight to voicemail. 'Hey, Jake, just as soon as you can, call me. It's important.' She looked at Holland. 'Nope, I couldn't get him, either. When did anyone last talk to him?'

'He called his office and said he'd be on the road and wouldn't have the best reception at all times, but that was almost five hours ago. They're getting a bit frantic and called over here, asking for you. They settled for me since you weren't here.'

'Do they know what he was working on?' Lucinda asked.

'They said he was involved in the search for Connelly.'

'What happened to Connelly?'

Holland ran down the bizarre events of that morning, from the visit to Dr Singh's office to the taking of two hostages.

'Hostages? You've got to be kidding. Is that just the FBI's language or is ATF seeing it that way, too?'

'We all are, Pierce. Our police department is lead on the search for the man. So far, nothing. Lovett was supposed to be helping us out.'

'Who's in charge here? Have you spoken to whoever is in charge?'

'Yes, I ordered him to make finding Lovett a priority but he went over my head and got the order countermanded.'

'Call dispatch. See if they know anything about where Lovett was going or what he was doing today.'

'I should have thought of that,' Holland said as he snatched up his phone. He asked, listened and jotted down a few notes. 'Thanks,' he said and disconnected. 'He went to the regional ATF office to see if anyone there had any idea of where Connelly might have gone. He never reported back.'

'I'll go there and see what I can find out.'

Holland slid the notations he had just made across the desk. 'Here's the address and name of the officer manager. Just call me if you go anyplace else. I can't have you disappearing on me, too.'

'You got it.'

'I'm serious, Pierce.'

Lucinda was already out in the hall but she hollered back, 'Yes, sir!'

*   *   *

Lucinda popped the bubble light on top of her car and tore off to the ATF office. When she reached the federal building, she bristled with impatience as the guard at the gate checked her identification and called in to confirm. As the gate slowly started to rise, she fought off the urge to ram right through it.

Would the office manager be cooperative, she wondered as she waited for the elevator, or would she get nothing but bureaucratic crap? She hated just standing around – but eight flights were a bit too much to handle.

Lucinda burst into the office, startling Maggie Lazarus to her feet. Lucinda held up her badge before Maggie could press the silent alarm. 'I'm here about FBI Special Agent in Charge Jake Lovett.'

'What about him?'

'No one has seen or heard from him since he left to come see you. Did he get here?'

'Yes. We talked about Agent Connelly and where he might have gone.'

'What did you tell him?'

'The only place that he indicated was a new lead was the cabin that Agent Connelly's brother owns over at Smith Mountain Lake. Give me a second and I'll pull up the address,' she said as she sat down in front of her computer and tapped on her keyboard. Maggie jotted it down on a piece of paper and handed to the lieutenant.

'Thanks. If you hear from Lovett, or hear anything about him, call me or Captain Holland at the police department,' Lucinda said.

When Maggie nodded, Lucinda headed out the door, down the elevator and back to her car. She punched the address into her GPS, reported in to Captain Holland and hit the road heading west.

She'd just finished the first fifty miles of her journey when her cell phone rang. She looked at the screen and saw Jake's name. Was it actually Jake or was someone else using his phone?

THIRTY-SIX

J ake stayed down but moved toward the rear of the car, brushing bits of glass and debris off his clothes as he went. 'What the hell's wrong with you, Connelly?'

'Nothing. It's the rest of you all who are wrong.'

'The rest of us. Jeez, Connelly, I come out here to help and you shoot at me. Damn, you shot your own freakin' car.'

'Don't bullshit me, Lovett.'

'If I didn't come out to help you, then why the hell didn't I bring back-up with me?'

A moment of silence and then Connelly said, 'You still have to throw out your gun. No need to put your hands on your head but I can't have you coming out here and shooting me.'

'OK, OK,' Jake said. 'If I toss out my revolver, will you stop pointing that shotgun at me?'

'I will as soon as your weapon is tucked into my waistband.'

Jake knew it was a risk to give up his weapon but it didn't seem as if he had any other choice except to start firing and hope he survived. He didn't much like his chances and he didn't care for the idea of shooting another member of law enforcement.

'Still got you in my sights, Lovett. Don't try anything,' Connelly said. 'OK, you can come out now.'

Jake stood and saw the shotgun still aimed right at him. He ducked down and shouted, 'C'mon, Connelly, we had a deal.'

'All right,' Connelly said. 'Listen, I'm opening the breech.'

Jake heard the distinct sound and stood again. He didn't take his eyes off Connelly, alert to any sudden moves, as he walked out from behind the SUV. 'OK, brief me on what's going on.'

The two men walked inside as Connelly ranted about the Muslim terrorists he had inside the cabin. Jake didn't argue with a single one of Connelly's crazy assertions; he just nodded his head.

'There they are,' Connelly said, pointing into the kitchen. 'Those bastards were casting spells and bringing curses down on my head.'

Jake shook his head. 'What do you mean?'

'You had to have been out there long enough to hear them. You heard that gobbledygook, didn't you?'

'Oh, that. Jeez, Connelly, they were praying. Weren't you, guys?'

The two men appeared very confused but nodded at Jake just the same.

'Muslims don't pray,' Connelly said.

'Now you know that's not true, man. You've heard the calls to prayer from the minarets – shoot, they answer the call to prayer five times a day.'

'That's what they tell us – but they're not really praying; they're bowing to Satan. That's all Mohammed is – another name for the devil.'

Jake looked hard at the two men cuffed to the appliances, hoping they'd get his message to play along with his plan without really knowing what he was doing. 'Well, see, that's just it, Connelly. These guys aren't Muslims.'

'Then why do they have that crap on their heads?' Connelly said as he snapped his shotgun closed again.

'Because they're undercover, man. And you just about blew their cover in this so-called doctor's office.'

'Undercover?' Connelly said. 'Why didn't they tell me?'

'They weren't allowed to tell anyone. They know how tricky those Muslims are. You could have been one of them. How would they know?'

'I don't believe you, Lovett. If there was an undercover operation, I would have known.'

'Yeah,' Jake said with a sigh. 'I'm sorry, Connelly, I really am. They told me I couldn't tell you. I argued against that decision but got nowhere. I had to follow orders.'

'They who?'

'The FBI, man. I can't tell you how stingy the home office is with information. I don't know how many times I've told them that we need to work with the ATF. But you know how the brass is – everywhere. They get all pissy about their territorial imperatives. You know that. But listen, Connelly, you and I – we can make a deal on the side. We can agree to share everything with each other. Screw those other guys.'

Connelly studied Lovett's face. 'OK, Lovett, say I believe you – what do you think we should do now?'

'Easy, Connelly. We've got to get back to work. We've got to get these special agents back to work. We've got to catch the damn Muslim bastards that blew up the high school. We sure can't do it out here in the middle of nowhere.' Jake prayed that he'd laid the foundation and struck the right tone to make his act credible. Dr Singh and his patient still appeared bewildered but at least they'd done nothing to give the lie to anything he had said.

'I can't say I totally trust you, Lovett. But what you're saying does make a lot of sense. But why did you just leave me there in his office? Why didn't you tell me then?'

'I was ordered not to tell you, Connelly, and I thought, for sure,

these guys would level with you if I wasn't around. So I left. I had
no idea they had this much discipline. You gotta admire men who
can maintain their cover when they're under adversity.'

Dr Singh finally spoke. 'I am sorry, Agent Connelly, that I felt
an obligation to continue in deception. It is my training, I fear. We
have been so indoctrinated that it requires intensive deprograming
for us to let down our masks.'

Ohmigod! That was brilliant, Jake thought. He flashed Dr Singh
a tight smile. 'So c'mon, Connelly, let's get this show on the road
– who knows what those terrorists have been plotting while we've
been away? Hand your shotgun to me while you get those cuffs off
and get the hell out of here.'

'Do your rear doors have automatic locks?' Connelly asked.

Jake snorted. 'I'm driving a sweet 1966 Impala Super Sport,
buddy – what do you think?'

'Then we're taking my car – just in case these guys have you
fooled.'

'Your car has no windshield, Connelly – remember?'

'I'm not real comfortable with this. You gotta put the top up on
your car.'

'Good idea, Connelly. And first sign of trouble, I promise, I will
pull over and we'll deal with it – you and I – and if they try running
off, I won't stop you from shooting them. Can we go now?'

Connelly looked around at the three faces, passed his shotgun to
Jake and walked over to unfasten Dr Singh's cuffs.

Jake stifled the sigh of relief that wanted to escape. He reached
out and pulled his revolver out of Connelly's waistband.

Connelly spun to face him. 'I knew I shouldn't trust you.'

'Oh, relax,' Jake said, sliding the weapon into his holster. 'I was
just thinking you were right to be cautious. What if they are double
agents? I don't think they are, but why take chances? One of them
could have grabbed that gun just as easily as I did. Now –' Jake
patted on the outside of his jacket – 'it's all tucked away so it's not
a temptation for anyone.'

Connelly squinted his eyes and studied Jake again. Then his
shoulders dropped as he released the tension. He patted Jake on the
shoulder and said, 'Sorry, man, I'm not used to having someone on
my side these days. I've been telling them about the problem and
no one takes me seriously.'

'I talked to your office manager; I think she did,' Jake said.

'Well, yeah, but I don't think she could shoot an elephant standing four feet away,' Connelly said as he chuckled. He stepped over to the patient and unlocked his cuffs. 'OK, Lovett, let's hit the road. You two,' he said, wiggling his finger at the two other men, 'you walk out first and get into the back seat.'

'Good thinking, Connelly,' Jake said, making sure he was behind Connelly as Dr Singh led the small procession down the dirt driveway to where the Impala was parked. Jake kept up his act, spouting anti-Muslim garbage until Connelly dozed off and filled the air with a loud snore.

THIRTY-SEVEN

Charley was surprised when she and Amber approached Amber's home. It was a cute little bungalow in a revitalized part of town. The lawn was mowed, daffodils lined the sidewalk with cheer, pots filled with amaryllis added color to the front porch, everything appeared neat and tidy. Knowing what happened to Amber, Charley had expected to arrive at a dark, miserable hovel – something more in keeping with the evil acts the four walls had witnessed.

Amber slid her key into the lock but before they could open the door, they heard Andy sobbing, 'No, no, no.'

Amber hurried inside and said, 'Andy it's me. It's OK.'

The little boy threw himself at her, wrapping his arms around her waist and sobbing into her shirt.

'Mom still asleep?' Amber asked.

Andy nodded his head up and down, wiping his nose on her clothes. Then he pulled back. 'I don't think I got it all, Amber.'

'That's OK,' Charley said as she pulled out her iPhone and flipped on her flashlight application. 'Look what I have. We'll find every little bit with this.'

'You sit down over here, Andy,' Amber said. 'We'll get it all. You just rest for a minute and try to calm down, OK?'

Charley and Amber peered at every centimeter of the fireplace, using a pair of tweezers to pick the smallest bits out of the mortar and uneven surface of the bricks. When they were satisfied, they moved on to inspect the carpeting around the hearth. That area proved a bit more difficult: extracting little glass slivers from the tufts was exasperating.

They stood back and sighed, rubbing on their lower backs when they finished. 'That's it, Andy,' Amber said. 'We got it all.'

Andy gave them a weak little smile from beneath his reddened eyes and runny nose. 'Thank you,' he whispered.

'Go get his things,' Charley said, 'and let's get out of here.'

'Go on, Charley,' Amber replied. 'We'll be OK.'

'You will not! Your mother is still conked out. That man will be back here any minute. You can't stay here. And we can't leave Andy. Get his things and let's go before it's too late.'

'If I take Andy away from here, we'll both be in trouble.'

'If your mother's boyfriend comes back, you'll both be in trouble.'

'Well, we got all the glass up,' Amber objected.

'But he's drunk, Amber. He could do anything. And if I go home and leave you here, I'll be in trouble.'

'Oh, Charley, you don't know what trouble really is. If I'm not here, he might do to Andy what he did to me. I can't let that happen. It was a mistake to leave. Andy's not safe.'

'That's why I said we need to take him with us.'

'If Mom wakes up and he's gone, she'll freak out.'

'Leave her a note – but hurry. We have to go,' Charley pleaded. She could hardly stand still to talk to Amber. Her knees wobbled; she felt shivers running up and down her spine. The urge to flee fought with her best intentions.

'I don't know,' Amber wailed.

'I do. Let's go.'

The snick of a key going into the lock froze them all in place for a second. Then Charley grabbed Amber's hand and reached out and latched on to Andy's as they ran down the hall. 'Which one is your room?' Charley asked.

'That one,' Amber said, pointing a little further down the hall. They ran into it and shut the door.

'Where's the lock?' Charley asked.

'He took it off,' Amber wailed.

Down the hallway, a male voice echoed. 'Andy! Where the hell are you? Come out, you little bastard!'

'Hurry. Help me, Amber,' Charley said as she pushed a chest of drawers toward the doorway.

Andy whimpered and stuck four fingers of one hand into his mouth.

'Sssh, Andy,' Charley urged.

A fist pounded on the door. 'You in there, you little bastard?'

'The bed,' Charley whispered. 'Help me push it.'

As they got the second piece of furniture into place, a crack appeared in the entry. 'Lean against it, Amber.'

Amber pushed with all her strength but she was losing ground. Charley jumped in and shoved as hard as she could.

'What the hell are you doing, you sniveling little snot? Let me in there now.'

To their great relief, the pressure on the other side eased and the door slammed shut. Charley pulled open the door to the closet and forced it all the way open, wedged against the bed. 'C'mon. Sit on the floor in front of the closet door.'

Amber, Andy and Charley sat with their backs against the door, their feet digging into the floor. Charley punched the screen of her iPhone, feeling the pressure on her back of renewed pushing from the hallway.

THIRTY-EIGHT

Afraid that it was not actually Jake on the other end of the line, despite the name on the screen, Lucinda answered, 'Pierce.'

'Hey, Lucy! Looks like I'll be back home tonight after all. But I've got a few things to take care of first, so don't expect me for dinner.'

'Jake, are you OK?'

'Sure, sure. Just took a drive. Everything's fine. Don't worry about a thing. Don't wait up. I'll snuggle you when I get there.'

'Do you need help?'

'Don't need a thing, Lucy. I'll see ya sometime tonight.'

'Jake, where are you?'

'Oh, you did? Well, I wasn't getting a signal out in the country so I never heard it ring.'

'Are you saying you're not alone and can't talk to me now?'

'You got it, girl!'

'So you're on your way back from Smith Mountain Lake?'

'Sure thing, sweetheart. Hope you get your errands done soon and get to head on home. I'll meet you there as soon as I can. Talk to you later. Bye.'

Lucinda pulled into a convenience store parking lot and called Captain Holland. 'Lovett is on his way back, sir.'

'Do you know where he is?'

'Just that he is somewhere between Smith Mountain Lake and home.'

'Is he in trouble? Does he need assistance?'

'He obviously wasn't alone and couldn't talk freely but he made it clear that he didn't want or need any help and had everything under control.'

'Well, you're needed back here anyway. Does the name Tom McCallister mean anything to you?'

'Yes, that's Brittany Schaffer's date last weekend. I interviewed three teachers and she was on the top of my list for possible involvement in the explosion. I was in the middle of writing a report to you when the crap hit the fan over Lovett.'

'He's here waiting for you right now. We told him we weren't sure when you'd get back from the field but he insisted that he was staying until you were.'

'What made him show up there?'

'He said that he heard you wanted to talk to him and he sure didn't need you showing up at his place of business and causing problems. So, here he sits.'

'I'll be there in an hour or less,' Lucinda said, then circuited the parking lot and pointed the car back toward town.

Back in her office, Lucinda sat down with an extremely attractive but obviously conceited Tom McCallister. 'Sir, I just have a couple of questions for you—'

'Yes, I did go out with Brittany Schaffer on Saturday night. Yes, I did spend the night at her place and left late Sunday morning. And, yes, I sure would like it if you could keep this very quiet. My wife won't be too happy to learn that I wasn't out of town on business.'

'My, my, my, Mr McCallister, you are full of surprises.'

'Yeah, yeah, can I go now?'

'Just a couple of additional questions. Did you see Ms Schaffer's truck when you were at her house?'

'No.'

'Could it have been parked in the garage instead of out in the drive?'

'Absolutely not. When I arrived, I parked in the garage. I didn't want anyone seeing my car there.'

'Did you stay in all night?'

'Nah. We went out for dinner and some dancing.'

'Was the truck there when you returned to Ms Schaffer's house?'

'No.'

'How about the next morning?'

'I wish it had been but no, it wasn't there.'

'Are you sure?'

'Yeah, I'm sure. I wanted her to give me a ride back to my car.'

'Back to your car?'

'Yeah, we had a bit too much to drink Saturday night and had to take a cab back to her place. So, the next morning, I had to get a taxi again to pick up my car.'

'What cab company did you call?'

'Darned if I know. Brittany called them and I didn't pay any attention.'

'Did you ask Ms Schaffer about the whereabouts of her truck?'

'Yeah, she said it was in the shop. You need anything else?'

That's one of Brittany Schaffer's lies uncovered – what else might she be hiding? Lucinda wondered. 'No, sir, that's just fine,' she said, rising to her feet. 'Thank you for your cooperation.' She stepped out into the hall and watched him walk away. He certainly was a rude guy but definitely fit in the eye-candy category. She returned to her desk to finish up her report to Captain Holland.

She was nearing the end when her cell phone rang. Before she could say a word, she heard Charley's voice yelling, 'Lucy, I need you. I need you now.'

THIRTY-NINE

Outwardly, Jake worked to appear calm and relaxed. His thoughts, however, sped down the road faster than the car. He had to release the hostages without raising Connelly's suspicion. Then, somehow, he had to get the unbalanced man into custody before he had any inkling that Jake was not his comrade-in-arms. Connelly appeared still to be asleep but Jake could not be certain if it was real or feigned.

Jake drove past the city limits sign and said, 'Hey, Dr Singh, I was thinking I should drop you off a couple blocks from your office in case anyone is watching your place – wouldn't want them to see you two with us.'

'Good idea, Agent Lovett,' the doctor said. 'There's a drugstore at Fifth and Market. We could go in there and buy something before we walked back to create more distance.'

Jake was impressed with Dr Singh's ability to fall into the role forced upon him with such ease. 'Good idea. Great cover.' Jake eased to the curb and said, 'Thank you, guys. I'll catch up with you later through the usual channels.'

'You got it, Agent,' the doctor said as he and his patient stepped out of the car.

Connelly started and sputtered awake. 'Where are we? Why have we stopped?'

'I just dropped off the undercover operatives a couple of blocks from their headquarters in case their place is under surveillance,' Jake said as he pulled back into the traffic. 'I'm going to give the office a call and make sure they don't need us to go anywhere else before we come in.'

Jake held his cell tightly to his ear. When the call was answered, he said, 'Hey, this is Lovett. What do you need from me now?'

'Oh, thank God, sir. We have been very worried. Are you on your way in? When can we expect you?'

'You've got a suspect in custody?'

'Excuse me, sir?'

'A person of interest from the Middle East? Very interesting.

Sure, sure, we'll be there in twenty minutes. Put him in interrogation room B. Connelly and I will conduct the interview,' Jake said.

'Sir, are you telling me you need me to put someone who appears to be an Arab or Pakistani in B within twenty minutes in order for you to do something I don't understand and you can't explain because you're not alone?'

'You got it,' Jake said. 'See you soon.'

As soon as he finished the call, Connelly said, 'A suspect? Really? They have a suspect?'

'Yes,' Jake confirmed. 'They picked up a man who is on the terrorist watch list. Had no idea he was here in town until someone spotted him going into a mosque. They are pretty sure it's our guy.'

Connelly's eyes glowed with self-righteousness. 'I told you, didn't I, Lovett? That incident at the high school was part of a master plan to bring us down and subject us to the Sharia law. That should teach that woman cop a lesson.'

'Woman cop? You mean Pierce?'

'Yeah, worthless local,' Connelly said with a sneer.

'Hate to tell you, Connelly, but that's one hell of a stubborn woman. I doubt that she'll come around to your way of thinking even now.'

'Like I said, worthless. So how do you want to handle this interview?'

'I thought you'd take the lead, Connelly. You're senior officer and you have more experience in this arena than I do.'

When they arrived at the FBI field office, Jake led the way inside. Standing by the door, Special Agent Jim Ford stood with folded arms. 'Agents, I am going to have to ask both of you to leave your weapons at the front desk. We'll lock them in the safe but you can't take them in that room.'

'What's the problem, Ford?'

'Homeland Security orders, sir. The bastard we brought in has a nasty history. Took a revolver off a federal marshal, shot him dead and escaped from custody the last time. They don't want us to take any chances of a repeat performance.'

'What kind of idiot would let someone in custody close enough to seize his weapon?' Connelly asked.

'Apparently, he was a twenty-year veteran with the federal marshal's office. Homeland figures if he can be taken by surprise, anyone can.'

'Not me,' Connelly argued.

'Connelly, I want to get in there. I don't want to get bogged down in negotiations with the damned bureaucrats in DC. I want to talk to this guy,' Jake said as he pulled his gun out of the holster and handed it to Agent Ford. 'C'mon, let's go.'

'I'm going to file a complaint,' Connelly threatened.

'You and me both. But, for now, let's just get in there.'

Connelly grumbled as he turned over his revolver. He pulled out a small notebook and jotted down Jim Ford's name. Shaking his head, he followed Jake down the hall.

Entering the room, Jake nodded to the armed officer in the corner and gestured Connelly to the chair opposite a swarthy-looking man, who appeared handcuffed to the wall and aware of nothing beyond the surface of the table in front of him. He didn't look up.

As Connelly eased into the seat, he said, 'You are in a deep vat of bubbling oil, buddy. Your only hope of survival is if you take the help I'm offering you. But you gotta be straight with me. I need the names of any accomplices and of everyone in your sleeper cell. Otherwise you're gonna cook to death pretty darned quick.'

Out of the corner of his eye, Jake saw the armed officer move into place behind Connelly. The man across from the ATF agent slowly raised his head and looked Connelly in the eye. 'Listen to me carefully. You are under arrest for the abduction of two American citizens. There may be additional charges.'

Connelly started to rise but was pushed down by a hand on his back. The armed officer grabbed his wrist and twisted until Connelly gasped in pain and bent forward. A cuff snapped on one wrist, Connelly bucked and pulled his other arm out of the officer's reach.

The supposed suspect reached across the table, grabbed Connelly's shirt front and jerked him forward. The armed guard moved fast to secure Connelly's other wrist.

Connelly raged like a frustrated toddler. He twisted his head to Jake and screamed, 'Judas! Judas! When I'm released, I'm coming after you, Lovett. You won't get the best of me ever again.'

Jake watched the other two men wrestling Connelly out of the room and down the hall. Jake felt like crap. He knew what he had done was in the best interest of the investigation, the two hostages and even Connelly himself. Still, he'd betrayed a fellow agent and even now, after all that had happened, it felt very wrong.

FORTY

C harley Spencer's plea for help upended all of Lucinda's priorities. 'What's wrong, Charley?'

'That man has us trapped. He's drunk. And he's yelling. And I'm scared.'

'Where are you?'

'Amber's house. Oh, please hurry, Lucy. I'm scared.'

'Are you alone with him?' Lucinda said as she sprinted down the hall.

'No. Amber's here and Andy and he—' A loud cracking noise echoed in the background as the children shrieked.

'What was that?' Lucinda said, running up to Sergeant Robin Colter's desk and motioning to her.

Robin jumped up and followed Lucinda.

'The door is cracking,' Charley wailed.

'Stay with me, Charley. Sergeant Colter and I are on our way,' Lucinda said as she climbed into the passenger's seat of Robin's vehicle.

Robin popped the bubble on the roof of her car and pulled out of the parking lot with a squeal of tires. She placed a call for uniformed back-up to meet them at Amber's home.

Lucinda heard another crack. 'Charley?'

'He's hitting on the door with something,' Charley said as Andy whimpered in the background.

As the car approached a busy intersection, Robin laid on her horn. Some vehicles pulled to the side of the road; others just braked to a stop where they stood. Robin weaved through and around them.

'Charley, we are still five minutes away. Is there a window?'

'Yes.'

'Can you open it?'

'Amber,' Charley said, 'can those windows open?'

'One of them can – the other's painted shut,' Amber said.

'Lucy, one of them can open but if me or Amber aren't pushing against the door, I think he'll be able to get in.'

'Can Andy open the window?'

'I don't know,' Charley wailed.

'Get him to try,' Lucinda said and listened as Charley instructed Andy to grab the chair from the desk, unlatch the lock and push up on the wood frame.

'Lucy, he's trying but—'

'Tell him to keep trying. As long as the door holds, I want you to stay in that room. But the second he breeches it, you all need to get out of there. We're only a couple of minutes away.'

'It's up, Lucy. Andy got it.'

'Tell him to try to kick out the screen.' Lucinda despaired at her current state of helplessness as she listened to the blended sounds of some tool pounding on the door, a little boy's feet smashing into the screen and the urgent words of confidence from Charley and Amber to Andy.

'It's bending, Lucy,' Charley shouted. 'Andy, keep kicking in that same spot. It's bending more, Lucy.'

Lucinda heard a clatter and scrape coming across the line and then silence. 'Charley? Charley? What's happening?'

'Andy did it!' she said. 'The screen fell out.'

'I don't hear the pounding on the door any longer. What's going on?'

'I don't know, Lucy.'

'Do you know where the man is?'

'No.' Charley's voice cracked as she answered.

'We're just a couple of blocks away.'

The voices of the children's screams ripped through Lucinda's ears. 'Hurry, Colter.'

Robin took the last turn at high speed, causing the wheels on one side to lift from the ground and then slam back down as she regained control. She drove straight up on to the lawn before applying the brakes.

Robin and Lucinda burst out of the car as if they'd been ejected. Robin went straight to the front door. Lucinda circled around to the side of the house. When she reached the back corner, she paused, raising her gun and spinning into a shooter's stance.

Eddie Springer had one leg raised up on the windowsill, his head jerked toward Lucinda.

'Lower your leg and get down on the ground. Now!'

Instead of obeying Lucinda's order, the boyfriend lurched forward and rolled inside the house. Lucinda was right behind him, pointing her gun straight at his head. The man grabbed a squealing Andy in one arm and held the boy up in the line of fire.

Lucinda heard muffled voices out in the hallway. Then she heard pounding, cracking and scraping as three policemen burst through the door, aiming their weapons at Springer.

'Set the boy down,' Lucinda said in a soft voice.

Andy screamed out as the man clutched him tighter.

'Sir,' Lucinda said. 'Right now, there are four guns pointing at you. The odds are not in your favor.'

'Make that five,' Robin said as she stepped into the frame of the window.

'I'll strangle the little bastard,' the man threatened, causing Andy to whimper.

'I promise you, we will kill you before you can kill him.' While keeping her eyes on her target, Lucinda spoke to the girls. 'Charley, Amber, please walk across the bed and out the door.'

'But my little brother—' Amber objected.

'We will take care of Andy,' Lucinda said, 'and it will be easier if we don't have to worry about you at the same time. Charley, get her out of here.'

Charley grabbed Amber's hand and tugged. Amber allowed herself to be guided across the bed. She took one last look back at Andy and followed Charley out of the room.

'Let Andy go, sir.'

'I can break his arm faster than you can shoot me.'

'Oh, I'm sure you can, macho man. I imagine you'll feel pretty good about yourself after hurting a little boy.'

'Shut up,' he said.

'You break anything on that child, big man, and you're dead before he can cry.'

At that moment, Andy sunk his teeth into the boyfriend's arm and held on. The man fell back screeching with the little boy hanging on like a pit bull. A uniform reached out, slinging an arm around the boy's waist. 'Let go, son. I've gotcha.'

Andy released his jaws and the officer swung him out of the danger zone. Another policeman pushed Springer against the wall and spun him around. Using one hand to press the man's face into the wall, the officer snapped a cuff on one wrist, then released the man's head to grab the other wrist and fastened it, too. He jerked on the chains.

'Oh, man, I'm bleeding. Cut me some slack. The little bastard bit through to the bone. I need medical attention. Little kids' mouths are filthy. I need a doctor. I'm going to get infected.'

The officer jerked harder on the chain connecting Springer's wrist and manhandled him towards the doorway.

'Wait,' Lucinda said. 'Get his ID.'

The officer pushed the whining man against the wall, face first. 'That a wallet in your back pocket?'

'I'm in pain, man.'

'Shut up. Anything sharp in that pocket?'

'No, man.'

'There better not be. If I get cut, you'll be in a world of hurt.'

'I'm hurting already.'

The officer wrapped his fingers around the man's wallet, slid it out of the pocket and handed it over to the lieutenant.

'Get him down to the station.'

'Man, I need medical attention,' the boyfriend said.

'Shut up. I'm tired of the yapping from your pie hole,' the officer responded.

Lucinda watched them leave and turned to Robin. 'We've got one more thing to do.'

'Mommie dearest?'

'Yeah, let's disturb her beauty sleep.'

Lucinda opened the closed door leading into the master bedroom. She walked up to the bed where a body was face down under the covers. Lucinda used her foot to push at the rump. 'Get up.'

'What? What the hell are you doing?' Teresa Culvert sputtered, flopping over on to her back. 'Who the hell are you? And what are you doing in my bedroom?' She looked over to Robin and pointed in her direction. 'Is that a damned gun? What kind of shit is this?'

Lucinda pulled out her badge and flipped it up. 'Get out of the bed, nice and easy. You are under arrest.'

'Under arrest? What? It's against the law to sleep one off in the afternoon?'

'Get. Out. Of. Bed. Right. Now,' Lucinda ordered.

'You tell me what the hell is going on first.'

Lucinda grabbed one of Teresa's wrists, twisted it and flipped her back over. Lucinda cuffed both of the woman's hands behind her back and hoisted her up by the chain. Teresa's feet scrambled for purchase on the floor. She swayed in place once she found it.

'What's the damn charge?'

'Child neglect. Child endangerment. And aiding and abetting the commission of a felony.'

'What?'

'We'll explain all to you back at the station. Colter, get her out of here.'

'I demand a lawyer!'

'Yeah, yeah, yeah,' Robin said. 'At the station.'

Lucinda walked out into the living room where she saw an over-stuffed chair filled with three bodies, clinging to each other as if their lives depended on it.

Charley said, 'Daddy's on the way.'

'You called him?'

'Yes, he said he'll pick up all three of us.'

She nodded at Charley. CPS was on the way and would probably get here first. All she had to do was talk them into breaking the rules. She looked heavenward and whispered, 'Send me a rebel, please.'

FORTY-ONE

As soon as Connelly was secured, Jake called Lucinda but his call went to voicemail. 'Hey, Lucinda, I've got a plan. I want to make sure you're OK with it before I take steps but I don't have a lot of time. Call me as soon as you can.'

Jake drove over to Dr Singh's office. The doctor was with a patient but Jake was escorted to a room in the back and asked to wait there. He tried calling Lucinda again without luck.

Dr Singh walked into the room with an outstretched hand. 'I want to thank you, Agent Lovett, for extricating us from that tricky situation. You were innovative and quick on your feet; we appreciate you very much.'

'Anything I could say in return would sound trite, so I'll just say that I am delighted that I was able to end this situation without any serious injury to anyone.'

'And where is Agent Connelly?' Dr Singh asked.

'He's in custody. He's being held on kidnapping charges.'

'Do you really think that is appropriate, Agent Lovett?'

'You don't want charges placed against him?' Jake asked, hoping that was exactly what the doctor meant.

'Agent Connelly appears to be experiencing a serious problem with his mental stability. Treatment seems more appropriate than jail time.'

'Really? But if you bring him to the courtroom to face those charges, it could be a golden opportunity to confront the bias and misconceptions about your faith.'

Dr Singh smiled. 'Yes, Agent, but it could be a trap that results in a backlash, making the situation even worse.'

'You don't want to publicly explain your beliefs and principles?'

'We find it far better to simply live them, Agent. We do not proselytize. We do not believe in cramming our faith down the throats of the unwilling. We believe that, if, by our example, people are drawn to our faith and ask questions about it, then is the time to discuss the essence of our beliefs. Not before.'

'What would you like to see?' Jake asked.

'I would like to see Agent Connelly evaluated by a neurologist, mental health professionals and a gerontologist. I would like to see him given the treatment he needs so that he can retire with peace of mind.'

'Sounds as if you have made a preliminary diagnosis, Dr Singh.'

'Not exactly, sir, but the more I observed his behavior, the greater my feeling that Agent Connelly's paranoia and delusions could be symptoms of Alzheimer's or another form of dementia. I think that possibility should be explored.'

'Do you think your patient, Mr Basra, will share your view?'

'I am relatively certain he will. But if you would step out of the room, I will gladly give him a call. After I have spoken to him briefly, I'll put him on speaker phone, with his consent, and you can hear his response.'

'Certainly,' Jake said, rising from the chair.

'And, Agent Lovett, I couldn't help but notice that you often looked down at your cell while we talked.'

'I . . .'

'No, no,' Dr Singh said, moving a hand side to side. 'No explanation needed. I just wanted you to know that if you need to make a call, the examination room next to this one is empty. You will have privacy there.'

'Thank you, sir.'

In the neighboring space, Jake called Lucinda. Once again, he heard the sound of her recorded voice. Where was she? What was she doing? He disconnected and paced the floor for less than three minutes before the door opened.

'Please, Agent Lovett, can you return now?'

Jake took a seat across from the doctor in the room where their conversation had begun.

Dr Singh smiled and pressed down on a button to reconnect the call. 'We are back now. I will put you on speaker phone.' When Mr Basra responded, the doctor laid out his viewpoint in succinct bullet points. 'Now please, sir,' Dr Singh said, 'tell the FBI agent exactly what you think of my opinion.'

'I am completely in accord with Dr Singh,' Mr Basra said. 'I would strongly prefer that charges against Agent Connelly be set aside and he be given the treatment he so desperately needs.'

'Thank you, sir,' Jake said. 'I'll do what I can to make that happen.'

Dr Singh disconnected the call. 'Agent Lovett, I understand that ignoring violations of the law goes against your nature. I am very pleased that you are willing to step outside those self-imposed boundaries and explore a more equitable solution.'

Jake stood and stretched out his hand. 'Thank you, Dr Singh. I'm not sure if I'll succeed in giving you satisfaction in this matter but I will do my best.'

On the drive back, Jake tried Lucinda again without any luck and then arranged for a conference call at the top of the hour with ATF Deputy Federal Security Director Franklin Wesley and FBI Assistant Director in Charge Sandra Fielding – his supervisor, also known as the Wicked Witch of the North.

Jake took a seat behind his desk and waited for the call to come through. When it did, he exchanged greetings with the other two and plunged right into the briefing about the situation with Connelly.

'Do you plan to move Connelly to a jail to await trial?' Wesley asked.

'I was hoping for a better solution to this problem, sir.'

'Excuse me! You don't plan on letting this lunatic run loose, do you?' Fielding objected.

Wesley snapped, 'Quiet a minute, Sandra. Let's hear what he has to say.'

Fielding expelled a noisy breath of air. 'Please, Lovett, entertain us.'

'It seems apparent to me that Agent Connelly is not mentally stable—'

'Oh, well, aren't you the bright one?' Fielding interjected.

Wesley said, 'Sandra, please.'

'As I was saying, I think that Agent Connelly should have a professional mental health evaluation before incarceration. And, in light of the public relations problem this situation presents for the ATF, perhaps that agency should be making the decision on this matter.'

Fielding expressed her displeasure with another noisy exhalation.

'What about the victims, Agent Lovett? Have you spoken with them?' Wesley asked.

'Yes, sir, I have. They are in agreement that Connelly needs consultation with a neurologist, a gerontologist and mental health professionals. They prefer that charges not be brought against him.'

'They were kidnapped. Restrained. Held against their will. Are they as crazy as Connelly?' Fielding asked.

'That is how they feel, ma'am,' Jake said. 'I got the impression that their opinion was grounded in their faith.'

Fielding sighed, 'Spare us all from the saints among us.'

'They are not Christian, ma'am,' Jake said.

'Whatever,' Fielding snapped back.

'Agent Lovett, I am inclined to support this action initially – at least until we have a professional assessment of Agent Connelly's issues. I will arrange for him to be transported to a secure facility. I can send in another agent to help with your investigation.'

'Sir, I need someone who is already in the loop – I really don't want to take the time to backtrack. And there is only one person I can think of – the only one who was conducting a realistic investigation.' Jake paused, hoping this was what Lucinda wanted. 'I would like the investigation turned back over to Lieutenant Pierce.'

Wesley and Fielding started talking at once, making most of what they said hard to understand – but one thing stood out: they were united in their disdain for local cops. Jake listened to their objections until they ran out of steam.

'May I remind you both that while I and Connelly were dedicating our time to chasing down his paranoid fantasies, Pierce was actually making progress?'

'She was taken off the case, Agent Lovett. I hope you were not providing her with unauthorized information,' Fielding said.

'I sort of had my hands full with Agent Connelly, ma'am. Hey, all I'm saying if we want to find the person who blew up the school, she'll get us there quicker than anyone. After all, I'm not exactly on top of the latest developments – I've been sidetracked and I'll have some catching up to do.'

'I think, Sandra, that this is a matter that requires further discussion between the two of us, don't you?'

'Yes,' she said. 'Lovett, we'll get back to you within twenty-four hours with our decision.'

Both connections terminated abruptly. Now, if he could only find Lucinda, they could start working toward a solution together – with or without approval from on high.

FORTY-TWO

L ucinda watched through the picture window in the living room as a young woman, who appeared under five feet tall, bustled up the sidewalk clutching a briefcase. When she stopped to speak to the patrolman at the steps, Lucinda opened the front door. 'CPS?' Lucinda asked.

'Yes, Estelle Lopez,' she said, extending her right hand. 'Are you Lieutenant Pierce?'

'Yes, come on in.'

'Is there a place we can talk privately?'

'Yes, Ms Lopez, there is a deck out back; follow me.'

The two women crossed through the house, Estelle glancing at the three children and smiling at them as she walked through the living room. As soon as they stepped back outside and Lucinda pulled the sliding glass door closed, Estelle said, 'I thought there were only two children.'

'There are – only two of the three children involved in this incident actually live in this home. The other is Charley Spencer, the daughter of Dr Spencer.'

'The timing of this is not optimal.'

'You know I didn't plan this, right?' Lucinda asked.

'Certainly, Lieutenant. My supervisor redlined the review of Dr Spencer as a suitable person for temporary custody of the two children but we'd only begun. And now we need to act without being fully prepared.'

'That is out of my control – and your control. But what we can do is make things as comfortable and as safe as possible for the two children, whose only guardians are currently in police custody.'

'Granted. That is why we are considering an exception to our normal operating procedure. We are prepared to escort these children to Dr Spencer's home for the night – maybe a little longer. However, we have already taken steps to identify any suitable family member to step in and care for them.'

'I trust you will exercise due diligence in ascertaining their suitability,' Lucinda said.

'Of course, Lieutenant. And we are well aware of the additional trauma we could inflict on these children if we make one false move. That is why we are reluctant to act on your recommendation, in case Dr Spencer is not as appropriate as he seems at this moment. We are doing so just the same, but when I take the children over, I will be making certain that they are OK in that environment and that Dr Spencer lives up to our expectations. If I have any doubts after talking to him, the children will not spend a single night in that home.'

'Thank you, Ms Lopez, for putting the needs of the children on the top of your priority list. I feel confident that Dr Spencer will not raise the slightest suspicion in your mind. I believe Dr Spencer is on his way here right now but I can call him and ask him to return home if you can give Charley a ride, too.'

'Naturally, but I will be evaluating her en route.'

Lucinda smiled at that thought. 'I think you'll find her to be the independent sort who questions authority at all times.'

'Good. The other two children need that kind of influence to help them get past the betrayal by their mother.'

'You certainly don't sound as if you popped out of the typical cookie-cutter mold.'

'Not in stature, not in philosophy and not in attitude. I don't believe in coddling the children under my charge. They need to be able to deal with their reality and move on. I want them to develop a strong sense of self and an independence of spirit to help them build a successful future.'

'Good; we're in agreement,' Lucinda said.

'Terrific. Now, can you introduce me to the children?'

Estelle explained to the three of them what would happen in their immediate future and gently addressed the long-term uncertainty. Then Lucinda, Estelle and Charley helped Amber and Andy pack up what they needed and put it in the trunk of Estelle's car.

Estelle turned to the sister and brother and said, 'I know you've gotten what you need for a few days, but is there anything that you want – anything that you will miss or that means a lot to you? Because, in some ways, you'll need those things, too.'

Both kids nodded and scurried back into the house. Andy returned with the shoebox containing his rock collection and Amber brought a framed photograph of herself, her mother and her brother as an infant – obviously taken in happier days.

Lucinda went back inside and waited for the arrival of Lieutenant Barry Washington from the sex crimes division so that she could turn the scene and the case over to him. She was exhausted and could think of little more than a shower and a warm bed. She knew she should check the messages on her phone, but it felt as if it would take too much effort to pull it out of her pocket and press the necessary buttons.

FORTY-THREE

Jake arrived at the apartment first. He was tired, hungry, worried about Lucinda and getting a headache from Chester's relentless high-pitched demands for attention. First things first. He scratched behind Chester's ears and down his back. The cat seemed to like the stroking but was still meowing like a maniac.

He pulled out a can of Chester's current favorite, Turkey Feast, and carried it over to the pet bowl. He knew he should clean out the dried-up remnants from the cat's last meal, but at that moment he didn't care. As soon as he dumped the contents, Chester was on it, making quieter sounds of contentment as he ate.

Jake opened the refrigerator, looking for something appealing and easy. He had a lot of options but all of them involved too much effort. He grabbed a hunk of aged cheddar, a knife, a box of stoneground crackers and a bottle of Killian's and carried it all out on to the balcony.

After washing down a couple of bites with a swallow of beer, he pulled out his cell and pressed Lucinda's name again, prepared to leave a more desperate message. He was surprised when she answered. 'Where are you?'

'In the car, in the parking lot.'

'Which parking lot?'

'Our apartment building. Where are you?'

'I'm up here – in the apartment. Why aren't you coming up?'

'I'm looking for the energy to walk over to the elevator.'

'You sound as bad off as I am.'

'Maybe worse,' Lucinda said. 'You made it upstairs. I'm still underground.'

'You need motivation?'

'Oh, yeah, but the usual stuff won't work. I'm too exhausted to play.'

'Me, too. So, how about this? I'm sitting on the balcony. If you're not up here soon, I'm apt to fall asleep in the chair. If you get up here after I doze off, your arrival could startle me and cause me to jump up, stumble, fall over the balcony and plunge down all those stories to the ground. Then you won't be able to sleep because the police will come and you'll need to identify the body and—'

'Enough! I'm opening the door. Swinging my legs out. Hold on, hold on, I'm summoning up the energy to stand. Oh, what an effort.'

'Lock the car,' Jake said. He heard the beep of mission accomplished.

'Got it,' Lucinda said. 'Walking to the elevator – got lucky, it's really close. Pressing the button. Now if I can only stay awake until it gets here.'

'Do jumping jacks,' Jake suggested.

'You are one sick puppy,' Lucinda said with a groan. 'Ah, it's here. Meet me at the top.'

Jake pushed up on the arms of the chair, plodded through the apartment and stood in front of the elevator door, arriving just as it dinged to a stop. He wrapped an arm around Lucinda's waist as she stepped into the hall. She threw her arm over his shoulders.

Once inside, Lucinda said, 'Shower and bed.'

'You need something to eat.'

'Too tired,' she said as she trudged down the hall.

'I've got cheese and crackers.'

'Bring them to bed. I'll eat them once I'm clean.'

'You're eating crackers in bed?'

'Oh, please, Jake. Admit it, you want to, too.'

'Want a beer?'

'Glass of merlot, please,' Lucinda said and shut the bathroom door.

In a moment, Jake heard the water running in the shower. He pulled out a tray, loaded up the snacks, another bottle of beer, a wine glass and the bottle of wine. He set it all down on the mattress and set his opened beer bottle on his nightstand. Then he poured a glass of wine and put it and the bottle on the table by Lucinda's side of the bed.

Jake went into the bathroom, disrobed and stepped into the shower.

'Ah, c'mon, Jake,' Lucinda objected. 'I told you I'm just too tired . . .'

'Me, too. I just don't know how long I can stand up, so I wanted to be ready to slip in the water as soon as you're done.'

'Yeah, well, I'm done. Inertia kept me from moving. It's all yours,' she said, stepping out and wrapping a towel around her body. In the bedroom, she wiped herself dry, pulled an oversized T-shirt over her head, plumped up her pillows and slid under the covers, sitting up against the headboard.

When a wet Jake emerged, he saw her munching and sipping and couldn't help but smile. 'Good, isn't it?'

'Better than that,' she said, refilling her wine glass.

Jake slipped into the other side, grabbed a hunk of cheese and a couple of crackers and said, 'You know, I really want to hear every detail of your day, but I'm afraid I might fall asleep in the middle of it.'

Lucinda smiled. 'Same for me, Jake. How about we keep it all till morning?'

'Deal – except for one important question?'

'What's that?'

'Do you want to be back on the case at the high school?'

'You know I've never really been off it, don't you, Jake?'

'Oh, yeah, but I'm trying to make it official.'

'Oh, sure, I can take orders from you for a little while.'

'Actually, I'm trying to get the case returned to you and your department. I want you to take the lead again. Are you OK with that?'

'If I wasn't so tired, I'd show you how OK I am with that.'

'Rain check?' Jake asked.

'Most definitely,' Lucinda agreed.

In a moment, they both were snoring, lights still on and the cheese and cracker tray on the bed between them. Chester eased up over the footboard and helped himself to a piece of cheddar before stretching out between their legs.

FORTY-FOUR

Lucinda awoke to the smell of coffee. She sat up in bed and saw Jake walking into the bedroom with two steaming mugs in his hands. She reached up for one of them and said, 'Oh dear, looks like I'm going to have to keep you around.'

'I should hope so,' Jake said with a grin. 'Now, tell me everything that happened yesterday.'

'Oh no, you go first – you were missing for a while.'

'What about you? I couldn't get hold of you for a long time.'

'But I wasn't missing. You could have called my office and found out. Your office, on the other hand, was in a state of panic.'

'OK, OK,' Jake said and ran down a summary of his day. 'Now, your turn.'

Lucinda had reached the point where Charley called asking for help when her cell rang. 'Pierce.'

'Lieutenant, there's a priest trying to reach you. He said that no one else would do. He has a Woodrow Wilson student down in his church this morning. I told him that the school case was turned over to the federal authorities, but he said that the girl knew you from a career day thing and wouldn't talk to anyone else.'

'You got a number?' she asked and jotted it down as he spoke. She disconnected and immediately made the call. 'Father Mark, please,' she said when the phone was answered.

'You got him.'

'This is Lieutenant Pierce.'

'Thank heaven. I've been worried she'd bolt since before I called you. It began in confession, then it turned into a counseling session here at Holy Redeemer. She's wracked with guilt and I told her the best way to alleviate that is to tell the authorities what she knows. She insisted that she talk to you and no one else. She's afraid of going to jail and believes that you might be able to help her avoid that.'

'Depends on what she has to say, Father.'

'Knowing what I know, Lieutenant, I do believe you will be willing. But you really need to hear it all from her.'

'I'll be there as quickly as I can but it might not be for half an hour. Can you hold on to her until then?'

'Sure, I'll fix her some breakfast. That should do it. But please come alone or she might spook.'

'Thank you, Father. See you soon.' Lucinda jumped up and started getting dressed.

'Whoa, whoa, whoa,' Jake said. 'You can't leave me hanging like that. Is Charley OK?'

'Yes, Charley is fine. Safe and sound home with her dad.'

'And, and . . .' Jake said, trailing behind her as she went into the bathroom and picked up her toothbrush.

'Just a minute,' Lucinda said. When she finished and rinsed her mouth out, she added, 'I'll tell you more if you can keep up with me while I'm getting ready. I really don't have a minute to spare. There's a Woodrow Wilson student sitting with a priest, feeling guilty and getting restless.'

'How 'bout if I come with you?'

'You can ride with me – and talk on the way – if you can get ready quickly enough and if you're willing to wait in the car while I conduct the interview. Father Mark warned me to come alone or she might run off.'

At the church, Jake decided to walk the six blocks or so to his office instead of sitting in the car while Lucinda was inside. 'Call me when you're finished here, OK?'

'Sure, I don't know how long I will be. See ya later.' Lucinda watched Jake walk down the street until he turned the corner. She approached the old stone church, pulled open the massive wooden doors and entered the sanctuary. The walls on the other side were lined with enormous stained-glass windows of biblical scenes – the old-fashioned kind that seemed to glow with the light without illuminating the interior much at all.

The smells of incense, mingled bodies and lemony wood polish tickled her nostrils. Usually, grand old churches with intricate vaulted ceilings stirred up a sense of serenity deep in her core. But today it felt both more ominous and more thrilling. She might be on the verge of uncovering the information she needed to crack the case. Or the girl could simply stir up questions without answers. Or she could change her mind and say nothing at all. People consumed with guilt can be very unpredictable.

She walked up the aisle past the gated pews. When she reached the halfway point, a man wearing a black cassock with a clerical collar emerged from a door on the left side of the altar. 'Father Mark?' she asked.

He smiled and nodded. 'Lieutenant Pierce?'

Lucinda said, 'Yes, Father.'

'Follow me, please.'

Lucinda walked behind the priest down a narrow hall. Outside a closed door, he stopped and said, 'I'll introduce you and then excuse myself. Please remember, she is very fragile. Be gentle with her.'

'If I can,' Lucinda said, not willing to stand in a house of God and make a promise she feared she might not be able to keep.

Father Mark opened the door to reveal a red-eyed, wet-nosed teenage girl wearing a Virginia Tech ball cap. 'Tamara, as you requested, Lieutenant Pierce is here. Lieutenant, this is Tamara Van Dyke. She's a sophomore at Woodrow Wilson High School. Now, if you two will excuse me, I have some phone calls I need to make.'

'Father,' Tamara blurted out.

'Yes, Tamara?'

'Am I doing the right thing?'

'Absolutely. This is not a burden you should carry. Hand it over to the Lieutenant and ease the pain in your heart.' Father Mark smiled and nodded at them as he backed out of the room.

Lucinda slipped into the chair opposite Tamara. 'Father Mark said you have information about the explosion at the school?'

'I don't know for sure that it is about that, but I know what I did and I know it might be.'

'What did you do, Tamara?'

'I'm in the marching band.'

Lucinda waited for the girl to continue. When Tamara said nothing more, Lucinda asked, 'What instrument do you play?'

'The xylophone.'

'Did you have a performance this past weekend?'

'Yes, it was a battle of the bands in Norfolk.'

'Did you do well?'

For the first time, Tamara smiled. 'Second place,' she said.

'That's nice. When did you all get back to the school?'

'It was after eight Saturday night.'

'What happened then, Tamara?'

'I changed out of my uniform and then I hid in the restroom until everyone was gone.'

Lucinda wasn't sure where this was leading but she had a difficult time imagining that the meek girl sitting in front of her could have set up the bomb. 'Why did you do that?'

'So I could duct-tape the latch on the door.'

'But, Tamara, I thought that the school doors all had safety bars that could only be unlocked with those ratchet-type keys.'

Tamara nodded her head. 'Most of them, yeah. But there is one in the back, by the shop, that has a regular lock on it.'

'And you duct-taped that one?'

'Yes, ma'am.'

'Why, Tamara?'

'It wasn't for me. It was for someone else who needed to get into the school on Sunday.'

'Who?'

Tamara dropped her head into her hands and sobbed. 'But he said he changed his mind and didn't go.'

'Who didn't go there?'

'He said someone else must have found the door I rigged and took advantage of the opportunity.'

'Who told you this, Tamara?'

'But, you see, that still makes me responsible. It doesn't matter. I created the opportunity and someone died. There's blood on my hands,' she said, stretching out her hands, palms up.

Lucinda knew she had to tamp down the drama or it would escalate. 'Take your guilty feelings to Father Mark and do penance. But right now I need you to keep your attention on the facts. I do not have time for your emotions.'

'I thought you would care about what I was going through. I thought you were different when I met you at the job fair. But you're just like everybody else.'

Lucinda slapped an open palm on the table. 'Cut the crap, Tamara.

You are involved in a serious situation and I need you to answer my questions.'

Tamara's jaw dropped and her face flushed. 'Are you going to put me in jail?'

'I don't want to do that, Tamara. But you need to tell me everything or I will have no other choice. Now, who told you to tape the door latch?'

Tamara's chin trembled. 'Jimmy. Jimmy told me. But he changed his mind and didn't go to the school that morning.'

'Jimmy who?'

'My brother,' she wailed.

'Jimmy Van Dyke?'

Tamara nodded her head and sniffled.

'Does Jimmy go to Woodrow Wilson?'

The girl shook her head. 'No. He graduated last year.'

'Did he tell you why he wanted to go into the school when it was closed?'

'Sort of, but not really.'

'What did he say, Tamara?'

'He said something about defending someone's honor. A girl, I think?'

'You don't know which girl?'

Tamara shook her head.

'Did he have a girlfriend?'

'Not since sometime before Christmas. I don't know exactly when.'

'What was her name?'

'I don't know. I asked but he wouldn't tell me. He used to tell me that stuff but this time he said it had to be a secret.'

'Any ideas?'

Tamara nearly shouted when she said, 'I told you: I don't know!'

Lucinda paused in the hope that a small break would dissipate some of the tension in the room. Then, in a quiet, calm voice, she asked, 'Is Jimmy a good big brother?'

Tamara nodded and her face glowed. 'He's super. He taught me lots of stuff when we were growing up. And he never lets anyone mess with me. One time, when this boy Billy was picking on me in sixth grade, Jimmy put an arm around Billy's shoulder and walked across the field, talking baseball. Then just when Billy wasn't expecting it, he spun around and sunk a fist into Billy's gut. When

Billy fell to the ground, Jimmy stood over him and said, "You leave my sister alone or next time I'll break something." And Billy never bothered me again.' Tamara smiled as she remembered. Then, abruptly, her brow furrowed and her mouth turned down. 'I don't think he really would have. He was just trying to scare Billy. He wouldn't have broken his arm or anything. Not Jimmy.'

'Does Jimmy still live at home with you?'

'Yeah. He wants to get his own apartment. He's been saving his tips.'

'Where does he work?'

'He does delivery for Pizza Barn. Sometimes he brings home prank orders.'

'So Jimmy has a car?'

'Oh, yeah. It's Mom's old Nissan. She got a new Honda and sold her car to Jimmy for ten dollars.' Tamara laughed. 'It is old and ugly but it's still running.'

'What color is it?' Lucinda asked.

'Once upon a time, it was shiny black but now it's all faded and icky-looking, and the first week he drove it, he had an accident. He had to get a new fender at the junkyard and the only one he could find was white. So I call it a skunk-mobile. Sometimes Jimmy thinks that's funny but sometimes it makes him mad.'

'Does he ever drive anything else?'

'Sometimes, Mom lets him drive her Honda – but only if she's in the car, too. And every once in a while, he drives this red pick-up truck.'

Lucinda sucked in a hard breath.

Tamara cocked her head to one side and said, 'What?'

'My very favorites – red pick-up trucks. I wish I had one,' Lucinda said.

'Really? You don't look like a pick-up person.'

'Well, I did spend a chunk of my high school years living – and working – on a farm. So, where does Jimmy get that truck?'

'He borrows it sometimes.'

'Whose is it?' Lucinda asked.

'Some friend, I guess.'

'Did Jimmy borrow the truck last weekend?'

'Ye—' Tamara began but slammed her lips shut before she could finish the word. Her eyes narrowed to suspicious slits. 'I told you Jimmy did not go up to the school on Sunday.'

'Because that's what he told you?'

'Yes, but it's true. I got home before he did Saturday night. I saw him pull into the driveway – and the truck was still there when I got up Sunday morning until he left to take it back after lunch.'

'Were you out late Saturday night?'

'No. I was home before *SNL* started but I was up kinda late online.'

'So did you get up to go to morning mass?'

'Are you kidding me? I was still online when the sun came up. I only got up when I did because Mom made me a grilled cheese sandwich for lunch and I smelled it in my sleep and realized how hungry I was.'

'So what time was it when you saw the truck out front?'

Tamara blanched. 'That doesn't matter. It was there. Jimmy didn't go up to the high school Sunday morning. He was out really late. He slept in, too.'

'Tamara, calm down.'

Tamara pushed back from the table and jerked to her feet. 'No, I won't calm down. I just wanted to help you and you're twisting my words and making things up. I'm sorry I told Father Mark to call you. You are not a nice person – that was just a big, fat, phony act.'

'Tamara, I'm sorry. I didn't mean to upset you. I really appreciate you coming forward about this. It took a lot of courage.'

Father Mark appeared in the doorway. 'Is everything all right?'

'No,' Tamara said. 'This was a mistake. I want to go now. I'm late for class.'

'Lieutenant?' Father Mark asked.

'I will need to get a written statement from Tamara, but that can wait until after school.'

'Then you'll have to talk to my lawyer,' Tamara snapped.

'Your lawyer?' Father Mark asked.

'I don't have one now, but I will,' Tamara said, pivoting on her heels and walking out of the room.

Father Mark called after her, 'Tamara! Tamara, wait.'

The girl didn't pause or look back.

'Oh dear,' the priest said. 'What happened, Lieutenant?'

'What did she tell you, Father?'

'She said that she taped the latch on a door at the school.'

'Did she tell you why?'

'She said that she wanted to see if it would still be there when she went back to school Monday morning.'

'She did it for someone else, Father, and I pressured her to tell me that person's name. She was very unhappy about that. Thanks for everything, Father.'

They shook hands and Lucinda left the church. As soon as she went outside, she called Jake. His cell phone went straight to voicemail so she punched his office number into the keyboard. When she asked to speak with him, she was told that he was in a conference call.

Lucinda drove back to the Justice Center to get organized. She decided she'd talk to Brittany Schaffer at the high school first. Then she'd go find Jimmy Van Dyke. She could be wrong but the coincidental absence of Brittany's truck the same weekend Jimmy was driving a red pick-up could not be ignored.

FORTY-FIVE

Lucinda was at her desk, making arrangements with Principal Rose Johnson for a second interview with Brittany Schaffer. As soon as she hung up, she heard the captain's voice coming from the doorway. 'My office now, Pierce.'

Lucinda sighed. She hoped whatever the captain had to say wouldn't take long. Rose expected her at the high school in half an hour. She sat down across from Holland's desk and said, 'Yes, sir.'

'Good news this time, Pierce. You are back in charge of the investigation at the high school.'

Lucinda smiled. 'Thank you, sir.'

'Don't thank me, Pierce. This was all Lovett's doing. So don't blow it.'

'Blow it, sir?'

'I've been warned, Pierce.'

'Warned?'

'OK, threatened. The police chief told me that all eyes will be on you and how you conduct this investigation. He's worried you won't be up to speed.'

'But, sir—'

'No, Pierce, I didn't dare tell him that I authorized you to proceed in that sneaky fashion we cooked up.'

'We, sir?'

'Don't push it, Pierce. He's also worried that you might not be up to the task – you might not be knowledgeable enough about terrorist plots.'

'But, sir—'

'No, Pierce, I didn't tell him that you thought this had nothing to do with any terrorist group or outside agitators. Just solve the damn case. Then he won't be able to argue. But don't forget: the police chief feels the whole department is on the line and our credibility with federal law enforcement is at stake. Try to follow all guidelines and don't do anything stupid.'

'Stupid, sir?'

'Don't argue semantics with me, Pierce. You got what you wanted – now go out and do your job.'

Lucinda walked out wanting to hug Holland – heck, she'd hug the police chief, too. But at this moment, more than anything, she'd like to wrap herself around Jake and give him the best thank-you ever. That would have to wait.

She returned to her desk, gathered up everything she'd need for the interview and headed for the high school. She went straight to Rose Johnson's office in the trailer, where Brittany Schaffer was already waiting for her.

When Lucinda walked into the room, Brittany raised her left wrist and looked down at her watch. 'My next class starts in forty-five minutes, officer. I need a little time to prepare.'

'This shouldn't take too long, Ms Schaffer. I do have some good news.'

Brittany gave her a sideways glance through narrowed eyes. 'What?'

'Your alibi checked out.'

'Of course it did,' Brittany said, followed by a faux yawn.

'There was just one little problem. Mr McCallister told me that when he arrived at your home initially, the truck wasn't there and it still wasn't there when he left the next day.'

'Tom is mistaken.'

'He said he was certain he would have seen it when he pulled up to your house.'

Brittany blew a breath out through extended cheeks. 'It was parked in the garage.'

'Actually, he said he parked *his* vehicle in your garage.'

'That must have been another time. He's confused.'

'No. He was certain. In fact, he said he asked you about it and you told him your truck was in the shop.'

'You can check with my mechanic. My truck was not in the shop – it is running like a top.'

'Why would Mr McCallister lie about something like that?'

'I did not say he was lying. I said he was mistaken.'

'Cut the crap, Ms Schaffer. Who was driving your car last weekend?'

'No one.'

'You are saying that it was at your place the whole time?'

'I certainly am and it certainly was.'

'Then why did Mr McCallister say that he had to call a cab to take him back to his car since you couldn't give him a ride because your truck was in the shop?'

'A cab? We got a taxi the night before because we'd been drinking and didn't want to drive.'

'Yes, he said that, but he also said you called a cab for him in the morning.'

'Tom had too much to drink. His memory is befuddled.'

'I doubt Mr McCallister will be pleased to learn you are calling him a liar.'

'I never called him a liar.'

'Do you recall a former student named Jimmy Van Dyke?'

Lucinda could have sworn she saw a flicker of panic in Brittany's eyes and a quickened tempo in her swinging leg before the teacher gave an answer.

'The name does sound a bit familiar, officer.'

'How about a current student? David Baynes?'

'Oh, that's such a tragedy. He was in my fifth-period class but I didn't recognize his name at first – not until Ms Johnson pointed out that he was one of my students.'

'The school year is nearly over and you still are not familiar with the names of the students in your classes?'

'Listen. There are a lot of periods in a day and a lot of days in a school year and even more names on those classroom rosters. I wish I could say I remember all my students, all the time. But, sadly, I don't.' Brittany turned on a plastic smile. 'And any teacher who tells you otherwise is a liar.'

'Seems as if there are a lot of liars lurking in your life, Ms Schaffer.'

'Everybody lies, officer. In your line of work, you should be well aware of that fact.'

Lucinda stared straight into Brittany's eyes. 'I am reminded of the frequency of dishonest answers every day, Ms Schaffer.'

Brittany turned away, uncrossed her legs and stared into space. 'Is that all, officer?'

'Who are you talking to, Ms Schaffer?'

Brittany jerked her head back to Lucinda. 'You, of course.'

'Then perhaps you could address me properly. It's Lieutenant – Lieutenant Pierce. I told you that the last time we talked. You seem to have forgotten – or is that just your little way of demonstrating your disdain for me?'

'Really, Lieutenant,' Brittany said, rising to her feet. 'I meet a lot of people with your level of self-absorption every day – but most of them are teenagers.'

Lucinda stood and looked down at the shorter woman, laughing long and hard. 'If you're trying to amuse me, you are succeeding. If not, you're even less self-aware than road kill.'

'How dare you?'

Lucinda tilted her head and smiled.

'I am so sick of dealing with envious women in positions of power. You're all the same – you, Ms Johnson, those management-level mothers – you make me sick. You take one look at me and turn green over your own physical inadequacies. I will be reporting you to your superiors.' Brittany pivoted on her toes and stalked out of the office, her heels tapping an angry staccato on the floorboards. She punctuated it all by slamming the door as she stepped outside.

Lucinda was now even more convinced that Brittany Schaffer knew something about the incident at the school. And she strongly suspected it had something to do with Jimmy Van Dyke. Perhaps Jimmy's parents would know who loaned him the truck. If not, maybe they'd know if he had a relationship with his teacher that was close enough that she would loan him her vehicle over the weekend. The question was: whom should she interview first? Who would be most likely to answer honestly and completely? She needed to know more about Mr and Mrs Van Dyke before she could decide.

FORTY-SIX

J ake wanted to coordinate his efforts with Lucinda, but when he
called, he was shuttled straight to voicemail. Rather than work
on another case in the pile on his desk, he decided to go to the
high school and search the student area of the parking lot for red
pick-up trucks.

Looking over the large space, he saw about a dozen scattered
throughout the other vehicles. He took them one row at a time,
jotting down the make, model and license plate numbers. Then he'd
look in the cab and take notes on the contents before moving on to
the next truck. The last one in the lot was parked in a far corner,
at the greatest distance from the school and with no other cars in
the spaces around it.

He was peering into the passenger window when he heard, 'Hey!
Hey! What are you doing? Get away from that truck!' Jake turned
around and saw a shaggy-haired young man in jeans and a T-shirt
running in his direction.

'Sweet-looking ride,' Jake said. 'Had to check it out.'

'Don't touch it.'

'What are you doing out of class?'

'What's it to you?' he said.

Jake whipped out his FBI badge. 'I think you'd better answer the
question.' Jake saw a bob in the teenager's Adam's apple as he swallowed his anxiety.

'Hey, man, I didn't do anything wrong. Here's my hall pass,' he
said, holding out a piece of paper. 'Mr Welch sent me out to get
an ink cartridge for the printer.'

'Mr Welch?'

'My journalism teacher.'

'Is this your truck?'

'Yes. No. Well, it's my dad's.'

'You drive it often?'

'No. This is the first time. He only let me use today 'cause he's
working on my car.'

Jake ran a hand across the right front fender. 'You've never driven it before?'

'Oh, man, don't touch it,' the boy said, pulling up the tail on his T-shirt and rubbing on the spot touched by Jake. 'If I bring it back with even a fingerprint on it, he will never let me use it again.'

'Let me see your driver's license.'

'Gee, FBI doing traffic checks?' he said as he pulled out his wallet.

'Gerald Fitzgerald Whiting the third,' Jake read from the card. 'Well, Gerald—'

'Fitz. Everybody calls me Fitz. My dad is Gerald.'

'What were you doing last Sunday morning?'

'Trying to fake sick so I wouldn't have to go to church with my folks.'

'Did it work?'

'Nah,' he said, scuffing the toe of his shoe on the tarmac.

'You sure your parents didn't fall for it and go to church without you in your mom's car and you decided to take the pick-up for a spin without them knowing it.'

'Yes. We did go in my mom's car – but I was with them.'

'You slip the keys to a friend to use during the services?'

'You crazy? My dad would kill me. Wait, are you saying this truck looks like one that was at the school when the explosion went off?'

'What if I was?' Jake asked.

'Well, somebody else has a truck that looks just like this one.'

'Here at the school?'

'Yeah. It's up in the teachers' parking lot.'

'Whose truck is it?'

'Ms Schaffer. I know 'cause I had her for English last year.'

'So you think Ms Schaffer had something to do with what happened here Sunday morning?'

'Ms Schaffer?' Tom said. 'You gotta be kidding. Have you seen her?'

'No.'

'She's hot. I mean, she's a very nice-looking lady.'

'If you don't think she was up here at the school, why are you pointing a finger at her, Fitz?'

'Not at her. At her truck. She loans it out to kids all the time.'

'She loans it to students?'

'Yeah. You know – her favorites.'

'What do you mean by "favorites"? The best students?'

Fitz snorted. 'Not exactly. I mean some of them are dumb as toothpicks.'

'Do you think there is something going on outside of the classroom, Fitz?'

'Somethin'. I just don't know what. Some guys say they did her. But you know how guys are – the ones that say they did a girl are probably the ones who didn't.'

'You think others have had a sexual relationship with her?' Jake asked as a tight ball of fury formed in his chest.

'You know, there's rumors,' Fitz said. 'I don't know anything for sure. It could be all talk. Like I said, she's hot. That makes guys talk – most of it's just a pile of crap.'

'Anyone in particular come to mind, Fitz?'

'No, man. It's just talk. Really. She's a nice lady. Listen, I gotta go or Mr Welch is going to be asking questions.'

'Give me your cell number and home address, and then you can go.' Jake jotted down the information with his notes on the truck and watched as Fitz backed out of his space and drove out of the parking lot.

Interesting new wrinkle, Jake thought. It will certainly add another layer of suspicion to Lucinda's concern about Brittany Schaffer. Was she having intimate relations with some of her students? Or was she just playing the flirt with the kids for the ego gratification she received? Is her inappropriate behavior somehow connected to the case?

Or is this whole pick-up connection just one rolling red herring on four wheels? He needed to talk to Lucinda. Maybe she'd cleared Brittany Schaffer already. He punched her name on his phone, listened to one ring and then heard the sound of her voice.

'Jake? Want to get together for lunch? I'm starved and I can give you an update on my morning's progress.'

'Yeah, sounds perfect. Where are you?'

'I'm just walking out of one of the temporary trailers at the high school. Where are you?'

'In the student parking lot.'

'At the high school?'

'Yeah.'

'I'll be back there in a flash. I'm driving.'

'Of course you are,' Jake said. *Sometimes she's just so predictable.*

FORTY-SEVEN

Over lunch, Jake and Lucinda established their priorities: find Jimmy Van Dyke and bring him in for an interview; find out more about Brittany Schaffer's relationships with students; and then confront the English teacher with the information they'd gathered.

They drove into a neat neighborhood of small, well-tended 1940s-era bungalows and pulled up in front of a tidy house with a front yard nearly filled with flowerbeds. Early-blooming daffodils and tulips added cheerful color; myriads of fresh green sprouts erupting from the ground promised more.

Ringing the doorbell, Jake and Lucinda were surprised when the door was answered by a dark-skinned, middle-aged woman with traces of a Caribbean lilt in her voice. They presented their badges and Lucinda said, 'We would like to speak with Jimmy Van Dyke.'

'My son is not here,' the woman said.

'Do you know where he is?' Lucinda asked.

'He's nineteen years old. What do you think?' the woman replied with a chuckle.

'Mrs Van Dyke?' Jake asked.

'Yes, sah, I'm Charlotte Van Dyke.'

'May we come in and talk to you for a bit?'

'Of course,' she said, pushing open the screen door.

She led them into her living room, where Jake and Lucinda sat down on a dark brown sofa. Mrs Van Dyke chose a tan upholstered chair perpendicular to them.

'Just before you got here, I started the coffee pot. Would you like to have a cup with me?'

'Yes, ma'am,' Lucinda said, 'that would be very nice.'

'I'll be right back then.'

While she was gone, Lucinda looked around the room. Vivid Caribbean paintings on the walls, multicolored books lined up on shelves and an array of school photos marching across the mantelpiece provided a bright contrast to the neutral tones of the furniture. Not a speck of dust anywhere and every single item in the room seemed to be exactly where it was supposed to be – maybe to an obsessive degree.

Charlotte walked through the archway carrying a large wooden tray with a carafe, sugar bowl, creamer, teaspoons and three cups. Jake jumped up, relieved her of her burden and placed it down on the table.

After pouring coffee for each of them and waiting until Jake and Lucinda had settled back into the sofa, Charlotte said, 'Now, how can I help you?'

'We accept your word that you do not know where your son is right now, Mrs Van Dyke, but do you know where he was Sunday morning?' Lucinda asked.

Charlotte sucked in a quavering breath. 'Is this about the explosion at the high school? Please tell me you don't think Jimmy had anything to do with that.'

'Do you know where he was Sunday morning?' Lucinda repeated.

Charlotte sighed. 'No, ma'am. He left here very early that morning before I even got out of bed.'

'Did he leave the house in his car?'

'No,' Charlotte said, shaking her head. 'He left in that red pick-up truck that he came home in Saturday night.'

Jake and Lucinda exchanged a glance. Jake asked, 'Whose truck was that?'

'I'm not so sure,' Charlotte said. 'I asked but all he said was that it belonged to a friend. I told him I didn't think any of his friends could afford a truck like that. He just snapped back that he had more friends than I knew about.'

'What about Jimmy's dad? Are they close?'

Charlotte rose up and walked toward the hallway. 'Just a minute,' she said, extending an index finger in the air. She returned with the portrait of a couple – a younger version of her and, by her side, a handsome white man in uniform. 'This is Jimmy's daddy,' she said, handing the framed photograph to the investigators.

'My Terrence was a fine man, a good father. He and Jimmy were very close before he died.'

'I'm sorry for your loss,' Lucinda said in a hushed voice.

'Been a long time now. Remember that awful ice storm in January of 1998? Terrence was up in Pennsylvania on business and tried to

make it home. He ended up in the middle of a multi-car pile-up.
He didn't survive. Somehow, Jimmy seems to hold me responsible
for that and blame me as if I engineered the whole disaster. He's
still carrying that anger, along with the memory of the taunts of his
classmates because of the color of my skin. I know of at least one
occasion when he told his friends that I was the family maid.'

Lucinda felt bile rise in her throat. The younger generation was
supposed to be beyond this superficial appraisal of a person's value
– and yet it persists.

'And Jimmy's not just angry at me,' Charlotte continued. 'He's
angry at his dad – for dying, for marrying a woman of color, for
not being here. That's why I keep that picture of my husband and
me in the bedroom. I used to have some photos of us on the mantle,
but Jimmy destroyed them one afternoon.'

Lucinda felt the woman's pain pressing on her. She didn't want
to add to it but it appeared to be the direction the investigation was
going. 'Mrs Van Dyke, can you give me the names of Jimmy's
friends?'

'I can't say I know any of their last names and not all of their
first names. He's been hiding a lot from me since that English
teacher broke his heart.'

'What English teacher?' Jake and Lucinda asked together.

'Ms Schaffer. I told him he was being foolish. But somehow he
thought that once he graduated from high school, she was going to
marry him. It was the craziest thing. After he proposed, she cut him
off. Blocked him from sending her texts, "unfriended" him on
Facebook and never answered his email. But I think she started
talking to him again just recently. I think she's back in his life. In
fact, I wondered if she loaned him that truck last weekend.'

'Ma'am, I hate to ask this but do you think Jimmy was sexually
involved with Ms Schaffer?' Jake asked.

'I know he wanted to be, sir, but I would think a school teacher
would have more sense than that. Wouldn't you?'

Lucinda and Jake looked at each other, and Charlotte read their
faces. 'You do think that's possible, don't you? Not just now but
back when he was still in school?'

'We don't know,' Lucinda said with a shake of her head. 'It is a
question that has crossed our minds, ma'am, but, honestly, we do
not know the answer.'

'Well, you'd better find the answer. If she did that to my son, she'll do it to someone else's son. Who knows how many boys she has manipulated? If that was her truck Jimmy was driving and that truck was up at the high school, she was behind it.'

'Ma'am, could we have a look in Jimmy's room?'

Charlotte stared at them and folded her arms across her chest. 'No. Not now. This is getting too serious, too fast. I need to talk to an attorney before I do anything or say anything else. I would appreciate it if you would leave now. I apologize for closing the door to the hospitality of my home but I have to think of my son's best interests right now. Obviously, no one else is.'

Jake and Lucinda mumbled appreciation for the coffee and apologized for upending her day but left without objection. Lucinda dropped Jake off at his car in the high school parking lot and returned to the Justice Center to file a Be-On-the-Look-Out for Jimmy Van Dyke and his car.

FORTY-EIGHT

After taking care of the BOLO, Lucinda checked for messages on her desk phone. One was from Leticia Fletcher, the CASA attorney handling Amber and Andy's case. Lucinda returned the call.

'Amber's abuser was denied bail for the time being. However, the judge did set a low bail for Amber's mother. As soon as she was released, her attorney took her over to family court where they filed a petition for an emergency hearing for custody. In the document, she stated that the abuse allegations were a misunderstanding,' Leticia said.

'You're fighting this, aren't you?'

'You think I should?'

'I can't believe you asked that,' Lucinda snapped. 'That woman wants to get her hands on those children to intimidate them into recanting their statements. She doesn't care what happened to Amber or she would have done something about it as soon as her daughter told her what was happening.'

Leticia laughed. 'I was hoping you'd feel that way. So I can expect you at court for the hearing tomorrow morning?'

In that moment, Lucinda felt overwhelmed, unable to meet all the demands on her, but she could not ignore this responsibility to a young girl. 'Yes,' she said, exhaling a deep breath to punctuate the answer.

'Good. And it might even get better. CPS located the family of the children's father in Maryland. He has absolutely no interest in Amber or Andy—'

'I thought you said this was good news.'

'Give me a minute. It gets better. His parents and his siblings are interested in these children. They are willing to step forward to assume permanent custody. In fact, they expressed interest in adopting the kids. Maryland CPS has started an inquiry into their fitness as foster parents. They all have decided that whichever family member does best in that analysis will be the custodial parents. As soon as that's determined, that couple will come down here and hire an attorney.'

'Can I share that with Dr Spencer?'

'Yes, but tell him that it wouldn't be wise for Amber and Andy to know just yet until we can be more certain of the likely outcome.'

'You got it. I'll see you in family court in the morning.' She hung up under the assumption that, while she was in court, Jake could follow up with Jimmy if he'd been located or bring Brittany Schaffer in for an interview if not. Or maybe he should go talk to Principal Rose Johnson about the possibility of sexual misconduct.

She was still mulling it over when her cell rang. 'Jake, I'm so glad you called. I was just—'

'You're not going to be glad when I tell you why.'

'What's wrong?'

'Well, it started out OK. When I returned to my office, the forensic tire expert had sent me a report by email that identified the type of tire on the red truck that was parked in front of the school. I rushed over to the school to get a look at the tires on Schaffer's truck and they were the same make and appeared to have the same wear patterns.'

'That sounds good,' Lucinda said.

'Yeah. Then I got a call from the Wicked Witch.'

'Oh dear.'

'Command performance time in DC. Apparently, ATF headquarters is bitching about getting shoved off the case and is trying to get back on it. She thinks that my presence is mandatory. My flight leaves in two hours.'

'Damn her. Get back as soon as you can. Call me when you get to your hotel.' Lucinda hung up, cursing bureaucrats and wondering how she'd handle it all on her own.

FORTY-NINE

Since Lucinda would be tied up in court in the morning, she moved her plans to visit Brittany Schaffer to that evening. She stopped by the apartment to feed Chester and grab a bite to eat.

Brittany's home, in a sprawling suburban community, was small but the lot was spacious. She pulled into the drive and parked behind Brittany's red pick-up truck.

Lucinda rang the doorbell and heard movement inside for a full minute before Brittany answered. 'What do you want?' she said.

'Just a few minutes of your time.'

Brittany stretched her arm across the doorframe, blocking entry. 'What about?'

'I thought you'd want to know that we did check with the taxi services about your alibi.'

'You found the one that gave us a ride home Saturday, right?'

Lucinda stared at her without responding.

Brittany dropped her arm. 'Oh, all right, come in. But I'm really busy. I have a lot of papers to grade, so you need to make this quick.'

Lucinda followed the teacher into her kitchen and sat across from her at a table in the corner of the room. 'The good news is that Commonwealth Cab did confirm giving you and Tom a ride home Saturday night.'

'Fine. I knew they would. And I know they didn't come back here on Sunday morning.'

Lucinda smiled. 'That's right. But the bad news,' Lucinda continued, 'is that City Taxi informed me that they did pick up a man here early that day.'

'Someone is fudging their books – covering up an unauthorized use of the cab.'

'Sounds like the whole universe is plotting against you, Ms Schaffer. But the other thing is that both taxi companies confirmed Tom's story that your truck was not here.'

'I told you: the truck was in the garage.'

'But Tom said that he parked in the garage when he first got here.'

'He's mistaken.'

'He's lying?' Lucinda asked.

'No, mistaken. Confused. Whatever.'

'There's another little problem, Ms Schaffer. You told me you never loaned out your truck and yet we have a witness who said that you loaned it to students quite often.'

'That witness is mistaken.'

'Oh, he's lying, too?'

'I didn't say that,' Brittany said.

'And then there are the witnesses at the high school on the morning of the explosion. They said the truck that pulled away in a hurry looked just like yours.'

'There are a lot of trucks like mine around.'

'I think the witnesses were pretty certain it was the same truck when they came up and looked at yours in the parking lot.'

'They are mistaken.'

'Wow, there are a lot of mistaken, confused people around here, aren't there? Either that or a whole bunch of liars.'

Brittany folded her arms across her chest and stared up at the ceiling.

'Unfortunately, Ms Schaffer, forensic evidence cannot prevaricate and we have evidence placing your vehicle at the high school that morning,' Lucinda said, stretching the truth a bit.

'That is not possible. My truck was here. So how could there be any evidence?'

'You ever watch *CSI*, Ms Schaffer?'

'Who doesn't?'

'You ever hear about tire track evidence?'

Brittany's face paled. 'Yes.'

'Well, the FBI analyzed the casts of the tire tracks in the grass in front of the school – and surprise! They are a match for the tires on your truck.'

'OK. So I did loan my truck to someone over the weekend. But it wasn't to anyone attending Woodrow Wilson High.'

'Who did you loan it to, Ms Schaffer?' Lucinda asked.

'I prefer not to answer that question.'

'This is a murder investigation, ma'am – that is not an option.'

'Fine. I refuse to answer any more of your questions without an attorney present.'

'That's your choice, Ms Schaffer. I can either take you to the station now or you can agree to come there voluntarily tomorrow afternoon with the lawyer of your choice.'

'What if I refuse to accept the boundaries of your arbitrary options?' Brittany asked.

'Then I will take you in by force – in handcuffs. Although it is quite possible that the media will find out that you came to the station of your own free will, I can guarantee that they will know about it if you arrive with your hands pinned behind your back.'

'You are a bully,' Brittany said.

'Your choice, Ms Schaffer.'

Lucinda heard a loud thump off to her right and turned her head in the direction of the noise. It seemed as if it came from behind the closed door – probably a bedroom door. 'Who else is in this house?'

'No one,' Brittany said.

'I'm not deaf – I heard someone in the other room,' Lucinda said, rising to her feet.

'You are imagining things,' Brittany said, leaning back in the chair.

'Would you like to ask that person to come out here right now?'

'There is no other person.'

A crashing sound was followed by the tinkling of falling glass. Lucinda raced to the door, pulling her weapon. She turned the knob but it was locked, stepped to the side and kicked it open. She spun into the space with her revolver drawn. 'Police! Step out and reveal yourself. Keep your hands visible at all times,' she said as she scanned the room.

'Excuse me,' Brittany said, 'you are violating my civil rights by searching my home without a warrant. I assure you that I will file a complaint.'

Lucinda ignored her and focused on a crooked venetian blind with bent slats hanging in front of a smashed window on the far side of the room. Lucinda rushed towards it. As she did, she heard the unmistakable sound of a rising garage door. She fled the room, running to the front door.

She reached the porch just in time to see a ratty old Nissan burst out of its enclosure and weave erratically down the drive. She raised her gun and aimed at it but pulling the trigger became too risky too fast. The driver fishtailed the car, turning on to the street, where the vehicle had a string of bungalows as a backdrop. She couldn't take the chance that a bullet might enter a home and kill or injure someone who lived there. She lowered her gun, certain that she'd just uncovered the hiding place of Jimmy Van Dyke.

Back in the house, she loomed over Brittany. 'Who was that?'

'I don't know. I imagine it is fortunate that I had a police officer here to uncover an unknown intruder in my home.'

'Cut the crap,' Lucinda snapped. 'That was Jimmy Van Dyke, wasn't it?'

'Who?'

Lucinda wanted to throttle the woman. 'Are you sexually involved with Jimmy Van Dyke?'

'My sex life is none of your business.'

'It is if the affair started while he was still a student.'

'Are you accusing me of unethical behavior with a student?'

'Not exactly. I suspect that you have been involved in an illicit relationship with Jimmy Van Dyke for quite some time but I doubt that he is the only student you have taken advantage of – that adds up to unethical conduct with multiple students. How many of them? And for how long?'

'As I said, officer, I am not answering any questions until and unless I have an attorney present to represent me.'

Lucinda stifled her urge to correct the woman for calling her 'officer'. Lucinda knew it was intentional and a deliberate sign of disrespect but she refused to take the bait this time. 'I will contact the sex crimes division and open an investigation about your behavior. Just the fact that we are looking into what you may have done with students should be sufficient to get you suspended – if we're lucky, the school district will make it without pay.'

'I will sue you and your department and the school district if this phony investigation becomes public information.'

'You do that, Ms Schaffer. Your case will wither away the

moment we find the concrete proof we need to file charges against you.'

'Oh no, officer, that will be the moment that my attorney will have the proof of harassment that she needs for a successful law-suit.'

Lucinda knew that the courts could look at the situation that way and it made her angry and even more determined to ferret out the truth. She pulled a card out of her pocket and set it down on the end table beside Brittany. With a saccharine smile plastered on her lips, she said, 'My card, Ms Schaffer. I'll expect a call if Jimmy Van Dyke shows up here again.'

Brittany wouldn't even look in the direction of the table. Lucinda wanted to grab her by the hair and force her to face the surface, but she knew better than to follow through on that impulse. She stared down at the other woman with as much disdain as her facial features could express. Then she turned away and set out in search of Jimmy Van Dyke.

FIFTY

Lucinda called the dispatcher as she walked to the car. After she provided information about the sighting of Jimmy Van Dyke, she was assured that a patrol car would be sent to his mother's home, the Walking Dog, the high school and any other place she might later specify.

After doing that, Lucinda drove off, checking for voicemail messages. She had one from Charley and another from Jake. She checked the time and saw it was still early enough to return Charley's call.

'Oh, Lucy,' Charley said. 'Amber and Andy are scared.'

'What happened, Charley?'

'Amber's mom called her and said that she'd be picking them up after she went to court tomorrow morning. How come she's not still in jail?'

'The judge granted her bond. And, right now, no one knows if family court will allow her to pick up her kids.'

'That's what the social worker said. She came by right after

Amber talked to her mom. Daddy said that he's going to tell the
judge what he thinks about that. The social worker said that maybe
they'd have to go with their mother but everybody was going to
fight that and try to keep them here.'

'That's right, Charley. I'm going to be there, too, to tell the judge
what I know. We'll do everything we can.'

'But Amber says she's going to run away tonight after Daddy
goes to sleep.'

'Did you tell your dad?'

'No, she made me promise not to before she told me.'

'Well, your dad sets the alarm every night, doesn't he?' Lucinda
asked.

'Yes, but that doesn't stop her from leaving.'

'If the alarm goes off, you call me right away. We'll find her.
Tell her that I talked to the CASA lawyer who is representing her
and her brother. She told me that she'd already drawn up a stay in
case the judge rules in favor of Amber's mom.'

'What does that mean?'

'It means that she will immediately file the paperwork requesting
a delay until the decision can be appealed.'

'So even if the judge says that they have to go with their mom,
they won't have to do it tomorrow?'

'That's right. So there is really no need for her to run off tonight.
She won't be going anywhere with her mother anytime soon.'

'For sure?' Charley asked.

'Absolutely. Amber and Andy don't have to worry about that – no
matter what their mother said. OK?'

'OK, Lucy.'

'You talk to Amber. And I don't want to scare her, but if that
doesn't convince her that she is safe for now, tell her that if she
runs away, the court will certainly remove her from your home.
They'll believe your dad could not provide her with the proper
care and supervision.'

'All right. You'll let me know right away what happens in court
tomorrow?'

'You'll be in class, Charley.'

'Text me. I keep my phone turned off in class. But I'll check in
between, OK? Please.'

'You got it, Charley. Now, go talk to Amber. I'll try to drop by
tomorrow after school.'

After ending that call, Lucinda called Jake. 'All settled in for the night?'

'Yeah,' Jake said. 'Surprisingly, the Wicked Witch put me up in a decent hotel for a change. Not sure if that's a good thing or just preparation for my execution in the morning.'

'I don't think she has that much authority, Jake,' Lucinda said with a laugh.

'She's like you in that way – another one of those don't-ask-permission-first-just-beg-for-forgiveness-after people.'

'Ha! You're as bad as I am – maybe even worse.'

'No one could be worse. Anyway, did anything new come up since I left town?'

Lucinda recounted her evening at Brittany Schaffer's house and laid out her plans for the rest of the night and the next morning. 'I'm just about a mile away from Jimmy's home right now so I'll need to get off.'

'I'm so sorry I'm not there to help you out with all this crap. Be careful, OK?'

'Oh, you know me.'

'Yes, I do. And that's the point. Please be careful.'

'Gotta go, Jake. Call me tomorrow when you get a chance.' Lucinda pulled up beside the patrol car in front of the Van Dyke's house. 'Any sign of him?'

'No, Lieutenant, and I checked with his mother when I first arrived. She said he wasn't there and she was worried about him. She offered to let me come in and search her home, but I didn't think there was a need for that. She struck me as cooperative and sincere.'

'I think you're right. Have you got my cell number in case things heat up here?'

'Sure do.'

'Thanks, officer. Call if you have any questions at all,' Lucinda said and drove off to the Walking Dog and then the high school. There was no sign of Jimmy at either location. Time to call it a day and grab a few hours of sleep – she owed it to Amber and Andy to do her best tomorrow. She knew her credibility in the court would suffer if she showed up looking like the walking dead. Nobody trusts a zombie these days.

FIFTY-ONE

S andra greeted Jake warmly when he arrived at her office the next morning. Her nice attitude raised his level of suspicion by several notches. She led him to the conference room where the acting head of the ATF, Darren Clothier, and Deputy Federal Security Director Franklin Wesley were already seated at the table. Wesley raised his eyebrows and grimaced when he saw Jake.

Jake nodded in response and then stretched out his arm to shake hands with both men. Sandra made the introductions, alarming Jake by calling him one of the department's most competent special agents in charge.

As a young woman entered the room bearing a tray with coffee supplies, Sandra said, 'Ah, thank you, Elizabeth. Just set it in the middle of the table. Coffee, gentlemen? Jake, if I recall correctly, you like a little half-and-half. I made sure we had some on hand for you. It's in that little pitcher.'

'Thank you,' Jake said, feeling even more certain that doom was about to descend on his head.

'Thank you for your hospitality, Sandra,' Clothier said. 'But I am not pleased with your decisions regarding this investigation. We are the federal explosive experts and our expertise is demanded in this situation. I am deeply troubled that you have shut us out of the investigation.'

'Oh, please, Darren, we did not shut you out. Your resident agent in charge was in the midst of a personal crisis. We just stepped in and relieved you of responsibility until you had time to put adequate personnel in place.'

'I find that difficult to believe, Sandra, since you have turned the investigation back to the local police department. I can't tell you how inappropriate and unprofessional that action seems to me.'

'It was all politics, Darren. After the unfortunate developments with your man on the scene, we had to appease the locals. They had to think they were in charge again. In reality, Special Agent in Charge Lovett is running the investigation. Their local detective, Lieutenant Pierce, takes orders from Special Agent Lovett. He has her firmly in control. Don't you, Jake?' she said, piercing him with a hard look that told him he'd better back her up or else.

Jake swallowed hard, grateful that Lucinda was not present for the conversation. If she even guessed what he was about to say, he was a dead man. 'Oh, of course. I let her think she's calling the shots. But, honestly, she's so easy to manipulate. She'll do anything I say.'

Clothier squinted his eyes as he stared at Jake, making him feel as if the man was strolling through his skull, examining every stray thought. 'Your assurances that the FBI is really in control of this operation are heartening, Sandra. I've told Deputy Director Wesley that I want him personally in charge of our operations down there, effective immediately. I expect he will be part of the investigative team.'

'Naturally, Darren. Special Agent in Charge Lovett will brief him on developments and consult with him daily on the division of tasks and next steps.'

Clothier drained his coffee cup and stood. 'Thank you, Sandra. I'm glad I requested this meeting. I feel certain we can work together and wrap this investigation up in no time. Wesley has to tie up a few things here and then he'll meet you first thing tomorrow morning at your office, Agent Lovett.'

'I am sure Special Agent in Charge Lovett will appreciate his assistance,' Sandra said, smiling and escorting them to the front door.

Jake trailed after them but Sandra stopped him before he could leave. 'We need to talk.'

Jake followed her to her office, shutting the door as she instructed. 'Yes, ma'am?'

'I will not have the effin' ATF effin' up this effin' investigation again. They put effin' lunatics in the field and we have to clean up their effin' messes. I am sick of it.'

'Umm, I'm confused,' Jake said.

'Of course you are. Those effin' idiots create confusion everywhere they go.'

'I'm not sure what you want me to do.'

'I thought I'd made myself very clear. Treat that effin' ATF goon like a mushroom – keep him in the dark and feed him shit.'

'What?'

'Busy work, Lovett. Busy work. Give him those boring assignments that no one wants to do because they're not going to lead anywhere. And don't tell him about anything that matters.'

'I don't think Franklin Wesley will be a problem—'

'I didn't tell you to think. Effin' Wesley could be just as nuts as that other guy. As I said, I don't want to give them a chance to eff this up again.'

'Yes, ma'am.'

'Make him think that you're feeding the busy work to the local cop. Play him, Lovett. I know you can. You've been playing the FBI for years.'

'Excuse me, ma'am?'

'Oh, look at you. Look at your effin' shoes. Different color for every day like a little pre-teen girl with her day-of-the-week underwear. You get away with that because you've been playing your supervisors forever. And your hair's been getting too long lately. You let the ATF eff this up and I'll have you in oxford shoes and a buzz cut before you know what hit you. Is that clear?'

'Yes, ma'am,' Jake said.

'Fine. Now, get back down there and get busy. And do not eff this up.'

Jake couldn't leave her presence fast enough. And he couldn't wait to get back to his office where he could pretend she didn't exist – at least until she called again.

FIFTY-TWO

Lucinda slid into a seat in the family courtroom of Judge Barbara Brickhouse. She rose when the Judge entered and sat impatiently with one leg crossed over the other, the suspended foot bobbing.

She listened as the attorney for Teresa Culvert expounded on his client's parental rights with regard to Amber and Andy Culvert. He then argued that sometimes children make up stories to get attention and cited a number of psychologists who concurred that this was particularly common in adolescent girls. The lawyer was only doing his job but Lucinda's anger toward him increased with every statement he made.

It was nothing, however, compared with the rage she felt when Teresa took the stand. She wanted to stand up and scream 'Liar!' or worse, as the woman talked about her love for her children and her overwhelming desire to protect them from harm. Then Lucinda's anger turned on Judge Brickhouse at the realization that the judge was nodding as if in agreement with that miserable excuse for a mother when Teresa said, 'If I believed there was any truth in the allegations made by my daughter, I would have taken action immediately, but unfortunately, Your Honor, the child has made a habit out of reading stories in books and newspapers and then claiming them as her own.'

Lucinda wasn't sure how much more of that crap she could take. She breathed a sigh of relief when the other side stood up to present their case. The state's attorney explained the reality of Amber's abuse at the hands of Teresa's boyfriend, Eddie Springer. He described Amber turning to her mother for help and being chastised for her honesty.

First witness on the stand was Dr Carson Winters. In sickening detail, she explained her findings from her examination of Amber.

When the questioning ended, the judge asked, 'Do you have any physical proof that Eddie Springer or any other individual is responsible for the damage to this child?'

'Not at this time, Your Honor. We did take samples but do not yet have DNA test results.'

'You may step down.'

Next up was a psychologist who had not yet had time to interview Amber but who did talk about the impact of sexual abuse and of a mother's betrayal in general terms. The judge asked her if she knew for a fact that Teresa Culvert rebuffed a cry for help from her daughter. She had to admit that she did not, making Lucinda cringe.

The state's attorney then called Dr Evan Spencer to the stand. He told the judge about Teresa's call the day before and then explained, 'Both of the children were very distressed after talking to her. Both of them expressed fear about the possibility of being returned to their mother's care.'

'Are you wanting to make the custody of these children a permanent situation?' Judge Brickhouse asked.

'No, Your Honor. I am merely caring for them until a family is approved to assume permanent custody and can arrive here to take the children back to their new home.'

'This court has not decided who should have permanent custody. You are being far too presumptuous, Doctor.'

'I'm sorry, Your Honor. I was merely thinking of the best interests of the children.'

'Are you implying that this court is not?'

'No, Your Honor.'

'Are you a pediatrician? A psychiatrist? Any kind of pediatric medical specialist?'

'No, Your Honor, I am an orthopedic surgeon.'

'Then you really have no standing here as an expert. You may step down.'

A fresh burst of anger brought a flush to Lucinda's face. She held her head down and struggled to compose her emotions as she walked up to the witness box. She told the judge about Amber's statements to her about Eddie Springer, her abuse and the reaction of Teresa Culvert. She then explained the sequence of events that lead to the arrest of Springer and Culvert.

The state's attorney asked, 'Do you believe it would be detrimental to the welfare of the children if custody were awarded to their mother, Teresa Culvert?'

'Objection,' Teresa's lawyer yelled out.

Lucinda barreled forward with her answer, 'Absolutely. She has betrayed their best interests for the sake of her boyfriend. She drinks excessively and neglects her children.'

'Objection sustained!' the judge shouted.

Lucinda continued, talking as quickly as she could. 'If Teresa Culvert gets custody, she will intimidate and manipulate those children into recanting their statements and—'

The gavel banged three times. 'Say another word, Lieutenant, and I will hold you in contempt of court.'

Lucinda swallowed and pressed her lips together.

'I am sure, Lieutenant, that this is not your first appearance in a court of law. And I am certain you know better. When anyone voices an objection, you will be quiet until I rule upon it. Is that clear?' the judge ordered.

'Yes, Your Honor,' Lucinda said.

'Very well. Continue.'

'I have nothing further, Your Honor,' the attorney said.

'You are dismissed, Lieutenant,' the judge said. 'I will remember your outburst if you ever appear before me again. I will not give you a second chance.'

'Yes, Your Honor,' Lucinda said as she stepped down to return to her seat.

Judge Brickhouse scooped up a handful of file folders and said, 'I will review these reports from CPS and issue a decision on this matter within the hour. For now, court is in recess.' She slammed down her gavel and stepped down from the bench.

FIFTY-THREE

L ucinda wanted to stay near the courthouse until the judge announced her decision but just standing around waiting was making her nuts. She called up the District Attorney's office and asked for an available Assistant DA to help with a search warrant for Brittany's pick-up truck.

The receptionist transferred her call to ADA Susan Judd. Lucinda had seen her around the building but had never worked with her before. She introduced herself and explained the search warrant she needed for tire track impressions and the connection to the explosion at the high school. Lucinda added, 'I'm tied up at court right now and can't draft anything for you but time is not on my side.'

'That's fine. I can handle it. What are the legal grounds for your request?'

'It's an investigative need and I'm hoping you'll say it is legally justified. Witnesses at the scene indicated that a red pick-up pulled away out of the grass in front of the school moments before the explosion. They have identified a truck owned by Brittany Schaffer as similar to the one they saw that morning.'

'Similar. I hope you have more than that.'

'The FBI tire tread expert has identified the tracks leading from the scene as a specific brand. That same brand is on the vehicle owned by Ms Schaffer.'

'Anything else?' Susan asked.

'The whereabouts of that truck on the night preceding and the morning of the explosion are unknown. Ms Schaffer has said she

loaned it to someone that weekend but will not tell us the identity
of that person.'

'Possible. Let me draw this up and take it to a judge. We probably have a better chance of success than usual because any kind
of bomb blowing up at any school is enough to make judges anxious
about public opinion. I'll get back to you when I know something,'
Susan said and then hung up the phone.

That accomplished, Lucinda had nothing to do but pace. She was
worried about Judge Brickhouse's decision. The questions the judge
had asked indicated she was leaning toward awarding custody back
to the mother. She couldn't think of anything that would be more
traumatic for Amber – and probably Andy, too. And if Teresa could
get them to recant their statements, Eddie Springer could be released
to abuse Amber again.

Lucinda tried to shove those worries out of her mind by thinking
about Jake. Rather than easing her anxiety, it elevated it. She
wondered what was happening up at FBI headquarters and what it
might mean to the investigation of the explosion. She hoped that
Jake's supervisor didn't hold him responsible for Connelly spinning
out of control – she wasn't sure how or why the Wicked Witch
could do that but that woman's attitude toward and treatment of
Jake did not seem justified and simply made no sense to Lucinda.

Realizing that the attorneys were making their way back into the
courtroom, Lucinda followed them through the double doors and
resumed her seat. Five more tense minutes passed before Judge
Brickhouse finally stepped up to the bench.

The judge stared out at the audience, waiting for the settling-in
movements to cease and the whispered conversations to end. Then
she began. 'The rights of parents to care for their children without
interference from the government are sacred.'

Lucinda felt a hard lump in her throat. 'Sacred' seemed such an
over-the-top word for this situation. She didn't like the sound of it
at all.

'We must, whenever possible, uphold and protect these rights. A
free citizenry has the expectation that we will do so except in extreme
cases where there is substantial proof that it is not in a child's best
interests. Have we reached that high bar? It can readily be argued
that we have not.'

Lucinda closed her eyes. She could not bear to look at the judge
one moment longer.

'And if we were discussing a permanent change in custody of these children, I would be forced to rule in favor of the rights of the biological mother. However, we are not. We are discussing a temporary arrangement – one that would not terminate the mother's parental rights; it would only put them on hold for a short period of time. In situations like these, we must always rule in favor of the protection of the children against possible harm.'

Lucinda's eyes flew open. Did she hear correctly? Was the judge about to rule against Teresa Culvert?

'It is the decision of this court that temporary custody be awarded to Dr Evan Spencer, who currently has physical custody of the children. This decision is to be in force until the CPS in Maryland and here in Virginia completes their investigation into the suitability of members of the biological father's family. After the submission of that report, we will hold another hearing where the biological mother can present renewed arguments to regain custody of Amber and Andy Culvert.'

Lucinda breathed a sigh of relief and looked over at Teresa. Her attorney had a hand on her shoulder. He appeared to be applying pressure to keep his client in her seat. Teresa's profile was shot full of anger. The lawyer leaned toward her, talking non-stop in a soft voice as if trying to prevent Teresa from doing anything rash.

Lucinda stepped out of the courtroom and sent a text with the good news to Charley. When she finished, Evan Spencer was at her side.

'When she called for a recess, I was certain she was going to rule against me and return custody to their mother. And they're just starting to settle into our home. Even Amber seems to be calming down a bit. She doesn't always startle when I walk into the room and watch my every move with suspicion.'

'The way she started the reading of her decision made me apprehensive, too,' Lucinda said.

Evan chuckled. 'Judges seem to like to create a sense of drama with every decision they issue from the bench. Makes me wonder if they're like that at home with their spouses and children.'

Lucinda laughed. 'I'll betcha anything some of them are.'

'I'm going home to deliver the news to the kids. You want to come along?'

'Sorry, Evan, I've got to check on the progress of a search

warrant – and serve it, I hope. Give them all my congratulations
and best wishes for the future.'

Lucinda watched him walk away, wondering if she should have
told him that she'd already sent a text to Charley. Then she smiled,
realizing that Charley would probably pretend to be surprised when
her dad delivered the news.

FIFTY-FOUR

ack in town, Jake called Lucinda as he drove to his office.
'Hey, Lucy! We need to talk.'
'Are you still in DC?'

'No, I'm back and I really want to talk to you in person.'

'Right now, I'm arranging for a tow truck and then heading over
to the high school to serve a warrant on Brittany Schaffer's
pick-up.'

'Good work.'

'You want to go with me? We can talk on the way. I can swing
by and pick you up.'

'I probably won't be at the office for another ten minutes.'

'That'll work, Jake. I'll call when I'm a block away.'

Jake was worried about Lucinda's reaction to his orders from the
Wicked Witch. *Will she agree to pretend to be taking orders from
me? Or will she bristle at the suggestion? Oh, well*, he thought, *I'll
find out soon enough.*

He arrived at the office just in time to let them know he had
survived yet another encounter with his nemesis up north before
Lucinda called back. As he left the building, he saw her pulling into
the parking lot.

He slid into the passenger's seat and leaned over to Lucinda for
a kiss. She obliged and then said, 'What's got you all worried, Mr
Special Agent Man? Did the Wicked Witch bully you again?'

'You're not going to believe this but she called me by my first
name and made sure that half-and-half was available for my coffee.'

'You're kidding? Did she follow that up with a firing squad?'

'Not exactly. But she did warn me not to eff up this
investigation.'

'Did she say "eff" or did she say—'

'No. She stuck with "eff" and "effing", but she certainly was angry enough to let the f-bomb fly.'

'Angry at you?'

'No, believe it or not. She was angry about the inter-agency politics. As often as she's pissed me off about that sort of thing, this time it was her turn.'

'Inter-agency? Problems with my cop shop?'

'Oh, no. Bigger deal than that – you guys she'd just brush under the rug. Her problems came straight from the Acting Director of the ATF.'

'Don't tell me they're trying to take the case back after the disaster with Connelly,' Lucinda said with a groan.

'They were trying but Sandra cut off that maneuver before they knew what hit 'em.'

Jake explained what was said in the meeting. When he repeated Sandra's statement that he had Lucinda firmly under his control, Lucinda interrupted. 'I certainly hope you set her straight on that.'

Jake looked out the window, trying to figure out the most diplomatic answer possible.

'Well? You did, didn't you?' Lucinda pressed.

'Not exactly. I agreed with her.'

'And you call that "not exactly"?' Lucinda said as she pulled her car on to the shoulder and came to a stop.

'Oh, c'mon, Lucy. She knows it's not true. She just wanted the ATF guys to believe it. She wanted them to think that even though you were called the lead investigator, I was really calling the shots.'

'And do you think that?'

'No. Absolutely not, Lucy. I was just playing along so that the ATF guys would back off.'

'Really? How do you know she wasn't serious?'

'Because, when they left and it was just the two of us, she told me to treat the ATF like mushrooms, to keep them in the dark and feed them shit. That was when she was "effing" this and "effing" that. She told me to give the ATF nothing but busy work – but to make them think that's all you were doing.'

Lucinda stared at him, making Jake squirm. She pulled the car back on to the road without saying another word. When they reached the high school, she said, 'And I suppose you all want me to go along with this little ruse? To pretend like I'm a bumbling fool, to act like a total idiot and kiss your damn ass every time the ATF is around?'

'Pretty much, Lucy.'

'Damn, you Feebs are all assholes,' she snapped as she stepped out of the car and slammed the door. 'Well, are you coming?'

'Yes, ma'am,' he said, opening his door and exiting the vehicle.

They went straight to the office and spoke to Principal Rose Johnson who led them to Brittany's classroom. 'I'll get her to step out into the hall,' Rose said before opening the door and slipping inside.

'Ms Schaffer, could I have a word, please?'

'What?' Brittany asked.

'Could you step out in the hallway for a moment, please?'

Brittany rolled her eyes. 'Class, turn to page one hundred and seventy-four in your anthology. Read "The Second Coming" by William Butler Yeats and be prepared to discuss it when I return.' She stepped through the door and saw Lucinda and Jake. 'Oh, Ms Johnson, you're running errands for the cops now?' She turned to Lucinda and said, 'I told you, I am not going to answer any more questions until and unless I have legal representation by my side.'

Lucinda smiled. 'I have no intention of asking you any questions, Ms Schaffer. In fact, I would be quite pleased if you would just shut up and listen. I came with a search warrant for your truck,' she said, handing a copy of the document over to Brittany.

'You can't do this. I'm calling my attorney.'

'You can call him if you like, Ms Schaffer,' Jake said. 'But by the time you reach him, your vehicle will be loaded up on the city tow truck. And by the time he gets here, your truck will be parked in a bay at the forensic garage.'

'You have exactly one choice in this matter,' Lucinda added. 'You can give me the key to your truck or we can drill out the lock at the garage. Which do you prefer?'

Rose stepped into the fray. 'Ms Schaffer, you can't stop this. You need to cooperate. If you do, they will not damage your pick-up. But if you fight them, they'll have to force their way in – I know it's difficult for you but this is for the school. A crime was committed here. A student died. A staff member died. You have to do everything you can to help.'

'You wouldn't believe that if they were targeting you, Ms Johnson. I think you'd feel a little differently if it was your property they were confiscating.'

'We are not confiscating your truck, Ms Schaffer,' Lucinda said. 'We are taking control of it for a short period of time in order to search it for any evidence. If you loaned it out to someone else, as you said, I would think you would want the assurance that it was not used in the incident that damaged the school where you teach.'

Rose continued. 'As a teacher, you have an obligation and responsibility to cooperate. Now give them the keys to your truck. And then I want you to rethink your decision not to answer their questions without an attorney mucking things up. If you are as innocent as you claim, there is no reason for you to hide behind a lawyer.'

'What do you mean "no reason"? Have you never heard of framing? Have you never heard of wrongful conviction? Have you never heard of prosecutorial misconduct? Have you never heard of water-boarding?'

'Oh, good grief, Ms Schaffer, you are so dramatic,' Rose said. 'Get in there and get your truck key and give to the Lieutenant or I will be forced to call the Superintendent of Schools and report your behavior. I am certain it is something he will want to take before the school board.'

Brittany glared at her and then shared her venomous gaze with Lucinda and Jake. 'Fine. I'll get the key. But I will be informing my attorney about your intimidation, Ms Johnson.' Brittany spun around and flounced back into the classroom where the subdued buzz of conversation cut off immediately. 'Go ahead, go ahead. Discuss the poem among yourselves. I'll be back in a moment.'

Brittany stepped back out and turned over the key. 'I am going to file a complaint with the police department about this harassment, so don't celebrate your victory too soon.'

FIFTY-FIVE

C harley and Amber sat across from each other in the cafeteria. Amber said, 'I can't go to the movies tomorrow. If I use my allowance, I won't have any money – and what if there's an emergency?'

'Daddy will give me enough extra money for both of us.'

'That makes me sound so pathetic.'

'No. Daddy always pays for the movies when I take a friend. And gives me plenty of money for snacks and drinks, too – plenty for both of us.' Over Amber's shoulder, Charley saw Amber's mother coming straight for them. 'Amber! Your mother!'

Before Amber could turn around, Teresa took hold of her upper arm and jerked her out of her seat. 'Time to come home, Amber,' Teresa said.

'But I'm not supposed to go with you, Mom,' Amber said.

Charley jumped to her feet. 'No. The judge said no.'

'Screw the judge,' Teresa said. 'C'mon, Amber, don't dawdle.'

Charley pulled out her cell, punched in nine-one-one. 'My friend is being abducted from the school cafeteria. Thomas Jefferson Middle School. Hurry! My name is Charley—'

Teresa slapped the phone with one hand, sending it flying across the room, and used the other hand to pull on Amber's arm. Although the girl planted her feet as hard as she could, she still slid across the room as her mother tugged her toward the door.

Charley grabbed Amber around the waist and tried to pull her in the opposite direction. Teresa swung around and punched Charley in the face, knocking her to the ground. For a moment, Charley was stunned. She wiped a hand across the end of her nose, pulled it away and saw blood. Charley felt her lower lip quiver. She wanted nothing more than to sit down and cry but she refused to surrender to the desire and give up on her friend.

'Help! Help!' she screamed. 'My friend is being kidnapped!'

A few boys rushed to help Charley but stopped in their tracks when Teresa said, 'I'm her damned mother, you idiots.'

'But today the judge said she can't do this,' Charley argued.

'If you listen to that dumb little girl, you are all going to be in big trouble,' Teresa said and continued dragging her daughter across the floor.

The boys looked at each other, unsure of what to do. Charley caught up with mother and daughter, climbed on a table and jumped on Teresa's back, grabbing the woman's ears and pulling hard. Teresa released Amber's arm and ran over to the closest wall and rammed Charley's back into the hard surface, knocking her loose. Charley slid down the wall and thumped on the floor.

Teresa reached out to latch on to Amber again, but Amber ducked under her mother's arm and ran off. Teresa chased after her but when she passed the pack of boys, one of them stuck out his leg.

Teresa stumbled, fell and her face slid a couple of feet across the floor before she came to a stop.

No one had noticed Principal Bowerman jogging towards them, but there he was, looking stern, tall and hefty. 'Everybody, stop what you are doing and stay right where you are.' He pointed at Teresa and said, 'You misrepresented yourself when you checked in at the front office. I've called the authorities and they are on the way.'

'But I am Amber Culvert's mother.'

'And you checked the legal guardian box but, according to the court order I received five minutes ago, that is not true.'

'I still have parental rights.'

'We'll discuss those in a minute,' Bowerman said. He then pointed to the boy who sent Teresa flying to the floor and said, 'Go to the office and wait for me. Now, who hit that girl over there by the wall?'

'She did,' the boys said, pointing at Teresa.

The principal looked down at the boys and said, 'I'm going to find out which one of you is responsible for giving that girl a bloody nose. And if I don't get the answers I need, all of you will be expelled. Now, go to my office and wait.'

'But they didn't do it,' Charley said. 'It was that woman. She was trying to make Amber come with her but the judge said she couldn't.'

'Amber? Where's Amber?' the principal said, looking around the cafeteria.

'She went thataway,' one of the boys said.

The principal turned to Charley. 'You go to the nurse's office and let her patch you up. Then come to my office. You guys, I told you to go to my office – now go.'

'But—' one of them said.

'I don't want to hear it. Just go to my office now.' The principal helped Teresa to her feet and, pointing over to Charley, he asked, 'Did you hit that child?'

'Of course not, sir. I am a parent. Amber's mother.'

'She did too,' Charley said. 'She punched me in the face and then slammed me into the wall.'

'You,' the principal said, pointing at Charley, 'go to the nurse's office now. And you, ma'am – Ms Culvert – please come with me.'

'I am sorry, sir. But I need to find my daughter. Do you need to see my ID again?'

'If you do have any rights to that child, we'll straighten this matter out and I'll personally help you find your daughter.'

'You can't do that,' Charley yelled from the doorway. 'The judge said no.'

The principal turned toward her. 'The nurse's office – now.'

Teresa looked down at the watch on her wrist. 'I'll have to come see you in the morning. I'm going to be late for an appointment,' she said and took off in a sprint.

The principal sighed as he watched her exit the building. He turned back to the doorway and realized Charley was still standing there. He pointed a finger at her but she took off before he could say another word. She heard sirens pulling up in front of the school and smiled even though it made her face hurt.

FIFTY-SIX

Lucinda and Jake observed while technicians made a visual examination of the tires of Brittany Schaffer's pick-up, searching for similarities and for any anomalies that might eliminate them as the ones that left the tracks on the grounds of the high school. Finding none, they next took measurements of the wheel-base length and width.

Everything pointed to a possible match – but it wasn't proof. The techs laid out four wide strips of paper, each one a bit longer than the circumference of the tires. Removing the wheels one at a time, they rolled them across the sheets as they visually searched for any wear patterns, defects or scarring that would eliminate them. Finding none, they replaced the tires and laid down an inked board, followed by a similarly sized board covered with a clear film to receive the impression. Carefully, they manipulated the truck into place and rolled the vehicle one tire at a time over the ink and then across the film.

When finished, they had four sheets of plastic to prepare for transport and a police officer drove off to deliver the evidence to the forensic lab in Washington, DC. There, a tire and track expert would superimpose the impressions on the actual tracks collected at the scene.

A new batch of techs took over to search for fingerprints,

explosive residue and any other trace evidence that might be lingering in the bed or the cab of the truck. The two investigators went back to their offices to file reports and update their supervisors.

Lucinda was diverted from her intentions when she walked into her office and saw an urgent note from the front desk. She returned Brubaker's call.

'Hey, Lieutenant. I thought you'd want to know that your little friend was in here filing an assault charge.'

'Assault? Charley Spencer? Against whom?'

'Teresa Culvert. Apparently, the woman barged into the school and tried to physically remove her daughter from the cafeteria. Your little buddy took exception to that and ended up with a bloodied nose, an aching back and a bruised backside.'

'Oh dear. Did they arrest Culvert?'

'At the scene. The woman denied everything, but when they checked on Charley's story about the judge's ruling, they hauled Culvert into the station. She's in lock-up and I hear a bond revocation hearing is set for Monday. Her attorney's been in here raising a ruckus about harassment and threatening legal action against the department.'

'Of course he is. Where's Charley now?'

'On her way home – or already there, I suspect.'

'What about Amber Culvert? Is she with Charley?'

'Nobody knows where she is, Lieutenant.'

'What?'

'She ran off. But we're looking for her. We've got someone posted at the Culvert home and the Spencer home and they're searching every inch of the school. No telling where she went,' Brubaker said.

'What about nearby parks or shopping centers?'

'Taken care of, Lieutenant. Along with libraries, hospitals and any other place anyone could think of. I imagine we'll find her before long.'

'A lot of harm can come to a twelve-year-old girl before long, Brubaker.'

'I know, I know. Trust me. We are doing all we can.'

'Is there anything I can do?' Lucinda asked.

'I think we've got all the bases covered, but if you think of something we might have missed, give us a call and we'll get somebody on it right away.'

Lucinda tried to go back to her report but she was too distracted to focus. Maybe a call to Charley would help.

'Lucy! Did you hear about all the excitement at the school today?' Charley said when she answered.

'Yes, Charley. I heard you were hurt.'

'I didn't need any stitches. Gotta big bruise on my face and my nose is a little swollen but that's it.'

'What about your back?'

'The doctor said it will hurt a lot tomorrow. But I don't care. Everybody from school is calling me – teachers, the principal, even boys. I can't wait to go to school tomorrow. I'm a hero.'

'Charley, you take too many risks. You could have been seriously injured.'

'But I wasn't, Lucy. Really, I'm OK. I couldn't just sit there and let that nasty woman take Amber away, now could I? You wouldn't let that happen, would you?'

Lucinda rubbed a hand across her brow. A young girl with a powerful sense of justice was a dangerous combination. 'Of course I wouldn't, Charley, but I am a police officer. And I'm a lot taller and stronger than you.'

'And you have a gun – don't forget that. You could have just shot her dead on the spot. Do you think I could get a gun?'

Oh, good grief. 'Did you ask your father that question?' Lucinda asked.

'Yes,' Charley said with a strong dose of disgust in her voice.

'What did he say?'

'The same old thing – "When you're an adult, you can do what you want, but while I am responsible for you, the answer is absolutely, positively no." He says that about all the fun stuff.'

Lucinda almost argued that her attitude about guns was not appropriate but she knew she'd get nowhere with that point right now. 'About Amber. Have you heard from her since she ran out of the cafeteria? Do you know where she is right now?'

'No, Lucy. I'm sorry. I didn't think she'd do that. I was defending her. It kind of hurts my feelings that she didn't trust me enough. If I had a gun, I bet she would have.'

For now, Lucinda continued to ignore the gun comments. 'Where might she go, Charley?'

Charley ran down a list of places that Lucinda had already discussed with Brubaker. Then she added, 'Maybe she went to a movie.'

'Which movie, Charley?'

'I don't remember the name of it. It was some dopey romance. I told her I'd fall asleep. I needed more action – and the kind of sappy action those love stories have just doesn't keep me awake in a dark movie theater. So we were going to see something else tomorrow. But maybe she'd go to see that by herself since I didn't want to go.'

'Did she have any money?'

'Some – Daddy gave her an allowance, just like me. He said a girl of her age should have some mad money in her pocket.'

'You have one nice daddy.'

'Yeah, most of the time. But he's pretty mad at me right now. And I don't get it, Lucy. Both of you are hypocrites. You tell me to do the right thing and when I do you get all on my case.'

'We'll talk about that later, OK? Right now, somebody needs to check out the movie theaters. I'll call you if we find Amber or later tonight even if we don't.'

'OK, Lucy. But you really need to work on that hypocrite thing.'

'Love you, Charley. Later,' Lucinda said as she ended the call.

Lucinda knew she was going to have to have a long discussion with Evan about his daughter. She didn't want to stifle Charley's spirit but she certainly wanted to keep her safe. She picked up the phone to call Brubaker, thought better of it and hung up. She couldn't stand sitting still a moment longer. She'd check out the movie theaters on her own.

FIFTY-SEVEN

Lucinda grabbed a copy of the BOLO with a photograph of Amber before leaving the Justice Center for her theater run. She stopped at the Cineplex 12 and showed the girl's picture to the ticket seller, the checker at the door and the two people behind the snack counter. No one thought they'd seen her that day. She walked the aisles in the room showing a romantic feature, looking down each one for Amber but with no luck.

She decided to come back to check the other eleven after she'd cleared the remaining three theaters within walking distance of the school. At the next movie house, she had better luck. Everyone thought they might have seen her that morning and one of the girls working the snack bar was certain that Amber had been there. 'She bought a soda and a box of Jujubes. I think I saw her running out about fifteen minutes ago but I only saw her from behind so I'm not sure.'

Lucinda didn't hold much hope of finding Amber but she walked the aisles just the same. No luck.

The third theater was a bust, too. By now, though, Lucinda thought it was possible she could have walked a little further. She called Brubaker and told him what she knew. She hung up when he started to give her a hard time about searching on her own initiative.

Brubaker called her right back. 'C'mon. I am not in the mood to argue,' Lucinda said when she answered.

'Not calling to give you a hard time. A pair of visitors just walked in the door to see you.'

'Amber?'

'No. A woman named Brittany Schaffer and her feminist warhorse attorney, Rita Younger.'

'Younger? Oh, geez. That woman hates me for being tall.'

Brubaker chuckled. 'I figured she must know you. The spike heels on her shoes are longer than her legs.'

'Get someone from my department to take them up to the floor and put them in an interrogation room. I'll be there in ten minutes or less.'

Lucinda had never worked a case where Rita Younger was the opposing counsel but the lawyer had been involved in complaints against her in the past. Rita produced any number of juicy sound bites about Lucinda. Rita liked to use her as an example of a woman who did not know how to succeed without acting more macho than all the men on the force combined. This interview was not going to be fun.

'The Rime of the Ancient Mariner' pounded in her head as she walked down the hall, wondering what she'd done to deserve this particular albatross. She opened the door with a smile that felt like waxed Halloween lips on her face. 'Good afternoon, Ms Schaffer. Ms Younger. What can I do for you today?'

'Would you please sit down?' Rita asked. 'Your abnormal altitude is putting a painful kink in my neck.'

Lucinda bit her tongue and slid into a chair on the opposite side of the table. 'OK. What does your client have to say today?'

'First of all, Lieutenant,' Rita began, 'I must tell you that if you hadn't been so absurdly confrontational with my client, you probably would have obtained her cooperation without any interference from me. You are your own worst enemy, as I imagine you've heard me say before—'

'Yeah, yeah, yeah, fine. What's the point? Why are we here right now?'

Rita closed her eyes and shook her head before continuing. 'Oh, Lieutenant, you make everything so difficult. It took my considerable skills to convince my client to come see you and tell you all she knows after you bullied her so badly.'

'Your client, Ms Younger, has seriously misrepresented our interactions; however, there is no need to argue this point. I will accept your argument, specious as it may be.'

Rita compressed her lips in a straight line. 'I told her you wouldn't make this easy.'

Lucinda threw back her head and looked up at the ceiling. 'Can we get on with this, please?'

Rita turned to Brittany. 'Ignore her hysterics, dear; just tell her what you know.'

Lucinda dropped her head to look straight at Brittany, noting for the first time the way the teacher was dressed. Instead of a plunging neckline, Brittany sported a business suit as if mimicking the attire of her attorney.

'As I told you before, officer—'

Rita interrupted, 'Don't stoop to the detective's level of being petty, Brittany. Address her by her proper title.'

Brittany appeared peeved but followed her lawyer's direction. 'As I told you before, Lieutenant, I did loan my truck. I did not loan it to a student. I did loan it to a former student. He told me he needed it to move his things out of his mother's place and into his new apartment.'

'And what is the name of this former student?' Lucinda asked.

'He is a very troubled young man. He lost his father in a horrible automobile accident when he was quite young. He has suffered through adolescence without a man to guide him. His mother has done her best but she is very limited in her ability to help him in any constructive way. She's not the kind of person he could take in public.'

'You mean, because she's black?' Lucinda said.

'He is not a racist. He just has other problems,' Brittany objected.

'Fine. So what is his name?'

'He needs help, Lieutenant. Not persecution. Quite frankly, I think it is impossible that he had anything to do with the explosion at the high school. If he was there, if my truck was there at the school, it was just a coincidence. And it frightened him.'

'His name, Ms Schaffer?' Lucinda insisted.

Brittany glanced at Rita who nodded and said, 'You need to tell her.'

After a long, dramatic sigh, Brittany said, 'Jimmy Van Dyke. Please be gentle with him. Deep inside, he's such a sensitive boy.'

'You seem to be quite close to this young man,' Lucinda said.

'He's bared his soul to me – and, believe me, it is a place of torment. I have every faith that once he climbs the great mountain of adolescence and reaches the summit, he will be ready to tackle all that the world has to offer.'

Lucinda thought she'd be sick all over the table. Does her lawyer know what a pile of crap her client is? 'And was this all pillow talk?'

Brittany furrowed her brow. 'Excuse me.'

'Post-coital pillow talk?'

'I do not like what you are implying, Lieutenant Pierce,' Rita snapped.

'All she has to do is deny it,' Lucinda said.

Rita turned to her client. 'Do not say a word.' The attorney pivoted back to Lucinda. 'This is so typical of women of your ilk. You always assume the worst of other women. You parade your superiority by turning every other woman's success into a sexual conquest.'

'Not another word about your client's relationship with Jimmy Van Dyke, then. I do have a few other questions if that is acceptable,' Lucinda said.

'You may proceed,' Rita said. 'But from now on, please direct your questions to me, Lieutenant.'

'Did your client teach a student named David Baynes?'

Brittany turned pale. 'Yes, I did. That poor, poor boy.'

'Nothing more, Brittany. Lieutenant Pierce, I believe you are fishing,' Rita said. 'That is the young man who died in the explosion at the high school and I do not appreciate your obvious efforts to upset my client. And besides, if I recall correctly, my client has already admitted to that. Asked and answered, Lieutenant.'

'I was not trying to cause distress to your client, Ms Younger. I simply wanted to know if her link to David Baynes was a typical teacher–student relationship or if it was something more.'

'That's it, Lieutenant. We're leaving now,' Rita said, rising to her feet. 'I can't believe that you are not expressing gratitude toward my client but have chosen instead to make baseless accusations. If I hear a whisper of this matter in the press, you will regret it – instantly and eternally. Let's go, Brittany.'

Lucinda now knew for a fact that Jimmy had possession of Brittany's truck at the time of the explosion. She thought it close to a certainty that the tire track comparison would prove that vehicle was at the school on that morning. She knew that Jimmy had access to the school – but did he have access to explosive materials? She hoped the lab would find some trace in or on the truck. She had to find Jimmy Van Dyke.

FIFTY-EIGHT

Jake and Lucinda sat out on their balcony overlooking the James River as they sipped on glasses of Pinot Grigio and tried to de-stress. They both said they wanted to talk about anything but work but soon slipped from the mundane to brainstorming ideas for finding Amber Culvert and Jimmy Van Dyke.

Jake asked, 'Are you sure that Charley will let you know if Amber contacts her?'

'A couple of days ago, I would have said that I am absolutely positive that Charley would call me right away. But earlier today she called me a hypocrite – and her dad, too – because we tell her to do the right thing and, when she does, we chastise her for taking so many risks.'

Jake laughed. 'That doesn't surprise me. She's learned well from you.'

'What does that mean?'

'How many times have you said that it's easier to ask forgiveness after taking action than to get permission beforehand?'

'But I never said that to Lucy.'

'Sure, you didn't say it. But actions speak louder than words. You're going to have to find a way to make risk assessment an intellectual exercise for Charley – challenge her reasoning power. You might make more headway with that tactic than pointing out the dangers she seems to run toward with glee.'

'Might work. But she may out-think me on that one. She's a scary-smart kid.'

'How about Charlotte Van Dyke? And do you think she will call if she hears from Jimmy or he shows up at her home?'

'I forgot to tell you. I got a message from her earlier today. She said she'd changed her mind about calling a lawyer. She said if Jimmy did something wrong, he needs to answer for it, and if he didn't, he needed to show up and clear his name. But I don't know, Jake. She seems to realize that, while he's on the run, he's taking a big risk and, because of that, she'd call me right away. But I worry that if she thinks her son is about to be charged with a serious crime, she might help him get far, far away to keep him out of prison.'

'It's a difficult position for any mother, I guess. But it might be tempered by wanting to set a good example for Tamara.'

'I wonder if Tamara told her mother that she talked to me. And does Jimmy know she did?'

'Maybe we ought to go see Charlotte this weekend,' Jake said.

'Be best to do that tomorrow. Sunday is Mother's Day – not likely to be very productive to talk to her about turning in her son on that particular holiday. Besides, I promised to take Charley and Ruby to a mother–daughter tea that afternoon. I was going to ask Charley to invite Amber to come along with us, but now . . . Damn, I am worried about that girl. Too many predators and users out there waiting to take advantage of a twelve-year-old's innocence.'

'Unfortunately, she's not as innocent as she should be. But perhaps her experience will make her more cautious.'

'It could also make her run from someone who actually wants to help her,' Lucinda added.

They both sighed and stared out over the river, lost in thought, making them startle enough to splash wine when Lucinda's cell burst into song. 'Pierce,' she said.

'Marguerite Spellman, Lieutenant. I thought you'd want to know right away that traces of the same material used to construct the bomb were found on the floorboard of the passenger's side of Brittany Schaffer's pick-up truck. We also found an excellent palm print on the driver's door as well as some good prints around that seat and picked up prints for both Todd Matthews and David Baynes and a host of others all over the truck – a lot of them smeared beyond recognition. I imagine that some of them belong to the owner, but until you bring me known prints, I can't do much else on that score.'

'Thanks, Spellman. I hope you're going home now and enjoying your weekend.'

'I'm going to try but one of you guys will probably find a body somewhere before it's over.'

'I'll put out a memo: "No dead bodies till Monday." Will that help?' Lucinda teased.

'Yeah, right. If they listen, they'll be sure to call me between midnight and one, Monday morning.'

Lucinda hung up and told Jake about the call. 'I just wish I knew what was going on with those three boys. What puts them all together at the same time in that truck?'

'We don't even know if they were there at the same moment, Lucy. We just know that they have all been in that vehicle. No date stamps on prints.'

'Damn. I need another glass of wine,' Lucinda said, going inside to retrieve the bottle from the refrigerator. When she returned, Jake was on the phone and he looked excited. As soon as he disconnected, Lucinda asked, 'Who was that? What was that?'

'That was the tire impression guru – and we have a match. Absolutely no doubt at all. A perfect match down to every little tiny defect.'

'But really we knew it would,' Lucinda said. 'It will be a great piece of evidence in the courtroom. But we need more to get us there.'

'Ah, c'mon, don't put a damper on it. We both got good forensic reports this evening. Let's celebrate that tonight – and move on tomorrow.'

'Honestly, Jake, until Amber is found, I won't feel up to celebrating anything. I'm terrified for her.'

FIFTY-NINE

After a quick breakfast of bagels, cream cheese and coffee, Lucinda and Jake drove over to the Van Dyke home. They noticed that lights were on in a few rooms and that probably meant that Charlotte was up for the day. For a few minutes, they sat in the car observing the house and neighborhood for anything that appeared out of the ordinary.

Standing in front of the door, they listened for any suspicious sounds before ringing the bell. Charlotte answered wearing a blue terry cloth robe and pink fuzzy slippers. 'Well, good morning, Lieutenant. You sure are up early today. I suppose you got my message. Or did you find my Jimmy? Is he OK?'

'Yes, ma'am, I did get your message, but we haven't found Jimmy,' Lucinda said. 'This is Special Agent Jake Lovett with the FBI. We were hoping you might have thought of something that would help us locate your son.'

Charlotte shook her head and frowned. 'No, ma'am, I sure do not know a blessed thing. I keep having these horrible pictures of Jimmy being shot by a police officer for resisting arrest. I am so afraid for him. I do believe this is all going to come to a very bad end. But come on. Come on into the house. I have a fresh pot of coffee brewing and I need to pull the biscuits out of the oven. We can all sit around the kitchen table and try to find a way to make it all work out.'

The two investigators followed Charlotte through the living room and into an immaculate kitchen. The aroma of coffee fought for dominance over the fragrance coming from the oven. They sat down and watched as Charlotte slipped the baking sheet out on to the top of the stove, used a spatula to transfer the biscuits two at a time into a basket lined with a red-and-white checked kitchen towel. That morning's bagels faded from memory as their mouths watered in response.

Charlotte put the basket on the table, slid a butter dish, a jelly jar and cream pitcher out of the refrigerator, small plates out of a cabinet, three butter knives out of a drawer and set them in front of Lucinda and Jake. Then she poured three mugs of coffee, carried them over and sat down. 'Now that's real butter, mind you, and real coffee cream – no substitutes allowed in this house.'

'I imagine, then, that's no decaf,' Jake said with a smile.

'Heavens, no. If God didn't want us to have caffeine, He wouldn't have put it in the coffee beans in the first place,' Charlotte said with a grin. 'Now, I don't think I know a thing that I haven't already told you. But perhaps if you ask some questions, something might come to mind.'

Lucinda thought for a moment about how to ask if Charlotte knew about her daughter's interview without betraying the girl. 'Do you think Tamara might know anything worthwhile?'

Charlotte smiled. 'You are a lovely woman, Lieutenant. I see what you are doing – protecting my girl's confidence. I am very pleased to know you'd do that. But, actually, Tamara told me all about her visit to see you. I don't think she knows anything else but you could ask her. But if we wake her up this early on a Saturday morning, she would probably bite my head off – and yours, too – and she would be grumpy all day long. I could give you a call when she wakes up. Would that be OK?'

'Oh, yes, Mrs Van Dyke, I do know enough about teenagers to realize that. Please, let her sleep and, yes, I was trying to find out if you knew without exposing Tamara. I'm glad you understand. But do you have any idea of where Jimmy would go to lie low.'

'I tried really hard to know those things before Jimmy was eighteen – sometimes I did; probably most times I didn't.' Charlotte sighed. 'Then on his eighteenth birthday he told me that he liked living at home and would like to keep staying here until he figured out whether he'd go to college or join the army or get a serious job; but if I was going to always be in his business, he'd live in the streets rather than put up with that. So I backed off. I guess that's the long way of saying, "No, Lieutenant, I have not one single idea." For all I know, he's left town – even left the state. Maybe he's been driving all night, heading for Montana or Idaho. He always said he wanted to live out where there were more acres than people.'

A flash of worry jagged through Lucinda's thoughts and she asked, 'Do you know if Jimmy knows that Tamara talked to me?' Lucinda asked.

'I don't believe she's talked to him since then. She hasn't mentioned it to me so I don't believe so. But I guess it's possible he called her last night after I went to bed. We'll have to ask her about that when she gets up.' Charlotte's head tilted to one side. 'Well, speaking of the devil, did you hear that?'

Jake and Lucinda started to form the word 'no' but stopped when a louder thump hit the floor above their head.

'Sounds like Little Miss Grumpy is up early today. She must have smelled the biscuits,' Charlotte said with a chuckle. 'I've told her if she sleeps too late, I might eat them all and leave her nothing but crumbs. I imagine she'll be down shortly. Maybe the two of us will be able to think of something else. More coffee?'

They both nodded and lifted their mugs. Charlotte filled the cups, turned around and was walking back to the table when she gasped and the cups fell from her hands and crashed on the floor. Hot coffee sprayed in the air and splashed all over Charlotte's legs but she seemed oblivious. She stared straight ahead, her jaw moving up and down but not a word coming from her mouth.

Lucinda and Jake spun their heads around to see what had alarmed her and both automatically put their hands inside their jackets and on the butt of their guns.

'Put your hands where I can see them,' Jimmy said. He stood in the doorway, looking dirty and disheveled. One arm was wrapped tightly around his sister. The other held a gun, pressed into the flesh of one of her cheeks. 'I will shoot her, I swear I will.'

The surprised detectives slowly pulled out their hands and held them out, palms up and open.

'Put both your hands on your head.'

Jake and Lucinda followed his orders without hesitation.

'Mom, go get their guns.'

For a moment, she didn't respond. Then she put hands on hips and said, 'I will not. You stop this nonsense right now.'

Jimmy shoved the barrel into Tamara's face, causing her to whimper. The force scraped the surface of her skin, causing a small trickle of blood to run down to her jawline.

'Jimmy, you look what you've done. You cut her. Now give me that gun right now. You know I have forbidden guns in this house. You've known that all your life. Where did you get that thing?' She stretched her hand out. 'Give it to me.'

Lucinda looked at Tamara whose eyes seemed about to roll up into her head. If she passed out, Jimmy might shoot her, thinking she was trying to escape from him. She then studied Jimmy. When she first looked at him, his eyes appeared dead and flat; now they were jumping. His mother was escalating not defusing the situation. 'Come on over to me, Mrs Van Dyke. You can take my gun. I will not try to stop you.'

'See, Mom, she has sense enough to know who's in charge here. Do what she says.'

Charlotte walked backwards toward Lucinda. She turned to face her. She reached one hand inside Lucinda's jacket.

'Just flip the snap on the top of the holster and it will slide right out.'

The snap filled the quiet room like an explosion. Lucinda, however, did not feel the revolver moving, even though Charlotte was acting as if she was withdrawing the weapon. Lucinda tried to get the woman to look at her but she seemed to be avoiding her gaze. Lucinda wasn't sure what Charlotte was thinking but she wanted to yell at her to stop. But she didn't for fear that it might prompt Jimmy to fire the gun. She sat there helpless as Charlotte spun around, slapped a hand on Jimmy's pistol and jerked.

As Charlotte and Jimmy struggled, Jake pulled Tamara away and shoved her back.

Tamara screamed, 'Mom!' and rushed toward her mother.

Jake and Lucinda circled Charlotte and Jimmy, seeking any small window of opportunity to wedge in between mother and son and disarm whoever had control of the weapon. Before they could do anything, the gun went off, echoing in their ears, and Tamara fell to the floor.

SIXTY

Charley pulled her iPhone out of her pocket when she heard the familiar sound of an incoming text message. She read, 'If I tell u where I am, will u promise not 2 tell any1?'

Amber! She knew if she said yes and then told her dad or Lucy, Amber would be angry. If she told her no, then she probably wouldn't hear from her again. If she agreed to keep the secret and kept her word, Dad and Lucy would be mad at her. Well, they don't need to know, do they? She typed back, 'Y.'

'Coffee shop 2 buildings away.'

'OMW,' Charley answered.

She headed out to meet Amber but the moment she unlocked the front door, her father shouted, 'Where are you going, Charley?'

'Down to the coffee shop for something with lots of whipped cream.'

'Why don't you take Ruby with you?'

'Da–aaa–ad,' Charley whined.

'OK, OK, just bring something back for her, OK?'

'Yes, Daddy.'

'There's a twenty in the box on the table.'

'Thank you, Daddy,' Charley said and ducked out into the hallway before he could change his mind. When she reached the coffee shop, she looked all around but didn't see Amber anywhere. She pulled out her cell and tapped on the keyboard, 'Where r u?'

'Ladies.'

Charley went into the restroom and still didn't see Amber. 'Amber, where are you?'

'Down here, last stall,' Amber said, pushing open the door.

'It stinks like disinfectant in here. Can we go talk out at a table?'

'I wanted to make sure you didn't bring anyone with you.'

'So, you don't trust me? Really? What's with that?'

'I'm sorry, Charley. I don't trust anybody. Ever. I'm sorry.'

'Well, c'mon, let's go get a drink.'

Amber stepped out of the stall and said, 'I don't have any money. We could go for a walk.'

'Daddy gave me money before I left.'

'He knows?' Amber said, stepping back into the small enclosure.

'Oh, c'mon, Amber. I told you I wouldn't tell him and I didn't. He gave me money so I'd come home with something for Ruby and he never asks me for change back. It's OK, really.'

Amber came back out and said, 'Thank you, Charley. You're a good friend. I shouldn't doubt you.'

Charley threw an arm around Amber's shoulders, noticing a tear in the sleeve of her shirt and the dirtiness of her hair. 'You can order anything you want. Double mocha, triple caramel, quadruple whipped cream. You name it, it's yours.'

The girls placed their orders and carried the largest size cups brimming with their fattening concoctions – Amber's chilled, Charley's hot – to a table. 'Girl, don't take this the wrong way,' Charley said, 'but you are a mess.'

Amber sighed. 'Duh. There are mirrors in the bathroom, you know.'

'We've got to do something. You can't live on the streets, Amber.'

'She came to the school. She'll come to your house, too. She'll get me. And she won't let up. She'll call me a liar. She'll make me feel so bad. All for him. All because she has to have a boyfriend so bad she doesn't care what a piece of crap he is. She doesn't care what he does to me. Or to Andy. All she cares is that he's there.'

'But that's just it, Amber. They put her back in jail.'

'They let her out before; they'll let her out again.'

'Not this time,' Charley said, shaking her head.

'You can't know that. Nobody can.'

'We can go see your CASA lady. She'll know.'

'Yeah, right. She didn't think they'd let her out last time.'

'You're going to get hurt out here.'

Amber snorted. 'Can't be any worse than what happened to me in my own home.'

'OK. I'll sneak you into my bedroom.'

'How can you do that? There's no way.'

'Easy peasy,' Charlie said. 'Just do what I tell you to do, every step of the way.'

'What about the doorman? I bet he's looking for me.'

'Sure, he is. So I'll go in, chat him up and then let you in the back door.'

'What if somebody sees me in the elevator?'

'I'll buy a newspaper and you can hide behind it.'

'Won't that look suspicious?'

'OK, how about a magazine? We've got enough change left for that.'

'Which magazine?'

'There's a bookstore a block from here – you can pick out whatever you want. Pick one big enough to hide your face.'

'I don't know. It sounds dangerous.'

Charley rolled her eyes. 'And you think it's safe roaming the streets?'

'OK. But if anybody says anything, I'm going to run and you'll never see me again.'

'Drama queen,' Charley said.

Amber stuck out her tongue and laughed.

Everything went as planned and without incident all the way up to the Spencers' condominium. 'Now,' Charley said. 'I'm going to leave the door open a crack. Put your foot against so it doesn't close and listen. I'm going to get everybody out on the balcony – you'll hear the door. Sneak in and go up to my room. I'll be there as soon as I can.'

'What if someone sees me out here?'

'Read your magazine. I'll only be a minute.'

Charley breezed inside. 'Daddy, Ruby, you gotta see this guy down on the street. He's got a monkey and his hair his purple.'

'The monkey has purple hair?' Ruby asked.

'No,' Charley said, 'the man has purple hair and a monkey.'

Ruby ran straight for the sliding glass door.

'C'mon, Daddy, c'mon. You gotta see this guy,' Charley urged.

'OK, Charley, I'm coming.'

Charley peered over the railing. 'He was right here. He couldn't have gotten far. Where is he?'

'I don't see no monkey, Charley,' Ruby whined.

'*Any* monkey, Ruby,' Charley corrected her sister.

'I don't see any monkey, either.'

'OK, Charley, is this supposed to be a joke?' her dad asked.

'No, Daddy. He was right there. That darned elevator is just too slow. Maybe if we went down on the street, we could find him.'

'He'll probably be long gone by then. C'mon, let's go back inside.'

'But I want to see the purple-haired monkey,' Ruby whined.

'The monkey doesn't have purple hair,' Charley snapped.

'But you said—'

'Girls, girls,' Evan said, 'it doesn't really matter. He's gone now.'

'But, Daddy,' Ruby pleaded, jutting out her lower lip.

'If Charley sees him again, she'll call me on her cell phone right away, won't you, Charley?'

'Yes, Daddy.'

'And that way we won't miss him next time.'

'That was stupid, Charley,' Ruby complained.

'Ruby, what did I tell you about calling your sister stupid?'

'I didn't call her stupid, Daddy. I just—'

'Enough,' Evan said.

'Well, I'm going to start on my homework. See you later,' Charley said, rushing off before anyone could object. She opened her bedroom door but didn't see her friend. 'Amber,' she hissed.

The closet door eased open and Amber's head popped out. 'Made it. No one saw me, did they?'

'Nope. I told you it would work.'

'What are we going to do now?'

'I have to get on my computer and do some homework. Don't you have some?' Charley asked.

'Yeah, I do – or I did.'

'What do you mean?'

'This boy stole my backpack and it was in there.'

'See, I told you it's not safe out there. You can't leave me again. Promise?'

Amber's brow furrowed. 'But—'

'No buts. I had your back. I wasn't going to let her take you. I never, never, never give up.'

'You sure had Mom's back,' Amber said with a giggle. 'If I hadn't been so scared, I would have laughed.'

'I bet that did look pretty funny,' Charley said with a grin. 'But you've got to promise.'

'OK, I promise.'

'Swear?'

'Swear.'

'No lying?' Charley asked.

'If I'm lying, I'm dying.'

'BFF forever and ever?'

'Forever and ever,' Amber said.

The two girls bumped fists. Amber curled up on the bed with Charley's iPad and Charley sat down at her desk and got busy on her homework.

SIXTY-ONE

Charlotte Van Dyke crumpled down to her knees and let loose a high, keening wail. Jimmy threw the gun across the room and screamed, 'I'm sorry. I'm sorry. I'm sorry.'

Lucinda and Jake went down on the floor on either side of Tamara. The girl still had a pulse. They searched but found no sign of entry. Puzzled, they looked at each other and then around the room. Jake spotted the point of impact. There was a hole through the crown molding.

'I think she just passed out,' Lucinda said.

Jake stood and checked the defect near the ceiling. 'Looks like the bullet went up through here. 'Mrs Van Dyke, are you hit?'

'No, no. Tamara. My baby . . .'

'Jimmy, were you shot?'

'I didn't mean to, I didn't mean to . . .'

'No one's injured?' Jake asked again.

'Tamara – get help for Tamara,' Charlotte pleaded.

Pulling out his cell, Jake said, 'I will. I will but it doesn't look like she was shot, ma'am. I think she just passed out.' On the phone, Jake identified himself and explained he was with Lieutenant Pierce, then requested an ambulance and a patrol car to transport Jimmy Van Dyke.

On the floor, Tamara came round and struggled to sit up. Lucinda placed a hand on her chest and said, 'No, Tamara. Lie still. You had a shock and you took a fall. An ambulance is on the way and it would be better if you didn't move until the paramedics are here. Do you hurt anywhere?'

'No. No. What happ— Mom? Jimmy? Who was shot?'

'Easy, easy, Tamara. No one was shot. Everyone is OK. Just lie still.'

Charlotte moved into the space vacated by Jake and grabbed her daughter's hand. 'Hush, hush, baby. You do what the lieutenant said. Oh my good, sweet Lord, praise his name – I thought you were dead, baby. You gave me such a scare when you fell to the floor.'

'I'm sorry, Mama.'

'Hush, hush. Be quiet now. Everything is OK.'

'What about Jimmy, Mama?'

'He's not hurt. But I suspect he'll be leaving for the jail soon.'

'Yes, ma'am,' Lucinda said. 'We do have to take him in for questioning. And there will be charges.'

'Ah, yes, the wages of sin – at least, no one is dead.'

'Jimmy,' Lucinda said, 'I really should cuff you and I'll have to when the patrol car gets here. But I thought you might want a few minutes with your mother and sister. Can I trust you not to do anything stupid?'

'Yes, ma'am.'

Lucinda rose to her feet and said, 'Here. Take my spot.'

Jimmy sank to his knees at his sister's side. Jake and Lucinda moved across the room where they could keep an eye on the young man but allow some measure of privacy for family interactions.

Jimmy, Tamara and Charlotte made a circle of their hands and Charlotte prayed earnestly and long. When sirens filled the air, Charlotte said, 'Amen,' raised her head and placed a hand on each of her son's cheeks. 'I love you, Jimmy.'

Jimmy sobbed and stumbled to his feet, holding his hands behind his back. Lucinda snapped on the handcuffs and led him outside, passing the paramedics who rushed in with a stretcher. She opened the rear door of the patrol car and, pressing down on the top of Jimmy's head, she eased him into the back seat. 'I'll see you at the station, Jimmy. Don't give anyone a hard time about anything between now and then. I don't want to have to explain any injuries to your mother.'

'Yes, ma'am,' he said, hanging his head.

Lucinda shut the car door and slapped an open palm on the roof of the vehicle. She watched as the marked car pulled out of the driveway and went down the street and out of sight.

SIXTY-TWO

Back at the Justice Center, Lucinda and Jake stood outside the interrogation room. 'You're ready?' Lucinda asked.

'Yep,' Jake answered.

'I'm pretty sure he did it.'

'Me, too.'

'I wish it wasn't Charlotte's son.'

'So do I. It's going to break her heart. She fell apart all over again when you left the house with Jimmy.'

'I wouldn't want to be her today. OK, let's go,' Lucinda said, twisting the knob and opening the door.

'Hello, Jimmy,' Lucinda said. 'They told me you refused an attorney.'

'Yes, ma'am, and I signed that paper.'

'You want a chance to reconsider?' Jake asked.

Jimmy shook his head.

'I'm going to read you your rights one more time, Jimmy. You think about it again while I do.'

'I'm not gonna change my mind.'

'Just think about it,' Lucinda said and recited the words she knew by heart.

When she finished, Jimmy said, 'No, ma'am, I don't want a lawyer. I just want to tell you what happened.'

'Are you responsible for the explosion at the high school?' Lucinda asked.

'Yes, ma'am.'

'How did you learn how to build a bomb?'

'Online. There's all sorts of ways online.'

'What did you use to build it?' Jake asked.

'Well, I got a thermostat, clothespins, some bare metal thumb tacks, batteries and string at the hardware store. Then I stole a bag of fertilizer from a barn out in the country.'

'Where did you build it?'

'Out in Ms Schaffer's garage. But she didn't know what we were doing. We just said we were working on a project and needed a workbench, and since she had one in her garage that she never used, I asked to use it. But she didn't ask any questions. She didn't know what we were doing.'

Lucinda and Jake exchanged a glance and then Lucinda said, 'We, Jimmy? Who is we?'

'Me and Todd Matthews. But Todd – he didn't know why I was doing it. I just told him it was a joke. We made rockets powered by gunpowder when we were kids and Molotov cocktails that we threw into cornfields in middle school. So he believed me when I told him that it would make a mess but that was it. He liked setting things off, destroying things, leaving a mess behind, but he never wanted to hurt anybody.'

'Is that why he took his own life, Jimmy?'

'Yeah. That was my fault, too. I didn't know he liked David Baynes. I didn't know he'd care. If I did, I would've gotten someone else to help.'

'How did you get into the school?' Jake asked.

'I tricked my sister. I told her that I needed to defend a girl's honor. I guess she liked that 'cause she didn't ask any questions. I was ready for the questions. I was going to tell her that the principal had confiscated some naked photos of the girl and I needed to destroy them 'cause the girl didn't know that they were being taken. But Tamara never asked.'

'What did your sister do for you, Jimmy?'

'Saturday night, when she got back from the battle of the bands, she just duct-taped open the door by the shop. So, I went in that way and set all the components in the file cabinet drawer, pushed it shut and pulled the string that was attached to a piece of plastic that separated the heads of the thumbtacks.'

'Weren't you worried that you'd set it off when you removed that barrier?'

'Yeah. I was sweating something wicked. I had to wipe my hands on my pants a few times and hold my breath. I said a prayer, too. That was pretty stupid but I did it.'

'Why did you do it, Jimmy?'

'I did it to kill David Baynes,' he said, his face devoid of emotion as he stared straight into Lucinda's face.

'Why, Jimmy? Why did you want to kill him?'

Jimmy shrugged and looked down at the surface of the table. 'Didn't like him much, I guess.'

'Why not? Why didn't you like him?'

'I don't know. I just didn't.'

'Jimmy, you had to have a reason to hate him enough to kill him.'

'Well, I didn't,' Jimmy screamed. 'I didn't have a reason. And that's that. No matter how many times you ask me, the answer is the same. I didn't have a reason. I just didn't like him.'

'OK, Jimmy, settle down,' Jake said. 'We hear you loud and clear. Take it easy.'

Lucinda knew from his strong reaction that there was a reason he wasn't willing to reveal. There was something between the two boys to stir up such a strong emotional response. 'So, Jimmy, how did you get David over to the school?'

'Todd told him about the girl and the naked pictures.'

'Did David go in alone?'

'Yeah, we drove over there together in Ms Schaffer's truck. When we got there, Todd walked him around back to the door. He told him it was pictures of my sister so I couldn't get caught inside and Todd said he was dating my sister so he'd be a natural suspect, too. So David went inside by himself. What a fool! He saw himself as some sort of white knight when it came to girls. He didn't even know my sister – but that didn't matter to him. He still wanted to protect her honor. I think he believed it would help him score some ass. I guess nobody told him that good guys finish last.'

'Was Todd back in the truck when you pulled away?'

'Yeah. Then we got past the traffic light and the whole place blew. We were laughing. But Todd – he stopped laughing later when he heard what had happened. He was really pissed. I told him if he told anybody, he'd go to jail, too. He kept saying, "You told me it would just make a mess. You told me nobody would get hurt." I told him to get over it but he just kept on and on. And then I got mad and I said, "Well, what happened happened and there's nothing you can do about it. If you can't handle that, then maybe you should off yourself." I really didn't mean it. I didn't think he'd do it.'

'Is there anything else you want to tell us, Jimmy?' Lucinda asked.

'Just that, like I said, Todd didn't really know what was up. And Tamara didn't know. And Ms Schaffer knew less than any of them. This is all on me.'

'OK, Jimmy, I'm arresting you for first degree murder and destruction of public property, and there will probably be a few more charges once the DA gets his hands on the case.'

'Yes, ma'am. Tell Mama I'm sorry.'

Lucinda stepped into the hall and asked the patrolman standing guard to secure Jimmy in a cell. Lucinda half expected Jimmy to turn around and add something – any little thing that made more sense than what he'd already said.

'What's wrong, Lucy?' Jake asked.

'I don't like this.'

'What's not to like? You solved the case. You've got the bad guy locked up. This is what you wanted, right?'

'Only partly, Jake. I wanted answers. All the answers. He's still holding something back. Right now, there's a great big, gaping hole in his story. And I'm going to have to find out what that is.'

SIXTY-THREE

Lucinda obtained a search warrant for Brittany Schaffer's garage where Jimmy Van Dyke claimed he built the bomb. She, Jake, Marguerite, a handful of forensic technicians and a pair of uniformed patrolmen descended on the teacher's place that evening.

When they pulled up, they saw a silver BMW in the driveway. Their arrival disrupted a candlelight dinner on the back patio. Brittany shrieked her objections to their presence and the owner of the car out front made a hasty retreat. Lucinda wasn't sure if it was to escape the police or to get away from the scene Brittany was making.

Before they started the actual search for objects connected to the bomb, two techs went inside. One wiped likely surfaces, including the floor in front of the workbench, to collect any explosive residue. The other followed in his wake, dusting for prints.

In the trash can, Lucinda and Marguerite recovered and bagged receipts and packaging for a thermostat and batteries. On the bench, they confiscated open packages of clothespins and thumbtacks, a ball of cotton string, plastic shavings and a single-edged razor blade. Underneath the bench, they found a half-full bag of ammonium nitrate fertilizer.

Still, Lucinda was convinced that, this time, the confession didn't hold up under close scrutiny. Jimmy Van Dyke left something unsaid, something hidden below the surface. Did Brittany Schaffer know what he was doing in her garage?

It was time for Brittany Schaffer to answer a few questions about what they had discovered. She refused to allow them inside her house and slammed the door shut. She screamed through the door, 'I've already called my attorney. She will be here shortly. Until then, I am not answering any of your damn questions.'

'I would really like to force my way inside, but it might have too many negative consequences,' Lucinda said.

'But,' Jake said, 'if she was knowledgeable about the activity in her garage, it would be totally justifiable.'

'Patience. If she wasn't, or if I can't prove she was, Rita Younger will nail me to the wall.'

'I thought Younger reserved her aggression for attacking men.'

'Apparently, with me, she's willing to make an exception.'

'OK, let's give the lawyer fifteen minutes. If she's here by then, fine. If she's not, we go in.'

Five minutes later, Rita arrived in a sapphire-blue Cadillac XTS. By the time she parked, Jake was drooling. Lucinda, however, was not impressed – too much car for that small woman and too ostentatious by far, she thought.

'Harassing my client again, Lieutenant?' Rita said as she stepped out of her car.

'Well, gee, Younger, I doubt that a judge would see it that way considering what we found in your client's garage,' Lucinda said.

'First things first, Lieutenant. I will, of course, be challenging your grounds for obtaining that search warrant. If I win that battle, what you found will be irrelevant. Now, if you'll excuse me, I'll confer with my client and see if we're willing to answer any of your questions.'

'Be clear on this, Younger,' Lucinda said. 'It's here or at the Justice Center – one way or another she's talking to me on tape.'

'We'll see,' Younger said and went inside.

'Whoa,' Jake said. 'If anything, she seems to dislike you more than any man I've seen her shredding to bits.'

'The feeling is mutual,' Lucinda said.

Lucinda paced around the front yard for ten minutes before she lost her patience. She balled up both fists and banged them on the front door. Rita opened it and said, 'Five more minutes, Lieutenant. We'll be ready for you then.' The door closed.

'Damn that woman,' Lucinda said.

'Don't let her push your buttons, Lucy. Let her play her games and think you don't care.'

'Easy for you to say.'

'Oh, yeah, I'm not in her gun sights. But you know I'm right.'

Lucinda shrugged and resumed her pacing. Four minutes later, the door opened and Brittany, saccharine smile in place, invited Lucinda and Jake into her home as if they were guests to a cocktail party. She led them to the dining-room table where Rita Younger was seated, appearing to be holding court.

'Before we begin the questioning,' Rita said, 'my client would like to make a statement. Are you recording?'

Lucinda pressed the red button and said, 'Yes, we are recording.

It is Saturday, May eleventh, 2013, at nine fourteen p.m. Present are Brittany Schaffer, her attorney Rita Younger, FBI Special Agent in Charge Jake Lovett and Lieutenant Lucinda Pierce.'

Brittany cleared her throat and straightened her posture. She held a legal pad and read from it. 'I did give Jimmy Van Dyke permission to use the work space in my garage to work on a project. I didn't ask him anything about what he was doing because, at that time, I did not care. I assumed if he was busy in there, he was not out on the streets getting into trouble. At no time, however, was I aware that he was involved in any criminal activity. I would not condone anyone using my property for illegal purposes. I also had no knowledge, at that time or since that time, of Jimmy Van Dyke's involvement in the explosion at the high school.'

'So, if you didn't know what he was doing, how did you know why we were here?' Lucinda asked.

Brittany blanched.

Rita came to the rescue. 'My client is not a stupid person, Lieutenant. She is an educated professional. The search warrant stated what you were trying to find and it wouldn't take much intellectual prowess for her or anyone to draw that conclusion.'

'Yes, exactly,' Brittany said, earning a glare from her attorney.

'What about the other person in the garage?' Jake asked. 'Why didn't you mention him?'

Brittany's eyes glanced sideways toward Rita. 'My client doesn't know what you are talking about, Lieutenant.'

'Ms Schaffer, are you aware that the other person is dead?' Lucinda asked.

Rita answered, 'As I said, Lieutenant, my client has no knowledge of a second person.'

'What is your relationship with Jimmy Van Dyke, Ms Schaffer?'

'I don't have one. Whatever he said, it was just his little fantasy; it had nothing to do with me.'

'Please, Ms Schaffer,' Rita said, 'don't answer any questions until I tell you that it is appropriate to do so.'

Brittany looked down at the surface of the table, appearing as chastised as a little girl who interrupted her mother's conversation.

'Ms Schaffer,' Jake said, 'did Jimmy talk to you about his fantasy? About what he wanted to do to you – with you?'

Brittany looked ready to jump up and run from the room. Rita placed a firm hand on her client's forearm and said, 'We have no comment at this time.'

'Did you know,' Lucinda asked, 'that Jimmy told people that you two were getting married once he graduated from high school?'

'That's ridiculous,' Brittany said.

Rita squeezed her arm. 'Lieutenant, I am going to have to terminate this interview. It's getting late. My client is tired and stressed from your invasion of her home and property and she wants to get some rest tonight so she can visit her mother tomorrow. It's Mother's Day, you know – oh, that's right, Lieutenant, you don't have a mother and you're not a mother so I'm sure it's irrelevant to you. But, for the rest of us, it is a very important day.'

Lucinda bolted to her feet, her hands clenched at her side. She glared down at Rita Younger and turned off the digital recorder. Lucinda heard Jake's sharp intake of breath. She smelled the stink of fear on Brittany and saw the self-satisfied smug on Rita's face. She spun around and walked to the door. 'Come on, Special Agent Lovett. We'll find what we need for an arrest warrant and come back when we have done.'

SIXTY-FOUR

Lucinda struggled Sunday morning to match Jake's upbeat attitude. Mother's Day was always a difficult holiday for her since it fell one week after she witnessed her father shoot and kill her mother decades earlier. She'd been in shock the day her mother died and all through the funeral. It was on that first Mother's Day that her anger had started to build into an uncontrollable fury. Her biggest wish that day was that her father hadn't died so that she could kill him herself. She knew the annual celebration of mothers wasn't any easier for Jake, either, since he had lost his mom to breast cancer. However, Lucinda thought Jake seemed to be more focused on her needs and her past trauma than on the early demise of his own mother. It seemed as if he was trying to soften the emotional impact of the day by waking her up with a steaming mug of coffee and then serving her breakfast in bed.

This year, though, in addition to the mournful thoughts about her mother, she was troubled by the outcome of the case at the high school. Like Jake, she was delighted to have identified and jailed the perpetrator, but she couldn't shake the conviction that there was more to the story – some subterranean motivation that turned a troubled teen into a bomb-building killer. And she strongly suspected that if she turned over enough rocks, Brittany Schaffer would slither out.

Jake blew off her concerns in that regard. 'Sometimes things are what they seem, Lucy. They're simple. They're direct. So simple and direct they seem too stupid to be true. But it is what it is. And nothing more.'

She was lost in thought when her cell rang. She looked at the screen and saw that the caller was Evan Spencer. 'Good morning, Evan. Are the girls OK?'

'Yeah, pretty much. You are still coming to take them to tea today, right?'

'Yes, Evan. I'll be there about three.'

'Could you make it two thirty?'

'Sure – what's up?'

'I'll meet you in the garage. I think I know where Amber is. Gotta run.'

'But, Evan? Evan?' *Oh good grief. If he knows where Amber is, why didn't he just tell me? What was up with him? Is something else wrong? Are the girls obsessing about their mom?* It had only been four years since Kathleen Spencer was murdered by her brother-in-law. Lucinda had to be prepared for almost any kind of reaction or acting out from the two of them.

Lucinda pulled into the garage of the Spencers' high-rise condominium building at two twenty-five and walked towards the elevator. Before she reached it, the doors opened and Evan stepped out. 'Hey, Evan, what's going on?'

'I'm not sure but I think Charley has someone hiding in her room.'

'You think it's Amber?'

'Might be. I thought I could check when the girls left with you. Then I worried that if it was Amber, I'd terrify her if I barged in on her.'

'You want me to barge in on her?'

'I thought that might be better,' Evan said. 'But maybe you could be subtle about it. Charley and Ruby are getting ready. You could just wander into Charley's room. You think?'

'Ask around, Evan. Subtle is not my strong point. But I'll see what I can do. Let's go do it.'

Evan and Lucinda entered the front door as quietly as they could. Lucinda went up the steps to Charley's room and rapped on the door.

'Not now, Daddy, I'm getting dressed.'

'It's just me, Charley.'

'Oh, Lucy. Oh, just a minute. Hold on. Just a minute.'

Lucinda eased the door open just in time to see Charley closing the walk-in closet. Charley leaned her back against the entrance and smiled. 'Hi, Lucy, you're a little early.'

'Yeah, a bit. Thought I could help you get ready.'

'Ruby and Andy need more help than I do. Andy can come with us, right?'

'Yes, I assumed Andy would come along with us.'

'Even though he's a boy and it's a mother–daughter tea?'

'He's just a little boy. He won't be a problem.'

'Well, you'd better go to Ruby's room and help them.'

Lucinda folded her arms across her chest. 'Why do I get the feeling you're hiding something, Charley?'

Charley shrugged. 'I don't know. Maybe you've just been a cop too long – makes you a little paranoid, don't you think?'

'Why don't you just tell me what's in the closet?'

'My clothes, my shoes – you know, that kind of stuff.'

'Could I have a look?' Lucinda asked.

'Oh, it's such a mess right now. I'd be embarrassed.'

'Don't be silly. I'll just straighten it up a bit while you finish getting dressed.' Lucinda walked toward the door blocked by Charley.

'No, no, no, Lucy. I can't have you doing that. Daddy would not want me to pass my work on to you. He'd be very disappointed in me.'

'Charley, you don't want me to call your dad up here, do you?'

'I'll never get ready in time if you do—'

'Step away, Charley.'

'This is so not cool, Lucy.'

'Charley, please . . .'

Charley's face grew dark and her brow furrowed. 'You're not the boss of me. You are not my mother.'

Lucinda sighed. 'Fine. We'll play it your way, Charley. I'll go get your dad.'

A pounding sound came from the other side of the door. A muffled voice said, 'Let me out, Charley.'

Charley squinched up her face and gave Lucy a red-faced smile. She stepped away from the door and it opened behind her.

'Amber,' Lucinda said.

With outstretched arms, Amber ran out towards Lucinda as if she wanted to embrace her but, two steps away, she stopped, dropped her hands to her sides, looked down at the floor. Lucinda crossed the gap between them, wrapping her arms around the young girl. At first, Amber resisted and Lucinda responded by holding her tighter. In less than a minute, Amber relaxed and fell into the hug. Her hands touched Lucinda and then she reached further, pressing her face into Lucinda's chest, clinging to her as if she'd fall to the floor without her support.

'I am scared. I don't want to go to my mother. Please don't make me,' Amber said, her voice muffled against Lucinda's body. 'She'll make me say I lied. She'll let him hurt me again.'

'Sweetheart, your mom is locked up in jail. You don't need to worry about her now.'

'Yeah. That's what you said before. And look what happened.'

'This time is different, Amber. She was charged with another crime while she was out on bond; the judge denied her bail this time. He said that it was obvious that she could not be trusted. And, on top of that, your CASA attorney got a restraining order against her for both you and Andy. So even if she does eventually get out, she can't come near you.'

Amber pulled back and said, 'I'm still scared.'

'Of course you are, Amber. I don't blame you for that.' Lucinda placed her hands on the arms of the girl and looked into her eyes. 'But why don't you get dressed and come to tea with us? You'll be safe with me.'

'Yeah,' Charley said, 'she's armed and dangerous.'

Lucinda rolled her eyes. 'Will you trust me, Amber?'

Amber's eyes searched Lucinda's face and finally she nodded her head.

'OK, then. I'll leave you two alone to get ready. I need to make a few phone calls to let everyone know that Amber is OK and then we'll go – all right?'

'You won't call my mom?' Amber said.

'Of course not.'

'We won't be long, Lucy,' Charley said.

'Amber?' Lucinda asked.

Amber nodded and tried to smile but couldn't quite make it happen.

SIXTY-FIVE

When Lucinda walked through the door of the apartment after the excursion with Charley, Ruby, Amber and Andy, Jake asked, 'Where do you want to go to dinner tonight?'

'I know we usually go out on Sunday night, Jake, but I'm beat.'

'I thought we could go someplace special to celebrate the resolution of the case.'

'First of all, Jake, I'm not in the mood to celebrate until I have my questions about Jimmy's motivation answered. Second, even if I were, I am too tired to go anywhere. Do you have any idea how exhausting a few hours with four kids can be?'

'OK. But I'm really hungry. Scrounging up something here just won't do it. Either delivery or carry-out, OK?'

Lucinda nodded. 'No problem.'

'So, how was the tea-house adventure?'

'Not exactly what I was expecting,' Lucinda said and burst into a laugh.

'Oh dear. What happened?'

'Ruby kept calling Andy her fiancé, much to the amusement of Charley and Amber – I did call you about Amber, didn't I?'

'Yes, you did. But her *fiancé*? Does she even know what that means?'

'Oh yes. And she even referred to herself as the older woman but informed us all that, by the time they were old enough to marry, the difference in their ages wouldn't seem like all that much.'

'And how was Andy taking all of this?'

'That boy fell right into line. He agreed with everything she said about their future. And he was very accepting of all of her corrections. When Charley took Ruby to the ladies' room, Amber asked Andy, "You always get mad at me when I tell you what to do. Doesn't Ruby make you mad?" And Andy said, "Oh no, I want to be the best man I can be for Ruby."'

'Where do they get this crap?' Jake said with a laugh.

'Got me. When I asked Ruby what would happen to the relationship if Andy had to move away to live with his family, she said, "When it's true love, distance doesn't matter."'

'How was Charley reacting to this romance?'

'She said, "I've been telling Ruby that she needs to stand on her own two feet before she gets tripped up by any man." And Ruby said, "You're just jealous." That about caused a sibling squabble right there in the quiet tea room. I settled that down but it is obvious that the sisters are definitely individuals. Charley the rebellious pragmatist, Ruby the hopeless romantic. It's only going to get more interesting as they get older.'

'I hope Evan knows what he's facing down the road.'

'Actually, it's probably better if he doesn't see it coming,' Lucinda said.

'Could be. It would be better for me if I saw dinner coming, though. I'm famished.'

'How about a couple of rolls from the Sushi place down on the ground level of the building?'

Jake agreed and called in their order: a dragon roll and a spiced salmon roll for Lucinda and then two bowls of soup, a pair of spring rolls, three more rolls and a half a dozen pieces of sashimi.

'And this is just for the two of us, Jake?'

'As I said, Lucy, I am really, really hungry. Do we have any saki?'

'We've got a bottle or two of Nigori.'

'Perfect. Now, while we're waiting, I'm curious about what you're going to do tomorrow since you've scratched basking in your success off your list of possibilities.'

'I'm going to run down Jimmy Van Dyke's associates. Somebody has to know something about what's going on here. Somebody can give me the information that positions Jimmy's actions into a logical framework.'

'Good luck with that,' Jake said. 'I know you like to think that logic is the answer but the majority of criminals don't operate that way.'

'Not knowingly, Jake, but underlying it all there is always logic – maybe in a perverted or distorted form – but it's always there.'

'Yeah, but it's not always easy to make your mind do the necessary contortions to match their reasoning. You may already know everything and just not be able to twist your logic into the necessary improbable shapes.'

'You could be right, Jake. But I have to try. I can't accept Jimmy's story at face value yet.'

'Let me know if I can be of any help. You can tap into the resources of my office any time. You want me to go with you to interviews?'

'Nah, you go to your office and bask in the glory. Not the kind of moment you usually get under the Wicked Witch's thumb. I'll let you know if I find anything interesting or if I run out of leads. Maybe by the time this day's over, you'll be saying "I told you so",' Lucinda said and sighed.

SIXTY-SIX

Lucinda went to the office, gathered names, home and workplace addresses and any criminal records for everyone she could locate with a connection to Jimmy Van Dyke. She mapped out a logical progression of stops and drove off to the spot the farthest distance from the Justice Center with plans to work her way back. Mike Petronis managed an auto parts store on the south side of town.

Mike was a waste of time. He said he and Jimmy had a falling-out six months earlier, when Mike wouldn't allow Jimmy to move into his apartment, and they hadn't spoken since. When Lucinda asked him about other people Jimmy knew, Mike didn't come up with any names that she didn't already have on her list.

She caught Jason Mourning at the seedy dump he called home. The smell of sour beer, unwashed nineteen-year-old and stale pizza nearly made her leave before she got a potentially important piece of information. She stuck it out, though, and got the name of a girl Jimmy had been seeing, Julie Troutman.

Jason added, 'I don't think it's serious – just a piece of ass.'

Lucinda bit her tongue to keep a lecture about respect for women from spewing out all over the guy. She moved on to a delivery store where she found Matt Halgorn behind the counter. He looked camera-ready in a company polo shirt, a pair of khakis and a winsome smile.

However, when Lucinda said she was there to talk about Jimmy Van Dyke, Matt's welcoming expression disappeared, his face flushed and he whispered his response. 'I can't talk to you here.'

'Can you take a break?' Lucinda asked.

'Five minutes. Give me five minutes. I'll meet you at the coffee place across the street.'

Lucinda entered the shop, got two lattes and slid into a seat in the most remote corner she could find. When Matt walked inside, she waved to him and slid one of the drinks across the table. 'What's up, Matt?' she asked.

'I've been trying to put the past behind me. But since I heard Jimmy was arrested, it's all been rushing back.' Matt sipped his coffee and stared down at the table.

'What's come back? Did Jimmy do something to you in the past?'

'Oh no, not really. I blamed him at first but it didn't take me long to realize he was not the problem.'

'What did he do?'

'It's not what he did; it's what we had in common.'

'And what was that?'

Matt blurted out a bitter-sounding laugh. 'A woman. Isn't that pathetic? That's why, after a while, I realized I couldn't blame him. He was just a dumb, horny kid, like I was. He was just another notch in her belt – another puppet to manipulate.'

'Another puppet for what woman to manipulate, Matt?'

'Brittany Schaffer. Our teacher. Like some stupid teen movie. We both fell for teacher. Pretty sad, when you think about it, isn't it?'

'A lot of people have crushes on their teachers. There's nothing new about that,' Lucinda said.

'Sure. That's not new. And I guess having sex with students is nothing new, either. We both did her. Not at the same time. I was first, then Jimmy came along later when she got bored with me. Hell, I don't know that I was first – kind of doubt that I was. Damn, she was a good teacher – in the classroom and in the bedroom.'

'How do I know you're not just bragging?'

'She has a tramp stamp. It's a blue swallowtail butterfly with curlicues and arcing; below it are three words: "Live. Laugh. Love."

Ask Jimmy. He knows. Or check out the tramp wearing it. She likes to flaunt it.'

Although the fact that Brittany was having sex with students was no real surprise, hearing it from the mouth of one of her conquests was unsettling. 'OK. So you both had sex with Ms Schaffer. What does that have to do with Jimmy's arrest?'

'He didn't do that by himself. She put him up to it. She has this sneaky way of sticking ideas into your head to get you to do things without you realizing it's really her idea – her way of showing how much control she has over you.'

'So you're saying, without her pushing Jimmy, he wouldn't have built that bomb – he wouldn't have set it off?'

'I'd bet my life on it. I heard he confessed to killing that boy – she must have wanted that kid out of the way for some reason. That's how she operates. She got me to vandalize another teacher's car one night – spray-painted "Bitch" on one side and "Whore" down the other. All to get revenge for her. She told me I shouldn't have done that but I knew she was pleased. She also got me to steal another teacher's grade book and a few other stupid things I'd rather not remember – and then there was the thing I wouldn't do and she dropped me and took up with Jimmy.'

'Where did you draw the line, Matt?'

'She wanted me to beat up this girl. I'm not sure what she had against her – she said she was causing her trouble by spreading ugly rumors, but who knows? Brittany and the truth don't hang together much. But I was not hitting a girl, not for anybody. That's why I'd bet anything that she put Jimmy up to it. See, David Baynes had replaced Jimmy. Jimmy said he didn't know why she dumped David but I'd guess she'd asked him to do something and he refused. But, anyway, about a month ago, Jimmy said that Brittany was going to take him back. I told him to run away as fast as he could. He said that he couldn't. All he had to do was take care of a problem for her and she was his. He said they were going to get married. I reminded him that she'd told him that before – that she told me that, too. But he insisted this time it was different.'

'Did he say anything more about the problem he was going to fix for her?'

'Nah, I asked but he wouldn't give it up. But I'd betcha the problem was David and the whole explosion thing was Jimmy's way of taking care of him for her.'

'Are you saying you think it was her idea that he blow up the school and kill David in the explosion?'

'She never was that specific with me so I doubt she was with him. She just hinted at stuff in a roundabout way – pointing me in the right direction to serve her purposes. It worked like this: she'd let me know about her problem, I'd suggest a solution, then she'd gently push me in the direction she wanted me to go. She was really good at that. She knew how to use people – particularly horny boys who always wanted more.'

'Thank you, Matt. This is all very helpful but you really need to do one thing more. You need to press charges against Ms Schaffer.'

'Not me, man. No way. You force me to come in and I'll deny it all.'

'Could you come in and give me a written statement of what we talked about today? You wouldn't need to file a complaint against her and you wouldn't get into any trouble over the vandalism – I'll see to that.'

Matt stood up. 'No. Can't do it. Can't get involved. It would freak out my mom. And I've got a girlfriend now – a decent girl, a smart girl. I think it's getting serious. I don't want to screw that up. I want to forget the past, not wallow in it. You're going to have to find somebody else. And I've got to get back to work.' He turned around and walked outside.

How would she go about finding someone else? Was there someone new in Brittany Schaffer's life? Or was there an old boy toy might be willing to go public? She pushed up out of her chair, got another latte for the road and continued her search for answers.

SIXTY-SEVEN

Back in her car, Lucinda called in and got an address for Julie Troutman's home and workplace, a Kroger grocery store. She called there, found out Julie was not at work and then went to her apartment building.

The four-story structure appeared to date from before the Second World War but the exterior and the grounds looked well maintained. Inside, the wooden banister by the stairs had a fresh coat of paint;

the wooden steps with their swayback of wear had to have been original.

Lucinda went up to the second floor and rang the doorbell by apartment 207. With the door chain in place, it was answered by a studious-looking young woman wearing lavender sweats and tortoiseshell eyeglasses. A pencil was balanced on the top of one ear. She looked more like a nerdy college student than anyone's 'piece of ass', Lucinda thought.

'May I help you?'

'Are you Julie Troutman?'

'Who are you?'

'Lieutenant Pierce. Homicide,' Lucinda said, flashing her badge.

'May I see that, please?'

Lucinda held the wallet with her identification close to the crack in the door and waited while the woman peered at it.

'Yes, I'm Julie Troutman. Just a minute, please,' she said and shut the door. Lucinda heard the clatter of the chain on the other side before the entryway opened and Julie invited her inside.

The room Lucinda entered was sparsely furnished with an old, fat television set, a bookcase filled with jumbled volumes and a seen-better-days green sofa that was partially covered by a multi-colored throw. Julie went to the far end of the sofa and sat sideways and cross-legged. Lucinda took a seat at the other end.

'Do you know Jimmy Van Dyke?'

'Yes. Is it true he's been arrested?'

'Yes, Miss Troutman. When did you last see him?'

'A week ago on Sunday evening – well, all night. He didn't leave until I went to a class at the community college. He dropped me off on his way home.'

'What time on Monday morning?'

'Class started at nine fifty that morning. I think he dropped me off a little past nine thirty-five.'

'Did you stay here in the apartment all that time?'

'Oh no, we walked up to the Walking Dog Sunday evening to get something to eat.'

'When was that?'

'I really don't know. But we weren't gone long.'

'And then you stayed in the rest of the time?'

'Yes.'

'Do you know David Baynes?'

Julie winced. 'I've heard his name but I never met him.'

'His name seemed to have struck a chord with you. Why is that?'

'That was the kid who was blown up at the high school, right? Him and Mr Fred?'

'Yes. Did Jimmy tell you about that?'

'Actually, Jimmy was with me when I saw it on the news.'

'Do you often watch the news together?'

'Not really. Jimmy is usually not interested in it.'

'But he was that night?'

Julie sprang up from her seat. 'Can I get you something to drink? I have Coke and Dr Pepper or I could make a pot of coffee or a cup of tea.'

'No, thank you,' Lucinda said.

'Well, I'm parched. I need something. Back in a click.'

Lucinda thought Julie was spending far more time in the kitchen than she needed to grab a can of soda. She rose to follow the girl in there but, before she took a step, Julie returned to the living room.

Sitting back down, Julie said, 'So, you were asking me about David Baynes?'

'Actually, we were talking about the news the night of the explosion. You were about to tell me about Jimmy's reaction to it.'

'I was? Oh. Um, you know, I was so shocked looking at that news footage, I don't know that I recall his reaction.'

Lucinda sighed. 'Miss Troutman, I could arrest you as an accessory after the fact but I really don't want to do that. It's all up to you. You have to decide to tell me the truth or you have to be willing to face the consequences.'

'You would arrest me?'

'If you left me no other choice.'

'But finals start tomorrow. I have to study. I have to show up to take the test. You can't do this.'

'As I said, Ms Troutman, I don't want to do that but . . .'

Julie got up again and went to the window overlooking the street, her back to Lucinda. Neither woman said a word. After a minute, Julie placed her hands on the sill and leaned forward, resting her forehead on the glass. In another moment, she shrugged out a sigh and turned around to face Lucinda. 'She put him up to it.'

'She?' Lucinda asked.

'Yes. That teacher, Brittany Schaffer.'

'Why do you think that? Is that what Jimmy told you?'

'No. But I was here. I heard everything he said to Todd.'

'Todd Matthews?'

Julie nodded.

'He was here?'

'First, he came into the Walking Dog and approached our table. He started yelling at Jimmy. Nothing he was saying made any sense to me but Todd was like that a lot – always angry, usually destructive, except when he was too bummed out to speak or move.'

'Why was that?'

Julie shrugged. 'I don't know. I know his parents made him crazy 'cause they were always bickering and he usually seemed to think it was all because of him. He didn't feel like he could ever please his dad. In some ways, even though there wasn't much age difference, he always seemed to seek Jimmy's approval, like he looked on him as a father figure.' Julie laughed. 'But maybe that's just my psych class talking.'

'Did Jimmy seem to understand why Todd was angry that night?' Lucinda asked.

'Yeah, right away and it made Jimmy mad. He jumped up and pushed at Todd and said, "Outside, Matthews. Not in here."

'Todd said he didn't care who heard. Jimmy went out the door anyway and Todd chased after him. I scooped up what was left of our food into a bag and followed. When I stepped outside, Jimmy grabbed my hand and said we were going home. Todd said, "You can't walk away from me. You tell me why you killed him." Jimmy shouted, "Shut up, asshole," and kept walking. Fast – he was half-dragging me.

'Todd kept coming and yelling about killing somebody and wanting to know if Jimmy did it on purpose and why he did it. Jimmy broke into a run, pulling me along with him. We got to the building, ran up the stairs. Jimmy slammed the door shut and threw the deadbolt. A minute later, Todd was there, pounding on the door, screaming.

'I told Jimmy, "Let him in. Talk to him. Somebody will call the police if you don't." And he said, "Good, let them take him away." But then a funny look went across his face and he went across the room and pulled open the door and jerked Todd inside and Jimmy said, "OK. Stop yelling at me and we can talk." And Todd stopped yelling. That's when I learned what really happened that morning.' Julie hung her head and threw her hands over her face.

'Tell me what you learned,' Lucinda coaxed.

'When we were seniors at the high school, Jimmy had a thing with that teacher.'

'Brittany Schaffer?'

'Yeah. I knew him then and I knew he was crazy about her but I didn't really know about their relationship until she dumped him. That's when Jimmy came to me the first time. I'd had a crush on him for years but he never seemed to notice I was alive. But although he started spending a lot of time with me, all he wanted to talk about was that teacher. Even when we were in bed together, he'd say, "Brittany would do this" or "Brittany would do that" to try to get me to try something new. I kept telling myself I needed to dump him, but every time I decided it was the last time, I caved again. Pretty pathetic, huh?'

'I'm sure we've all made stupid relationship decisions. When did Jimmy start seeing Brittany again?'

'A couple of months ago. He even told me about it. He said that she told him that David Baynes was a mistake and she wanted Jimmy – wanted to marry him. I told him that would never happen. He got really mad at me and left. I didn't see him for weeks until he showed up the night after David died.'

'OK. That brings us to a week ago. Now, tell me what you learned that Sunday night when Todd and Jimmy talked.'

'According to Todd – well, that's not exactly right since Jimmy didn't deny anything, so I guess that was the same as him admitting it – but, anyway, Todd said that he helped Jimmy build the bomb because Jimmy said that nobody would get hurt and it would just make a mess. Todd was mad at the principal about something and the idea of her office getting trashed gave him a kick. Like I said, Todd was always mad about somebody or something – either that or he was depressed as hell. Jimmy admitted that he lied about the reason for setting the bomb. Jimmy said that David had become a problem for Brittany – that David found Brittany in bed with a freshman and got really angry. He said it was over between him and the teacher and that he was going to report her for having sex with students. Jimmy said that was why he had to kill David to protect Brittany. Jimmy said she was all upset and crying and saying that if he really loved her, he would make sure that David didn't get her in trouble.

'She knew they were building a bomb. She just let them do it.

Jimmy said she didn't know any details but she knew he was going to take care of David for good. Todd said, "Why did you drag me into this? I didn't want David dead – I didn't want his blood on my hands." He swung at Jimmy and Jimmy pushed him to the floor.

'Jimmy said, "I needed you. David wouldn't trust me but he would trust you. I needed you to get him to the school."'

'Do you know how they managed that?'

'Oh, yeah. Apparently, Todd told David that someone had taken naked pictures of Jimmy's sister Tamara and her reputation was going to be ruined and that she was going to be kicked out of school and Jimmy's mom was going to throw her out of the house. Todd told David that Tamara didn't agree to having the pictures taken, didn't know they were taken at the time and couldn't stop crying about it.'

'He fell for that story?'

'From what I could gather, he balked at first and then Todd told him that Ms Schaffer always said that David was a knight in shining armor. And that she was sorry about having sex with that other boy. If she only could win David back, she would be faithful forever and they could live happily ever after. I can't believe he fell for it but apparently he still had a thing for her.

'So Jimmy drove them over there Sunday morning, dropped David and Todd at the back of the building. Jimmy told him he couldn't go inside to steal the photos of his sister because he would be the first one suspected. Todd told him that he'd been dating Tamara so he'd be second on the list and, since David didn't know Tamara, no one would ever think he did it. So Todd showed David how to get inside and then ran around to the front and got in the cab of Jimmy's truck. Todd kind of freaked out when Jimmy started leaving without David, but Jimmy joked him out of it. Made funny remarks about David being stuck at the school and caught in the act with vandalized file cabinets. When Jimmy dropped Todd off at home, Todd was laughing, too. Thought it was all a big joke. Then Todd heard the news.'

'Did Jimmy's explanation Sunday night calm Todd down?'

'Sort of – but more like it made him really depressed. When he left, he was mumbling about the blood on his hands – David's blood, Mr Fred's blood. I swear if I'd thought he was going to commit suicide, I would have done something about it that night. But it never crossed my mind. I was kind of in shock just knowing what Jimmy did and not really wanting to believe it.' Julie's lower lip quivered and tears rolled down her cheeks. 'I know I should have said something before now but I felt so guilty about Todd, I just pretended like it didn't happen.' She let her arms hang limp and silently sobbed, her shoulders heaving with effort.

Lucinda put an arm around the girl's shoulders. 'I'm going to need your written statement, Ms Troutman. I do have this interview on tape so it can wait until tomorrow after your test. Can I trust you to come in then?'

Julie nodded.

'And are you going to be OK?'

Julie pulled a tissue out of her pocket and blew her nose. 'Probably never again. But I'm not going to do anything stupid, like kill myself.'

Lucinda pulled out a business card and scribbled on the back. She handed it to Julie and said, 'I wrote my personal cell number on the back. You get any stupid ideas, you call me before you do anything, OK?'

Julie nodded her head and whispered, 'Yes.'

'Maybe you shouldn't be alone tonight.'

'Hey, I'll be OK. Honest. In fact, I didn't really expect this but I think I feel a little better now that I've told somebody.'

SIXTY-EIGHT

Lucinda called Rita Younger. 'I need to speak with Brittany Schaffer. You can make the arrangements or I can pick her up. If I pick her up, handcuffs will be involved. Your choice.'

'You are such a drama queen, Lieutenant. I will be delighted to make my client available in my office in an hour and a half if you will tell me what is on your mind.'

'I need clarity on a few items. I have had one young man tell me of his sexual experiences with Brittany Schaffer while he was one of her students. I've had a young woman tell me about her boyfriend's escapades with your client. And I've also had a statement that she knew the boys were building a bomb in her garage and did nothing to stop them or alert the authorities, making her a suspect in a terrorist attack.'

'My, my, my! You do dredge up the strangest things. I'll tell you right now, without talking to my client, a few things that everyone knows. First of all, teenage boys brag about conquests that only happened in their minds. Second, teenage girls whose boyfriends develop a crush on a teacher tend to feel inadequate in comparison and therefore they are jealous and will stop at nothing. Third, quite often when someone points a finger at someone else it is done to divert attention from their culpability. Nonetheless, I will have my client here in one and a half hours to dispel your odd notions.'

Lucinda showed up a few minutes early and had to wait. When the door to the office opened, Lucinda entered, shut it behind her and turned on the tape recorder. She walked out forty-five minutes later with exactly what she wanted – an audiotape of Brittany ripping Jimmy to shreds.

When she arrived at the jail, Jimmy was waiting for her in an interview room. 'Jimmy, you have admitted to the murder of David Baynes, correct?'

'Yes, I have. Do I need to do that again?'

'No, not just now at any rate. Matt Halgorn told me you could describe the tramp stamp on Brittany Schaffer's back.'

'Matt is a liar.'

'Julie Troutman told me that you killed David for Brittany Schaffer.'

'Julie is a liar.'

'Supposedly, Todd Matthews said that you were just playing a joke on David Baynes and he wouldn't get hurt.'

'Todd's dead.'

'Yes, he is. Does that bother you?'

'It was stupid. I wouldn't have given him up.'

'Maybe he felt guilty,' Lucinda suggested.

'Well, boo hoo.'

'I heard that David was sharing Brittany's bed and that's what this was all about.'

'You were misinformed. Brittany had nothing to do with this.'

'Do you call all your teachers by their first name?'

'She hasn't been my teacher for nine months.'

'Did she promise to marry you?'

'Do you want me to take back my decision to waive my right to an attorney?'

'Wouldn't blame you if you did, Jimmy. But before you do that, I'd like to play you a recording I made just a little while ago.'

Jimmy shrugged. 'Whatever.'

Lucinda pressed the button and Brittany's voice filled the room. 'Jimmy is a troubled boy. I knew he needed help. And putting him in prison was not a place he'd get that help.' Lucinda stopped the tape. 'Do you recognize that voice, Jimmy?'

'Should I?' Jimmy said.

'I would think you would, if for no other reason than the fact that you sat in her classroom for all of the last school year. Who is it, Jimmy?'

'Ms Schaffer. Brittany Schaffer. English, third period.'

'Very good, Jimmy. Now, I'd like you to listen a little longer.'

Brittany's voice continued, 'That's why I didn't report what happened. I told his mother he needed counseling. I wished she'd listened to me.'

Lucinda's voice said, 'Exactly what happened, Ms Schaffer?'

'It was the middle of the night. About two months ago. I was sleeping – very deeply. I didn't hear a thing but suddenly felt a heavy weight on top of me. It was Jimmy Van Dyke. He was tearing off my clothes. I fought him. I screamed. But you've seen where I live – with the windows shut on a cold March night, the people in all the other houses were too far away to hear a thing.'

Lucinda stopped the tape and asked, 'Do you remember that night, Jimmy?'

Jimmy's jaw was slack, his eyes unfocused and his hands shook. He looked at Lucinda with an expression that screamed, 'Why?'

'Jimmy, answer me. Do you remember that night?'

Jimmy's head slowly moved from one side to another.

'Maybe a little more will freshen your memory,' Lucinda said and pressed the button.

Brittany's story started again. 'He punched me in the face. He pounded on my body. And then he raped me. Cruelly, savagely. He called me a bitch and a whore. He told me I belonged to him and I had no right to speak to any other man. Then he left. I took a long shower and cried myself to sleep.'

'I didn't. I swear I didn't,' Jimmy said, his voice sounding weak and far away.

'Why did you kill David, Jimmy? Was it because he was sleeping with Brittany?'

'No, no.'

'You want to know what she said when I asked her about why she allowed you to use her workbench in the garage?'

Jimmy shook his head.

Lucinda cued it up to the right spot and pressed play anyway.

Brittany said, 'He came to my house with a drawing of a tattoo that I have in a private place. He said that if I didn't let him use my garage to work on his project, he would pass copies of it all over the school.'

Lucinda's voice spoke from the recorder. 'I thought you said you were facing him when he raped you. So, how did he see your tramp stamp?'

'That is such vulgar slang, Lieutenant,' Rita remonstrated.

'Everybody calls it that,' Brittany said with a sigh. 'I just didn't tell it all. It was too embarrassing. But after Jimmy Van Dyke raped me vaginally the first time, he flipped me over and took me the other way. It was so horrible.'

'No, no, no!' Jimmy shouted and pounded on the table.

Brittany continued. 'If he distributed that at the school, my career would be over. I couldn't explain it away. So I let him and that other boy work in the garage. I didn't know what he was doing. And poor little David Baynes. I was trying to help him with composition because he'd fallen behind in class and somehow, in his sick little mind, Jimmy decided that David and I were lovers. I think that's why he killed him. I should have reported Jimmy to the authorities immediately. But I didn't want to ruin his life.'

Lucinda stopped the tape again. 'She's throwing you under the bus, feeding you to the lions, sacrificing you on the altar – whatever cliché you want to use, Jimmy. Are you going to let her get away with it? Are you going to let her use and manipulate more boys? Or are you going to tell me the whole story? All of it?'

For a long time, Lucinda sat and waited while Jimmy sat stone-faced, staring at the wall.

Lucinda interrupted his contemplation once. 'Jimmy, you killed David and there will be consequences for that. Brittany Schaffer's manipulation will provide your attorney with a strong mitigation case and I will do everything I can to get your sentence minimized, maybe down to as little as twenty years. But I need to know everything and I will need you to testify against her in court when she goes to trial.'

Jimmy sighed. 'If I tell you everything, do you promise she'll be charged?'

'Yes, Jimmy, with everything I can think of.'

He stared back at the wall for another couple of minutes. Then he turned to her and said, 'OK. Where do you want me to start?'

'At the beginning, Jimmy. Tell me how it all began.'

SIXTY-NINE

Lucinda left her interview with Jimmy Van Dyke stunned by his revelations. On the one hand, it was nothing more than the age-old story of a lovers' triangle but, on the other, it was flat-out bizarre.

Brittany Schaffer was a garden-variety sexual predator, using and discarding the adolescent boys who gratified her ego and did her dirty work. Unlike any similar case of an authority figure taking advantage of their position to manipulate their charges, Brittany set off a chain reaction that led to homicide, suicide and a federal terrorism investigation.

The time was now here for the climactic closing of the law enforcement case. After the next step was accomplished, she would turn the responsibility for justice over to the prosecutor's office – always a bittersweet moment.

Lucinda spent the rest of the day meeting and making plans with Lieutenant Barry Washington of the sex crimes division. They decided to serve the arrest warrant on Brittany Schaffer and execute the search warrant for her home at the same time, but they did not want her in the house when they did it. They decided upon ten a.m. the next morning and arranged for two uniformed back-up teams and a team of techs led by Marguerite Spellman.

'You want me to take care of the house?' Lucinda asked.

'Absolutely not,' Barry said. 'It may not be a homicide but this is your collar. I would not think of depriving you of handcuffing that Schaffer woman.'

'Are you sure?' Lucinda asked as she felt a jolt of adrenaline speeding through her system at the excitement of publicly arresting a woman who had lied to her and violated the public trust.

'I should be at the house, anyway. I have more experience with evidence collection in sex crimes. It makes sense.'

The next morning, Lucinda drove up to Woodrow Wilson High School, followed by two marked patrol cars containing four uniformed officers. She stopped first in the main office and requested that Principal Rose Johnson accompany her.

Rose was full of questions but Lucinda didn't say a word. She just handed her the arrest warrant to read as they walked the halls to Brittany Schaffer's classroom. At the door, Rose raised her hand to knock. Lucinda wrapped her fingers around Rose's fist and pulled it away with a shake of her head.

Lucinda opened the door and entered the classroom followed by the patrolmen.

'Well, class,' Brittany said, 'It appears as if we have visitors this morning.' Turning to Lucinda, she added, 'There are a few seats in the back of the room. Feel free to join in our discussion.'

Lucinda was not amused. 'Brittany Schaffer, you are under arrest for the sexual exploitation of minor students and for your involvement in the bombing at this school. Please face the wall and put your hands behind your back.'

'I will not,' Brittany said. 'I'm not going anywhere without my attorney.' She pulled out her cell.

Lucinda plucked the phone from Brittany's hand. One of the uniformed men grabbed Brittany's shoulder, spun her around and pressed her face into the wall. It took two officers to secure her flailing arms and make them accessible for Lucinda to snap on the cuffs.

A man on either side of Brittany grabbed her elbows and led her out of the room. As Brittany passed Rose, she shouted, 'Ms Johnson, you need to call my attorney. Rita Younger. Tell her what happened here. Hurry.'

'I don't think so, Ms Schaffer,' Rose said.

Lucinda walked into the hallway realizing the classroom behind her was in uproar. Students were standing, shouting questions, sending texts, making calls and milling in clumps for whispered conversations. She heard Rose raise her voice to speak over the hubbub, 'Class, everyone, please take your seats and I will answer your questions the best I can.'

Epilogue

The following Sunday, at Evan's invitation and Charley's insistence, Lucinda and Jake went to the Spencer home to say goodbye to Amber and Andy Culvert and meet their new guardians, Aunt Livie and Uncle Zach, and their two children. As she drove, her mind wandered to the resolution of the mystery behind the explosion at the high school.

The aftermath of a case always left Lucinda in a pensive mood. She was pleased that Brittany's predation and manipulation of high school boys was at an end and that, unlike many other cases, Brittany couldn't use her good looks and gender stereotypes to squeak out of the situation with a mild rebuke from a judge. The cost of that, however, was high. Two people – David Baynes and Fred Garcia – were dead as a direct result of her instigation. Another boy – Todd Matthews – died by his own hand, indirectly driven to his suicide by Brittany Schaffer.

The parents of David and Todd would carry an unnatural burden of pain for the rest of their lives – outliving one of your children furrows deep rows of unending sorrow. And Fred Garcia's children would grow up without a father. She vowed to remember those kids every year at Christmas – a small gesture, but she remembered how the tiniest gestures had meant so much to her after her parents died.

Charlotte Van Dyke lost a child, too, albeit in a very different way. Jimmy would still be alive but he'd be behind bars for a long time to come. Charlotte would suffer a sense of loss that at times would swamp her heart. And what of Tamara? How would she cope with the guilt of what she did that weekend? She had no way of knowing that her action would lead to a fatal conclusion, but still . . .

By the time they reached the Spencer home, plans had changed. Evan had suggested that the children might have an easier transition if they stayed with him until the end of the school year. Livie and Zach agreed. The farewell party had evolved into a celebration of justice and the best interests of the children. The kids ran between rooms, drinking soda and stuffing themselves with snacks, and the five adults sat out on the deck, sipping wine and getting to know one another. Jake and Lucinda left feeling very good about the people who would take over responsibility for Amber and Andy once school was out for the year.

On the ride home, Jake said, 'All six of those kids are great but, for me, they were a persuasive argument for birth control.'

'Are you saying if you got married, you wouldn't want children?'

'I don't think I do, Lucy. What about you?'

'Leaving my job would be like cutting off an important part of my anatomy. Not leaving my job wouldn't make me a very good mother – running out in the middle of the night, sometimes gone for forty-eight hours at a stretch. I'd have to marry a good candidate for Mr Mom – but, honestly, I've never met a man like that. I meet victims who are in a state of shock, criminals who belong in prison and law enforcement types like you. Not much hope there.'

'So, you want children – you just haven't found the right guy? Is that why you've avoided answering me when I've suggested marriage?' Jake asked.

'There was a time when I really wanted kids badly. That's how I felt the first time I married – but that was a bust. When that happened, I wasn't able to think about allowing a man into my life again – I didn't want to take the risk. Instead, I focused on my career and built it – through ups and downs, joy and despair – until it became such an integral of my personality that I can't imagine me without it. Now, it's a bit late for me to start a family under any circumstances. But you're younger. With the right woman, you could have your career and a family. You can have it all – just not with me.'

'It's not what I want, Lucy. I am not interested in raising children – that's where the risk lies, in my opinion. There is no risk worth considering in a relationship with the woman I love. And whether you're comfortable with it or not, you're it. I'm not going to go away. If you push me away, it won't change anything in my mind or in my heart. Simply put, I belong to you.'

'You poor thing. I've never been good at taking care of my belongings.'

'I'm serious, Lucy. I want to marry you.'

'We've only been living together for six months, Jake. By the time a year is up, you could tire of me.'

'So, are you saying that after we've lived together for a year, you'll marry me?'

Lucinda winced. 'I can't say that, Jake.'

'What can you say?'

'I love you. How's that work for ya?'

'I like that, Lucy, I like that a lot – but it's a very evasive answer. What can I expect six months from now? What can I expect then?'

'What can any of us expect six months from now? People always make the mistake of thinking they know someone well only to realize they've developed a relationship with a monster. This case and Amber's situation and all the other shattered lives I have encountered have taught me a lot about human motivations and I can't say I like what I've learned. With the experiences I've had and the knowledge I've gained, how can I pretend to believe two people can live happily ever after till death tears them apart?'

'Stop the car, Lucy, please.'

Lucinda pulled over into the parking lot of a closed furniture store.

'Look at me.'

She turned in his direction and he took both of her hands in his. 'You've always believed that the biggest risk in an investigation was not taking any risks. You should give yourself – give us – the same opportunity. No, it won't come with a guarantee but it does come with a promise. I know you won't turn into a manipulating fiend like Brittany Schaffer. And I trust that you know I won't become a child-molesting creep like Amber's mother's boyfriend. There's no good reason for you not to give us a chance – nothing but a weakness buried deep in your heart. I've never thought of you as a coward, so please don't act like one. What will you be willing to tell me in six months?'

Lucinda chewed on her lower lip and darted glances at Jake. 'I can say this, Jake. For the next six months, I will think about it a lot – instead of avoiding it as I have been doing. And when the time is up, if you are still interested, I will seriously consider your proposal and try to give you an answer.'

'Thank you, Lucy. It's not exactly what I wanted but, for now, it's enough.'